Evelyn, After

"Hands down, the best book I've read this year. Brilliant, compelling, and haunting."

—Suzanne Brockmann, *New York Times* bestselling author

"Readers will cheer on Evelyn when the power dynamic with her lying, cheating husband shifts, even while they watch her flirting with disaster in her steamy affair with Noah. A solid choice for Liane Moriarty readers."

—*Library Journal*

"Stone (a nom de plume of romance writer Victoria Dahl) . . . ably switches to darker suspense in a compelling story exploring what lurks behind a seemingly perfect life."

—*Booklist*

"Stone pens a great story that will have readers wondering what will happen next to the characters involved in this mysterious tale . . . Fascinating tale told by a talented storyteller!"

—*RT Book Reviews*

"Victoria Helen Stone renders the obsessions and weaknesses of her characters with scorching insight. Her sterling prose creates a seamless atmosphere of anticipation and dread, while delivering devastating truths about the nature of sex, relationships, and lies, often with a humor that's rapier-sharp. *Evelyn, After* reads like *Gone Girl* with a bigger heart and a stronger moral core."

—Christopher Rice, *New York Times* bestselling author

Half Past

"A gripping, haunting exploration of the lengths to which we'll go to belong, *Half Past* will hold you in its thrall until the very last page. Stone's expert storytelling, vivid characterizations, and tantalizing dropping of clues left me utterly breathless, longing for more—and a newly minted Victoria Helen Stone fan!"

—Emily Carpenter, bestselling author of
Burying the Honeysuckle Girls and *The Weight of Lies*

"A captivating, suspenseful tale of love and lies, mystery and self-discovery, *Half Past* kept me flipping the pages through the final, startling twist."

—A. J. Banner, #1 Amazon and *USA Today* bestselling author of
The Good Neighbor and *The Twilight Wife*

"What would you do if you found out that your mother wasn't your biological mother? Would you go looking for the answer to how that happened if she couldn't provide an explanation? That's the intriguing question at the heart of *Half Past*, Stone's strong follow-up to *Evelyn, After*. [It's] both a mystery and an exploration of what family really means. Fans of Jodi Picoult will race through this."

—Catherine McKenzie, bestselling author of *Hidden* and
The Good Liar

Jane Doe

"Stone does a masterful job of creating in Jane a complex character, making her both scary and more than a little appealing . . . This beautifully balanced thriller will keep readers tense, surprised, pleased, and surprised again as a master manipulator unfolds her plan of revenge."

—*Kirkus Reviews* (starred review)

"Revenge drives this fascinating thriller . . . Stone keeps the suspense high throughout. Readers will relish Jane's Machiavellian maneuvers to even the score with the unlikable Steven."

—*Publishers Weekly*

"Crafty, interesting, and vengeful."

—*NovelGossip*

"Crazy great book!"

—*Good Life Family Magazine*

"Stone skillfully, deviously, and gleefully leads the reader down a garden path to a knockout WHAM-O of an ending. *Jane Doe* will not disappoint."

—*New York Journal of Books*

"*Jane Doe* is a riveting, engrossing story about a man who screws over the wrong woman, with a picture-perfect ending that's the equivalent of a big red bow on a shiny new car. It's that good. Ladies, we finally have the revenge story we've always deserved."

—*Criminal Element*

"Jane, the self-described sociopath at the center of Victoria Helen Stone's novel, [is] filling a hole in storytelling that we've long been waiting for."

—Bitch Media

"We loved being propelled into the complicated mind of Jane, intrigued as she bobbed and weaved her way through life with the knowledge she's just a little bit different. You'll be debating whether to make Jane your new best friend or lock your door and hide from her in fear. Both incredibly insightful and tautly suspenseful, *Jane Doe* is a must-read!"

—Liz Fenton and Lisa Steinke, bestselling authors of *The Good Widow*

"With biting wit and a complete disregard for societal double standards, Victoria Helen Stone's antihero will slice a path through your expectations and leave you begging for more. Make room in the darkest corner of your heart for Jane Doe."

—Eliza Maxwell, bestselling author of *The Unremembered Girl*

"If revenge is a dish best served cold, Jane Doe is Julia Child. Though Jane's a heroine who claims to be a sociopath, Jane's heart and soul shine through in this addicting, suspenseful tale of love, loss, and justice."

—Wendy Webb, bestselling author of *The End of Temperance Dare*

"One word: wow. This novel is compelling from the first sentence. An emotional ride with a deliciously vengeful narrator, Jane's tale keeps readers on the edge without the security of knowing who the good guy really is. Honest, cutting, and at times even humorous, this is one powerhouse of a read!"

—Brandi Reeds, bestselling author of *Trespassing*

False Step

"[A] cleverly plotted thriller . . . Danger and savage emotions surface as [Veronica] discovers that she's not the only one whose life is built on secrets and lies. Stone keeps the reader guessing to the end."

—*Publishers Weekly*

"Intense and chilling, *False Step* wickedly rewards thriller fans with a compulsive read that'll leave readers wondering how well they know their loved ones. I was riveted!"

—Kerry Lonsdale, Amazon Charts and *Wall Street Journal* bestselling author

Problem Child

"Outstanding . . . Readers will find vicarious joy in Jane's petty vengeances and unabashed meanness to anyone who tries to take advantage of her. Stone turns some very dark material into an upbeat tale."

—*Publishers Weekly* (starred review)

"This installment is highly recommended for fans of edgier psychological fiction."

—*Library Journal*

The Last One Home

"Stone gradually reveals her multifaceted characters' secrets as the intricate, fast-paced plot builds to a surprising conclusion. Fans of dark, twisted tales of dysfunctional families will be satisfied."

—*Publishers Weekly*

"The story gives just enough detail each chapter to keep the reader intrigued about where it is going to go next . . . family secrets will never be looked at the same."

—*The Parkersburg News and Sentinel*

"A slow burner . . . *The Last One Home* takes its time to set the scene for the twists and revelations that will come in the last chapters of the book."

—*Mystery & Suspense Magazine*

"*The Last One Home* is elegant and chilling, an indelible novel of family secrets. I couldn't put it down until I learned the truth about these finely drawn characters—the ending left me absolutely shocked and amazed, and I can't stop thinking about it."

—Luanne Rice, *New York Times* bestselling author of *The Shadow Box*

"Gripping and relentless, *The Last One Home* stalks you like the serial killer within its pages: you know danger is right around the corner, but you don't know when it'll strike. And just when you think you have the story figured out, Victoria Helen Stone rips the rug right out from under your feet. Highly recommended!"

—Avery Bishop, author of *Girl Gone Mad*

"In *The Last One Home*, Victoria Helen Stone weaves another sure-handed story, this one about mothers, the fierce love they have for their children, and just how far they will go to protect their progeny. This is a suspense novel that's in part a love story, as well as a chilling mystery. But it's the kind of tale that sneaks up on you, revealing discoveries in the last scorching chapters that flip the whole narrative on its head. Full of shifting family loyalties and recollections of the past, and creepy, alone-in-the-countryside vibes, this book held me, start to finish, in its mesmerizing thrall."

—Emily Carpenter, author of *Reviving the Hawthorn Sisters*

AT THE QUIET EDGE

ALSO BY
VICTORIA HELEN STONE

AT THE QUIET EDGE

A NOVEL

VICTORIA HELEN
STONE

LAKE UNION
PUBLISHING

Text copyright © 2022 by Victoria Helen Stone
All rights reserved.

Published by Lake Union Publishing, Seattle

www.apub.com

Amazon, the Amazon logo, and Lake Union Publishing are trademarks of Amazon.com, Inc., or its affiliates.

ISBN-13: 9781542037327
ISBN-10: 1542037328

Cover design by Damon Freeman

Printed in the United States of America

AT THE QUIET EDGE

CHAPTER 1

The police officer stared at her from behind mirrored sunglasses, his blond brows raised high enough to crease his forehead into deep wrinkles. Lily couldn't make out his eyes behind the lenses, but she tried her best to hold his gaze and look innocent.

The smile lines around his mouth seemed like a good sign, but the dimples she glimpsed when he spoke remained inert now despite her attempts at friendliness. He showed no interest in returning her smile, and she'd convinced herself he must be able to see the frantic thud of her pulse in her throat.

"No," she said again, repeating her answer as if saying it twice would make it more true.

"You're sure about that?" he pressed. "You didn't see anything?"

"I'm sure. Nothing strange around here last night, not that I noticed." Her smile trembled at the edges when his straight mouth stayed firm. "And obviously we're pretty focused on security. Have to be." Her wide gesture toward the storage lockers behind her felt far too dramatic, a hostess showing off prizes on a game show.

"Obviously," he said, finally removing the shield of the reflective glasses. His eyes angled purposefully toward the camera mounted above the gate. Hazel. He had kind hazel eyes and more smile lines to frame them, and the sight eased her fear down by the tiniest fraction.

"Yeah," she offered lamely, following his gaze to the unblinking black of the camera's lens. It perched high above the sad lilac bush she and her son had planted five years earlier. The damn thing had only grown scraggly leaves and hadn't flowered yet, and when her eyes drifted to the branches, she couldn't help but see it as a sign of her failures.

"How many cameras are there? Do they all function?"

"Yes, they work." She pulled her gaze from the shrub to force herself to meet his eyes. "But the gate never opened after hours last night, Officer. I would have received an alert if it had. It was quiet out here, and the gate is completely disabled after six on Sundays, so the only way in is over the razor wire."

"It's 'Detective.'"

"Pardon?"

"It's *Detective* Mendelson. I don't think we've met, but I've seen you around, I think. Perils of a small town. I've probably stood in line behind you at the hardware store."

"Of course!" she said brightly, though she didn't remember him, and he was handsome enough that she probably would have. Was it possible he recognized her from the police station? But there had been only two detectives on the force the last time she'd been called in, and he hadn't been one of them.

She cleared her throat. "Are things that serious? You only said someone reported a car lurking around. Was there a break-in?" Angling her neck, she looked past the gate toward the business park on the other side of the street.

Movement drew her gaze, and she spotted Sharon in front of the upholstery shop, crossing her arms, head craned to the side as she tried to spy. Of course.

Sharon waved cheerfully when she caught Lily staring. The woman had never once expressed any chagrin over what she called her "attention to detail" and Lily called "general nosiness."

"Detective, if Sharon was the one to call, you should know she has a tendency to overreact. She's very nice, don't get me wrong, but . . ."

"You haven't noticed any parked cars on the road? Maybe people meeting out here at night? Perhaps a woman you've never seen before?"

Alarmed at this sudden shift in questioning, she quickly shook her head.

"The lack of lights on this street can encourage unsavory activities," he added.

Lily was very aware of how dark it could be here after the sun went down. Her place was lit every hour of the day to protect the storage units, but the constant light made her home stand out like a beacon.

It felt eerie driving down the deserted road at night, the facility that housed her apartment spotlighted in the blackness for all to see. Every other business in the isolated development closed at five, six at the latest. On slow Sunday mornings Lily could walk the road for an hour without seeing another soul.

"The street is kind of a catchall," she said with a shrug. "The UPS guy sometimes sits on the road to have his lunch. People pull over to text or make phone calls. At night . . . I'm not sure. Maybe it's the latest version of Lover's Lane for local teenagers? I wouldn't be surprised. It's probably a good spot for a meeting place."

"There's a back gate?" he asked, ignoring her theories.

"Yes, but it's only for emergency use and also has an alarm. That's the reason for the on-site apartment. I'm on call twenty-four hours a day to address any security problems."

"You live here alone?" He looked past her again, toward the office this time, and the hair rose on the back of Lily's neck. She got this question surprisingly often, and she hated it every time, but a law enforcement officer like Detective Mendelson was probably the only person who had a good reason to be curious.

And Lily really needed to keep him focused on her and not the maze of hiding places lurking at her back. She needed him to look at her and believe her, so that he would go away and never come back.

"My son and I live here." She flashed a purposeful grin, determined to make herself believable. "Yes, I know it's an odd place to live, but it's a nice, quiet location to raise a family. It's just us and the pigeons."

He didn't laugh as he took a business card from his pocket and handed it over. He didn't even offer the smile she'd worked so hard for. "The world can be a dangerous place on your own, ma'am."

"Oh boy, I know."

He finally met her eyes again, studying her until she had to force herself not to squirm. His sharp jaw ticked once, then twice before he finally nodded. "I'll be sure to drive out more often now that I know you and your boy are here. Call me if you see anything."

Oh, damn it. She'd only been trying to seem harmless, not helpless. But she'd taken her acting too far.

"Thank you, but we're really fine. Like I said, it's quiet!"

He started to turn away, then changed his mind, his shoulders softening a little. "I know Herriman seems safe and quaint, but there are dangerous people in every community."

A moment of new worry for Everett broke through the red buzz of Lily's fear. "Was this more than a tip about a car?"

At long last, Detective Mendelson offered a smile, and his dimples were just as charming as she'd imagined. "Just keep your eyes open, since you're alone out here at night. Do you have cameras pointing outward? We could review the footage together."

"The cameras are focused on the gates and the buildings, but I'll be sure to take a look. The company is pretty strict about customer privacy. We're part of a big chain, and you know how that goes." She rolled her eyes as if she considered their rules a burden, but in this case it was a blessing.

"Got it." He glanced around one last time, then pointed at her hand. "You've got my card. Get in touch anytime. I mean it."

For a brief second she got the impression he might be flirting, but maybe that was why he kept the dimples under wraps. He was pretty cute, and certainly not out of her age range for dating. He looked maybe forty-five? Forty-six?

As if she could risk a cop hanging around.

As if it mattered when she hadn't dated since college.

She knew thirty-two wasn't old, but good God, she felt old. Tired of all these years dangling from a cliff's edge. She couldn't add new risks to her world. She had to fight her own impulsiveness for the sake of her son. If she drew police attention back into her life . . . If she lost her job . . .

Lily raised her hand in a small wave as the detective took a backward step toward the sedan he'd parked outside the gate. He hadn't pulled in to one of the visitor spots. Cop instincts, maybe, wanting to leave himself a quick exit in case of an emergency. She admired the watchfulness. She could understand it.

Staring hard until he slipped back into his car, Lily managed another friendly wave of appreciation as he shut the door behind him. He was done. He was leaving. She was safe.

Detective Mendelson had barely made the turn out of the entrance when Sharon Hassan's foot hit the street. She stepped off the curb to hurry across the road toward Lily.

"Is anything wrong?" she called with far too much excitement in her voice.

"No, nothing."

"Is Everett okay?"

Lily's irritation faded a little at the concern for her son.

"Everything is fine! The cops were just checking on that car you saw hanging around last night."

"Me?" Panting from her near jog to get a little gossip, Sharon pressed a hand to her chest. "No, I didn't call. Was there a robbery? A break-in?"

Lily frowned at that surprise. "Nothing like that. Just a suspicious car, maybe."

"Wasn't that Detective Mendelson? There must be something going on if they sent an actual detective."

Lily watched as his car disappeared up the road, wondering if she'd been too quick to focus on her own worries. She'd assumed Sharon had been in her shop for a late appointment and had seen the delivery dropped off for Lily after dark. And that definitely would have looked suspicious. But if it wasn't that?

A little icy fear trickled along her nerves. Were her old ghosts back to haunt her? Had Mendelson only been testing the waters?

She dragged a sleeve over her forehead to wipe off the nervous sweat. "He didn't offer any specifics. Just asked if I'd seen anything out of the ordinary. A car, people, he wasn't really clear."

"Well, I'll keep my eye out, and I'll remind Nour to keep the alarm set when I'm not around. She always forgets, and she wears those dang sound mufflers when she's using power tools. Someone could walk right in and steal the whole place right from under us, and she'd look up an hour later to an empty shop."

Lily suspected Sharon was actually right about that. Nour was nothing like her wife. She kept her head down and her eyes focused on upholstery and woodworking, and she cared nothing for gossip. Then again, Sharon's penchant for loose talk fit in perfectly with her front room job of going over fabrics with interior designers and their clients. She always had local stories to pass along, even if Lily had no idea who most of the people were.

Lily had been a part of the community when she'd first moved here, but trying to keep up with cleaning a house, cooking meals, and entertaining a toddler had consumed her free time. The only people she'd known had been other moms with young children.

And her husband's clients, of course, but they made a point of not knowing her now.

"I hope this wasn't about that big break-in at the pharmacy last week," Sharon said with something suspiciously like glee. "Pill fiends! Maybe they're looking to unload some goodies." She glanced past Lily with narrowed eyes. "Anybody suspicious rent a locker recently? They could be hiding their stash while they wait for the heat to die down."

"I hate to disappoint, but I haven't rented out a new space in the past week. Things will probably be slow until summer moving season."

"Well, keep your eyes peeled."

"I will."

Sharon started to turn, and Lily was sighing with relief when she abruptly swung back. "I almost forgot! Guess who my latest customer is? You'll never believe it!" Without waiting for a response, she plunged into a breathless answer. "Kimmy Ross, Dr. Ross's new wife! Oh my God, that has to be a big change after Francesca. No one was more shocked than I was that he got married so quickly after her death, but I suppose he *is* still a young man at fifty-one. And a thirty-year-old wife makes him even younger, I guess. Good Lord, she is not a fan of Francesca's design aesthetic, let me tell you."

Lily pressed her lips together, unwilling to reveal that she'd already suspected part of that story. Dr. Ross had moved some of his first wife's old furniture into a storage unit just the month before. *I can't keep staring at it forever,* he'd explained with a sad smile. Lily had suspected he'd happily keep the furniture if not for his new bride, and Sharon had just confirmed that.

"She's tearing everything out," Sharon added. "New kitchen, new bathroom, new paint, and some very expensive drapes and bedding. Gorgeous stuff. Teal and gray with brushed-nickel accents. Amazing they can afford that with his daughter in rehab, but that's how it goes.

Nour is making these stunning box valances for the bedroom. You should come over when they're done."

"Absolutely," said Lily, taking a sidestep toward her office door. She'd try to avoid the visit, though. She didn't enjoy oohing and aahing over furnishings she'd never be able to afford. Hell, she currently daydreamed of buying one of those basic Ikea beds with the attached bookshelves, so she definitely wasn't springing for custom work anytime in the next twenty years.

Though maybe she could watch a few videos and learn how to make cute throw pillows. Sharon had offered scraps of her best fabrics in the past. Everett was twelve now. A better mom would've already upgraded him from his *Adventure Time* posters and SpongeBob pillowcases. His funny joke T-shirts rarely found their way to the laundry anymore. Her baby was growing up.

She could paint his bedroom and fix it up with more-mature décor, but . . . She sighed. Not until she'd finished her latest online coursework. Another bullet point of guilt to add to her endless list.

After waving a definitive goodbye, Lily escaped through the glass door of the storage center office, but it was only an excuse to get Sharon to leave. What Lily truly needed to do was head right back outside to check on the grounds and the fencing . . . and on the status of last night's delivery.

Adrenaline flooded her blood again, and her heart sped right back up to its previous frantic beat. Why had she agreed to this? The first time had been an accident. The second time, her ego had gotten caught up in saying yes. This time she'd barely given it a thought, and now she felt sick with the risk she'd taken.

Managing this storage facility wasn't just Lily's job; it was her and Everett's world. Their home, their security, their future. Their bubble.

She'd started feeling too safe. That was the problem. She'd landed this gig six years before, and she'd lost her gratitude for it somewhere along the way, distracted by her guilt over making Everett live like this, and resentful of how small and dingy her place in the world had become.

But small and dingy was better than out on the raw streets, exposed to every sight, sound, and threat that came along.

She may have fallen far, but she'd clawed her way back up to this ledge, and she'd be damned if she'd let her tired hands rest now. One more year and she'd be past the worst of it. She'd have her degree. She'd be ready to take on the world.

But not yet.

After standing quietly for a few minutes, she grabbed her keys and stepped outside, pausing to look for anyone watching or approaching. Things were usually quiet on weekdays before lunch. Though Saturdays could be busy enough to make her scream, nobody moved on a Monday.

She set off along the first row of large units, walking briskly, pretending to check the doors, but she was only eating up ground until she could get her eyes on her goal. She walked another row before cutting over to the high exterior fence. The top spiked up in razor wire, but none of that would make a difference if someone simply cut through the thick chain link to break in.

Everything looked secure, just as she'd suspected, the only anomaly the scraggly black cat that strolled past her without even a glance. When it wasn't chasing field mice, it often lounged on the tops of stored trucks and cars, tolerating Lily's presence as if Lily were the interloper.

She felt like one today, skulking around the property, eyes shifting at every shadow and whisper of wind. But this was part of her job. Checking on things.

Ears straining for the sound of approaching cars, Lily finally turned toward the open storage area of the facility. The maze of RVs and cars and covered boats never inspired a feeling of safety. It was a warren of hiding places and deep shadows, like a scene from an abandoned city in a zombie movie. A rabbit had once bounded out from a hiding spot and torn a genuine scream of terror from Lily. But today she already felt clammy with fear as she took a left turn into the deepest aisle and then another left into the next row of vehicles.

Nothing stood out about the RV she approached. The curtains were drawn tightly and the steps retracted just like all the others in storage. But her skin still prickled at the sight of it.

Lily looked to her right and her left and strained her ears for visitors again before she held her breath and tapped quietly on the door.

Nothing happened. Skin tingling with alarm, she tapped harder, quicker. "It's me," she whispered. The latch finally clicked and then turned before the door opened out two inches and revealed a pale oval of face in the dim interior. Thank God.

"Are we leaving?" the girl whispered.

"Not yet. I just wanted to check and make sure you're okay. Did you hear anything strange last night?"

"No. Why?" The girl's throat clicked loudly when she swallowed. But she wasn't a girl, of course, despite her slight bones and wide eyes. She was a grown woman in her twenties, at least. "Did something happen?" she asked, voice pitching up as the door swung farther out.

"No, everything's fine," Lily reassured her. "I'm just making the rounds. The phone's not here yet, so . . . if anything happens with you or . . ." Lily inclined her head toward the woman's taut belly.

Amber. Her name was Amber, and she seemed to be at least seven months pregnant, if not more, looking for all the world as if she'd stuffed a basketball under her pink T-shirt.

Lily wasn't supposed to know anything about her. The less any of them knew, the better. But the woman had introduced herself the night she'd arrived.

"We're fine," she said, her eyes arcing past Lily to scan the area behind her as her hand curved over her abdomen.

"I could bring fresh food if you need it."

"What you left is good. Thank you. Will the papers be here soon?"

"Hopefully tonight." Lily stepped back. "Just sit tight."

The woman glanced around one more time before closing the door. The lock snicked quietly into place.

Lily backed all the way to the next RV before sucking in a deep breath. She counted in for five, then blew out for ten. Everything was fine. One more night at the most. After another breath of dusty, diesel-scented air, she felt steady enough to move.

As soon as she got back inside the office, she'd review all her footage; then she'd finish up her Monday paperwork and see if her restocking order had been approved by corporate. By the time she finished sweeping out the two newly vacated lockers, Everett would be home from school. Homework for him. Then dinner. Then homework for her. If—

"Hey there!" a graveled voice barked from her right.

Lily jumped, spinning around, one hand out, the other sliding up to protect her neck from fatal blows.

"Whoa!" the guy croaked, raising a beer in salute. "It's just me!"

At the sight of the white-haired man rising up from the captain's seat of his stored boat, Lily's limbs weakened and her eyes burned with a hint of relieved tears. "Jesus, Mac!"

"Sorry. Didn't know you were lost in thought."

The adrenaline hurt now, too much to absorb into muscles she no longer needed for fighting or fleeing. "You scared the hell out of me!"

"Well, I see that! Sorry, Ms. Brown."

She waved a shaky hand. "It's fine. I should've expected you when you didn't show up yesterday."

Mac snorted. "My wife had a big bingo potluck. Said she couldn't spare me."

"Well." She looked pointedly at his beer. "Enjoy your fishing."

"I will. No baseball game on the radio today, though."

"You'll have to settle for the sounds of nature, then." She tipped her head toward the nearest metal doors and the pigeons cooing from the roof above them.

Mac laughed uproariously at that, and Lily would've wondered how many beers he'd already had, but she knew he only brought two for each visit. Anything more and he wouldn't be able to bike home.

At first she'd assumed Mac had lost his license to a DUI, but after a few weeks of him visiting his beloved fishing boat, he'd spilled the truth. He'd had two unexplained seizures and couldn't drive until he was cleared by his doctor. He'd lost work and had to sell his shiny black half-ton pickup, but he'd refused to give up his boat.

Still shaking, Lily waved goodbye and walked away. As soon as she turned a corner, she fell against the side of the storage building and waited for her world to steady.

When had Mac arrived? Had he seen anything? Though she'd been listening for a car engine, surely she would have heard his bike wheels crunching over stray gravel if he'd come anywhere near where she'd been.

Once the ache had left her muscles, she pushed off the cement block wall and cut through a narrow alley between two buildings to head straight back to the office. She needed water and a moment of peace to regroup.

She got neither. When she returned to the office, a young man was waiting, but he was the first person today who didn't ratchet up her tension. His pimpled hangdog face was too forlorn to cause any alarm as he watched her approach.

"Hey, man," he said dully when she reached the bench where he waited. "I need a place to store my gear. My woman kicked me to the curb."

Lily pasted on a sympathetic expression, though she wanted to laugh at his choice of phrase and the old-fashioned hippie ponytail that hung limply to the middle of his back. "Short-term locker?" she asked, looking back toward the small mound piled at his feet.

"I guess. I've got a gig lined up in June, but I'm a free spirit until then. You ever heard of the Farm? It's down in Tennessee, man. I might go check it out."

He followed her inside, telling her all about a permanent commune still full of hippies, though she had to interrupt him to explain that without a billing address, two months of fees were due in advance. She handed him a list of prices.

By the time he'd signed all the paperwork and she'd given him a quick tour of the facilities, she was nearly over the morning's panic. Maybe it was the calming effect of the pot fumes that wafted off the new client when he moved.

Once he left, Lily sank gratefully into her squeaky office chair to sip her room-temperature coffee and fire up the security footage.

This video review felt like overkill now that the cop was gone and her nerves were quiet. The road that led to the business park and storage facility was nearly a mile long and connected to a state highway. Whatever his worries were, these loiterers had nothing to do with her.

First things first, she pulled up the front gate footage from 8:00 p.m. and watched her own ghostly figure approach the closed gate. Headlights swept across the background of the shot, though a car never pulled into view. Instead, a small, hunched figure scurried toward Lily before Lily led her off camera. She highlighted the footage and immediately deleted it.

Done. That moment no longer existed for anyone except her and Amber.

It took nearly an hour to carefully scan the other camera feeds, but absolutely nothing popped up aside from a possum that waddled past with a few babies on its back. Lily allowed herself a faint smile as she made a note of the timestamp to show to Everett.

Her son had morphed from a cuddly little boy to an awkward, slightly standoffish tween, but she could still suck him in with cute animal content, and she'd mercilessly use any tactic to keep him close.

They were close, weren't they? Despite everything?

Lily slumped back in her chair and rubbed a hand over her eyes. On good days she thought she was doing okay, raising a fatherless son the best she could. On bad days when one or both of them were in a foul mood, and she felt like she was failing him . . . Well, on bad days she turned on music and cried quietly in her bedroom while he played video games online.

There was no reason for this to be a bad day. She'd throw some frozen cookie dough in the oven as a warm welcome after his nearly mile-long walk from the bus stop, and she wouldn't even be resentful if he forgot to compliment her baking.

And once she handed off her special delivery, she'd lie low, stop taking risks, and everything would get back to normal.

CHAPTER 2

"Is it true you live in a storage unit?"

Everett stiffened at the girl's voice behind him, raised high to be heard over the rumble of the school bus as it pulled away and abandoned them on the desolate corner.

He felt his shoulders climb toward his ears with tension, but he didn't turn around. He'd gotten through all of elementary school and most of his first year of middle school without being bullied, but this was it. After all those years of warnings and role-play at school, it was about to happen in real life.

When he took two steps away, he heard the rasp of her footsteps follow. "Hey! You're Everett, right?"

Pausing, he turned his head slightly toward her, limbs tight and poised to react. "Yeah."

"Do you really live in a storage unit?"

"Jesus," he muttered before resuming his walk. Her footsteps shuffled behind him.

"Hey," she said, "I'm not trying to be rude. I'm sorry. That came out wrong. I mean, it's sad if you do live in a storage place, but I hope that's not true. I just can't figure out . . ." Her words trailed off, and though he kept walking, she quickly overtook him. "You live out there, right? And there aren't any houses!"

Everett glanced at her past the corner of his eye. Josephine Woodbridge. A Black girl about his size, with a pretty, round face. She wore purple clothes a lot.

They'd never been in the same elementary classroom, but he thought she'd moved to Herriman about two years earlier. She usually got off the bus with a girl named Bea, but Bea didn't ride the bus during soccer season, and he hadn't seen her in a while. Both girls lived in the tiny strip of houses that ran along the highway a few feet from the bus stop. Everett was the only kid who lived in the business park way down the road.

The perfect poof of Josephine's natural hair bobbed with every step. She watched him intently, seemingly paying no attention to the road. "Where's Bea?" he asked.

"She moved."

Bea had seemed a little snooty to him, so he wasn't exactly sorry, but that explained how he'd suddenly drawn Josephine's attention.

"Her dad got a job in Missouri. State government or something. She's so mad."

"I bet."

"I have Mr. Rose's class right after you," she said, changing the subject.

"Yeah."

"That last quiz was ridiculous."

"Yeah," he answered.

"I can't keep walking this way or I'll get home late, and my mom will lose her mind."

He stopped without even deciding to, and she immediately took the opportunity to move into his path and offer a big smile. "So you *don't* live in a storage unit? I only asked because when I see you walking home, it makes me worry, and I hate worrying. Like, *hate* it."

"I don't live in a storage unit," he snapped.

"Okay, good."

Her face was so chubby and sweet, and her tiny white earrings were enamel bits of popcorn, and that must mean she was okay, right? He had plenty of friends to hang out with at school, but no one ever thought to come out here to the edge of town all the way past the landfill to hang out with him. Except Mikey. And Mikey had turned into a stupid gamer this year.

He eyed Josephine again, concerned about her motivation, but equally tired of being bored to death. "There's an apartment behind the office of the storage facility. Two bedrooms. A kitchen. A patio. It's normal, all right? It's not a frickin' storage unit."

"Seriously? That's so cool. You live in a hidden apartment!"

Everett shrugged. It wasn't cool, actually. It was a crappy apartment like any other crappy apartment but without other kids to hang around. And no pool or park either. He felt suddenly self-conscious again. "I've gotta go," he said.

"Sure. Anyway, I'm Josephine." She held out her hand like they were breaking up a meeting or something. After frowning for a moment, Everett reached out and shook it.

"See you tomorrow," she said as she let him go.

If she was a bully, she was playing a very long game.

"Wait," she shouted when he was twenty feet away. "Give me your number!"

Everett shook his head at the sight of the phone she held up. Another thing to be embarrassed about. "I don't have a phone yet."

"That sucks! Tell your mom you're afraid of kidnappers. That's what finally worked for me!"

A laugh popped from his mouth. "Not bad. I'll try it." This time when he turned back toward his walk, Everett was smiling. Maybe Josephine was all right.

He picked up his pace, eager to get home and get through his history homework so he'd have free time before dinner while his mom was still working.

He'd discovered a new locker to check out.

As hobbies went, he'd found an exciting one, though he knew it was wrong. That was probably what made it exciting, of course, but Everett had promised himself he'd use up all his illicit thrills on this and not experimenting with pot or alcohol or something.

At first it had started out as a good deed. Or not quite a good deed, since he got an allowance for it. But he had volunteered to help out his mom around the storage facility for a couple of hours every week. He helped sweep or pick up litter. He changed the garbage bags from the common areas and broke down boxes for recycling. And he checked the locks on the storage doors.

The first time he'd found an unlocked door, he'd simply locked it and moved on, but lying in bed that night, he'd regretted it. He'd watched that *Storage Wars* show. He'd seen the weird characters who rented space in this town. There could be anything right there, a few yards away from his bed. Gold coins, ancient documents, wild photographs. *Anything.*

Not that he was a thief. He didn't take things . . . or nothing that valuable, anyway.

His arms prickled at the idea that he might have inherited something bad from his father. Did criminals pass on badness through their genes?

But truly Everett was only curious. In fact he could even convince himself he was helping people, because when they left locks open, thieves could take their stuff. He locked up their valuables. He protected them. Mostly.

Once he'd started watching for opportunities, he'd run out of unlocked units pretty quickly. They popped up on occasion, especially during the summer when more people were moving in and out, but they weren't common.

Still, he'd noticed something else during the downtime between open locks: a lot of people really didn't try hard to scramble the numbers on their combination locks. His mom sold two kinds of padlocks in the office. The more expensive, sturdier version came with keys, but you could also buy a cheaper one with a four-digit combination. Once it was engaged, the owner had to spin the numbers to jumble them, but most people were too lazy for that, and Everett could just nudge them forward in a straight line until the lock opened.

Yesterday, he'd discovered an even more special kind of laziness: an actual sticky note with the combination written right on it. The bright-yellow paper had caught his eye, the corner poking out beneath the bottom of the roll-up door like a tiny flag designed to alert only him.

He'd tugged it out, and as soon as he'd seen the four digits, he'd taken a careful look around. Once he'd verified that the security camera on the side of the building pointed slightly away from him, he'd lined up the combination and popped open the lock. There hadn't been time to explore, so he'd relocked it in the hopes of sneaking in tonight.

Anticipation fizzed through him even though he'd never found anything all that interesting in the previous spaces. What if it wasn't curiosity that got him pumped up? What if he just liked being bad? Wasn't that exactly who his father had been?

Shoving away thoughts of a father he barely remembered, Everett sniffed and put his earbuds in to distract himself with his ancient iPod. The truth was that he mostly just shifted things around in the units, shining a flashlight on random junk. He opened boxes to check for treasure, of course, but the best thing he'd discovered was a cool old car he'd been able to sit in.

Maybe he'd get bored and outgrow his evil criminal phase. Or else he'd need darker and darker thrills until he became a career criminal who ruined people's lives forever, and when everyone discovered the truth, they'd say, *What did you expect from a con man's son?*

"No," he said before turning up his music louder. That wasn't how these things worked. His dad had fled when he was only six, and if he'd taught Everett any bad habits, he couldn't remember them now. In fact, what he did remember of his dad seemed fake. He'd been fun, he'd laughed a lot, he'd taken Everett to the park all the time. And then he'd run away and disappeared. How could those things go together?

Everett inched the volume up until his mind was too blanketed with music to let anything else through.

He wasn't supposed to listen to his iPod while walking on the road, because his mom said a driver distracted by texting could race up behind him and he wouldn't hear the engine. But she worried way too much, and Everett was already breaking rules, so why not one more?

With a quick glance over his shoulder, he removed one earbud just in case.

When he got home his mom was on her office phone, fingers clacking away at an ancient keyboard while she argued with someone about the late notice they'd received. She had to do a lot of that. Had to threaten people that their prized possessions would be sold if they didn't pay. That was what happened on those antiquing shows, though that part wasn't discussed much. "You got poor and couldn't pay your bills, so we're taking your things" wasn't a selling point for a show.

His mom hated that part of her work. He knew she hated it. He knew she sometimes shifted things around so she could wait another month before calling the auctioneer. He'd heard her make phone calls, begging people to pay just one month of rent to stave off the eviction. And he'd once heard her crying in her bedroom after a confused old lady came in looking for her belongings a full year after her lease had lapsed.

Everett was never going to have a job like that. He was going to be a vet, probably. Or maybe a cop. He wanted to help people or animals or both. He didn't remember much about his dad, but he remembered the many, many times the police had come around those first few years, and the comforting feeling of his mom telling him not to be scared, they were only trying to help.

Could he be a cop if he got caught in someone's storage locker? He was pretty sure juvenile records were secret, but maybe they weren't secret to the police.

He added that to his mental list of things to google when his mom wasn't over his shoulder at the family desktop. He added another note to delete his history afterward.

She'd promised he could finally buy himself a phone when he turned thirteen *if* he saved up for it. He would. All his friends had phones already, and their grimaces of sympathy were so embarrassing.

After dropping his backpack on the floor by the computer, he went straight to his room and opened the window. Shadow immediately jumped down from the privacy fence that surrounded their tiny cement patio as Everett reached for the container of cat food he kept hidden beneath his bed.

"Good girl," he whispered. She watched for him to come home now and was always waiting nearby. He spread some food across his windowsill, and she leapt up effortlessly to eat.

"Hey, Shadow," he cooed, scratching between her ears as she purred and ate and rubbed into his hand all at once.

They couldn't keep a pet here. It wasn't allowed. But Shadow was definitely his, even if his mom didn't know. He pressed his forehead to her warm body for a moment and let her pleased vibration shiver through him. Sometimes when he felt really lonely, he opened the window late at night and let Shadow curl up into a tiny warm circle between his feet on the bed.

If he got fleas, his mom would kill him.

"You won't give me fleas, will you?"

She bumped her head against his hand in answer. Everett sighed and closed the window before his mom could finish her work and walk

21

in. She always made a ridiculous show of asking about his day after school when all Everett wanted to do was listen to music and play video games and *not* talk about the boring seven hours he'd just survived. It wasn't his fault they were out here at the edge of civilization with no one to talk to.

But no goofing off today. Today he had to be sure to finish his homework early. He dropped into the chair at the tiny desk in their living room and unzipped his backpack. A one-page history essay was due tomorrow. No big deal. He hated writing, but it wasn't exactly difficult for him.

He quickly scrawled out half a page on early Kansas settlers, then closed his pen and stuffed the paper back into his folder. He could finish the last paragraph on the bus no problem. He got through the math he hadn't completed during the bus ride home; then after a split-second glance at his science vocab, he checked it off, signed the paper, and left it out so his mom would see proof that he'd done something.

Finished.

Free.

Everett shifted the wobbly office chair slightly, wincing at the pained squeak. It was some old piece of shit his mom had salvaged when the corporate office had sent her a new one. Most of their furniture was salvaged, often from renters desperate to get rid of their old stuff. They were lucky to have it, she told him. He didn't feel lucky.

Holding his breath, he shifted his squeaky chair one more time, then listened for the click of his mom's nails on the keyboard.

Thirty seconds later he was logged in to Discord. **Hey Mikey,** he typed, then waited. And waited.

What up? his best friend finally responded.

You busy?

Yeah I'm on Twitch. When are you gonna upgrade that pos computer?

Haha whatever.

Everett's *haha* was one hundred percent fake. Mikey had been his best friend since second grade, but he'd turned into a stupid gamer since he'd gotten a new computer with a ridiculous graphics card at Christmas. They rarely hung out anywhere except school now, and Everett couldn't even text him because he didn't have a phone. He felt like a stupid little punk trying to keep up with the big kids these days. Mostly he just wished Mikey was still a stupid little punk too, and he could get him to come over and build a fort in the field out back like they'd done every other spring.

Listen, he typed, wanna come over tomorrow? He hadn't told Mikey about the storage lockers because he was afraid his friend might blab during one of his dumb livestreams, but he'd since gotten tired of being wise about it. It was way too cool to keep quiet.

Nah man I can't.

Everett slumped, sighing so loudly he missed the sound of his mom walking into the apartment. By the time he'd closed the screen, she was on him.

"What was that?" she demanded.

"Nothing."

"If it was nothing, you wouldn't have closed it."

"It's just Discord."

"Aren't you supposed to be doing your homework?"

"I already finished it." He gestured at the perfectly placed sheet of vocabulary.

"Oh yeah? What if I quiz you?"

"Go ahead." They stared at each other for a moment until she finally scrubbed a hand over her forehead. "Fine. What's this Discourse thing?"

"Discord. It's like online texting. It's no big deal."

"Come on, Everett. Online texting? That doesn't seem safe. You could be talking to *anyone*. How would you even know if they were dangerous?"

"Oh my God, *Mom*," he snapped.

"Seriously. Let me see it."

"Jesus," he snarled. "If you really think it's not safe, you should let me get a phone so I can text my friends like a normal person."

"Everett—"

"It's bad enough we live twenty miles from civilization and all the kids think I'm homeless and live in a storage unit! You don't want me to talk to anyone now? That's just *great*."

As Everett's words faded he realized he'd accidentally yelled all that. He'd never yelled at his mom before.

An ache began to rise up his throat as her silence sang in his ears. Or maybe the pain was the effect of her glaring daggers at him. Whatever it was, the longer he sat there, the thicker the clog in his throat.

Holding his breath, he waited for her to say something, say *anything* to break the horrible silence. He couldn't even hear her breathing.

When he couldn't take it anymore, he sprang to his feet and walked past her to the office. "Forget it! I'm going for a ride."

"Everett, don't walk out. Let's talk."

Did she sound like she was crying? Oh God. He'd expected yelling after his outburst, or maybe a lecture, but crying? He bolted through the office and out the door.

"Shit," he spat as he raced toward his bike. As soon as he reached it, he hopped on and pedaled for the open pedestrian gate. She couldn't get more mad after that, could she? He may as well get away for a little while. She was always begging him to get out and ride more anyway.

He pedaled hard down the road, but his roiling emotions wore off quickly. Maybe he'd overreacted. Five minutes later he just wanted to go back home.

When a loaded pickup passed him and turned into the storage facility, Everett circled back hopefully, imagining she'd be too busy to notice him.

Sure enough, the pickup was stopped in one of the front spaces. His mom would be occupied with a customer for a while. Perfect.

Everett biked back through the pedestrian gate. His mom might see him, but she couldn't follow him when she had a customer. He parked his bike against an RV and tugged a flashlight from a small pouch at the back of the seat; then he sprinted toward the locker in question, tugging the sticky note from his pocket before he even got there. He'd checked the camera's feed yesterday while his mom was working. Only the very edge of this door was visible, and only if you looked closely.

The lock opened with a click, and Everett raised the door a few feet and ducked inside before closing it behind him. His pulse sprang into panic in the second before he fumbled the flashlight switch on, and it wasn't completely calmed when the circle of light appeared. Flashlights were pretty creepy in his opinion, creating way too many shadows that shifted and writhed with any movement. It was a hell of a lot better than the dark, but he really, really wished he could leave the door open.

He'd had bad nightmares as a kid, and he still sometimes "forgot" to turn off the light after a late-night trip to the bathroom. He liked the comforting glow sneaking under his door.

As he swung the beam of light over the unit, he frowned a little. It looked like most of the others he'd seen. Lots of cardboard boxes stacked up like little condos for spiders and silverfish. A few pieces of old furniture. Some plastic storage bins. It surprised him how many people were willing to spend money on keeping things like these instead of throwing them out.

He walked a little deeper into a narrow pathway between boxes, sliding his light over every surface. When he caught sight of a woman staring at him, he yelped and jerked back, the beam shaking, shifting her face from smile to sneer to mad-eyed grin.

"Aah!" he cried out as he grabbed the flashlight with both hands to hold it steady. It still shook, but he could see that the woman stared flatly from a photograph; it wasn't a ghost or even a creepy mannequin.

"Oh, thank God," he whispered, then tried to catch his breath and calm himself down before his heart burst right out of his chest like the *Alien* monster.

When something tickled his neck, he jumped and slapped at it, anticipating a dangling spider, but finding only sweat. The light shifted, and there was another woman. A girl, actually, smiling weakly against the sickly blue background of a school portrait. There was a third picture too. And a fourth. He couldn't see the rest of the board they seemed attached to.

He cleared his sticky throat, took a deep breath, and picked his way through the forest of boxes toward the wall. It wasn't only photos. It looked like a big old-fashioned bulletin board, filled with pictures, notes, and newspaper clippings.

Everett bent closer, squinting to read the small print of one article.

An area woman reported her sister missing after she failed to show up for her scheduled shift at a chicken-processing plant for the second week in a row. Bridget Baumgarter says that her sister, Yolanda Carpenter, told her she was going to catch a ride to visit a friend in Salina. The friend has since reported that she never arrived. Yolanda Carpenter, age 19, was last seen leaving the Baumgarter home on October 2, 1999, at 3:00 p.m. She was wearing jeans, a red T-shirt, and a jean jacket. She is 5'5", about 120 pounds, and

has long blond hair. If anyone has any information,
please contact Lieutenant Nord at the Herriman Police
Department.

He scanned another thumbtacked article and glanced at a third
before stepping back to shine his flashlight in a wider circle.

There were five photographs of five different girls, and all of them
were missing.

CHAPTER 3

She'd forgotten to make the cookies. Their first teenage-level fight complete with yelling and storming off, and all Lily could think was it wouldn't have happened if she'd made cookies.

Nodding at the long story her customer was telling about a flooded basement, Lily hit PRINT on the contract and tried to concentrate on her work instead of on guilt and hurt feelings and that aching loss of watching the easy connection with her son begin to crack with brittle age.

"Of course," the woman continued, "the good news is I'm finally getting the basement refinish I wanted. Greg kept telling me the indoor/outdoor carpet and wood paneling were *just fine*, because who the hell ever saw it but him? And I kept telling him no one else saw it because no one else wanted to go down there! If—"

"Here we are!" Lily slid the contract across the counter and handed over a branded pen. "One month up front, and then hopefully by month two you'll be ready to move into your gorgeous new basement!"

"Did I tell you we're putting in a craft room? I'm so excited. Greg gets his home theater, and I get my craft room, and a full bathroom for when my sister comes to visit with her whole brood. Four kids. Can you imagine? But now I'll just be able to throw them all downstairs and say good night!"

"It sounds amazing. Bring pictures when you return to move your stuff back home." The woman's cheeks went pink with excitement at that, and she signed the contract with a flourish before grabbing the lock she'd purchased and practically jogging out to the big red pickup where her husband waited.

Lily gave them a moment to drive deeper into the complex; then she hurried outside to see if she could spot Everett. His bike was still gone as expected, so she moved past the open gate to look up and down the road. No bike there either.

Still, it was better that he was gone and not wandering the grounds when Amber was hiding. She'd promised not to crack a window or door, but people did thoughtless things sometimes, and kids were so curious.

The business road dead-ended past the storage facility, and Lily headed that way toward the thin dirt paths that snaked through dried grass and mounds of construction debris. The developer had made big plans for this business park ten years earlier, before a couple of local manufacturing companies closed down and shipped overseas. Now the existing buildings were surrounded by lumpy, barren fields, power lines to nowhere, and some distant copses of trees.

Still, this part of their world had been heaven for Everett and his best friend a couple of years ago. They'd even managed to scrape some of the dirt into small ramps for their bikes. They'd built forts. Lived out entire epics of battles and wars and entrenched siege life, complete with picnic lunches Lily had packed for them. The landscape had provided a scene as idyllic as one could imagine in an abandoned construction area.

Lily climbed up on one of the tiny hills and gazed over patches of grass just starting to green up. There was a lot of mud and a few wide puddles, but no bike and no boy. Sighing, she told herself he was fine. She nagged him to go ride his bike nearly every day, and now he was out there. He'd wear himself out and come home, and she'd apologize for pressing him so hard about that stupid texting app.

But were kids really saying he was living in a storage unit? Were they teasing him? Making up cruel stories?

Everyone had problems. It wasn't the end of the world. But it killed her that he might be embarrassed by her choices. Her job. Her status. It was bad enough he had to be embarrassed by his father. Not that he talked about that much.

Whatever else he'd been, Jones had been a good father when Everett was little. And Everett had missed him terribly those first couple of years, suffering nightmares at night and racing to peer hopefully out the window at the sound of unexpected visitors during the day.

Lily wasn't sure he remembered Jones at all anymore. She couldn't remember anything about her childhood before kindergarten.

"Hey there, Lily!" a soft voice called.

She spun to see Nour walking out of the big garage door of her shop's loading area. Nour, the opposite of her wife, was quiet and studious and introverted. She was softness personified with her piles of black curls and plump shape. She had been born in Egypt and had learned some woodworking from her grandfather before moving to the States at eleven. What an age to be dropped into a strange, new world. Everett didn't have it so bad, surely.

"Have you seen Everett ride by?" Lily called out.

"Not today! But he dropped by yesterday to RSVP for the crawfish boil!"

"Oh . . . right. Of course."

The damn crawfish boil. Lily had gotten into such a habit of excusing herself from any invitations that Sharon pulled off an end run around her. First she'd asked when Lily was done with classes for the semester, and then she'd invited her and Everett over for a crawfish boil in mid-May. And she'd done it in front of Everett.

Lily had murmured that she'd check her schedule, though she had no social life at all and certainly no money for a vacation. Everett had asked her about it three times and then dropped it. Now she knew why he hadn't bothered asking again.

Apparently they were going to the crawfish boil.

"Bring a side dish or dessert or beer, it doesn't matter. We'll have all the essentials."

"Will do."

Lily waved and turned to carry on with her search, but as soon as she stepped off the hill, she let her frown snap back into place. It wasn't that she wanted Everett to live in isolation. She just wanted it for herself.

When Sharon had realized who Lily was, she'd asked about her ex-husband a few times until Lily had managed to carefully orchestrate distance. She imagined what Sharon must have said about her to every person who stepped into the store. She would have been thrilled beyond measure to be in such close proximity to a walking scandal like Lily. Lily's only recourse had been to avoid Sharon like the plague.

Everett, of course, had wandered over to their shop often, craving any friendly company near his lonely home, and they'd welcomed him with open arms.

Face screwed up in frustration, Lily circled back around to the end of the road and peered as far into the distance as she could, searching for Everett's bike. And then searching for strange cars, just in case. One hatchback approached and turned into the lot across the street to park in front of the plumbing supply place. Probably just a contractor, though everything looked suspicious to her after that visit from the detective.

She finally gave up and headed back inside to wrap up her work and preheat the oven for dinner and for the cookies that felt suddenly vital to saving her relationship with her only child.

Still, the walk had done her good. She felt calmer now. Everett was growing more distant because he was supposed to at his age, and their fight was a blip in their life together, not a tragic turn. After all, things had been perfectly rosy between her and Jones when their life had blown up in her face. She should see calm happiness as more of a warning than a mild argument might be.

Ten minutes into reviewing delinquent accounts, her memories of the argument were blotted out by her tortured stress over customers who were going to lose their belongings. She hated to watch the moment lumbering slowly toward her as she sent out warning after warning, silently begging each person to respond. She'd lost nearly everything once, and the scars burned when she got too close to other people's hardships.

When her phone buzzed with a text from an unknown number, her distracted brain served her the briefest flash of Everett's bike wrecked somewhere, but then she saw the text.

It's in your mailbox.

What? What was in her mailbox? She had just opened her email app to search for new notifications when she sat straight with a sudden jerk. "Oh," she said on a breath. *That* was in her mailbox.

Lily sprang up and walked as fast as she could out the door and toward the large black box perched crookedly near the road. Another repair on her list of things to fix. Heart hammering, she opened the off-kilter door and drew out an unaddressed manila envelope.

She started to tuck it under her sweater, then glanced toward the front window of the upholstery shop and decided hiding it would look more suspicious. She was allowed to get envelopes, just like she was allowed to have visitors late at night. What she wasn't allowed to do was use a client's property as if it were her own.

What if Sharon had seen a strange car pull up and leave an envelope? What if she was putting little details together and passing them around like treats to every friend and acquaintance? Lily could lose her job and her home, and all her careful plans to get a better job, a better home, a better life for her son.

By the time she made it back to her office, she was wiping nervous sweat off her forehead again.

Unlike her ex-husband, she was clearly not cut out for a life of crime.

Worried that another customer would arrive or Everett would choose the worst moment to make his return, Lily quickly sliced open the heavily taped envelope and looked inside. Then she did tuck it beneath her sweater before she grabbed her keys and locked up.

A murmur of voices rose from the building to her right where she'd just directed the latest renters, but she headed left toward the vehicle storage area with only a quick glance toward the gate. Instead of hiding her route, this time she relied on speed as she zigzagged through the trailers and Jet Skis and motorhomes.

After a quick knock on the door of the only occupied RV in the lot, Lily's head pivoted back and forth until she was dizzy. She knocked again. "It's me!"

When the lock clicked, she pulled the door open herself and slipped in, causing the woman to quick-step backward in a panic.

"I'm sorry. The grounds are open right now, and I can't be seen. Your papers arrived." She thrust the envelope forward. "Make sure everything is there. We can leave tonight."

The woman immediately dumped the contents onto the dinette table. Before Lily looked away, she saw a driver's license, a debit card, and a cheap black cellphone. A few moments later, the woman whispered, "It's all here, I think."

"Okay. Let's go around eleven. There's a bus that leaves at eleven forty-five. Are you ready?"

Amber looked around in resignation, her hand smoothing over pale strands of hair that had snuck out in all directions from a ponytail. "It's not like I have much to pack."

Lily reached out to pat her shoulder. "You look like you got some sleep, anyway."

"Not much else to do. It's been good for me. Good for us." She touched her belly again, her eyes softening with grief.

"Do you need any food? For now or to take with?" When Amber shook her head, Lily gave her arm a gentle squeeze. "Then I'll see you in a few hours."

She slipped out the door and raced back toward the office, lighter now that she didn't have the documents on her. This would be over tonight.

After cutting down a narrow lane to dash toward the nearest building, she stepped clear of the last RVs and glanced toward the sound of an engine. And just like that, disaster struck.

She nearly collided with another body before it jumped away with a yelp. Lily drew in a breath so sharp it hurt; then her heart clenched with pain when she realized it wasn't a stranger she'd almost run into. It was her son.

"Everett!" she gasped, as if he didn't know his own name.

Had he seen anything? Had he followed? His face looked pale and stricken, lips parted and eyes wide with shock.

"I'm sorry," she stammered. "I was just . . ." Her mind blanked. This was her place of work. She did . . . *things* around here every day. Vital things. But now she couldn't think of *one* task to throw out for cover? "I was just . . . Are you ready for dinner?"

"Huh?" he grunted.

"We'll keep it simple with grilled cheese tonight," she managed to say in an almost-normal voice. "And tater tots. We haven't had tots in a long time." She forced a smile and kept talking. "We can count the ketchup as a vegetable just this once, all right? I won't make you eat a salad."

"Yeah." He laughed, though it cracked with nervousness. Why? Because he'd seen something he shouldn't have?

"Okay," she said, mind spinning between addressing the issue or ignoring it. She finally grasped on to the excuse of their fight. That was probably why he was acting strange.

"Okay," he repeated, before hurrying past her to grab his bike.

Even if he'd seen her go into the RV, that couldn't mean anything to him. The woman would be gone tonight. He wouldn't have time to snoop around. Unless he did it right now. "I need you to unload the dishwasher before I start dinner," she blurted over her shoulder as she walked away. "Can you do it now?"

"Yes. Sure. I'm coming." She heard the scuff of his shoes and then the crunch of tires. He would follow her home, and by tomorrow, if he had any time to poke around, there would be nothing left for him to see.

But she couldn't forget that moment of stark alarm on his face.

She'd emphasized to him over and over again how important it was to follow the rules in life, to stay out of trouble, to be honest. She could never tell him the truth she hid from everyone: that she worried about Everett's morals no matter how nice a boy he was. That she feared he'd inherited more from his dad than dark hair and a tendency to freckle.

Something had been deeply wrong with his father, because Jones had lived a friendly, normal, open life while he'd been embezzling money, hiding it away, and planning his escape. Some dark flaw had allowed him to do that, and on her loneliest nights, Lily wondered if Jones had been born that way . . . and what that could mean for Everett.

She could never tell him that. She could barely admit it to herself.

She needed to set a better example for her son, and she couldn't put her livelihood in danger, and now this damn cop was sniffing around? No. She'd been blessedly cop-free for a few years now, since they'd finally given up their fantasy that she was hiding Jones under their noses.

No, this had suddenly gotten too dangerous. She'd call Zoey and put a stop to this tomorrow. No more risks. They just weren't worth it.

CHAPTER 4

"Everett," she whispered softly, barely a breath of sound in the dark. Her son didn't stir, so Lily kissed his messy brown curls and backed slowly out of his room.

He'd been so cuddly tonight, more like the little boy he'd been last year than the teenager he'd been this afternoon. After dinner she'd finally made those cookies, and they'd snuggled on the couch and watched some old *Steven Universe* episodes. In the end neither of them had apologized because neither had brought up the argument at all. Not healthy, maybe, but she'd been relieved.

This day had been far too much to handle already, and there was only more stress coming before she could fall into bed. She'd just wanted to feel his warm little shoulder snug against her side, and his head tipping to rest on her when he got sleepy.

When she teared up at the memory, she knew without doubt that the day was breaking her down.

"Keep your shit together," Lily whispered to herself as she tucked her license into her pocket and grabbed her keys. She'd only be gone half an hour, forty minutes at most, he'd be fine, and then she'd be in bed, and tomorrow would be as normal as she could make it.

After turning off every light except the bathroom, she locked up and practically tiptoed to her car, as if anyone else lived within shouting distance. When she pulled up as close as she could to the RV, the door swung out and the woman hurried out to open the passenger door.

"Thank you," she gasped as she buckled up.

"It's nothing," Lily lied, and handed her the bus number and time she'd written down. "That one leaves at eleven forty-three, heading south. You set up an anonymous email account on the new phone?"

She nodded.

"Okay, go ahead and buy a ticket now. Once you get to a big station, you can head anywhere from there. I'm told there should be three hundred dollars on the debit card, so keep track of that."

Lily scanned the dark road as they drove, but she didn't spy any cars, and then they were on the highway, heading into the brief, black lull of isolation between this town and the next. Buses parked at the big truck stop there for a meal break.

The young woman next to her put off waves of fear that ratcheted Lily's own muscles into a tight ache. Amber kept looking back at the road behind them, though Lily wasn't sure if she was watching for cars or saying goodbye to Herriman. Whichever it was, she was sure they might both explode with tension before they made it past the wheat fields to the faint glow on the horizon beyond. The fear and uncertainty, the haunting terror of an utterly unknown future . . . Lily hadn't faced what Amber was facing, but she'd dealt with that sick feeling of losing the ground beneath her and fearing she might lose her grip on her own child.

She'd come to this town hoping she might re-create her own childhood, even hoping she might re-create some family. But her stepmother had looked right through her whenever they'd crossed paths, and she'd only seen her teenaged half brothers from a distance. With her father dead, no one was interested in bringing Lily into the fold, not even when she'd desperately needed help.

But Amber wasn't just alone. She was running for her life.

When they finally emerged from the darkness into the first sprawl of lights and houses, Lily glanced over to see a glint of silent tears on pale skin. "Amber?" she said gently. "Are you okay?"

She shook her head first; then she nodded, but she didn't say a word; she only took a band from her pocket, pulled her blond hair into a low ponytail, and tugged up the hood of her sweatshirt to hide as much of herself as she could.

"You ordered the ticket just fine?"

"Yeah."

Lily reached past her to pop open the glove compartment and withdraw a travel pack of tissues. "Take these."

That surprised a watery laugh from the woman. "Thanks. I guess I'll need them."

Lily wanted to ask a hundred more questions as the giant sign illuminated with food-court choices finally peeked up in the distance. *Do you have family? What's your plan? How will you take care of your baby? Will you really stay gone?* But she asked nothing even as she pulled into the huge, glaringly lit parking lot.

"Can I . . . ?" The woman swallowed hard. "Can I wait here in the car? Until the bus arrives?"

"Sure." Lily didn't pick up her phone, but she wanted to. Everett was fine. If he woke up and looked for her, he'd call. But when was the last time he'd searched her out in the middle of the night? Maybe a year ago after a nightmare? Two years?

He'd had so many at first. He'd cried for his dad, who'd been such a force of nature and charisma when he wasn't caught up in work.

Work. She almost laughed at the idea as she pulled into the dimmest spot she could find. Jones had been working on lining his own pockets and not much else.

Just as Lily reached to turn off the ignition, the sleek silver bus turned into the lot, brakes hissing in protest as it slowed. The woman beside her opened her door almost immediately, clutching her backpack tight to her distended belly as she swung her legs out. "Thank you" was all she said before she stood and slammed the door. The bus door accordioned open, people poured out to flock toward the bright-white glare of the station, and Amber rushed across the cement to climb the steps as soon as the doorway cleared. No shopping for snacks, no last-minute bathroom break; she desperately wanted to be gone.

Lily sighed with her own relief at escaping all this trouble. It was over, and she wouldn't do it again. She hadn't ever had the right motivation, anyway. Of course she'd wanted to help women in trouble. Who wouldn't? But she'd also wanted to convince herself she hadn't lost all her daring and guts in the past six years.

She pulled away from the station, away from the frantic waves pouring off Amber, and away from the lights of civilization. It didn't feel like escaping, though. It felt like being swallowed by a deep, dark mouth.

Amber's fear had left Lily feeling vulnerable and restless. She needed to reach out to someone, so she dialed Zoey. The screaming volume of the phone blasted over her car speakers, and Lily winced, but she didn't turn it down. She was still connected to the world, even if she felt entirely alone as she moved farther into the night.

"Lily?" Zoey answered. "Is everything okay?"

"Everything's fine. I'm done. She . . . I mean, I'm heading home."

"That's good. It's great, actually. Thank you so much."

"Zoey . . ." She hesitated, pride warring with fear. Zoey was so brave and so indefatigable, and Lily was just . . . scared. Hiding like a wounded animal. But she *was* wounded, and she had a son to protect. "Zoey, I can't do that again. I can't put my job at risk."

Her best friend was silent for a moment, and Lily wondered if she was nodding or frowning or rolling her eyes. After all, Zoey put her actual life on the line helping people every day, and she sometimes got exasperated with Lily's refusal to open her life back up. "You didn't do anything wrong," she'd said so many times. "Get your chin up, girl!"

"I get it," she finally responded. "I'm so sorry if I asked for too much."

"No, it's not that. I volunteered. Everything just felt intense this time. I got spooked. That's all."

"Are you okay?"

"I'm fine," Lily said. And she was. She relaxed a little into her seat. "Things are normal. Everett is going to explode if he doesn't get a phone, my class is boring but I'm pulling an A, and my love life is still nonexistent. How about you?"

Zoey chuckled, and the warm, raspy sound melted even more of Lily's tension. "Omar's new foster puppies are finally sleeping through the night, so I feel like Superwoman these days."

"Congratulations! Are you still up for a cup of coffee sometime this week?"

"I'm always up for a cup of coffee."

When they disconnected Lily felt like herself again. Tired, yes, but the normal kind of tired she always felt.

Zoey had been the first friend she'd made when she'd moved to Herriman as a little girl, and she'd been her first friend when Lily had moved back as a married woman with a tiny baby. After the police raid, Jones hadn't been there to face the consequences, so everyone had turned on Lily. Everyone except Zoey. She knew way too much about bad husbands from running the shelter, and she understood that Lily had been another victim of Jones's crimes.

She was amazing, and Lily wasn't, and she couldn't try to keep up with her friend's bravery. She'd get back to living a safe, quiet life and keeping her damn head down, down, down.

If Everett had seen anything, it would be nothing but a curiosity now. Things were back under control, and she could keep her life in order while she figured out how to navigate the next few years.

"One more year," she whispered to herself, pleased at the way the number had decreased to almost zero. One year and finally the foreclosure would fall off her report, she'd have her accounting degree, and she could get a better job, buy a house, and move to a real neighborhood. The bankruptcy would hang around a bit longer, but she'd have seven years of paid bills and decent credit to offset that. She could get Everett out of this town and out of this lonely apartment.

They could even take a vacation, drive all the way to the gulf, rent a little condo on a Texas beach. She'd never seen the ocean, and neither had Everett, and she wanted to show him that before it was too late. Before he grew up and moved away and told stories of the strange, isolated life she'd given him.

And he would move away. She knew that. When his father had first vanished, Everett had wailed at the idea of leaving their house and moving. "Dad will come back and we won't be here!"

She'd cried with him, but it had been a simple grief, because she couldn't fix the problem. After three months of missed mortgage payments, the bank had swooped in, and they'd been homeless. This job had put a roof over their heads.

But now . . . now life was more stable, and she'd lived through a few years of Everett's complaints about "this stupid town," and she wanted something better for him.

They were so close. Another year and she could move up instead of over. With a better credit score, she could find work in accounting, pretend the past six years hadn't happened, and even tout her long, steady commitment to one company. One more year and they would escape this town for something better. All she had to do was not fuck it up.

The town no longer seemed as idyllic as it had when her father had moved them to Herriman, settling in his old hometown to raise a family. Lily had spent three happy years here before Dad had decided he didn't want a wife and child anymore. Well, not the *same* wife and child, anyway. He'd found comfort in the arms of another woman pretty quickly, and then he'd found comfort in having two strong sons.

Her mother, barely treading the waters of emotional stability before the divorce, had needed a job and an apartment—and above all else, a new man—so she and Lily had moved to St. Louis.

If Lily had returned to Herriman with her own husband and child in an attempt to re-create her old happiness, that effort had failed spectacularly. It was time to move on. Or almost time.

When she eased off the highway exit toward the dark road to the business park, she noticed the car right away. It was parked on the frontage road that stretched out like a tail along the small neighborhood of shuttered houses, but outside the reach of the closest streetlight. The dark-colored sedan faced the road, but if there was someone inside, Lily couldn't see them. It was all one twisted lump of shadow and reflection.

She rolled past the corner, straining to look, but then she snapped her head forward and drove on. It was none of her business. She'd left her burden at that truck stop, and now she was free and clear. Goose bumps shivered over her skin, but she made it home, closed the gate behind her, and refused to look back.

CHAPTER 5

When the boy sitting next to Everett got up to exit at his stop, Josephine plopped right down into the vacated seat and leaned close. "Hey," she said.

"Hi." He'd passed her in the hallway at school that morning and dared to tip up his chin in greeting. She'd smiled and said hello, and he felt like maybe they were edging toward friendliness.

She bumped him with her shoulder. "I asked my mom if I could hang out at your place after school, and she said that's fine if your mom calls her."

Everett drew his head back in alarm at this sudden acceleration. "*My* place? Why would you want to come to my place?"

"I want to see your *environs*." She drew the word out, sounding like a comic-book villain. "Your apartment sounds cool."

After a nearly sleepless night of thinking about what he'd found in that locker, Everett felt too tired to navigate this minefield, so he decided to just ask. "Are you doing this to make fun of me or something?"

She rolled her eyes and slouched down in her seat, staying quiet for so long that Everett began to squirm. She finally sighed and tipped her face toward him. "Okay, like I said, Bea moved, and I'm stuck way out here for three more years until I get my driver's permit. You seem like a nice guy. You're the only one around. We should be friends. That makes sense, right?"

He kept staring at her until she rolled her eyes again. "Are you racist?"

"No!" he practically shouted.

"So your social calendar is full way out here? You have secret woodland friends or something?"

It took effort not to crack a smile at that. He crossed his arms tight over his chest as a reminder to play this cool. "No, I don't have secret woodland friends."

"Then invite me over, dummy."

Everett didn't know what to do. He hated that she'd brought up his living arrangements last time, but a lot of that was self-consciousness rubbing his insides raw. The way he lived was weird. There were definitely no other kids in Herriman who lived in a business park, so it burned like fire that she pointed it out. But he was better than that, wasn't he?

He could give Josephine a chance, if only because Mikey had become so entranced by the demons of online gaming. Everett uncrossed his arms cautiously. "All right, fine. You wanna come over?"

"Yes, I certainly do," she answered formally. They didn't say another word about it. When the bus stopped with a whine of brakes and the door whooshed open, they stepped off and turned down the long road toward the cement block buildings in the distance.

"Walk on the wrong side of the road," Everett said, nudging her toward the left. "That way you can see trucks coming."

"My mom always says that too."

"Does she tell you not to have your earbuds in when you're outside?"

"Yes."

They both bit out hard laughs before they settled into quiet. His mom had been acting so weird the night before that he'd convinced himself she'd seen him coming out of that locker. When she hadn't exploded in anger, he'd spent their whole evening together worried about her quiet disappointment and when she might spring it on him.

The relief he'd felt when she'd kissed him good night and sent him off to bed had lasted one blissful hour. Then he'd been awoken by the sound of his door closing. A quiet sound. Noticeable in its sneakiness.

He'd heard the same sound from the front room then, the purposefully soft closing of a door followed by the distant jingle of keys.

What the hell?

Everett had tiptoed at first; then he'd raced to the living room to look out the window when he heard a car start. His mom drove into the maze of the storage facility, and two minutes later, the gate had opened and she'd sped out into the night.

An emergency trip for milk, maybe. Or eggs. Laundry detergent? But why had she gone deeper into the complex before driving away?

He'd lain in bed for nearly an hour, first just weirded out about his mom's behavior. But then he'd started thinking about what he'd found that afternoon in the new locker, and he'd clutched his covers over his face and squeezed his eyes shut.

There were innocent explanations for a board papered with information about missing girls. He knew that. Maybe the renter was a cop or a private investigator. Maybe even a reporter. At first he'd been thrilled with the discovery, though he'd only spent a few minutes poking around before he'd worried his mom might come looking for him.

But then, lying in the dark, the only person within one square mile of a pitch-black night, he'd started imagining more dangerous possibilities. What if the renter was obsessed with the missing girls because he'd taken them? What if Everett had been poking around the belongings of a serial killer? What if there were cut-up body parts in those storage bins?

At long last, he'd heard the creak of the gate rolling open, then the rumble of a car, the engine ticking loudly in the familiar way of his mom's ancient hatchback, and his eyes had actually burned with thankful tears. He'd turned over on his side, ears straining at every sound of her unlocking the door, setting down her keys, then slowly opening his bedroom door to peek inside.

Where had she gone? Was something wrong?

His mind stuttered over the question again and again, because he couldn't imagine his mom doing anything bad. She'd always been so steady, *too* steady, too attentive and present and *there*. She hovered and checked up on him, and said no to sleepovers more often than not.

"Are you taking Spanish next year?" Josephine asked, breaking through his thoughts as though she couldn't take the silence any longer. "My parents want me to take Spanish, but I want to learn French. That doesn't start until high school, though, which is stupid. So I may have to take Spanish first."

"You'll be trilingual."

"True. Which would be kind of cool. And it would look good on college applications. I want to go somewhere far away for school. Georgia, maybe. That's where my folks are from. Where are you from?"

"Here," he said, though that wasn't quite true. "Actually, I was born in St. Louis."

"Oh, cool. A world traveler."

Everett laughed, the last of his dark thoughts blowing away. "That's me."

By the time they made it home, Everett was laughing so hard at Josephine's stories he forgot to be worried . . . until they walked into the office and his mom's surprised eyes went wide and locked right on them. Everett always had to make complicated arrangements to get friends dropped off and picked up afterward because no one could just walk over. He'd never shown up with an unexpected guest.

"Mom," he said, "this is Josephine. She lives over at the highway."

"Well, hello, Josephine."

"Hi, Mrs. Brown."

"It's Ms. Brown, but you can call me Lily."

Josephine glanced at Everett and lifted her eyebrows in a signal.

"Oh, right. Could you call Josephine's mom and let her know everything is cool and that you're here and we're safe and stuff?"

His mom leapt toward the office phone, all eager energy now. "Absolutely!"

Did she think he didn't have friends because Mikey didn't come over anymore? She looked way too happy at the prospect of a new visitor. Josephine gave her the information, and they wandered into the apartment, ignoring the overly cheerful parental conversation left in their wake.

There wasn't much to show off. A big living area with a drab kitchen that looked nothing like the kitchens in decorating shows his mom watched on cable. Though he supposed the space was "open concept."

He wondered what Josephine saw. The beige couch was nicer than the one they'd tossed last year, but it wasn't exactly stylish. Then again, they lived in Herriman. There weren't a lot of apartments, but there was a big trailer park. It wasn't as if Everett was the only poor kid in town.

Still, on Josephine's street, the houses were two stories with little front porches. She probably had a real dining room with a chandelier. Maybe she had a big yard and a trampoline, and one of those—

"Aw man," Josephine sighed. "It's just an apartment. I don't even see any hidden doors."

"Well, they're hidden, duh." He heard his mom laughing on the phone and tipped his head toward his bedroom. "Come on. I need to feed my cat."

"I'm not allowed to go into boys' rooms."

His skin blazed hot in a moment of embarrassment at the implication of what that worry implied, so Everett blurted out, "I'm gay," before he even realized he might say it. "I mean . . . I'm gay."

Her eyes went wide with the same surprise he felt over his sudden out-of-context declaration, so he stammered out an explanation. "I'm just saying that I'm not, like, going to try to kiss you or something. You don't have to worry. That's all I meant. It's safe. To come into my room."

Josephine laughed, a quick, loud bubble of amusement that popped in his ears, and for one single heartbeat, worry imprinted on him like a camera flash. Would she mock him? Tell him he was going to hell? Most kids around here went to church, though only their parents still cared about grimacing at the gays. And there wasn't much to say, anyway. It wasn't like he was old enough to go on dates.

Then her laugh turned into a sweet grin. "Well, *I'm* not gay. Aren't you scared I'll try to kiss *you*?"

The alarm he'd felt must have finally appeared on his face, because her smile softened into concern. "Hey, I'm just kidding. I wouldn't do that."

"I know. I mean, I don't really know, but I didn't think you would. Not because girls can't start things, of course. Just . . ." He shook his head, unable to think of a single logical conclusion to that sentence. *Because I trust you?* He barely knew her.

But her shrug ended his stuttering thoughts. "Can I tell my mom? She'll be much happier about us hanging out. She was a *little* tense. But I won't tell her if you don't want me to."

"No, that's fine. My friends know. And my mom. It's not a secret or anything."

"Good. Because my mom is super paranoid about boys."

Teen pregnancy was the one thing his mom didn't worry about, so Everett decided to be thankful for that small mercy. "Well, stand in the doorway at least. Mom doesn't know about the cat, so if she comes into the apartment, give me a signal and keep her busy."

"She doesn't know about your cat?"

"It's a stray. It stays outdoors. Mostly."

He hurried over to put out the food, apologized to Shadow for cutting things short, and was back in the living room by the time his mom popped in.

"Can I make you two some cookies?"

Everett rolled his eyes at her, pretending he was suddenly too old for cookies. "We're going outside. I'm going to show Josephine around."

"Just stay out of Mr. Mac's boat!" she called as they hustled toward the door.

He led Josephine through the RV area, pointing out the sports cars draped with car covers. Several owners had debuted their toys for spring, and all he could do was point to a blank spot of flattened weeds where a bright-yellow Porsche had once crouched. Mikey had been impressed with all this stuff, but Everett had no idea what Josephine must think. Maybe it just looked like he lived in a junkyard.

But it was all he had. Not a trampoline or backyard Jacuzzi in sight.

He saved the best for last, leading her to an old gray-green tank with rust eating at its edges. Anyone would think that was cool, right? "Look at this. Some guy bought a frickin' tank at an auction, and he's been hiding it from his wife here for eight months. People are so weird."

"Wow!" Pride sizzled through him at her open mouth and wide eyes. "That's crazy! And how long is he going to try to hide it? Though I guess the tank is smaller than I'd expect."

"Yeah, I looked it up. It's some sort of light tank? Still pretty cool."

"Definitely cool."

More confident now, he smiled. "Are you afraid of heights?"

She looked up and around before answering. "I don't think so."

"Come on." He led her to the tallest building on the grounds, built high for people who wanted to store their motorhomes and boats indoors. He gestured toward a metal ladder built into the rear of the building and out of sight of the security cameras. "Want to?"

"Heck yeah." She grinned when he began to climb and immediately followed behind him.

"This is so cool!" she said when they got to the top. The whole neighborhood lay before them, though it really wasn't much to see.

He pointed toward the huge field out back. "There are some good trails back there, if you've never been. I saw a porcupine once. And skunks. Do you have a bike?"

She nodded and turned in a slow circle. "I can see my house! My room's on the other side, though. I have a view of the stupid highway. Hey, what's the coolest thing you've seen here?"

"Here? You mean in storage?" At her nod, he frowned. "I don't know. That tank, I guess. Oh, someone had a coffin once, but it was empty. They were just waiting until they needed it for themselves, which is pretty weird."

"Yeah." A breeze carried up the scent of spring mud. She looked out over the meadow to the trees beyond before turning toward the sound of a motor. A car drove up the long road and turned into the front gate before making its way to another building.

"You should get a listening device. You could spy on everyone."

Everett held his breath for a moment, wanting to tell her he didn't need any technology to spy. He could break into units and dig through people's things whenever he liked. The words pushed at his teeth, wanting out. *I might even learn how to pick locks.* Her eyes would go wide again; she'd gasp and beg him to tell more.

He opened his mouth. Took a breath. But when she glanced over her shoulder at him, Everett closed his teeth with a snap. He couldn't say it. None of the kids at school ever talked about his dad, because it was ancient history. But history lived forever in a town like this, like a hovering ghost, and what if she told someone that Everett was a criminal too?

"Look!" she gasped, pointing back toward the highway. "My dad's truck!" A fire truck slid down the highway, lights flashing, though he could barely pick out the whine of the sirens. It moved through traffic like a toy, reminding Everett of a museum his mom had once taken him to that was filled with toy trains looping through miniature tunnels and over tiny bridges.

"Your dad is a firefighter?"

"Yeah."

"That's so cool! It must be scary, though."

"Sometimes. But mostly it's car crashes or other emergencies. There aren't many fires in a place like this. He's good at his job, so I don't worry much. He's just a great dad, honestly." She suddenly stood a little straighter, and her eyes snapped toward Everett as if she'd just realized something important.

He sighed at the regret he could read clearly in her expression. "I guess you've heard the story, huh?"

"Um . . . About your dad? Yeah. Sorry."

He shrugged. "It happened a long time ago, and a lot of fathers take off. It's not that different for me. He left my mom to take care of everything like any other deadbeat. But I'm glad you have a great dad." He moved closer to the edge of the roof, where a three-foot-tall edge protected them from falling.

He did miss having a dad, but nothing could be done about that. His dad couldn't come back even if he wanted to. And probably he didn't want to.

Josephine bumped his shoulder with hers. "Even great dads aren't perfect, just so you know. My parents broke up three years ago. Mom says he had a midlife crisis. I honestly thought I'd never be happy again, and I was so mad at him. So . . . I know it's hard."

"But he came back?" Everett asked, trying to keep the question as light as he could. He remembered telling his mom that Dad would be back. He remembered waiting. For years. He wasn't waiting anymore, though.

"Yeah. We moved here to start over."

"To *Herriman*? Doesn't seem worth the trade-off."

She shot him a narrow look.

"Hey, I'm sorry your dad came back and you had to move to Herriman!"

She tried to glare but broke into laughter. She seemed to get his sense of humor. She seemed . . . really nice.

Maybe next time he'd tell her about the storage units, because he desperately wanted to tell *someone* about what he'd found yesterday. Anyone.

In the bright daylight, he felt less certain about what he'd seen, and way less scared. He'd go back in as soon as he could, and this time he'd write down the names of the girls and look them up online. Maybe it was all a gross joke. Or a crime that had been solved a long time ago.

That was probably it. That was why it was in storage.

"Hey, do you like mysteries?" he asked her.

Josephine smiled.

Yeah, he'd tell her as soon as he found out more.

CHAPTER 6

Lily was thrilled to have Josephine over for dinner, though she hadn't been to the grocery store that week, so she'd had to order pizza. Not that the kids had complained. They even liked the same kind: ham and pineapple.

The two seemed to have fallen easily into friendship, already calling each other Ev and Josie and bending their heads close together to look at Josephine's phone every five seconds.

The girl's mother, Barbara Woodbridge, had promised to have the kids over soon, but she'd explained that she was working seventy hours a week during tax season and her husband was a firefighter on rotation for twenty-four-hour shifts at a time. Lily wondered if she could tap Barbara for career advice someday, though any accounting jobs she might take would likely be far from here.

Despite the pizza, she got out real plates and made the kids sit at the table with her so she could get to know Josephine better. The girl was funny, polite, and smart, though she seemed to hate English class as much as Everett did. They both loved reading and absolutely hated writing. A friendship made in heaven.

When the phone rang, Lily excused herself to answer it. There was no rest for the weary when you lived on-site.

"Ma'am, this is Detective Mendelson. I'm following up on your security footage."

She was struck by an immediate bolt of relief that she no longer had anything—or anyone—to hide. "Oh. Hi, Detective. Yes, I checked through everything as promised, and there was nothing there. Quiet as a mouse." When she glanced toward the kids, they were both staring right at her, so Lily walked out of the apartment to the office.

"And since then?"

"Since then?" she parroted. "It's calm as ever out here."

"You haven't seen anything odd when you're out and about in the evenings?"

"I'm not," she said quickly. "Not really. I have a young son, so our evenings are quiet, and we go to bed early. I haven't been wandering around in the dark. Is there something dangerous going on?"

"I'm not sure, Mrs. Arthur. Is there?"

Her body jerked straight, touched by the electric shock of his words: *Mrs. Arthur.* Her married name.

"It's . . . it's Ms. Brown," she said faintly. But he knew that. She'd told him her name.

"Of course. My mistake."

It hadn't been a mistake at all. It had been a warning. But a warning about what, exactly? Sheltering a person running from abuse was hardly a crime; it only violated the rules of the business and a few building codes. If this was all about Jones . . .

She shook her head, her hand gripping the phone so hard that her knuckles ached. *Mrs. Arthur.* It hadn't even been his real name. Or it had, in a way. Jones Arthur had started out life as Arthur Jones. He'd reversed the names as a way to leave his juvenile history behind. Start fresh. Or just fool everyone, including his wife.

Another reason she'd changed her son's name. No child should inherit a scam for an identity.

"What do you want?" she finally asked past clenched teeth. He didn't answer, and she imagined him staring, waiting for her to squirm, just like all those other cops had.

Mendelson hadn't been a detective back when she'd been in and out of the police station for interviews, but he could have been a patrol officer. She'd been in such a daze for those first interrogations she could have been in a room with him several times and remember none of it.

"I spoke to quite a few people in the area yesterday, Ms. Brown," he said, finally deigning to speak. "You were the only one who seemed nervous. You wanna tell me why that is?"

No, she definitely did not. "I really don't have any answers for you, Detective," she forced out. "I didn't see anything. I don't even know what you're looking for."

"You have an interesting history in this town," he continued as if she hadn't spoken.

"It's not my history. It's something I was witness to."

"Is that right?"

"Yes. I didn't steal anyone's money. I didn't run away. I'm still right here, aren't I?" She took a deep breath, trying to calm the bitter panic in her voice.

"Regardless . . . I think I'll drop by sometime and go over a few details with you. See if we can't jog that memory. Have a good evening, Mrs. Arthur."

She stood frozen for a long moment after he hung up. His voice had been perfectly pleasant, but his words had held threat. Of what?

But she knew exactly what. Her husband's case was still unresolved. *He* was unresolved.

She stared straight ahead, teeth grinding until her jaw ached. Had Detective Mendelson meant he would come tonight? Tomorrow? She registered a shadow from the corner of her eye and whipped around to see Everett's head poking past the door of the office. He watched her, a shallow frown marring his forehead.

"Ev! I didn't see you there!"

He took her in for a long moment before silently retreating back to the apartment. Lily frantically reviewed her side of the conversation. She hadn't mentioned Jones but she'd obviously been talking about him.

She didn't speak of him with Everett. Not that she wouldn't if he asked, but because she couldn't bring herself to broach the topic. She'd lied to her son over and over, and the guilt of it burned through her. He'd find out someday. She knew that. He'd find out that his dad had been in touch and she hadn't told him.

She'd been sure she was doing the right thing when he was nine, but now she didn't know. Now it felt wrong, like she'd taken something from him, when it had been Jones who'd taken everything. Jones who'd abandoned them so he wouldn't have to go to prison. Jones who hadn't sent a card or letter for two years and thought he could just drop back into a child's heart with no obligation, no commitment.

Lily swallowed hard several times, choking down her alarm and grief.

She had nothing to offer that cop about Jones. Nothing that he could know about at least, so she had nothing to fear. And if Everett wanted to talk about his dad, she'd keep up her charade.

Pasting a smile on her face, she walked stiffly back into the apartment. "Should I make those cookies now?" she asked, hoping a treat would distract them, but Josephine groaned.

"My mom already texted that she'd be here in ten minutes. No cookies for me, I guess."

Lily busied herself with cleaning up the already clean kitchen while the kids sat tight together on the couch, watching another video on Josephine's phone. One more thing to feel guilty about. Everett just wanted to watch YouTube videos and follow his friends on Snapchat like all the other kids. But he wasn't like all the other kids.

What if his father found him and pulled him into his twisted world of secrets and crime and lies? Jones was so goddamn charming. He lied like other people breathed.

But Everett's thirteenth birthday loomed before her, only three months away now, and she'd promised he could finally buy a phone. Then he'd have access to the world, and the world—and maybe his father—would have access to him.

"She's here!" Josephine chirped suddenly, and Lily tossed aside her towel to walk her out.

Barbara was parked outside the gate, and she rolled down her window as they approached. "I like your home security!" she called.

"Thanks! It's a nice benefit to the job." They shook hands and chatted for a while until Barbara finally waved goodbye.

"Thank you so much for letting Josephine come over."

"It's my pleasure. We get a little lonely way out here."

Lily waved as they pulled away, but her hand paused in midair as she registered another vehicle behind Barbara's. It wasn't on the road but parked across the street in front of the plumbing supply place. Maybe somebody broke down and left their ride. Or perhaps an employee got picked up by a friend for the night.

Lily stared hard, watching for any sign of movement, but the store lights were off, and she couldn't see anything but the shape of a dark SUV. "Shit," she cursed. Detective Mendelson had made her paranoid. A vehicle might have been parked there once or twice a week for the past six months and she wouldn't have noticed until now.

"I need a drink," she muttered, thinking of the red wine she'd stashed under her bed. She didn't particularly like red, but it didn't need refrigeration, and she didn't want to leave alcohol in the kitchen for her son to experiment with. She tried to protect him in every way she could, reading all the pamphlets the school sent home about alcohol, drugs, depression.

Don't keep alcohol in the house. Don't drink in front of your kids. Set a good impression. Hide your wine in your bedroom like the pitiful parent you are.

Lily huffed out a bitter laugh. When she'd met Jones, she'd never even tasted wine, and she still had yet to taste the good stuff. Her bottles were eight dollars max, and most were closer to six, and being at room temperature didn't help the quality.

God, it felt like a movie she'd watched once, that brief moment of her life she'd spent in a beautiful two-story house with a nuclear family on a reasonable budget. They'd been planning a trip to Disney World. She would've seen the ocean on that trip. She would have insisted on it.

She'd had wine by then, of course. She'd even had a martini at a neighborhood party, though she hadn't liked it. If everything had gone as planned, she would have been an established neighborhood organizer by now, volunteering for the PTA and maybe working in the school office for a few hours, with Everett already in middle school. Or maybe they would have had more kids.

She winced away from the idea of what might have become of her if Jones had gotten away with his crimes for another year or two. They'd been halfway through finishing the basement, anticipating the space they might need once Everett had a little brother or sister. She would've had another child. A baby to take care of in addition to a young boy. She didn't want to think about how much more hopeless she would have felt.

Lily glanced at the glass door, hesitating before she went back in. But she couldn't hide outside forever, wondering what the hell her ex-husband's crimes had dragged to her doorstep this time.

"Homework hour for both of us," she declared once she was back inside and locked up tight behind two doors. To keep the peace, she ignored the window he'd closed on the desktop when she'd walked in. At least he got out his backpack without arguing with her, and he retreated to the couch so she could work on an online assignment.

He seemed entirely back to normal. "I really like Josephine," she tried, testing the waters of his mood.

"Yeah. She's cool." He didn't seem inclined to offer more, so she dropped it. She knew there was no chance it was a romantic involvement, since he'd blurted out at age ten that he liked boys and not girls. He'd been clear on it since then, so what more could she ask about Josephine? It's not like he would volunteer answers anyway.

She was too strict to be one of those moms who got treated as a best friend. That was what she'd chosen, but she did occasionally yearn for adolescent giggles and whispered tales. Hell, she'd barely left those behind when she'd had him at age twenty.

When an alert buzzed on her cellphone, Lily looked up from her work to find that Everett had retreated to his room and she was all alone. A glance at her phone revealed that it was five minutes to eight, and her gate alarm was ringing.

Mendelson. Heart hammering, hands shaking, she lurched to her feet and raced to the office. When she glanced at the security feed, she was sure it was him, appearing just as promised. A white man leaned out the open window of an SUV to push the buzzer again. A second glance revealed that he looked nothing like the detective. This man's hair was shaggy and brown, not blond. Just a stranger here to give her a heart attack.

She glared as she turned on her microphone. "Can I help you, sir?"

"Oh hi!" he said, his eyes flashing up to the camera. "I'm here working on my uncle's storage unit. I misplaced the note with his gate code on it, so I was hoping you could buzz me in?"

"Sorry, sir, I can't open the gate without the code. You'll have to call him."

"I just tried. He didn't pick up."

"Please come back between nine a.m. and six p.m. tomorrow after speaking with your uncle."

He winced, his eyes crinkling. "I really need some stuff out of there, and I have appointments tomorrow. Any chance you could let me through for just a moment? I remember the combination for his lock. I'll be quick."

She glared at his hopeful smile, suddenly thinking about that SUV she'd seen across the street. And Amber's palpable fear over her abusive partner. This guy could be anyone, and she wasn't about to let him in.

"The office is closed. I'm not allowed to let anyone in after six p.m. without a code. No exceptions." That wasn't quite true. But she'd be damned if she'd take any chances this week.

She watched the man run a hand through his dark hair, but it fell back over his forehead immediately.

"No exceptions?" he pressed.

"None," she answered, not bothering with any apology this time. It was dark, she and Everett were alone, and she wanted him gone.

"Okay, I'll be back in a couple of days."

She crossed her arms and watched until he backed up and turned around. Then she watched the cycle of all the security cameras to make sure he was truly gone. Creep.

Unwilling to deal with more stress, she locked everything up tight again, then tapped on Everett's door. "I'm going to bed early with a book. Lights out at nine thirty tonight!"

"Got it," he called. She successfully resisted the urge to open the door and give him a tight hug that he'd try to squirm out of. He hadn't brought up his dad or his eavesdropping, so she wouldn't either.

Two glasses of wine later, her own lights were out at 9:30, and she fell into the dead sleep of a woman who was no longer smuggling other human beings on and off her property.

The cordless phone in her bedroom woke her at ten. Since it was the business line, she ignored it and let it go to the messaging system. When it rang again five minutes later, she silenced the ringer, but past the closed door of her bedroom and the front door of the apartment, she heard the line ring again. And again.

Every speck of sleepiness vanished as worry shone a bright, merciless light into her brain. She thought of the SUV across the street, the man at the gate, the woman in the trailer, the police detective and whatever had him so worked up.

Two minutes later, she finally snatched up the phone. "Who is this?" she growled. When there wasn't an immediate answer, she let her anger out. "What the heck do you think you're doing, calling over and over? If you're outside my property, I'll call the cops right now."

"Lily," a voice murmured, all hush and gravel in her ear.

Frowning, she turned on her bedside light and sat up. "Who is this?"

"It's just me. It's fine." His voice cleared up on the last words, as if he hadn't used it for days. And she knew exactly who it was.

"Jones?" she croaked, her own throat going dry as a bone.

"Yeah. Hi."

Her hands tingled. Her breath came too fast. The light she'd turned on seemed to multiply and spin around the room. Yes, he'd called her a month ago, asking about Everett, but he hadn't sounded like this. Like he was hiding somewhere in the dark. And before this, he'd only called twice in two years.

"What . . . what are you doing? Why are you calling again? You can't . . ."

"Oh, you know. Just checking in."

She shook her head. "You can't call me. What if they're listening? They're going to think I'm . . . This isn't safe. A cop was just *here*. Right here."

"It's okay. It's an internet call. They can't trace it."

"Trace it?" she snapped. "I'm not worried about *you*, you arrogant asshole. If you get me into trouble again . . . No. I can't do this. I haven't even gotten out of the bottomless well of shit you threw me into six years ago, and *I can't do this.*"

"I know. I'm sorry. I'm just . . ."

"Just stay away."

"What if I can't?"

"What?" She was endless anger now, the fear all burned away. "What does that even mean?"

"Nothing."

Lily groaned, unwilling to dance in circles with him. "What the hell do you want, Jones?"

"You know what I want."

Her anger dipped into uncertainty. She had no idea what he was talking about. "I don't know. I have nothing, so I couldn't give you anything even if I wanted to. And I *don't* want to."

He paused for a very long moment. So long that she wondered if he'd disconnected. "Jones?" she whispered.

"There's Everett," he answered softly.

Her lungs froze at that, her throat shut. It was the tremble in her jaw that broke her free, because she'd been scared for so many years, and she desperately wanted to be brave instead. "How *dare* you? How dare you threaten me like that?"

"It's not a threat. I just want to speak to him. That's all. I hoped he might answer the phone since he's older now. Twelve."

"I know—" She closed her mouth and took a moment to lower her voice on the off chance Everett didn't have his earbuds in. "I know how old my son is, Jones. I don't need you to tell me."

"I know how old he is too, Lily. He's still my son. When I called last time, you said I could talk to him when he's older. I've been thinking about it, and I think he's old enough to keep a secret."

"You want your son to be in on the *conspiracy*? You want him to help you hide? Live with the lies? That's disgusting. You left us. You *chose* that. You burned down our whole world and didn't even look back to see if we were okay."

"I knew you'd be okay. I never involved you in anything. Never had you sign any forms or open any accounts for me—"

"That's your standard? I'm not in prison? Everett's not in foster care? So we're *fine*?"

"Well, you're better off than I am."

She actually felt an urge to laugh at that absurdity. "Jesus Christ, *we* didn't do anything wrong, Jones. *You're* the criminal. You're the lying, thieving piece-of-shit fugitive who's never been honest one day in his life. You deserve to live how you're living. We don't. We didn't deserve any of this."

He had the nerve to sigh as if she made him tired. "Can we please not do this again? I just want to talk to my boy."

Madness. That's what this was. Pure madness that her fugitive ex-husband thought he should be able to drop into their lives at any moment without being hassled about it.

"A boy needs his father," he said, and she swallowed hard to keep from belting out a wordless scream of rage.

"Jones," she growled. "You sent Everett a card on his seventh birthday, and I gave it to him. I did. And then two *years* passed before you wrote again. He waited. He waited for you to write again, or to come back for him, and you didn't. A boy doesn't need a father he can't count on. I won't let you slide in and out of his life like the slimy little secret you are. You already let him down in the biggest way possible. He loved you so much and you abandoned him."

"He's old enough to make his own decisions about me now."

"No, he's not. He's a child."

"I was working at thirteen, supporting myself, making my own money."

"You'd already been in juvie once by then, from what the cops told me."

"Lily—"

"Don't call here again. If you do, I'll hang up and call the police. If I hear one hint of you, *one hint*, I'll turn you in. Maybe then they'll finally believe I didn't help you steal anything."

He stayed quiet for a long moment. "Didn't you?"

Her hands shook. She'd made one mistake. One. She wasn't going to sacrifice her son's well-being over that. Jones could go straight to hell.

"If you're still alive when Everett is eighteen, go ahead and reach out. I'll take the fall for being the mean mom who kept you at bay, because I'm an adult who accepts responsibility for her actions. Right now all my responsibility is for him. Goodbye, Jones."

She hung up, ears buzzing with adrenaline, eyes wide and darting over every surface of the room. Oh God, had Everett heard any of that?

Leaping from bed, she hurried to her door and cracked it open. The front room lurked dark and quiet, Everett's door still shut tight. The bathroom between them would have muffled her words before they could leak through his wall. He was safe. Or she was.

Lily got herself a glass of water and raised it with a shaky hand. She hoped that would stop her tears, but they still came, and she had to cover her mouth and rush back to her room before a sob could escape.

Everett had only the one birthday card. He didn't know about the others. Didn't know about the calls. Jones had gotten more persistent recently, but she'd keep him from Everett as long as she could.

Another sob broke free. How could she have been so completely taken in by a charlatan?

It's not fair. The phrase echoed through her head with slightly less volume than it once had. *Not fair not fair not fair.* It had been the mantra of her every breakdown once, but now it was only weary anger. Life wasn't fair to most people, after all. At least she'd chosen that man, even if he'd withheld very important information. Everett had been given no choice at all.

Jones had walked into the downtown St. Louis coffee shop where she'd worked the summer after her first year of community college. He'd immediately introduced himself, saying, "You're new here!" like she was a big surprise.

He'd only been three years past his own degree in accounting, so he'd stood out from the other white middle-class business guys who worked in St. Louis during the day before fleeing in a panic for the suburbs at night.

In fact, Jones had rented a cool little loft apartment in the minuscule tourist area of town, near the arch. Lily had been sharing an apartment in the much larger and shittier area of downtown past the railroad station, so he'd started offering advice about nearby take-out food. Then he'd asked if she'd like to grab take-out with him.

He hadn't been the most handsome man in the world, but he'd thoroughly seduced her. At twenty-five, he'd seemed light-years ahead of boys her own age. He'd taken her on real dates, planned weekend trips, he'd turned all his charm and focus on her, on Lily, and she had soaked it up like a plant growing toward an open window.

When she'd started classes in the fall, it had felt so much harder than before. All her time spent on dry homework and her minimum-wage job just so she could pay for more boring classes. When Jones had asked her to move out of her roach-infested sublet and into his bright and airy loft, she'd voiced only a token resistance. With no rent payment, she could cut her work hours and spend more time with Jones. Then when she'd gotten pregnant . . .

God, she'd fallen head over heels for that man, and she'd tumbled along for years, blindly in love.

She could see now how he'd wheedled his way into every nook and cranny of her many dysfunctions. A girl with a faint memory of a steady father who'd come home every night to their beautiful house . . . until he hadn't. Until he'd left for a younger, less volatile woman and started a new family. A father who'd drifted in and out of Lily's dull life before disappearing completely once the new kids had been born.

She'd craved stability. She could see that now. She'd dreamed of her own perfect nuclear family as her mom moved from shitty boyfriend to shitty boyfriend and her dad forgot her birthday year after year.

Jones had offered Lily her dream before she was even out of her teens. It could have been raining red flags and she wouldn't have noticed past their weekend trips to look at model homes, then their weekend trips to big-box furniture stores, then the emotional trip to an obstetrician to confirm the pregnancy test.

She'd walked away from college and friends and her job, and she'd sunk herself deep into the world of Jones.

The *fictional* world of Jones.

She'd been steeped in it, completely submerged. When her father had died unexpectedly from a massive heart attack, she hadn't been sure she wanted to attend the funeral, but Jones had insisted, and so they'd gone. And that had been the start of a dream that had morphed into a nightmare while she wasn't looking.

Once he'd clapped eyes on the idyllic little town of Herriman, he'd begun talking ceaselessly about giving Everett the perfect life, and Lily had been a dry sponge primed to soak up the fantasy.

Yes, a smaller town would be better than the St. Louis suburbs. Yes, there'd be a stronger sense of community and deep ties. They could build something in Herriman. Give their son security and love and roots. She still had family there, after all. Her father was dead, but he'd left a wife and sons behind.

Before Everett was a year old, they'd packed up for the Kansas plains. She'd never said it out loud, but she'd expected a mildly warm welcome from her father's family. She hadn't gotten it. Someone had finally broken the news to her that her half brothers had been unaware of her existence until she'd arrived for the funeral. She'd crashed her own dad's funeral, adding to his new family's grief.

Later she'd added to the grief of a whole small town, because she'd led a wolf to their door.

She could still feel the cold water from the kitchen tap splashing over her fingers. She'd been washing grapes for Everett when that echoing knock had boomed through the house, banging off hardwood floors and tasteful beige walls. She remembered cocking her head, only vaguely concerned. Then armed officers had swarmed onto her deck and approached the back door, and the twisted world of Jones had swallowed her whole.

Lily had been left with a son, a foreclosure, forty-five thousand in credit card debt, four civil lawsuits to settle, and an entire town that hated her. Not to mention years of questioning and surveillance from the police.

The least she could do for Everett was stop his father from damaging him the way her dad had damaged her. Promises broken over and over. The absolute heartbreak of realizing he just didn't love you enough.

No. Better for Everett to know a simpler truth: his father had broken the law and he'd run to avoid arrest. He was in hiding, and he couldn't come out.

Her son barely remembered his father now, and Lily meant to keep it that way.

CHAPTER 7

"Thanks for coming to dance practice with me," Josephine said as they made their way slowly back to school from the small dance studio off Main Street. "It was cool to have an audience."

"It was way more fun than doing chores." Everett had called his mom from the office before his last class of the day and begged to go to an after-school meeting for a new robotics club. She'd immediately said yes, of course, thrilled at even a hint of interest in STEM and asking what time she should pick him up.

Everett wasn't the least bit interested in engineering, so he had no idea when the robotics club met, but it had bought him a free afternoon to walk to Josephine's class with her and use her iPhone while she practiced.

He'd hoped to drum up the nerve to tell her about the storage lockers and the missing women, but so far the idea of it stuck in his throat like dry rice. Still, the afternoon had paid off. He'd been able to research the missing girls' names on Josephine's phone and confirm that he wasn't crazy and the bulletin board wasn't a joke.

"Hold on," Josephine muttered. "It's my dad." She stopped on the sidewalk to type out a text. "I've got to meet him at the station in ten."

She walked on, but Everett felt frozen to the cement, caught between the desperate need to share and the terrible fear of doing so.

"Can you keep a secret?" he blurted out, skin burning with hot regret before the words were even finished.

That got her attention. Josephine jerked to a stop and spun toward him like she was still in front of studio mirrors. "Are you kidding? Heck yeah, I can."

"I mean a real secret. Something that could get me in trouble."

She raised a hand to touch the little gold cross at her neck. "I swear," she said solemnly. "I won't tell anyone."

Everett glanced around as if someone might be lurking nearby hoping to eavesdrop on two sixth graders. "I found something weird in one of the storage units," he whispered.

"Weird?" she whispered back.

"Yeah. Sometimes people don't lock their units. And sometimes I . . . go in them." When her lips parted in shock, he shook his head quickly. "I don't take anything. I wouldn't do that. I'm not a thief."

"Okay," she breathed. "But what did you find?"

"I opened a new locker this week, and . . . well, there's a bulletin board inside, just leaning against the wall, and it has all this stuff on it about missing women."

Josephine gasped, her hand flying to cover her open mouth. "You mean like *Unsolved Mysteries*?"

"Yes. Exactly like *Unsolved Mysteries*."

"I love *Unsolved Mysteries*!" she squealed into her hand.

"This morning I snuck into the unit to write down their names, but I couldn't do much more than that." He could have done more, but he'd felt paranoid and vulnerable, sure every time he turned his back that when he looked again, the locker's owner would be standing in the doorway. He'd scrambled out and sprinted through the gate and toward the bus stop as quickly as possible. "I think they're all still missing," he said. "The girls. And they're all from Herriman."

"What? How is that possible? I've never heard anything."

"It was a long time ago. Like 1999, 2000."

"How many are there?"

"Five, I think. Maybe just four. The fifth one maybe ran away."

"Is it police detective stuff? Old records and files?"

"I'm . . . I'm not sure. There were a lot of boxes and some furniture. I don't know who owns it."

Josephine grabbed his arm, and in that moment he knew he'd done the right thing, telling her. Telling someone. He wasn't alone with it now, which made it seem cool instead of scary. "I want to see it," she said.

Everett grimaced. He'd risked his own ass going into lockers, but it didn't feel right to risk getting Josephine in trouble. "Maybe. If we get a chance. I'll send you the list of names. I was looking some of them up on your phone while you were dancing. Here."

He took her phone and typed in "Marti Herrera." A photograph of a dark-eyed young woman popped up. She was laughing, her frizzy blond hair blown back by the wind. He angled the phone so they could both see it.

Herriman police are asking for help finding local woman Marti Herrera. Her husband was out of town, working for a national moving line, when he arrived home last Tuesday evening to find that Marti Herrera, age twenty-one, had not returned from her work at the Free Throw Sports Bar the night before. She clocked out at 12:32 a.m. on Monday, March 13, and her car has since been located in the Free Throw lot. It is unknown if she was forced to leave her car or if she may have gone somewhere voluntarily.

"The police said she probably ran off with some guy, but she'd just gotten married the year before."

Josephine took her phone back and peered at the snapshot. "And she's never been found? I've listened to crime podcasts, and if a woman is still missing twenty years later, she didn't run off. That's something lazy cops say. Like, who stays gone forever?"

"Even from Herriman?"

"Even from here. Hey, can you figure out who's renting that space? Get into the records?"

"Yeah, I think so."

"I'll ask my mom if I can come over tomorrow, okay? We can go back in, see what else we can find."

Everett winced at the idea of heading back into that dark locker, but he kept his face turned away to hide his worry. He'd wanted someone to know his secret, and now it wasn't just his secret anymore. Now he had a partner, and he didn't want to let her down.

But something felt so off. Or maybe that was his conscience. But also his mom was sneaking around, and he'd heard her lie to that cop who'd called, pretending she hadn't been out the night before. All of it struck a strange chord of fear in him that he'd never felt before. Whatever else went on in his life, his mom was always the same, always the floor beneath him. Unyielding, maybe, but *steady*.

"Aw, man. I've only got one minute," Josephine complained after checking her phone. She picked up her pace, racing toward the school grounds and the fire station just beyond it. "I'll ask my mom," she reassured him, and Everett tried to feel reassured.

"Okay."

"I can't wait!" She grabbed him in a quick hug before sprinting away.

Everett's heart warmed, turning soft. He'd denied it to his mom, but he had felt kind of lonely lately, and not just because of Mikey. A sense of isolation had prickled through him now that he was hitting puberty in this stupid small town. There was only one other boy out in his school, and well-meaning classmates had already tried subtly pushing them together, despite that the guy was a dumbass with a mean streak who thought it was funny to wear a Trump hat to school. Everett couldn't stand him.

He hunched over on the bench, head in hands while he waited for his mom to pick him up. He dreaded the ride home, the questions she would ask and the lies he'd tell. But she wouldn't have taken a half hour out of her workday to pick him up just because he wanted to hang out with his friend. Or maybe she would have, but he hadn't wanted to risk her saying no, so a lie had been better.

And his mom was telling lies too.

Why had she implied to the police she'd gone to bed early when he'd heard her leave the house? What had the police even been calling about in the first place? Maybe his mom had seen him coming out of that storage unit after all. Maybe she was trying to protect him.

He'd taken only a couple of things from a couple of lockers. Nothing that anyone would notice. A cool pocketknife. A few comic books. One little plastic case of British coins. And one game disk for his ancient Wii, and he hadn't even liked the game. But maybe those comic books had been valuable. Maybe he should put them back.

His stomach began to ache, but he knew it was only guilt. There wasn't some elaborate law enforcement scheme to trap a misdemeanor criminal. He'd already looked up what a felony was, and no way had he stolen over a thousand dollars. But if it wasn't about Everett's criminal activities, there was one other criminal connection Everett could think of: his dad.

She never talked about him, so Everett never talked about him either, but he knew the whole truth. He'd used school computers to search for his dad's name years before.

Despite the flashes of bright and happy images Everett glimpsed in his own memories, his father had been a bad guy. A thief, a liar, a coward. He'd stolen from dozens of people and abandoned his family.

He'd disappeared completely, unlike his friends' divorced dads, who at least saw them a few weekends a year.

It had to be about his dad. Or . . . maybe there was another man. A boyfriend. Everett thought of the TV shows he watched when his mom was busy on the grounds. Sex seemed like a complicated subject, lots of sneaking around, lots of tangled lies. What if she was involved with a married man and he'd gotten into some kind of—

"Ev!"

He jumped at his mom's voice, jerking his head up to spy her parked in the school pick-up lane. "Hey!" he yelped before jogging over to slide into his seat.

"Lost in thought?"

"Yeah."

"Does that mean it was good?"

Frowning, he stuffed his backpack between his feet and slammed the door. "What?"

"Robotics!"

"Oh." His stomach burned. "Yeah, it was fine."

"So you're going back?" she asked, all high-pitched hope for a profitable future in technology.

"Probably."

"That's great, Everett. You really should find something to replace the Green Gardening Club."

"Oh my God, Mom, I only did that for the volunteer credit."

She mumbled, "You said you liked it," as she pulled into traffic.

"Whatever. But I need to follow up with some robotics stuff, so I'll be online a lot tonight."

"No problem. I'm meeting the auctioneer to cut a lock when we get back, so you can have the computer. Are there going to be fees involved?"

"I don't know."

"All right, give me the bad news when you get it."

Everett slid down in his seat and stared out the window as they reached the highway and sped up.

"Everett . . . are you okay?"

He could ask her if he wanted. Ask her about that cop and where she'd gone. Or he could confess his own secrets and see if his stomach felt better. But that was a terrible idea, because that might heal his stomach, but it would absolutely destroy any chance he had of ever going outside again. He'd be on house arrest for sure, his mom constantly muttering about her stupid job and how he'd put it in danger. Watching him with that worried look that made him feel more like his dad than anything did . . .

"I'm fine," he bit out. "But if we lived anywhere else I could just walk home. This is so stupid."

"Not true," she snapped back. "Plenty of kids around here live on farms way farther out than our place. Maybe I should wake you up at five a.m. to do chores, and see if you think they have it better."

"Jesus," he whispered, crossing his arms tight and glaring out at the highway signs as they whipped past.

As soon as they got home, she told him to start his homework, and Everett happily retreated to his room. He dropped his backpack in front of his door so he could buy himself a second of warning; then he opened his window and left it open. Shadow hopped right up, and Everett slid a food bowl to the floor on the far side of his bed where it wasn't visible from the doorway. Once she was happily settled, he joined Shadow on the floor and reached beneath his mattress for the one yellowed piece of newspaper he'd smuggled out of that storage unit.

Lynn Cotti. She'd been missing for two years when the article was written, but the snippet of text was just a brief story clearly prompted by the poor woman's mother. "She left for a week or two before, but that was nothing like this," Maria Cotti had said. "I just want answers."

There was no specific investigator mentioned in the story, just a general response that the Herriman police had followed up on every lead they received.

Lynn Cotti had been at a party in town on the night of May 21, 2002, and then she'd left. Alone or with someone else, nobody seemed to know. She'd been at the party, and then she'd never been seen again, and that was the whole story.

Her absence hadn't even been noted for over a week, but when her roommate had called her mother, her mom had phoned the police. Lynn had been twenty years old, a high-school dropout, and a big sister who loved playing gin rummy with her two younger siblings.

Everett briefly wondered what might be said about him if he disappeared. It would probably wind up being a story about his dad. Maybe they'd accuse Everett of running away to join him. Maybe he should. It would be way more exciting than this place.

He immediately felt guilty for the thought. He knew his mom had been the one to take care of him all these years. He loved her; she was just always so *there*.

When Shadow finished her food and climbed into his lap, Everett cuddled her close and absorbed her purring into his body as he imagined an article starting with his newfound love for robotics above a picture of him in his Green Gardening Club T-shirt. He managed a laugh at that.

Then he imagined his mom looking for him like Maria Cotti had looked for her kid. What would his mom even do with her time if Everett wasn't around? More online classes? Or maybe she'd get married or something.

He froze when he heard the office door open. When his mom's footsteps creaked closer, he carefully lifted Shadow and set her outside before yanking the blinds down.

"Ev?" she called through his door. "I'm heading out to snip a lock for an auction. You doing okay?"

"I'm fine!" he yelled back.

She'd be gone for a good while. She had to document the belongings removed from a locker, so she couldn't just snap off a lock and leave.

Everett tiptoed to the apartment door and listened as his mom left. Then he listened harder before he dared to crack open the door to the office. He glanced toward the security camera mounted above the front desk to confirm it was still pointed straight at the door, and then he crept over to the computer.

It was password protected, but he'd sat at this desk next to his mom often enough, smelling the bitter coffee smell that always wafted from the mug next to the keyboard. He knew she used the same password they used on their personal computer.

"*Yes,*" he whispered when it fired up. But his victory quickly deflated into cold defeat. He'd expected a helpful app with the storage company logo, but at first all he could find were spreadsheets. He finally found an icon for something called Star Logistics, but it only opened a primitive program asking for codes and IDs he couldn't puzzle out.

"Shit."

Everett turned to the metal filing cabinets instead. The top drawer seemed filled with mostly blank forms, but the second yielded better results. He immediately grabbed the file labeled *B Building Leases— Current* and slapped it open on the desk.

"B8," he muttered as he flipped through the dozens of sheets. "B8, come on." And there it was, finally. The last page in the file.

Lease Application was typed across the top of the form. The lessee name was filled out in blocky blue ink: Alex Bennick. He recognized his mom's handwriting below that, naming the unit as B8 and listing the monthly and annual rent charges. That application was stapled to a signed one-page contract. The third sheet was a photocopy of a driver's license.

An old man.

Everett stared at the unsmiling face for a long time, hoping for a hint. The guy *did* look like he could be a murderer. And he was right here among them. He'd stood in this room a few feet from their home; he'd spoken to Everett's mom. Everett shuddered as he looked at the man's pale skin and narrowed eyes. His flat, hard mouth and short white buzzcut. The copy was grayscale, so Everett couldn't see the color of his eyes, but the license said blue.

Were they in danger?

Everett blew out a hard breath. Probably not. He could be a bad guy. But he could also just be one of the grumpy old men who got coffee at McDonald's on school mornings. A grizzled farmer. A bitter retired cop. The guy they brought in to drive the school bus when the regular driver got sick.

Then again, he supposed any of those men could be murderers too. That was the point, wasn't it? They were always neighbors and fathers and coworkers.

Everett winced when a distant bang of hollow metal chimed from somewhere deep in the complex. He darted to the window to look through the blinds, but the only movement was the nub of a stray dandelion bobbing from a crack in the sidewalk.

He quickly slipped the page into the copier and waited for the flash before stuffing it right back into the folder. One second later, he'd slammed the file drawer, grabbed the copy, and strode straight back to safety. When he got to the desk in their apartment, he hurriedly jotted down the date of the lease agreement before he forgot. It had been rented only two years before.

With his mom out of the office, he could check absolutely anything online, because he'd have plenty of time to close windows and delete history before she made it all the way inside the apartment. Hunching over the keyboard, he began his search.

Alex Bennick was still alive as far as Everett could tell, and he'd been in the Herriman paper multiple times. Not for anything criminal, but he'd been an associate superintendent for the school district. That was incredibly creepy because instead of a cop investigating disappearances, he was a school employee obsessed with missing girls. Yikes.

Everett immediately opened his text app and typed out everything he'd found for Josephine.

OMG! Did these girls all go to school here??? she wrote back immediately.

Not sure. There are three high schools in the county??? I'll try to check it out.

First things first, though. He looked up the man's address online. He knew the names of only a few streets in town, and as he zoomed out, he didn't recognize anything. After shifting the map around a bit, he finally spotted a highway down the road. From there, he found his own street.

Frowning, he glanced back and forth between the two spots, then requested directions from his address to Alex Bennick's. Weird. It said the drive time was fifteen minutes, but on the map it looked so much closer.

He zoomed out again, tilting the map in a different direction, and suddenly he saw it. "Holy shit," he whispered before racing into his mom's room for the phone. "Josie," he panted as soon as she answered his call. "This guy lives on the other side of my field! Less than two miles away! He's right there!"

"No way. And he's still alive?"

"I think so."

"Everett, he's so close to you! That's scary! What if there are bodies in his house? Oh my God, what if there are bodies in the storage unit?"

Everett blinked in shock, then blinked harder. "No. There were some boxes, but I'd be able to tell, I think. There'd be a . . . smell?"

"Yeah, that's true. We'll find out more tomorrow, for sure. Send me everything you find on the missing girls. I'm in full detective mode now."

He hung up the phone, then stood there, caught off guard by Josephine's renewed insistence on helping investigate. He didn't really want to go back into the locker. What if this man actually was a killer? But if he was, shouldn't they find out? Tell somebody? They could solve a half-dozen cases. They'd be famous. Maybe there were even rewards.

When the phone blared in his hand, Everett dropped it, then jumped back when it hit the floor with a hard crack of plastic. "Oh no," he whispered, crouching down to examine the damage. But only the battery case had popped off. The ringer kept going. When he turned it over, an unknown number appeared. It wasn't Josephine. He snapped the case back on and set it on the charger. It finally stopped ringing, though it started again before he left the room. Everett closed the door and backed away.

That was weird. He'd just called his friend to talk about a murder, and now someone was being creepy.

He sat down at the computer, and when he searched for Lynn Cotti, he found the digital version of the exact article he'd hidden beneath his bed. He googled the next name he'd written down: Yolanda Carpenter. The articles about her were shorter, and he'd read most of them on Josephine's phone.

He was pasting both links into an email for her when the phone began pealing again. Eyes darting toward the sound, he clicked SEND and then slowly rose to his feet to face his mom's bedroom door. The electric chirp shrieked over and over. Finally it stopped.

He held his breath, waiting. Nothing happened. It was just a telephone call after all. "Wuss," he scolded himself when he finally let out a breath. But when the phone rang again, he jumped, his whole body jerking into the air in shock.

Heart hammering, he took one careful step toward his mom's door, then another.

When he heard his mom's voice outside the window, talking to someone just before the gate squeaked open, Everett felt stupidly relieved.

He wiped his search history, closed the windows, and then retreated to his room to hide behind his closed door until dinner.

Tonight was game night, and they'd already agreed on Monopoly. For once, he felt glad his mom had read too many articles about quality time with kids. He wasn't sure he wanted to be alone once it got dark.

CHAPTER 8

Lily had Thursday afternoons off, and she woke that morning with a desperate need to get out of the house and off this track of worry over Jones. She just wanted to leave behind her churning thoughts of what he might be up to and think about herself for an hour or two. She also had a half-price coupon for her favorite café, and that was as luxurious as her world got these days.

The Silver Spoon at 12:30? she texted Zoey.

When Zoey texted back with an enthusiastic YES!, Lily cracked a relieved smile and finished up her morning chores. She even sent Everett off to school in a good mood, handing him a couple of dollars for an extra slice of pizza at lunch.

Spring had definitely sprung, and the seventy-degree forecast inspired her to put on a yellow skirt and a shirt that wasn't made out of sweatsuit material. To add to the excitement, the Silver Spoon had a new summer menu, and Lily was scrolling through the choices as she hiked a bag of office trash up and shoved her way out the front door.

"The face behind the ominous voice!" a man called, and Lily nearly dropped the bag when she whirled toward him. He looked respectable enough in jeans and a clean button-down shirt.

"It's me from the other night," he said.

For a moment she could think only of the barrage of calls from Jones. Then the guy said, "I lost the code," and she recognized the flop of dark hair over his brow. The man from the gate intercom. He certainly looked harmless in the bright light of day. Thin and fit but only about three inches taller than she was, and he was keeping his distance so far, hanging back toward the pedestrian gate.

She offered a careful smile. "You made it back. I'm sorry about the other night. Security is tight around here."

"No worries," he said easily. "My uncle's belongings are stored here, so the high security is comforting." He walked closer to reach for the bag of trash, and she waved him off. This was her job.

"I'll show you where the trash cans are in case you need them. We don't allow any large amounts of garbage, but I can give you directions to the municipal dump if you're cleaning out."

He followed her around the corner, still keeping a respectful distance that inched her guard down a tiny bit. "Can I get the gate code from you now? I seem to have misplaced my sticky note."

She grimaced at his request. "Are you an authorized user? If not, I'll need your uncle to fill out a form and sign off on it."

"I'm . . . not sure, honestly. And my uncle forgot the code again."

She glanced at him. Midthirties, maybe. Cute despite the circles under his eyes and a pallor that spoke of too much office work. "Are you moving his stuff out? I can give you the termination paperwork too if you like."

"Not quite yet. He's moving from assisted living to memory care, so he's stopped arguing that he'll be getting back home soon."

"Ah." Lily winced. That happened a lot around here, especially with the demographics of this part of Kansas skewing older and older. "I'm sorry."

"He has great caretakers and help, but I'm between gigs right now, so I figured this is as good a time as any to get a start on helping sort his belongings. I know how much regret people feel when they find amazing personal stories and it's too late to ask any follow-up questions."

She smiled at that, but didn't press further. "I think that's a great idea," she said. "Let me get you that form."

Aware of him following behind her, Lily felt suddenly grateful that she'd dressed in something besides ancient jeans. He was kind of cute and maybe not a creep, and even if she didn't date, she still had an ego.

She dug out a form from the filing cabinet and handed it over. "You've been by already, you said? So you know the unit number?" When he told her, she typed it in and asked his name.

"Alex Bennick."

"That's odd." She squinted toward him. "You're the name on the lease."

"That's my uncle. I'm Alex C. Bennick. He's Alex Q."

"So you're Alex Conrad?"

He looked surprised at that. "Yeah."

"Congratulations. He listed you as an approved user when he filled out the lease. You're in."

He snapped his fingers. "Hot damn, what a day!"

Laughing at his exaggerated excitement, she took his license to confirm his identity and noticed the address in Tennessee right away. "Memphis? You're a good nephew, coming so far from home."

"He's done a lot for me. I lived with him for a few summers during college when I didn't have anywhere else to go. Are you from Herriman?"

"Kind of. I lived here during my childhood before we moved away."

"Maybe we knew each other."

"I was seven, so unless you were in my Brownie troop . . ."

"Pretty sure I'd remember that adventure." He held out his hand. "Like I said, I'm Alex."

She took his hand, still cautious about this stranger but aware that any other reaction would be rude. "I'm Lily."

"It's great to meet you, Lily."

When his smile widened to a grin, she actually blushed a little.

"I'll be here on and off for at least a week, but I'll try not to bother you after hours again."

She slid him a slip of paper with the gate code printed on it. "We lock down at eight during the week, office hours go to six."

"Got it."

He left but not before giving her a wink so subtle she couldn't quite tell if he was only squinting. She'd definitely tell Zoey it was a wink, though, just to liven things up a little.

Speaking of . . . She got out her laminated sign explaining the afternoon procedures and listing her cell number, grabbed her purse, and headed out for a few hours free of work and motherhood.

Zoey was her closest friend, though that wasn't saying much since she was Lily's only friend. And Zoey was close with everyone, throwing her arms and heart wide open to the world despite the kind of work she did. She'd just been born that way, apparently. When Lily had moved to Herriman at age seven, Zoey had marched right over from her house three doors down and introduced herself.

She'd been a bit busier since Lily had moved back with Jones and Everett, but they'd reconnected in fits and starts. Like everyone else in town, Zoey knew all about Jones's crimes, but she didn't know that he'd been in touch since. No one did.

When Lily spotted the café, she relaxed into the driver's seat, letting go of the worst of her tension. The patio was open, and it had been a long and dreary winter. They could sit outside and imagine themselves somewhere more adventurous than a small-town deli that called itself a café. But she supposed the espresso machine gave them that right.

Before she'd even stepped fully from the car, she heard her name called from the patio and looked up to see Zoey waving both arms like an overenthusiastic parking guide. Lily scooted between two fake potted plants and gave her a big hug.

"Mm," Zoey hummed, emphasizing her hug with sound effects. "You look great and ready for spring. How's Everett?"

"Annoyingly independent but otherwise fine. How are the puppies?"

"Mind-numbingly needy. Kids these days! Let's splurge and get cake for dessert. No arguments."

"Like I've ever said no to cake." She slapped the half-price coupon on the table. "And half your sandwich is on me, so you're welcome."

Thank God for Zoey. Lily wasn't sure she would've had the heart to build this life without her. On the days she felt like she was trudging through bare survival, Zoey reminded her that she was building something sweeter and that so many others had survived worse.

"So," Zoey started once they were settled, "what happened the other night?"

For one moment, she thought Zoey knew about Jones. That slight threat in the way he'd said that Everett was something Lily could give him. The additional threat of Mendelson and whatever new dirt he thought he'd dig up. But she didn't talk to Zoey about things like that. She kept their relationship light.

It wasn't that she didn't trust her friend. It was that she didn't trust anyone. How could she? Her judgment was atrocious. Her gut had failed her. She was truly her mother's daughter, and she couldn't risk bouncing from one disaster to another until she finally gave up and settled in the wreckage.

"Lily?" Zoey reached for her hand. "Did you run into trouble?"

She was asking about Amber and the drop at the bus station, not the other problems pressing down on Lily like gravity. "No, everything went fine. I just got spooked. I started thinking about putting my job on the line. I'm so close to leaving my past behind me."

Zoey didn't know about Jones getting in touch, but she sure knew the origin story. And when Lily spotted part of that story sitting on the other side of the patio, she gasped involuntarily. Zoey sat up straight and curled her hands into fists. "What's wrong?" she demanded, head pivoting to identify the threat.

"It's nothing," Lily said stiffly. "Just Cheyenne."

"Oh." But she had already craned her neck around to look behind them, and of course, Cheyenne glanced toward their table at exactly that moment.

Lily forced herself to hold still until Cheyenne was the one who turned away, her mouth twisting a little in distaste. She couldn't bear to look at Lily for very long.

They'd never had a heart-to-heart, so Lily couldn't be sure, but she'd put together bits and pieces over the years. Apparently Cheyenne hadn't known that Lily's father was married when they'd first met. Lily suspected she didn't like the blatant reminder of her transgressions. Because at some point she'd known and hadn't cared, and she'd somehow failed to ever mention to her own children that they had a half sister somewhere.

Lily had assumed her stepmother's cold shoulder at the funeral had been the result of grief. She'd been wrong. The cold shoulder was a permanent accessory.

"Sorry," Zoey whispered from her newly scrunched position in her seat. "Is she still looking?"

Lily waved a dismissive hand as Cheyenne and the woman she was having lunch with gathered up their shopping bags and stood to leave. "It's fine. Let her be uncomfortable. I didn't do anything to her."

She hadn't wanted to ask Cheyenne for help. When the bank had repossessed their home, Lily and Everett had even stayed at Zoey's shelter for one night. After that, they'd stayed at Zoey's own house for a week until Lily had swallowed her pride and finally contacted her stepmother for help.

Cheyenne had helped. A little. She'd given Lily the site manager job, after all.

Her stepmother didn't give the impression of being a cruel woman. When she interacted with other people, her face opened with friendliness, and her bob cheerfully bounced with her happy gestures. But it was different with Lily, almost as if she was jealous, and definitely as if she was resentful. Maybe she'd come to Herriman for the perfect life too, and Lily's existence had ruined it.

"Is she gone?" Lily asked, reluctant to turn toward the parking lot behind her.

"Yeah."

"You know she only gave me that job because it saved her money?"

"What do you mean?"

"When corporate bought back her location, my pay got bumped up fifteen thousand dollars. And that was only the *starting* pay for other site managers. So she got me out of sight of the rest of the town *and* she saved herself over thirty thousand in those first two years."

"Wow. That's . . ."

"Yeah. I guess it was her way of shuffling me aside. She tried to get me to apply for a different location after the first year. I should have, but Everett had started second grade, and things had finally settled down for him. I should have just done it. Gotten the hell out of here." Lily shook her head. "Maybe I had something to prove. To her. To everyone. To my dead father. Jesus, the dysfunction of it all."

"Well, you proved it, I guess. Literally no one else cares now. Look around. You're not the town pariah anymore." She held up her iced tea in a toast. "Congratulations!"

Lily laughed. "I'm living the dream." Their food arrived, and Lily moved her pickle to Zoey's plate. She meant to drop the topic. She really did. But doubt gnawed at her. "I didn't know where else to go, you know? Everett was so traumatized when the bank kicked us out of our house; he said Dad wouldn't be able to find us when he came back. I thought . . . Well, I was scared to drag Everett out of Herriman just because I wanted to run away."

Like his dad did, she left off.

"Hey." Zoey ignored her food to reach out to Lily. She squeezed her hand in a gentle grip. "Are you okay?"

"I'm good." Lily nodded. "Seriously," she said when Zoey raised a doubtful brow. She finally eased her hand away to pick up her sandwich. "Just didn't expect to see her."

"Well, you seem stressed. And you sounded scared the night you called me. Is everything all right?"

Lily made her voice cheerful. "That was nothing. The woman was terrified, and obviously the circumstances were dire if you sent her to me, and I think I let her fear get to me. That's all. It sort of oozed out of her pores. Poor thing."

Zoey nodded. "You know I can't say anything, but I wouldn't have asked if . . ."

"I know that."

"I won't call again, not for that. Okay?"

Lily bit into her sandwich to avoid having to answer.

A year before, she'd been making her normal tour of the facility when she'd heard a metal door lowering somewhere around the corner. A totally normal occurrence, but she'd rounded the building and seen nothing. No one leaving, no one locking up, and no car pulling away. She'd walked up and down the lane several times before giving up. But it had nagged at her brain until she'd decided to review the security footage. She'd discovered a woman leaving through the front gate in the afternoon and then returning an hour later, not long before Lily had made her rounds.

No matter how closely she watched, Lily couldn't find any evidence of the woman leaving the grounds again. It seemed as if she was still there.

Lily had tiptoed outside at dusk, and sure enough, she'd spied light coming through a crack beneath one of the rolling doors.

When she'd opened her phone to call the cops, the door had flown up, and a small woman overwhelmed by a cascade of wild black curls had nearly fallen outside to beg Lily not to kick her out. That had been the start of all this. That and Lily's own craving to prove that she could be strong again. She could be brave.

But she wasn't brave, not like Zoey.

"You know I want to keep helping," she said, her voice dark with guilt. "I really do. I just got scared."

"You're amazing," Zoey said as she reached to squeeze her hand again.

Lily huffed a laugh. "Come on, Zoey. This is your whole life, and you're never scared. You'd take on the entire world if you could."

"Bullshit. I get scared all the time."

Lily didn't think that was true, but she held her tongue. When that first woman had confessed to camping in her storage unit because a boyfriend had promised to shoot her if she left him, Lily had known exactly who to call. Unfortunately, at that late hour all three bedrooms in Zoey's county shelter had been occupied. It had been Lily who'd thought of the RV, the only one in the complex that she had the keys to, thanks to a forgetful owner now living overseas. Lily was the one who'd volunteered to break every facility rule and let her stay.

Zoey had asked for her help only twice since, and Lily squirmed with regret at begging off now. "It was honestly nothing," she said.

Zoey screwed up her face in a grimace. "Nonsense. You have to trust your instincts. You know I tell people that every single day. I won't ask again. I'm sorry."

"It's . . ." She blew out a long breath. She couldn't live her entire life as a mouse, could she? A cowering victim afraid to step out of place? "Please ask," she finally said. "You can ask, and if it doesn't feel right, I'll say no." Zoey shook her head, but Lily nodded back. "I know you won't ask if it's not necessary. I can make my own decisions."

Zoey didn't commit, but she let it drop and moved to sharing news about long-delayed local funding that had come through and the testimony she would give in the statehouse later that month.

She'd become a hairstylist after high school, but all that had changed when Zoey had lost her sister, Moira, to murder. Moira's husband had shot her when she was six months pregnant, and Zoey had agonized over every single thing she might have done or seen before that final, terrible attack.

She'd started her organization just a few months before Lily had moved back to Herriman. They'd both been too busy for much more than a chat when they ran into each other in town. But when the news about Jones had exploded in the town paper, Zoey had reached out to offer help, and Lily had finally accepted.

Zoey had been through so much worse than Lily had, dealing with her only sister being assaulted and abused and finally murdered, and she'd only grown stronger, more sure of herself. Lily was desperate to do the same.

"I think someone winked at me today," she said to change the subject.

Zoey raised her eyebrows. "You *think?*"

Shrugging, Lily raised a cocky brow in response. "I mean, I'm ninety percent sure. Maybe eighty-five."

"Was he cute?"

"Cute enough."

"I still can't believe you don't meet guys out there all the time. Aren't people always asking their big, strong friends to help them move shit? Tell me it was a big, strong himbo."

Lily snorted. "No, it wasn't a big, strong himbo. This guy was normal sized and seemed nice. And he's only in town helping his uncle, which is perfect for my taste."

"Your taste for not actually dating, you mean?"

Lily rolled her eyes.

"How are you ever going to meet a soul mate like that?"

She ignored the question, because she'd already answered it a hundred times. As if she'd ever trust a man again. "How the hell are you still a romantic with the kind of work you do?" she grumbled.

Zoey grinned. "I met *my* soul mate, didn't I?"

She groaned at Zoey's smug smile. Yes, Zoey had somehow met her perfect match the old-fashioned way, just going about her business at the natural foods store two towns over. The beauty of their three-year-old relationship was supremely annoying, and Zoey had somehow become an evangelist for real dating, in direct opposition to Lily's refusal to even consider it.

"Come on, Lily. You're still young."

"Old enough to know it's better to be single than deal with an asshole."

"Well, obviously I'll drink to that."

They clinked water glasses and dug back into their food. "This is nice, Zoey. It's been too long." Lily leaned her head back to let the sun glow over her face as she chewed.

"Jesus, girl, it's half-price sandwiches with county highway sounds included. You need a vacation."

That part was definitely true. A couple more years and she might actually be able to afford one.

By the time Lily returned home, she felt like she *had* been on vacation, complete with the slight warmth of a bit too much sun on her arms. She put more swing in her step as she stowed her purse in the office and headed back out to make the rounds. Bring on the detective's questions about her ex. It wasn't like she hadn't dealt with them a hundred times over, and she was tired of being scared.

It had all felt so dire when he first disappeared. When the police had come back day after day, then started pulling her into the station just when she thought they'd given up. But there weren't many big stories in Herriman, and they'd been humiliated by Jones's escape.

Lily had been too, in more ways than they knew.

But she couldn't go back to living like that. Couldn't suffer through the sleepless nights and the sobbing and the wild-eyed feeling that she might lose her mind at any moment.

Jones couldn't hurt her anymore, not really. Definitely not more than she could hurt him.

Could he?

CHAPTER 9

As far as he could tell, she never stayed away from the property long, and therefore never left him much opportunity. Instead, Lily seemed to be always lurking around the complex, or in the office, or at least inside the shitty little apartment behind it.

Today's unexpected departure had given him the chance to put on a jacket, pull a baseball cap low to shield his face, and explore the grounds for a few minutes.

It had been easy enough to peel back a section of fencing before zip-tying it back into place, since he'd carefully chosen an isolated corner that seemed safe from cameras. Once inside, even with the cameras rolling, he doubted she would suspect him of anything at all. He was only a random renter, an average white guy walking through the complex as if he owned the world. He noted every nook and cranny in the place in case he needed a quick hiding spot, but made his way steadily toward the office.

A six-foot-tall wooden privacy fence jutted out from the wall of the brick building that housed the office and the family living quarters. Knowing she was gone, he made a show of walking up to the office door and knocking as if he needed help. Keeping his chin tucked to hide behind the cap, he pretended to scroll through his phone for a moment while he peered in at the office layout and the heavy white door behind it that probably led to the apartment. He finally feigned losing patience for the camera aimed toward the door, then wandered down the walk as if he were still looking for help.

After following a turn in the concrete path to step around to the side of the apartment, he peeked through the slats of fencing. A cement patio hid behind the planks, hosting a couple of cheap chairs and a grill. A sliding glass door provided entry, and the open blinds allowed him to see into their home.

Though he didn't dare linger, he was able to catch sight of a flimsy dinette table and chairs, as well as the edge of a couch inside. He knew from long experience that opening a sliding door was as easy as taking candy from a baby. If he needed to get inside—

Something heavy thudded into the wood next to his ear, and his heart was still in midexplosion when he registered a bitter scratch of claws and a line of sleek fur. A black cat turned and glared at him before hopping into the patio area.

"Shit, that can't be good luck," he drawled, laughing with relief that he hadn't been caught prowling.

Taking the cat as a sign, he backed off and worked his way around the entire building before hitting the exit button on the gate. Whatever might happen in the coming days, he needed to get the lay of the land so he'd be ready for anything.

CHAPTER 10

"This is so exciting," Josephine whispered as they left Everett's mom behind in the apartment and rushed outside. School had felt interminable, waiting for the moment when he could finally show Josephine the locker. Fear still skittered beneath the excitement, but it felt distant now as his body pumped out adrenaline.

"Speaking of . . . ," Everett said as he shrugged his backpack on. "Follow me closely to avoid cameras."

"Everett! Hey there!"

He jumped in guilty shock when he heard the shout.

It was Sharon from across the street, hurrying over. He shot Josephine an apologetic look before they headed toward the pedestrian gate to meet her.

"Where are you kids off to?" she asked.

"Oh, you know. Just hanging out."

"Hanging out, huh? Well, I saw what you were up to, and you'd better be careful."

He felt all the blood drain from his face, and suddenly realized that was a real thing that happened, not just a punch line in cartoons. He dared a glance at Josephine's wide eyes, then jerked his gaze back to Sharon. "Wh-what?"

"Don't worry. I won't tell your mom."

They hadn't even visited the locker yet. Had she somehow seen Everett going in? "Oh," he ventured. "Okay?"

"That said, you really shouldn't be up on that roof. It's not safe. If I see you again, I'll have to say something. All right, Everett?"

A warm wave fell over his body, sliding from his head to his toes and leaving his knees weak as noodles. "The roof. Right. Yes. Of course, Mrs. Hassan."

She turned to Josephine. "I'm Mrs. Hassan from the shop across the way. It's nice to meet you . . ."

"Josephine," Everett supplied quickly.

"And Everett, the crawfish boil is in three weeks; do not let your mom squirm out of it. She needs to get out more often."

He nodded, shifting from foot to foot.

"Well, you kids stay out of trouble now," she said. "I'll be keeping my eye out."

"Yes, ma'am," they both chanted before spinning to hurry away.

"Jesus Christ," he rasped.

"Yeah, no crap," Josephine whispered. "Thought we were dead meat."

"My mom would absolutely kill me if she knew about this."

"Mine too. Though my dad might be willing to smuggle me to another state."

"Hell, I've got a leg up. My dad's already in hiding. I'd just have to find him."

A laugh burst so loudly from Josephine that Everett found himself joining in. It felt good to laugh about it, to let out the energy that had hardened and curled inside him. He still had the birthday card his dad had sent. *Happy 7th Birthday, Big Boy!* He hadn't signed it, but his dad had drawn a little cartoon bunny that he'd sometimes sketched on napkins for Everett.

"So . . . that's all true?" Josephine asked as they moved deeper into the complex.

He hadn't planned on talking about this, but Everett couldn't exactly avoid the subject now. "I'm not sure what you heard, but yeah. He stole a bunch of money from a bunch of places. The Ford dealership. Some trucking company. The hospital. I don't really know how it worked, but he took over a million dollars." Everett swallowed a thick pain stuck in his throat. His cheeks warmed until he was sure they must be glowing. "Then he left."

"Wow. I heard he was one of the FBI's most wanted."

He laughed a little just to break the clog in his throat. "I don't think that part is true. I never saw that online, anyway."

"I'm sorry."

"Thanks. It's not really that interesting. He just moved numbers around on computers. I didn't think anyone talked about it much these days."

"I don't think they do," she reassured him. "Bea told me because you got off at our bus stop so we saw you all the time. But I don't think my mom knows. She's never said anything."

He nodded, hoping that was true. He didn't have his dad's name anymore, and people seemed to have short attention spans for gossip. He knew his mom had always worried about repercussions for him, but kids didn't care about the stuff adults did. If his dad had murdered someone, sure. He'd be famous at school. But an accounting crime? Boring.

He did vaguely remember some boy saying, *Your dad's a thief*, in first grade, but the insult had rolled away forgotten, likely because it made six-year-olds picture some kind of ninja jumping from roof to roof, and that was actually pretty cool.

"Almost there," Everett said, and that was the end of the conversation about his father, thank God. Instead, Josephine began listing what she'd found about Alex Bennick, and Everett was glad. He didn't want to think about his dad. He wanted to think about anything else for a while.

"This guy worked for the school district for thirty years! So the first girl who went missing . . . Yolanda Carpenter? It was 1999, and she'd only graduated the year before. Or she was in school, at least. I don't know if she graduated. I know some of them didn't."

"I was thinking about that," Everett said. "If these were girls who caused trouble, they might have been in contact with the school district people, you know? Not just teachers and principals. Maybe that has something to do with this."

"That's right. Mary Elizabeth Sooner dropped out. That was in one of the articles you found. And then she disappeared less than a year later."

"So he could have been hunting girls at *school*?" Everett grimaced at his own words as they finally reached the right unit. He crouched down at the lock to turn the digits to the correct code.

"Turn on your phone light," he said, before rolling the garage-style door halfway up with a wince. This was always the worst part. The noise, echoing off concrete and metal siding. It was even more terror-inducing on the way out, when he couldn't see who might be coming.

She ducked in and he followed, lowering the door again after them. "Sorry. I can't leave it open or she might notice."

"All these boxes!" she said. "Jeez, that's a lot of stuff." Everett pointed out the bulletin board, and she drifted toward it, pulling him along with her phone's light. The scent of old newspapers and aging cardboard pressed in from the darkness.

The huge corkboard sat propped against file boxes on the cement floor. At first glance it was a muddle of photos and scraps and thumb-tacks, but after examining it several times, Everett could see it had been an organized grid before extra notes had been piled on, obscuring the original lines.

"Wow," she whispered. "This is spooky."

It was spooky, but it felt less so today with his partner in crime.

"There's Mary Elizabeth Sooner." Josephine pointed to what looked like a school photograph of a white girl with big blond waves and a bow in her hair. "And Lynn Cotti." This time she pointed to a photograph of a laughing teenage girl whose frizzy blond hair was in a high ponytail.

Everett leaned closer to look at the yellowed paper tacked next to her picture. It was the second page of the article he'd folded up and taken with him.

> Though initial stories indicated she'd had an upcoming court appearance and might have left town to avoid legal problems, it has since been revealed that the court date was a minor issue involving a traffic ticket. Lynn Cotti has not been seen or heard from in the two years since. Her mother says it's unlikely she would stay out of touch for so long. "She struggled a bit in high school, but she is a good girl. She came home every Sunday for dinner and games with her two little sisters. Gin rummy. Monopoly. Things like that. We always had lots of fun. She was arrested a few times, yes, but the stuff in the newspaper has been so wrong. My little girl has a family who loves her, and a room always waiting for her at home."

Sadness sank into his skin. "It's weird," he said. "Those women were all young. Nineteen, twenty, twenty-one. It seems like there would have been a bigger deal made. Five women in four years? That's a lot, especially in Herriman."

"It seems like most of them were dropouts or druggies. Cops don't care about women like that."

"Even here? *White* girls?"

She shrugged. "When I started looking up information, there were a lot of articles about girls that disappeared in the '80s and '90s and no one cared. Some serial killer recently confessed to, like, a hundred murders, and no one ever bothered connecting them because of who the women were."

Everett looked around, his skin crawling. "Seriously, are we in a serial killer's lair?" He'd meant it as a joke, but as soon as the words were out of his mouth, they both fell silent. He was holding his breath, and he thought Josephine might be too. The hairs on the back of his neck stood up until he couldn't take it anymore and swung around to check the space behind them.

No one was there, though the flash of Josephine's light off a mirror made him jump. "Whoever it is, he's probably just an amateur detective."

"Yeah," Josephine agreed. "Or maybe a relative of one of the girls?"

"I guess we don't even know that they're dead. They're only missing. Maybe they got the hell out of this town and never looked back."

Josephine scowled, but she agreed it was possible. "But whoever made that chart didn't think they were missing. Maybe because he *knows* they're dead."

"Still, he's really old now. And the murders stopped a long time ago."

"True."

When she started snapping pictures, Everett turned away from the flash to look for the light he'd stowed near the door. His vision had turned into patches of blue from her phone's glow, and he had to inch his way slowly back through the boxes. He still couldn't see it when he reached the corner, though.

Confused, he turned toward Josephine. Then he saw the flashlight. In front of her. Placed carefully on a shelf. His gut clenched tight with fear, shooting alarm through his body.

"Stop!" he shouted, the word far too violent against the metal walls.

Josephine froze, eyes wide, hands rising in defense. "What? What's wrong?"

"Someone's been in here. I left my flashlight right by the door. It's on that shelf now. I didn't put it there."

She took a step back toward him. "Are you sure, Ev?"

"Yes. We need to get out of here right now."

She looked wildly around. "There's not a camera, is there?"

"I don't . . ." He cleared the painful dryness from his throat and tried to get out more than a croak of sound. "I don't think he would suspect anything, right? He would've put on a new lock if he did."

"Right," she agreed, but her eyes still touched on every surface, her nervousness ratcheting up Everett's fear. He'd thought himself brave and angry just a few minutes before, but attracting the attention of an actual murderer suddenly seemed like a bad idea even for a rebellious kid.

He waved Josephine toward him so they were both near the door. Gesturing toward her phone, he whispered, "Turn that off and we'll look for any lights."

A starless midnight fell over them when she turned off the phone. His voice dropped to the barest breath. "Do you see any LEDs or a glow or anything?"

They were so close he could feel her head swiveling as she looked. "No. Do you?"

"I don't think so."

She turned the light back on, and they both sighed out a relieved huff of air. "Okay, this is officially dangerous and *not* okay. Let's go."

Everett put his ear to the metal. They held their breath for a long time, and he listened so hard he could hear the static fuzz of silence in his aching ears.

"Ready?" he finally asked.

When she nodded, he yanked the door up as quickly as he could, and they both ducked to clear it before he lowered the metal more slowly so it wouldn't bang against the concrete. He engaged the lock, and they rushed back the way they'd arrived.

"Have you seen him around?" Josephine whispered as they made it to the far fence line and slowed to a more normal speed. "Has he been here this week?"

"I don't think so, but I'm at school most of the day. He looks like a regular old white man, so he wouldn't stand out either."

"What if he'd caught us?"

"Yeah, we can't go back in there now."

"No." She shuddered. "We can keep looking online, though. And if we find anything, police take anonymous tips, I think."

Everett nodded, but his heart fell a little. For some reason, this had felt like something he needed. Like he could have been a hero, and then he wouldn't just be the son of a criminal anymore. His mom wouldn't have to hide and always try to keep pulling Everett back behind her for safety.

Josephine seemed to sense his mood and gently shoved his shoulder. "Let's go do that reconnaissance. See if he's even still around. He might have moved, and that's why he rented the locker."

"Yeah, good point. Let's go."

They slipped out the front gate and cut across the road to where it dead-ended at the field. Everett was already hitting the trail when Josephine said, "That's weird."

"What?" he yelped, imagining an old man with white hair walking toward them. But Josephine was craning her neck to watch over her shoulder as they walked, and the only thing he saw was a dark-colored car parked down the street. "It's just a car."

"There are those hidden lights in the front grille, though. That's a cop."

Everett's foot slid out on gravel, and he had to catch himself as he spun back to look again.

"Don't look, dummy!"

"Why the hell would a cop be here?"

"Can't be for us. They would've grabbed us when we came out. Haven't you ever watched *Hawaii Five-0*?"

Everett shook his head.

"Really? Because Daniel Dae Kim is my guy. So cute."

Everett didn't say anything as they walked along the dirt trail toward the distant trees. The police were back. Maybe the same cop who'd been calling his mom. Sweat prickled along his neck.

"Aren't police records public?" Josephine asked.

"Um. I guess. Why?"

"Maybe we could find out more about those cases. Just send a request or something."

"Maybe."

The trail dipped into a small gully, then back up. Josephine opened her phone map, and their little blue dot was moving closer to the address she'd marked. "Keep your eyes open," she said. "There could be bodies *right here*."

"I doubt it. I've ridden all over this lot." Still, she brought his attention back to the task at hand, and he began scanning the matted grasses for evidence. They walked only a few minutes more before they came to a barbed wire fence dotted with NO TRESPASSING signs.

"Shit," Everett cursed.

"You brought the binoculars?"

He dropped his backpack and dug out the used binoculars his mom had bought at a pawnshop back when he was in Boy Scouts. He peered through the sights, focused the lenses, then handed them to Josephine.

"I don't see the house."

"I couldn't find it either." He looked around. "Let's walk over to the trees. There's a rise there. I bet we can see better."

They followed the line of fencing along uneven ground, stepping around ruts and occasional piles of rocks that had been tossed out of the field. One of the fields had been tilled already, but not yet planted, though he remembered the way the wheat looked swaying green in the summer wind.

The cottonwoods were just starting to leaf, and they looked like they were misted with green fog that caught the sun every once in a while. When they stood beneath the closest tree, they could just make out a couple of roofs past the horizon.

"Want to climb?" Everett asked. Josephine tucked her foot into a V before he'd even finished. Ten feet up, they both reached a solid spot with a perfectly placed branch just in front of their chests and balanced there while Everett passed her the binoculars.

"I think that's it," she whispered, as if Alex Bennick might hear her. "The green roof. It had a green roof on satellite view."

Everett took his turn and nodded. "That seems right. It's just past that brown farmhouse."

"Do you see anyone there?"

Everett watched for a long time but saw no movement, though there was a gray SUV in the driveway. They took turns watching for fifteen minutes, but no one ever appeared.

"If he's dead we would have found that online, right?" he asked.

"I think so." She turned back to stare at the house. "Do you think we'd feel it? If someone evil were right there?"

"I have no idea."

She slapped her arm. "A spider! No way, I did not sign up for spiders, Everett Brown." She reached for the tree trunk. "I don't think anyone is there, anyway. Do you?"

"It's pretty quiet."

"I brought my Switch. Want to go back and play Mario Kart for a while?"

A little defeated now that the fear and excitement had settled down, Everett hesitated. "Tomorrow afternoon is teacher meetings. Can you come over again after our half day?"

"I have a dentist appointment at one, but I can bike over later. Do you think the teachers really have meetings, or do they just take a long weekend?" Josephine was already starting down.

Everett let her begin the climb by herself. She moved carefully, and while she was concentrating on the slow reach for each branch, Everett swung the binoculars around toward the storage center.

His strange and sprawling home sprang into view, closer than Bennick's house. He stared at the crisp details for a long while, expecting his mom to sneak out of the office and slink her way toward some hidden secret as he watched.

He shifted his view to the road and the parked vehicle that Josephine had said was a cop car. Maybe it was only a security guard. Shadows swallowed all the driver's features whole.

"You coming?" Josephine called up.

"Yeah." But as he watched, the cop car suddenly blazed to life, blue and red lights strobing. Everett startled, one foot skimming off the bark he stood on, his elbow cracking hard into a taller branch. He dropped the binoculars to windmill his other hand out in desperation, and his fingers miraculously found a grip. The strap around his neck jerked as it caught the binoculars, scraping his skin. His elbow burned, and so did his pounding heart.

"You okay?" Josephine's voice was a squeak of alarm.

Everett rolled his eyes up toward the road, and for one moment he was utterly confused at the distance. Through the binoculars, it had felt as if the cop were looking right at him, had turned on the lights just so he could hit the gas and rocket through the meadow toward their tree. But of course, the car was far away, and in the moment of Everett's slip, it had made a U-turn and was now just a speck racing away from them toward the highway.

"I'm okay," he croaked, but his knees shook so hard he had to rest for a long minute before climbing down just as slowly as Josephine had.

For one soul-freezing moment Everett had thought the cop was coming for him. Because Everett was a thief and a burglar just like his dad.

He ducked his head as they walked so she wouldn't see the tears in his eyes.

CHAPTER 11

Everett's scream echoed through the dark apartment and snapped Lily from restless sleep into immediate, rigid terror. "Ev," she rasped, her body jerking upright in a tangle of sweaty sheets. She pulled in a wheezing gasp, praying his cry had been only a part of her vague nightmare. It wasn't real, it couldn't be real.

But then it came again. "Mommy!"

Lily leapt up, stumbling on the bedding as she pushed off into a run toward her open door. He hadn't called her Mommy in years, and hadn't had one of his nightmares since at least fourth grade.

What if it wasn't a nightmare at all? What if it was Jones, come to claim his son?

"Ev!" she yelled as she flew through the hallway and launched herself into his door, banging it open. "Everett?"

A cold swipe of air whipped past her as she snapped on the light. Everett sat up, back pressed to the white rails of his headboard, blanket clutched high against his face. Only his eyes were visible, locked tight on his window.

"I saw someone," he croaked.

She rushed toward the window, registering that it was open to the night, the blinds rocking in the breeze as her joints went stiff with terror. "Someone opened the window. Get in the hallway. I'll call 911."

"I opened it."

"What?"

"I left it open."

She reached up and pulled the window down until it closed with a crack. After she locked it, she spun and switched off his light again so she could peer outside.

Moonlight shone weakly in, though the glow burned brighter the longer she stared and let her eyes adjust. "What did you see?"

"A man, standing there."

Her heart felt split in two at that. "A man? *Inside?*"

"No. Outside."

The light suddenly shifted, shadows writhing across the floor. Lily jumped with a yelp that made Everett whimper in response, but she shook her head and moved closer to the glass. "It's just clouds," she explained, angling her face to catch a glimpse of the moon. "Are you sure it was a man? What did he look like?"

"I woke up and something was blocking the light and then moved away."

Lily deflated with relief as she watched their tattered patio umbrella flap in the wind. "I think it was only a shadow, sweetie. A cloud or that old umbrella. It's really blowing out there. Have you been having bad dreams again?"

He shook his head, eyes still locked on the window. But then he looked at her and shrugged. "A few, not many."

"Were you having a nightmare tonight?"

Another shrug, which was a definite confirmation in tween language.

His nightmares had started the same night the police raided their house, looking for his dad. He'd had them every night for the first week; then they'd died down a bit. But when they'd been forced to leave their home, his bad dreams had returned with a vengeance for a whole year. Monsters coming to get him, monsters taking his dad, monsters coming for his mom too. Slowly, slowly, Everett had left them behind, stopped screaming for his father's help, and eventually they'd gone altogether.

Or maybe he'd just become too embarrassed to tell her.

She kissed his head. "I'm going to go turn on the porch light. I'll be one second. Are you okay?"

He nodded, but he still clutched his covers like a scared boy.

Lily circled out to the hallway and around to the sliding door near the kitchen to hit the light switch. The patio sprang into view, revealing a square of cement stalked only by the stray cat, who hunched in a corner, glaring right at her.

"Everett, I think it was that cat!" she called.

"It wasn't!" he responded as she hurried back to his room.

"The cat's sitting right outside."

"It wasn't the cat!" he snapped.

"Fine, but you only saw a shadow. Right?"

He looked a little calmer now, irritation with her distracting him from his bad dream.

She lowered his blinds tightly. "Better?"

He waited a moment before nodding, and she paused, feeling awful for him and not quite comforted herself. He wasn't a little boy anymore, but he was still a boy and he was still her baby. "Want to bring your blankets to my bed?"

His second of hesitation revealed exactly how spooked he was, but he finally shook his head.

"We can make you a place on the floor."

"No, it's okay."

"Well, leave your door open at least. It gets warm in here, and that helps the circulation." But then she noticed the extra blankets piled on top of him. "Everett, why was the window open? It's cold tonight." She glanced at the blinds, then back to him. "Everett. The *cat*?"

"What?" he snapped. "She's nice."

"You know we're not allowed to have pets."

"She doesn't live here! And she's good for keeping rats and mice out of the units. You know that, Mom."

"Everett . . ." She sighed, shaking her head, but she couldn't bring herself to scold him when he looked so much the scared little boy hiding under the covers. "Are you sure you don't want to sleep in my room tonight? We could put on a podcast for a while. Something funny."

"I'm okay," he said, and he did look better. But then his eyes slid away from hers, and his lips parted and closed a couple of times before he spoke. "Mom . . . are the police asking you about Dad again?"

Damn it. He'd heard her on the phone with Detective Mendelson, and she'd been too cowardly to talk to him about it. Now he was having nightmares again? It was her own fault. She shouldn't have left him alone with his thoughts so he could worry over them.

"Sweetie, it's okay. Unfortunately, the police won't ever stop looking for your dad. He has to go to trial and have his day in court, even if he doesn't want to. The authorities think I know where he is, and they like to check in and ask every once in a while."

"So everything is okay?"

"Everything's fine. The police can ask me about your dad all day long. That's their job, and it's okay. You understand?"

He nodded, the smooth skin of his forehead still creased, but he tugged the covers up a bit as if he were ready to settle back down.

"You're sure you don't want to sleep in my room?"

When he shook his head, she gave him a kiss and tucked him in tightly, but she left his door open and turned on the bathroom light for good measure. He didn't object.

After checking all the locks and turning off the rest of the lights, she was shocked to realize it was only a few minutes past midnight. She felt so exhausted and aching with adrenaline that she'd been sure it was three in the morning.

She poked her head into Everett's room one last time, but he'd already put in his earbuds and closed his eyes.

Of course Lily was wide awake when she climbed back into bed. For one terrible moment she'd been convinced someone was in Everett's room. Maybe a bogeyman or maybe Jones.

Climbing out of bed again, she padded to the living room and through to the office to review the video. It wasn't until that moment she realized none of the cameras pointed at their patio. Of course they didn't. No one wanted their employer watching them every day and peering into their windows. But she cycled through all the exterior cameras and saw nothing. Headlights had come down the road around ten, but they hadn't gotten close enough to reveal anything. It had probably been that damn cop spying on her.

Lily sighed and turned off the monitor.

It was only the ghost of Jones again. Everett had been thinking about the phone call, and it had been a trigger for him. He wasn't dealing with new nightmares; he was dealing with old ones. Her poor baby.

Fucking Jones. She hated him so much. And she hated that she hated him, because that meant she still felt something, when she wished he was just a blank void inside her. A vacuum in her heart that would eventually seal itself closed.

All that emotional energy for a man who hadn't ever loved her. He couldn't have.

It had felt real, but so had his steady-provider routine. It had *all* felt real, so one thing must have been as fake as the other. She'd obviously been married to some kind of sociopath.

Lily knew she'd never have another normal romantic relationship after what he'd done. Never. She couldn't even have a normal friendship.

Jones had been her one chance, her best attempt at creating the family she'd wanted back. A mother, a father, a child, a house, all of it planted smack dab in the middle of the hometown she'd been dragged out of at age ten. She was a textbook case of family dysfunction, come to life and lurching around the countryside like a tragic monster.

Or she was just tired and being melodramatic because she was worried about Everett.

Lily sighed, ordered herself to get her shit together, and checked all the apartment locks one last time. When she reached the patio door, she remembered the sawed-off broomstick that had been there when she moved in. She dug around in the pantry until she found it, then dropped it into the track of the door as an extra precaution. Now that she knew the camera system didn't have quite the all-seeing eye she'd thought, she felt more vulnerable.

She tiptoed to Everett's room to look in, and he seemed to be sound asleep. She wished he'd agreed to at least sleep in her room so she could reach down to the floor and smooth a hand over his warm head, for her own comfort if not his. He'd been ten before he'd stopped the occasional nighttime snuggles, and she'd mourned the change. But she supposed she should be proud he'd grown braver. She'd thought herself wise and independent at his age too.

Wiser than her own mother, certainly.

For all the stability in Lily's life until age ten, her later childhood had spun into chaos. The modest child support payments had helped financially, but nothing had been effective at pulling her mom back from her emotional tailspin. She'd been angry and ranting and weeping at first. Then she'd been single-mindedly determined to show up her ex-husband. There'd been an endless march of new boyfriends and all the trouble they brought along, interspersed by the occasional volatile marriage, and always, always spiced with way too much drinking.

It was no wonder Lily had fallen so completely for the ideal fantasy Jones had created. What a crock.

At least Lily had been determined not to spiral the way her mother had. She'd been absolutely committed to calm stability for Everett, and she'd managed it so well that his entire life was one endless boring stretch after another, apparently.

Well, boring was exactly what he needed.

She craned her neck out into the hallway to listen for a moment, then quietly closed her door. After checking that her curtains were shut tight, she opened her closet. It was stuffed too tightly with clothes and piled high with the miscellanea of their lives.

She reached up and, careful to lift each ancient shoebox with precision and set them down just as quietly, unloaded the highest shelf in her closet until one box sat alone.

She eased it free, then sat cross-legged on the floor, hunched over the cardboard. A harmless pile of old receipts lay in a jumble, but she pawed those aside, digging until her fingers touched thicker paper.

The envelopes emerged with a whisper, just a few accumulated over the years. One had been postmarked from California. Two from Mexico. Another from Costa Rica. All were addressed to EJA, the initials Everett had been born with. They weren't his initials now.

Lily had saved the cards, unsure whether she'd give them to him someday or hide them forever. But now she knew she should have destroyed them from the start. Even a hint of his father had brought Everett's nightmares roaring back.

Maybe her instincts had been right after all. A child needed stability, not a constant push and pull of affection given and then removed.

And if Jones really did bring the police back into her home, she couldn't have anything that would throw her story into doubt.

With a glance at the door, and a quick prayer that whatever he learned in the future, her son would forgive her, Lily began to tear up each card, and then the envelope it had come in. When she was done, she tore each piece smaller, then scooped them all up into a plastic shopping bag.

When Everett left for school the next day, she would open the rusted charcoal grill she'd inherited with the patio, and she'd burn it all.

CHAPTER 12

Everett's hand shook as he cleaned up the lunch his mom had set out and put his orange juice glass in the sink. He was excited. Really excited. And a little scared.

Josephine was done with the dentist—No cavities!!! she'd messaged—and was on her bike now and heading over. This was happening.

"I'm meeting Josephine at the trail!" he called out.

"Have fun and be careful," she responded, her normal parting caution, and then Everett was out the door and racing toward their meeting place at the dead end of the road. Josephine didn't look nearly as excited as he did, but she waved and led the way into the meadow, whooping a little when she barreled up a small hill and raced down the other side.

The narrow dirt trail they took ended near the tree they'd climbed during their last mission, so they rode straight toward it, then walked their bikes over and leaned them against the trunk.

Josephine pulled an ancient towel from her backpack and handed it to him. "You sure about this?" she asked.

"Absolutely. I need to know if there's someone dangerous here. I'm at school all day, and my mom is just on her own. What if he really is a killer?"

"Yeah. You're right. But let's hurry. I have to be back before four to go to dance or I'll be in deep doo-doo."

"Got it." Everett looped the towel around the top two strands of barbed wire, then twisted it tight to pull them up. Josephine tossed her backpack into the gap before easily sliding under. "Josephine Woodbridge, girl detective!" she yelled when she jumped upright, fists in the air.

"Hey, your boy detective is waiting," he said, gesturing with the ends of the towel.

"No one cares about boy detectives, Ev, come on. A dime a dozen."

He tossed his backpack right at her, rolling his eyes at her laughter as she let the pack fall and grabbed the towel.

Everett joined her in the field, and they set off, sticking close to the fence in case their presence agitated the cows or a farmer came tearing after them. But the cattle stayed quiet, and no farmers appeared.

"Did you read that link I sent about Marti Herrera?" Josephine asked. "She was the last one to go missing, you know."

"Yeah, and her family didn't let it drop. There were a lot more articles about her."

"I think maybe they scared the guy. No more women disappeared after that."

Everett frowned at his feet, watching to make sure he didn't step in any fresh cow poop. "I keep telling myself that means he's not dangerous anymore. Or that he's not really the killer." He dared a quick glance back toward the business park. "I mean, you can see my place, even from here. He's so close."

Josephine's fingers brushed his shoulder. "It all happened a long time ago. You don't really need to worry."

But Everett could hear the forced lightness in her words. If he didn't need to worry, they wouldn't be out here.

They paused at the barrier of another fence. Josephine pointed. "If we cut across that field, I think we can sneak up behind the brown house."

They ducked through the barbed wire, then hobbled across a plowed field that was alternately muddy and clumped with dried lumps of soil. But Josephine had been right. They were able to travel diagonally across it until they were behind the brown house that shielded Alex Bennick's home.

There were only three houses in this cluster, each of them on lots of at least a couple of acres. The brown house was protected from wind by a row of tall, thin evergreen trees, so Everett felt pretty sure they wouldn't be spotted as they crept toward the corner for a better view of the Bennick property. Most of Everett's earlier excitement had settled into a low buzz of anxiety, and his mouth felt coated with dry grit.

He stuck his head out. "Looks quiet," he whispered, but as soon as the words left his lips, the side door of the Bennick house sprang open, and a man stepped out. Everett yelped, grabbing Josephine's arm to tug her more securely behind the edge of the last tree.

After a few heartbeats, she pulled her arm free and leaned back out again. "Is that him?"

"No, that guy is a lot younger."

"He's getting into that truck."

Everett leaned carefully past Josephine to look, narrowing his eyes as the man started the SUV and backed out. He looked exactly like a normal person. Suspicious. The vehicle turned onto the road and drove away, leaving them in utter silence. Even the birds weren't singing.

He took a deep breath and said, "Let's go look," determined to be brave.

"Everett, I don't know . . ."

"That's what we came out here for."

"But we don't even know who that is!"

"Whoever he is, he's gone now, so this is the perfect time."

After studying his face for a moment, Josephine tipped her chin in agreement. "Okay. Let's do it."

For one shuddering heartbeat, he realized he'd hoped she would at least try to stop him, to give him a minute to reconsider and think. But he had to be sure for the sake of his mom, didn't he? She'd talked to Alex Bennick when he'd rented the place. She might have walked him over, stood alone with him in that echoing, shadowed locker . . .

And then Josephine was taking Everett's hand and pulling him from his hesitation. They ducked low to race across the broken grass, and there was no more time to think.

He focused on the bright-green spot of a dandelion sprouting ahead and tried to pretend he was in a movie. It didn't quite feel real, especially with her hand wrapped tight in his. He hadn't even known Josephine two weeks ago, and now she was his closest friend.

And his partner in crime.

He steered her toward the back wall so they wouldn't be in full view of the neighbor in the brown house, and they both pressed themselves close to the siding near a window. For a long while they just breathed, settling their hearts, until Everett finally nodded.

"I'll look," he whispered, braver now that his heart was pumping hard. He eased his face just far enough over to see into the house with one eye. "Kitchen. It looks empty."

Josephine popped up next to him to look too. "Lights are off."

They tiptoed to the next window to look, then dared to slide around the side of the house. Every window showed dark and unoccupied rooms. A few minutes after they arrived, they were at the side door. The wooden interior door stood open, and only a storm door protected the home.

He reached for the handle.

"You're not going in, are you?" Josephine whispered.

"We're only twelve," he responded so softly he could barely hear it himself. "They can't arrest us, right?" But then he thought of everything he'd seen on the news about people of color and the police and shook his head. "You should stay here," he said to Josephine. "I don't want to get you in trouble."

"Oh, *I'm* not dumb enough to go in there."

He eased the door open, wincing at the faint squeak of hinges. His mom never left anything unlocked, but he knew it was common practice for other people. He slid inside and froze to listen but heard nothing except his own terrified pulse and his brain screaming at him to *stop stop stop and get out right now.*

Trying to ignore his sudden need to pee, he took a couple of steps toward the living room, wincing at the crackle of old linoleum beneath his shoes. The kitchen still smelled of bacon and a faint hint of dish soap. But even serial killers had to wash dishes, he figured. Still it was a warning of how near he'd come to crossing paths with someone in this house.

When a floorboard creaked beneath him, he winced and held his breath until he saw stars in his eyes. Nothing happened. No sound of anyone else.

Once he caught his wind again, he moved on, stepping as lightly as he could. He crossed the threshold onto carpet and found himself in a big rectangle of a room packed with shelves and an easy chair and lamps and even a piano.

The giant cube of an ancient TV hulked in one corner, large enough to have pictures perched on top of it. Everett headed straight for the pictures.

A young man standing on a lawn in a graduation cap. A small child held in a woman's arms. The third picture seemed to be the older guy he'd seen in the license photo, though he was much younger in this snapshot, his arm around a dark-haired boy about Everett's age.

"Everett," Josephine called in a stage whisper.

He spun to find her head stuck in the back door and waved her off.

"This isn't okay," she hissed.

He picked up a Polaroid picture of Alex Bennick with two young boys, one a teenager and the other a bit younger. The man smiled hugely in the picture, and the teenage boy smiled along, but the younger kid looked blank. Everett stuffed the picture into the pocket of his jeans.

"What are you doing?" Josephine demanded.

"Shh." He moved on to a framed picture of a couple getting married a long time ago. In the '70s or '80s, he'd guess. He thought it was the same man, Alex Bennick, but what had happened to his young, curly-haired wife? Had he killed her? She was a blond white woman like all the girls on the bulletin board.

"Ev, come on," Josephine said, "we should—" Her words broke in half like cracking ice when a soft thump vibrated through the ceiling just above him.

They stared at each other, mouths frozen open in matching horror until they raised their faces in unison to stare up at the ceiling. A faint plop of water pinged somewhere nearby. A dozen heartbeats passed. Then another plop of water. A faucet leaking, maybe. Or just noisy pipes above them.

And then a door squeaked open somewhere on the second floor. A footstep creaked, weight settling onto old wood over Everett's head. He thought of those girls, their smiling faces, their pale, dead bodies. That wasn't the sound of plumbing or popping joists. Someone was in the house.

The old man.

The *murderer*.

Everett's hand spasmed, and the frame dropped to the floor with a hard crack. Mouth agape, he looked toward Josephine one more time, just a split second of shared fear, and then Everett broke into a mad dash, scooting around an ottoman, a stack of books, a little silver dog sculpture, racing for the kitchen and the door she held open to the cement steps outdoors.

The door smacked shut behind them, sending them sprinting across the lawn toward the welcome shelter of those skinny green trees.

But that wasn't good enough. It wasn't far enough. "Go, go," he urged as they kept flying past the brown house and out across the field.

Josephine pointed left, and they veered over to follow the closest fence line instead of running at an angle across the field, and Everett was immediately thankful for her quick thinking. Staying close to the fence would keep them out of view of whoever might be looking out.

They were far beyond the sightline of Alex Bennick's house by the time they dragged to a painful, panting walk at a barrier of wire fence.

"Did he see us?" she wheezed.

"I didn't even . . . look back." He paused to lean over and pull air into the fire of his lungs. "Did you?"

She craned her neck to look as far past the brown house and the trees as she could, but the Bennick house was no longer visible. "I don't see anyone."

After taking a few minutes to recover, they scooted through the wire and began to trudge along the last of the plowed field toward the cow pasture and the little group of trees beyond it.

"Was it him?" she finally asked. "The old guy?"

Everett had no idea. Or actually he had a few ideas, and they were all awful. "I don't know. I didn't see him."

"Well, thank God for that."

Josephine drew the towel from her backpack again and looped it around the barbed wire before turning her narrowed eyes on him. "That wasn't safe, Everett."

Nodding, he slipped past the threat of tearing metal and grabbed the towel to pull it tight for Josephine. But he didn't meet her gaze. It hadn't been safe, and now he felt awful to have risked it, especially with her along.

"I'm sorry," he muttered as they walked with the fence line toward the little stand of trees.

"Why did you *do* that?"

"I don't know." There was something wrong with him, maybe. Regret rolled over him. But the answers felt so close, and if he could figure it out, he could do something really good.

"Maybe we should stick to online research. I mean, it's not like we're going to identify DNA if we find something, right?"

"Yeah."

"No more stupid stuff, okay? I'm serious. Promise me." His body flushed at that, because she didn't seem mad; she just seemed worried. And no one ever worried about him except his mom. Shame settled over him with smothering heat.

"Yeah," he agreed. "I promise."

She glanced back over her shoulder several times, but the house stayed hidden behind a slight rise. "What if he saw you?"

He wasn't sure what to say to that. Because what if he had?

CHAPTER 13

Lily was entirely out of sorts, and she had been for the whole morning. She'd gotten only a few hours of sleep after last night's drama, but once Everett had gone to school, she'd shooed away the black cat and dumped the torn-up cards into the rusted grill.

She needed to throw the whole damn thing out at some point. She wouldn't dare set food onto the grill for fear of cooking up a new form of tetanus, but it had worked for the task of destroying evidence. She felt like the smoke still clung to her, marking her with guilt.

That was the reason she'd cried out in shock when Everett had shown up at lunchtime. She'd known about the half day of school at some point, but she'd entirely forgotten it by the time he'd raced into the office at noon, bursting through the door like a banshee. Thank God she'd finished with burning the cards early.

After Everett had lunch and set off for an adventure with Josephine, Lily had found two dead rats in traps behind one of the buildings, and one had been crawling with maggots. Still shuddering at having to clean up that squirming death, she'd locked up the office and taken a quick shower to regain her composure.

She felt better once she was back in her office chair, cleansed of both grill smoke and the rat incident. The third cup of coffee she'd brought to her desk helped too.

She got through messages and mail within five minutes, then moved on to her spreadsheet of overdue notices. For once there was good news. None of the renters would reach auction status this week. Most were one month behind, with a few two-month notices in there. She merged the file with her letter form and began printing them out. She would print out the labels too, but she always handwrote the envelopes for the two-month notices so they wouldn't get overlooked as junk mail.

The printing window sprang to life, but movement attracted her eye just as the printer alert covered it: something in the security camera window.

Curious, she opened the full screen and scanned the nine images. As she slowly reversed, she found what had caught her attention. A man passed by one of the cameras in the middle of the complex. The cheap system made for jerky video, but she could clearly see a white man in a pale baseball cap walk along one of the buildings.

She kept backing up until she saw that a car had entered when she was in the shower, but it had disappeared off camera at some point. To where?

A grinding clank sprang to life behind her, and Lily spun around with a gasp, but when the printer whirred more softly, she realized it was just starting to spit out letters. Despite having been the one to prompt the printing job, she cursed out the machine.

It would take a good five minutes to finish, so she grabbed her keys and walked outside. There was nothing wrong with a tenant walking around, but it was her job to keep an eye on everything, no matter how small.

Heading toward the camera that had caught the picture, Lily relaxed at the faint scent of sawdust that rode the breeze from Nour's shop. It was a soothing smell that brought to mind Nour's kind eyes.

Sometimes on slow winter days, she would burn wood scraps in a metal drum and invite Everett over for cocoa. Lily would always beg off with too much work, but she sometimes spied through her bedroom window, and it had looked as cozy as any campfire. Not quite the same as a neighbor with a backyard firepit, but close, right? He certainly seemed to love it every time.

When she got to the end of the building the man had walked past, Lily found no one. She moved on to the building next to it, walking more slowly as the sun dipped behind the roof.

When a rustling tickled her ears, she paused to listen. Raccoons? Mice? Sometimes the wind made all the doors tremble like metal ghosts, but this had been much more subtle. Like someone sneaking around.

She thought immediately of that cop and whatever suspicious activity had brought him out the first time. Pill fiends, Sharon had proposed. But if anyone was sneaking around, it was more likely to be someone with a bolt cutter, looking for Grandpa's coin collection.

The rustling floated back to her ears, so she moved toward the sound, tugging her phone from her pocket in case she needed help.

A few spaces down she spotted a rolling door that wasn't quite closed. Six inches of space gaped at the bottom. Kneeling, she held her breath and squinted into the strip of darkness that suddenly looked like an open mouth waiting for prey.

And then a shadow moved, casting midnight in a space she'd already thought black.

Fuck, she mouthed silently, easing her body up as carefully as she could. What the hell had made that cop so nervous the other night? Did she really have a damn ring of thieves around?

Or maybe it was just a renter in their own locker. It wouldn't be great customer service to sic the cops on them.

She glanced toward the office, searching out help or the sight of a car or any sign she wouldn't be attacked and left for dead with no clues to follow. But that was stupid. Armed robbers hit up stores or pharmacies or banks, not storage units. This was more petty thief territory.

Closing her eyes, she shook her head. She'd always been a little impulsive, and now she was tired of waiting, so she cleared her throat, pushed back her shoulders, and spoke as forcefully as she could.

"*Who's in there?*"

The rustle bloomed into a scuffle of fabric and grit, then the slap of something hitting cement. A bare foot? A limp body? Lily cursed and unlocked her phone, ready to call for help.

The ridiculous thing that stopped her panic was a sneeze. A remarkably small sneeze, squeaking out with all the gravitas of a sick mouse.

Her frown eased a little, and she dared to step forward. "Hello?"

"It's okay," a man's thin voice said, bouncing off the metal door and echoing back. "It's my unit."

The door rose to reveal running shoes followed by thin, hairy legs that seemed to pose no threat to anyone. She dipped her head a little to catch a quicker glimpse of the man as the door slid past running shorts and up to expose a windbreaker.

His narrow face popped into view with a scowl.

Lily scowled back. "Dr. Ross?"

"Yes. Hello."

She'd used his office a few times after Everett's original doctor moved. Then she'd stopped after the charges against Jones. Dr. Ross hadn't been personally involved, but he'd commented snidely to her about the money Jones had stolen from the county hospital system. Lily had found a new doctor.

If he hadn't stood there so awkwardly, she might have apologized for disturbing him and been on her way, but his stiff posture forced her eyes to the space beyond him. A burgundy Turkish rug spread across the floor. Two beige recliners faced a large oak china cabinet. A sturdy end table lurked between the two chairs and held a large electric lantern that glowed weakly in the gray space.

An "oh" of surprise escaped her lips when she spotted the paperback novel on the cold cement next to one of the chairs. That had been the slap she'd heard. His book falling to the ground.

"I . . . I was out for a run, and I thought I'd check on things," he explained, clearly lying. His voice had gone breathy. One of his hands shook at his side.

"Of course," Lily said immediately. "No worries, Dr. Ross. I was only concerned you were a thief."

He nodded but otherwise didn't move, his eyes hard on her, his cheeks reddening with embarrassment. Or was it anger?

"It's your space," she assured him again. That wasn't quite the truth. There was no "occupancy" allowed in a unit, but he was obviously only there momentarily. "Let me know if you need anything."

When he didn't respond, she spun on her heel and marched away. She wasn't moving toward the office, but she didn't care. She just needed to escape the awkwardness.

He was a busy doctor, and his first spouse, Francesca, had been the type of wife who'd done everything else for the family, at least according to Sharon. She'd raised the kids, kept the house, planned the vacations, cooked the meals, and scheduled every appointment. Lily imagined he'd been lost without her, a restless widower, wandering the rooms of his big house alone.

He'd seemingly jumped at the chance to marry Kimmy, who was twenty-one years younger, but Lily imagined that Kimmy wasn't the least bit interested in bleaching his dirty whites and making sure the cars got their oil changes. And she clearly wasn't interested in sitting in overstuffed recliners with him and enjoying a good Western. Apparently he did that in his solo time now.

"Yikes," Lily whispered as she finally made it around a corner of a building and out of sight. With the way he'd set it up, Dr. Ross clearly meant to visit repeatedly, probably pretending he was going out for a long run. Another drop in the huge bucket of her phobia of commitment. Kimmy Ross likely had no idea.

When she got to the far edge of the complex, Lily finally spotted Ross's car, or she assumed it was his. A gray Lincoln sedan sat just inside the back gate, beyond the view of the camera that pointed out toward intruders instead of in toward embarrassed visitors.

He'd recognized her when he'd first come to rent the unit. She'd seen the flash of recognition in his eyes, but then he'd pretended to be a stranger.

She hadn't seen that reaction in quite a while, but it had happened often during that first year. She appreciated it because the other reaction had been anger and sometimes yelling. Still, part of her had been relieved by the yelling. Part of her had welcomed it. She'd brought Jones to this town, and she'd had his biggest accounting clients over for summer barbecues as he'd dedicated himself to embezzling every cent he could.

These weren't big corporations with extra padding built into their profits. They had been small-town places that could be ruined by a bad year. The county hospital. An ob-gyn practice. A car dealership. Even the Town of Herriman itself. It had seemed as if every single person in Herriman had known someone affected.

As she approached building B, Lily heard noises, but this time they were the normal rhythms of the storage business. Cardboard sliding over cement, a car door opening, the thud of something heavy being dropped into place. She heard music as she walked past the wall to see an old SUV with the liftgate raised high. A few seconds later, Alex Bennick stepped out of the unit with a cardboard box.

"Hey!" he said when he saw her, his face immediately lighting with a smile.

"Hi. How's it going in there?"

He slipped the box into the back of the SUV and dusted off his hands.

"I'm making progress."

"Let me know if you need any tips. I know every junk dealer, pawn-shop, and mover in the county."

"It's mostly papers," he said. "I'm just trying to go through a few things a day. My next gig fell through, so I might stay for a couple of weeks."

"What do you do?" she asked, drawing a little closer. She liked the feeling of someone else being here after Dr. Ross's weird skulking around.

"I'm a reporter," Alex said. "I worked for a local paper in Memphis, but the newspaper industry is . . ."

Lily winced. "Yeah. Not exactly upwardly trending?"

He smiled. "Not so much. But I'm putting together some freelance work, so hope springs eternal."

Lily found herself smiling back, which probably wasn't the appropriate response to his talk of job loss, but he did have a rather infectious grin.

The music from his SUV faded, and a new song started up. Lily felt immediately transported back to college, floating down a slow river with friends during spring break of her freshman year. "Is that Brooke Waggoner?" she asked.

"Oh yeah. I've seen her a couple of times. Amazing stuff. You like her?"

"I was obsessed with her second album in college."

"I covered the music beat for a while in Memphis. She's a great performer."

"Cool," she said, still smiling. When his smile slowly returned, Lily felt a jolt of connection, and the warmth of it startled her. She'd used Tinder a couple of times in the past few years, but she'd barely felt anything at all, even during sex.

She cleared her throat and stood straighter.

Alex said, "Hey, do you want—" at the exact same time she said, "Well, I'd better get going."

She took a couple of steps past him, and he glanced quickly toward the storage unit. "It's a mess in there," he said before backing up to reach for the door pull.

"It's supposed to be," she said on a laugh, a little flattered that he wanted to make a good impression.

He tugged the door halfway down and shook his head. "It's giving me flashbacks to my college apartment, I guess. Never a good look when you're trying to impress a girl."

Now she was more than flattered. Now she was slightly alarmed and *definitely* warmer. "I'll let you get back to it," she said too loudly before rushing away down the lane, moving fast toward the fence so she could take a sharp turn toward the office.

"Thanks!" he called after her.

She was actually a little shaky as she forged a path back toward the safety of her desk, nearly jogging the last bit. Her cellphone rang a moment before her foot hit the walkway, and she hadn't even had a chance to answer the call when she spotted a woman waiting at the door.

Noticing the phone at her ear, Lily called out, "Hello! I'm back. Sorry about that. I was making the rounds."

It wasn't until the woman turned fully toward her that Lily recognized her. It was a Neighborhood Storage director. They'd met at a company gathering a few months earlier.

Lily's feet froze, and she rocked to a stop. Had Detective Mendelson contacted this woman about . . . well, what, exactly? He didn't know she'd been breaking company rules.

"Lily Brown? Hi, I'm Gretchen. We've met before."

"I remember! I'm sorry, have you been waiting long? I was helping a client with something at his unit."

"It's only been a moment. I didn't call ahead because it's a surprise audit."

Audit? Lily's stomach dropped, weighted down with the sharp tug of awful guilt and the burning knowledge of all those gaps she'd created in the surveillance video. And the knowledge that if Detective Mendelson wanted to turn the screws, he could've called corporate and asked a few pointed questions about her history. What if he told them she might be hiding a fugitive on the property? What if the audit was just an excuse to get rid of her?

She met Gretchen's smile as best she could and patted her pocket twice before realizing she held her keys in her hand. "Let's get started!" Lily said, hoping for reassuring brightness even as she watched her own hand tremble at the lock.

Gretchen didn't respond.

CHAPTER 14

His mom was being weirder than normal when he got home, or maybe Everett was just on edge from fear and guilt. He winced when she called his name in an oddly bright voice as he rushed through the office door. "You can go on inside and get yourself a snack!" she added.

He stopped and stared at her overly cheerful tone, then a woman whose head had been hidden by the monitor scooted to the side to wave at him.

"This is Everett," his mom said, "my son."

"Hi, Everett, I'm Gretchen."

He murmured a polite greeting, then moved carefully toward the apartment, eyeing his mom in question. She simply raised her brows too high and smiled, but as he opened the door, he noticed the other woman had a company logo on her shirt. His mom's boss, maybe.

A few steps inside the apartment, he dropped his backpack on the floor and was heading toward the kitchen when his limbs froze at a terrible thought. What if that woman was here because of Everett? What if he hadn't been careful enough about the cameras? What if someone had complained about missing items?

He stared wide-eyed at the fridge for a long moment before tiptoeing back to the door. When he pressed his ear against it to listen for accusations or hushed tones, he heard only the notes of normal conversation. The back-and-forth of questions and answers, then a moment of laughter. The woman said something about low carbs. His mom mentioned coffee.

Everything was fine.

Relieved, Everett grabbed a yogurt and headed for the computer. When he logged in to his email, he opened a note Josephine had sent earlier.

People are so gross, she wrote above a screenshot of a comment left on a Herriman High School reunion page.

> Tiffany Miller? Did she graduate with us? She was in foster care or something. No parents. She never talked to no one except her pot dealer. Is that guy invited to the reunion? Haha! Not surprised no one tracked her down. She probably ODd on something, right??? Girl was always high. Hot ass tho. Hey Tiffany if you see this, message me or hit me up at the reunion!

Tiffany Miller. She'd been included on the board of missing women, but there had been no accompanying newspaper article. Even online, there was hardly anything. The girl had just vanished from the world sometime in 2000. Maybe she'd only run off from a bad situation.

Or maybe Alex Bennick knew something no one else did.

When the apartment door swung quickly open, Everett jumped, convinced for half a second that the cops were here.

"We're doing a tour of the facilities," his mom said. "Just call my cell if you need me."

"Sure," he answered, doing his best not to reach guiltily for the mouse to minimize the window. She couldn't see the monitor from there, and she was already closing the door anyway. When he heard the office door open and both voices fade, he relaxed and started searching for Tiffany Miller online again, just in case he'd missed something the first time he'd looked. But the name was way too common. Maybe she was just one of the Tiffanys living in Minnesota or Iowa. He forced himself to look a bit more carefully just in case, studying pictures and birthdays.

When the phone in his mom's bedroom rang, he ignored it until it stopped. Then it rang again.

On the third round of ringing, it occurred to him that it could be his mom trying to reach him. Maybe she was on the far side of the complex and needed something? Still anxious about how his own behavior could've caused her harm, he walked into her room. The ringing stopped. Then it started a fourth time.

Everett finally reached for the phone. "Hello?" he said, then thought better of that and tried again. "Hi, this is Neighborhood Storage." He'd heard his mom on the phone often enough.

"Everett?" a voice asked after a long pause. Not his mom. A man, his tone deep and hushed.

"Yes?" Everett responded.

"Everett! Wow. It's your dad."

For a moment the words meant nothing. How could they? This wasn't his dad, because he didn't have a dad anymore. Then his brain ticked through a few notches of thought, and he realized it was a stupid prank call. "Yeah right," he snapped.

"Everett, I'm serious. It's your dad. I've been trying to reach you for days. Well, for months, really. How are you, little man?"

Little man.

That struck something that rang through his mind like a bell. *Little man.* Hadn't his dad always called him that? The words were more solid than a memory. They were buried too deep to actually recall, but he could *feel* them trembling through his muscles, his bones.

And who would prank call a business line? Who would try to reach him there? "Dad?" he croaked, as the possibility expanded inside him, pressing too hard against his heart and throat.

The man laughed. Or . . . his *dad* laughed. "Jesus, I've missed you! You're twelve now, right? You're probably almost as tall as me!"

Everett shook his head and whispered, "Dad?" again.

"It's really me. I've been hoping you would answer the phone, Ev. I wanted to hear your voice. I mean, jeez, what I really want is to see you, but that's a bit harder to arrange."

His eyes fluttered in blinks so rapid his vision looked like a stop-action film, so Everett turned his head away from the hard sunlight streaming past his mom's bedroom curtains. It didn't help. He still felt dizzy.

"My God, Son, I can't believe I'm finally talking to you. I've wanted to. I've tried."

"You did?"

"Every time I try to call, I think . . . Well, I don't know. Maybe this isn't a good idea."

Everett's body felt strange. Limbs heavy but also tingling and numb. His chest felt constricted, as if he were strapped down. He couldn't think, and his throat had squeezed itself shut. He closed his eyes and heard a slow sigh in his ear.

"You probably don't even want to talk to me."

"No," Everett rasped. The tight knot of his heart eased a bit, though it hurt more now, as if the lightened pressure had let pain in. "I do want to talk to you."

"You know that means you can't tell anyone, right? It's a big secret for a twelve-year-old. I'm still . . . Well, I did some bad stuff, and I guess you've heard all about it."

"Yeah." His *dad* was on the phone, and Everett felt like all he could get out were caveman grunts. But he'd never thought about what he might say if they talked, because he never thought he'd have the chance.

It seemed . . . not real. Like a dream where something weird happened and everyone carried on like it wasn't weird. Including Everett.

"I'm sorry, little man. Though I guess you're not so little anymore."

Everett's eyes started blinking again, this time to stop the burning of tears. "Dad, where are you?"

"I can't really talk about that. But maybe you could tell me about your life. Do you like school?"

"It's fine." He couldn't believe they were finally speaking and they were talking about school. He didn't care about school. He wanted to know a hundred things about his dad. Wanted to know everything. Yet he couldn't think of one single question.

"Play any sports?" his dad asked. "Do you still have that glove I got you?"

"Yes. I have it," Everett said quietly. "It's too small."

"Maybe I can send you a new one."

"Oh, sure."

"Do you have a special girlfriend?"

He frowned hard at that. "No." An engine started somewhere outside, and he jerked in shock before racing to the living room to look out the window. He heard voices somewhere around the corner. "I think my mom's coming back," he said, nearly panting the words.

"Okay, all right, it's fine. Just give me your cellphone number, and I'll call again."

"I don't have one." Now he really was crying, afraid this was their last chance and they'd only talked about the dumbest stuff like school and sports and *girls*, of all things. "But I want to talk to you, Dad! Can you use Discord? It's an app. We can text there. We can even do calls on it. I can—"

"I can get Discord," his dad said quickly. "Absolutely."

Everett gave him his username, then repeated it, just in case. "You promise?" he asked. "You'll find me there?"

"Absolutely, little man. I won't let you down."

When he heard his mom's voice outside the window, talking to someone just before the gate squeaked open, Everett couldn't catch his breath. "She's here," he whispered.

"Okay, we'll talk soon. Bye, Son."

"Goodbye," he stammered. "Bye, Dad." He didn't want to put the phone down, and he held it to his ear even as he heard the office door open. He held it there until it made a strange sound before going quiet. Then he finally sprinted to his mom's room to put the phone back on its charger.

After tumbling back out to the living room to close all his windows and wipe his search history, Everett retreated to his bedroom, closing the door tight behind him.

His stomach ached. His throat burned. Because now he had more secrets. Bigger ones. And he couldn't tell anyone, not even Josephine.

He changed his mind at the last moment and jumped from his bedroom to the bathroom just as he heard the knob on the apartment door turning.

Everett turned on the shower, sat down on the toilet, and cried. But they were happy tears. Mostly.

CHAPTER 15

Lily scowled at the missed call from Detective Mendelson. It was Saturday, her busiest day of the week, and she could not deal with his bullshit right now. Every time a car approached, her head jerked up to see if he was back. The audit was enough for her to worry about. One damn crisis at a time.

Not that the audit had gone badly. It had gone fine. She and Gretchen had even clicked a little, she thought. Or maybe Gretchen was extra nice to people who might be losing their job.

At least Everett had finally had a peaceful night, though Lily hadn't. This time, she'd woken up at 2:00 a.m., sure she'd heard a sound outside her window. It had probably only been the cat. Or possibly the family of raccoons she'd spotted just that morning on camera.

But she'd been too busy to be tired today. There'd been four new renters and almost that many moving out. Summer season had arrived early this year.

She glanced at the clock. "Five thirty!" she called out to Everett. "Are you ready? Barbara will be here to pick you up any minute."

"I know! Josephine messaged me on Discord."

Lily rolled her eyes, realizing she'd lost that battle by declining to fight it. Oh well. At least Everett had been in a great mood today. His hormones were surging in the right direction for once.

"She's here!" Everett called as he hurried out of the apartment and raced for the outer door. "See you later!"

Lily's hormones were not surging in the right direction. Once Everett left to get burgers and shakes with Josephine and her mom, she felt strangely unmoored, wandering around the apartment, touching a book, straightening a lampshade. She was wound tight and aching with tension, and she was still obsessing about that damn audit.

Gretchen had assured her it was routine, but they'd never audited her before. If she was in trouble, if they'd noticed the discrepancies in her security feed . . .

But they weren't tech wizards or hackers, and Gretchen hadn't even checked any video files. Why would she? Nothing was missing and her books were in order. *Beautifully* in order. Facing even one tiny financial error felt like risking a scarlet letter in this town, so Lily triple-checked her numbers every month.

Still, this all felt too coincidental, and she was half-convinced Detective Mendelson had alerted the company to Lily's past, the part that *wasn't* included in the credit file, like the extent of her ex's theft and all the terrible things they suspected of her.

"Stop it," she muttered to herself as she refolded the moss-green throw blanket and arranged it more neatly on the couch. She was used to being alone here during the day, but it felt odd in the evening as chatter and noise from the business park tapered into silence.

Lily glanced at the clock. It was six now. She was free. Barbara had told her to enjoy her night off, and Lily had played along, as if she might do something fun. Now she felt pitiful because she had no idea what to do with a night off. If she stayed home and sat at her table alone with a tuna sandwich, she wouldn't even be able to deny to herself that she'd turned into a hermit.

Mouth set in a grim line, Lily grabbed her car keys and decided to run a couple of errands to fill the time. Still, setting off toward town didn't feel relaxing. That wordless encounter with Cheyenne at the café replayed in her mind as she drove toward Main, watching for any familiar, unfriendly faces.

Had she stayed in Herriman to prove something to Cheyenne? She hadn't really thought about it that way, but now . . . it almost made sense. Lily had loved Herriman as a kid, and then one day her dad hadn't wanted her or her mom anymore and they'd been shunted aside. Cast out.

Maybe taking that job from Cheyenne had been a childish tantrum on Lily's part. A refusal to be tossed away again. Maybe this had all been a stubborn, selfish mistake and she should have taken Everett and gone anywhere, even if it meant instability.

Or maybe she was just feeling sorry for herself.

Sighing, she pulled into an open parking space on Main Street and turned off her car to sit for a moment.

They were doing okay, weren't they? It was just that life was supposed to be *easier* by now. Jones was supposed to be far behind her, the police should have forgotten her, and she desperately wanted to be normal and boring.

At least she had the boring part nailed down even if she'd never be normal. Time for a hot Saturday-night trip to the hardware store. Jesus, she was really going to have to find a few hobbies before Everett left for college in six years.

She lingered in the hardware store, but it still took only a few minutes to grab a couple of lock hasps and a pack of wood screws. She threw in a new paintbrush for some touch-up work she'd been putting off. Then she was back out on Main, tucking the receipt carefully into her billfold to file for expenses later.

She hesitated on the sidewalk. Maybe she could get a puzzle at the dollar store. Would doing a puzzle on a Saturday night be worse than doing nothing at all?

It could be relaxing, though. She could have a glass of wine and listen to music. Put on that old Brooke Waggoner album, maybe, and remember how normal her life had been before she'd met Jones. How she'd slept with fumbling college boys and smoked a cigarette or two with friends at keg parties off campus.

Life had been hard then, young and unsupported by family, but she'd felt capable in her own body. She'd felt strong enough to risk everything for her dreams. She wasn't sure she'd risk anything these days.

"Lily?"

She startled at the sound of her own name and whipped anxiously toward whoever had spoken it.

"Hey!" Alex Bennick called, letting go of the open door he'd been holding. "How's it going?"

How was it going? She had no idea, so she just shook her head. "Hi."

He walked toward her, tucking his hands into the pockets of his jeans and ducking his head a little. "I'm going kind of stir crazy tonight. Thought it'd be nice to get out and grab a real dinner."

"Hotels can be a little claustrophobic."

"Yeah. That's true. Is this place any good?" He gestured up to the sign.

"Absolutely. Mia's Taqueria is one of the best."

"Would you . . . ?" He raised his eyebrows. "Would you want to grab dinner with me?"

"Oh, I'm . . ." She held up her bag, and he glanced at it with a puzzled look on his face.

"Shopping?" he prompted.

"Yeah. Running a few errands."

"Well, if you're busy . . . but I'd really love some company. I've been talking to myself way too much this week."

"I . . ." She glanced at her phone, about to say that she needed to get home. But somehow only twenty-five minutes had passed since she'd set off in her car for an evening out.

And he was kind of cute. And watching her hopefully. And he was also leaving town in a week or two, which meant he was safe. *She* was safe.

"Sure," she finally said. "Dinner would be great."

Grinning, he swept an arm toward the door. "Let's see if we can get a table."

There was a large group standing inside the entry, but the host walked them right through to a table for two. Lily felt stupidly thankful it was tucked near the back and not in the middle of the room. Alex didn't know anything about her, and she wanted to enjoy being unknown.

"Any recommendations?" he asked, and then she was grateful they got through the first few minutes discussing only the menu, and she had time to calm her racing thoughts.

The server arrived to take their orders, and Lily liked that Alex made clear he was only having one beer since he was driving. She ordered a margarita to go with her enchiladas, though she would've happily had the special *gigante* version if not for her own drive home.

"So you live here in town?" he asked.

"I . . ." She winced but decided everyone else knew exactly where she lived, so it was hardly a secret. "I actually live on-site. It's one of my responsibilities. There's an apartment inside, and you can't beat the commute."

He tapped the table. "I forgot about that! I covered a case once that involved trafficking and a city official's storage company. That seems like a cool place to live."

Lily laughed. "I guess you could say that."

"It's full of secrets, right?"

"You know what? It really is. We get some characters, that's for sure."

"What's the weirdest thing you've ever seen?"

When the server set her margarita down, Lily took a big sip. She discarded the idea of telling him about Dr. Ross, since it felt too sad and private. "When people don't pay their fees, their property is auctioned, which is awful, and I hate it. But one time we opened a locker that had been rented for nearly five years. Then the man went to prison and stopped paying. When we opened it, the unit was full of taxidermied cats. Stuffed and mounted with glass eyes and everything. Probably forty of them."

"Wow, that is truly, truly disturbing."

"It was. But the weirdest part was that the only other thing in that space was a creepy Victorian doll. She was sitting on a stool, and all the cats were facing her."

"Jesus, I'm going to have nightmares now!"

"I'll just say I was extremely glad there were two people from the auction site there with me. And they took the cats! Made more than a thousand dollars on them. I will never understand people."

"And the doll?"

She laughed at his attention to creepy detail. "They took that too, thank God. People pay good money for old toys."

"Even obviously haunted ones?"

"*Especially* the haunted ones."

He shuddered a little, making her laugh again, and she realized this was surprisingly easy, talking to him, relaxing into the moment.

"So have you found anything creepy in your uncle's belongings?"

He coughed hard at that, seemed to think for a moment, then shook his head. "Just all the normal stuff, really. Lots of old documents. Pictures. That sort of thing."

"Is your uncle the keeper of family history?"

"You could say that. My mom is still alive, but he's the only one left on my dad's side."

"It's great that you're doing this. It's usually something that falls to women in the family."

"One of my best friends has hit that place in her life. She's got three kids and a mom who's moving in with her."

"So tough. I see so many customers like that, moving stuff out to make room for an aging parent. Or storing things like your uncle has done."

"You witness a lot of life in transition," he said.

That was very true. Maybe that made her comfortable, knowing she wasn't the only person just filling in the gaps until her life resolved itself.

"So," he said. "It's Saturday night. What do you do for fun around here?"

"Don't ask me. You're out on the town, and I was just running errands, so you probably know better than I do. You said you spent some teenage summers here, right?"

"Right. So . . . cow tipping? Wait a minute." He snapped his fingers. "Didn't there used to be a drive-in theater? I swear I took a date there once."

"That's where the business park is! The drive-in sat vacant for a long time. As a matter of fact, I think when you were here . . . Almost twenty years ago? That was an attempted revival. It didn't work, and someone bought the land to bring in business and revitalize the area. Of course, that didn't work either."

"The American dream," he said, and they toasted.

The server brought their food, but Alex didn't let it drop. "So you never said what you do for fun."

Lily stayed silent, trying to decide what to say and what to hide. But he was leaving town soon, which was the only reason she'd even agreed to dinner, so she let herself speak. "I have a son. I was married a long time ago. He's twelve now, so that's basically my free time in a nutshell. I am *amazing* at old Nintendo games and Wii bowling, and I have a black belt in nagging about homework. What about you? Any kids?"

"No kids, but I was married once long ago myself."

"The American dream," she echoed, and they clinked glasses again, laughing.

Lily actually felt good. He was easy to talk to, and she imagined it was a skill he'd nurtured at his job. She even found herself stealing glances at him as they ate. He wore a blue plaid button-down, but he'd rolled the sleeves up to his elbows, and she liked watching the muscles of his forearms as he moved. She no longer believed in love, trust, or romance, but she wasn't a robot.

"Do you run?" she asked. "Or ride a bike?"

His eyebrows rose and disappeared beneath that thick wave of hair. "Yes, I ride. How'd you know?"

"You look the part. Lean muscles."

Blushing, he smiled like a little boy at that, and delight fizzed through Lily's veins.

"Thanks. Do you ride?"

"No, I get all my exercise doing maintenance, I guess. And I've been busy with classes the past few years."

"Classes?"

"I'm almost done with my BA in accounting. I plan on being a CPA."

"You're going to abandon your Neighborhood Storage post?"

"I am *absolutely* going to abandon my post."

After her $15,000 raise, Lily had been able to enroll in an online degree program. Now she was one semester from finally graduating, and she was already studying for the CPA exam.

She'd been in school for accounting when she'd met Jones, after all. It had been their first commonality, something to talk about. She still loved it. A silly career to love, maybe, but numbers made sense, and they never betrayed you. Her deepest, unspoken desire was to get into forensic accounting and catch problems.

Problems like her ex-husband.

"Do you have family here too?" He raised his beer to drink the last of it.

"Not anymore. My dad was from here." She left it at that.

"And your mom?"

Lily shook her head. "I haven't seen her in a very long time. When I was eighteen she took off for Florida with a new boyfriend, and frankly, it was kind of a relief to be on my own. Then she spent a long period falling into crazy political crap on Facebook, so . . . I guess I didn't cut her out so much as mute her."

She left out the part where her mom had mocked and shamed her at the worst moment in Lily's life, getting petty revenge for all the times teenaged Lily had berated her mother for the men she chose. *Oh, I'm the one who makes bad choices, huh, Lily? I'm the terrible mother in this family?*

She shoved that thought away. She'd learned to stand on her own two feet, and there was nothing to be done about the rest. She found herself staring forlornly into her empty margarita goblet.

"If you want to have another, I'll be happy to drive you home," he suggested.

"I can't. Everett is at dinner with a friend, but he'll be home soon."

"So no sopapillas either?"

"Oh," she responded, mouth actually watering at the idea. She hadn't had sopapillas in years.

Alex winked. "Sopapillas it is." He immediately flagged down the server, though she noticed he did it politely, like a man who'd worked in food service at some point. He seemed like an all-around great guy. Cute and polite and smart. She felt a little sad looking at his smile.

"This was nice," she said. "Thank you for asking me."

"Thank you for saying yes." His eyes crinkled so perfectly when he smiled.

When the sopapillas arrived, she drizzled on too much honey and took a huge bite. "You're a genius," she said with an impolite mouthful of food. "So good."

Alex was describing a documentary about privacy in the internet age when her phone buzzed with a text. As she quickly wiped off her hands, her mind flashed to Everett and that invisible low-level worry in every parent's mind when a child was out. But when she flipped her phone over, it was a text from Barbara. The kids wanted to stop at the library, so I'm giving them thirty minutes to browse; then we'll head home.

Lily sent back a thank-you with five full exclamation points, then looked up to find Alex's lips curved up. She realized she was grinning. "Sorry. Everett and his friend are out for burgers and they wanted to stop at the library. I'm just feeling very pleased about that."

"That's pretty damn cute. I absolutely adored the library when I was a kid."

"It was like a wonderland, right? I still remember when my library started carrying DVDs. My God, the thrill. Now it's all online." She winced. "Sorry, that must be a sore spot for a newspaper reporter."

"It's a bit like being a carriage driver when cars came along, I'm sure. But raging against automobiles didn't make them go away. We adapt or we die. I'm figuring it out."

"Gonna start a podcast?"

He barked out a laugh. "Don't think I haven't considered it."

"You have a nice voice."

His eyebrows disappeared beneath his hair again. "Thanks. So do you."

"Oh yeah?"

"You sounded cute that night you were telling me to get the hell off the property."

They smiled at each other until the server dropped off the bill; then they both reached for it. "Let me get this," he said, but she shook her head.

"We'll split it."

He protested for a few more moments before finally laying down cash for his half. "And I've got the tip," he insisted.

She agreed, and they walked slowly out to the street before starting their goodbyes.

"Can I talk you into another meal sometime? I'm really tired of my own company."

She hesitated, meaning to say no, and somehow saying, "I don't have much free time," instead.

"I'll check back, then, if that's all right."

Was it? Maybe. Maybe it was, but only because he was passing through Herriman and not staying. And it gave her something fun to think about. She gave him her number, and he texted her so she'd have his.

When they paused next to her car, Lily wasn't sure if she should offer a hug, but Alex reached to shake her hand; then he pressed his other hand over the top of hers. "Thank you very much, Lily. I had a wonderful time."

She felt like melting into a stupid puddle at that and could only give a strange little wave before she spun and fumbled with her car door like a flustered teenager.

She pulled away from the curb before she let herself sigh at the delicious sparks of excitement floating inside her chest.

It hadn't been a real date. It was more like a tiny crush on a stranger, really. Still, she just felt . . . *light*. A pure anticipation she hadn't felt since she was young. Frankly, she hadn't thought she had anything that fun and fizzy inside her anymore, and the sensation soon faded into a strange sadness. Something like nostalgia, maybe. Or perhaps it was just that she was driving back toward her home and all the worries that waited there.

She turned on her ancient stereo and shoved in a Fiona Apple CD as she hit the highway out of town. As always, she'd barely managed to push her shitty car from thirty-five to sixty when it was time to exit and take a left to the underpass that flooded every spring. There was new graffiti again, ACAB spelled out in big red letters. Maybe that was what had Mendelson so pissed off.

She spotted the lurking car as soon as she cleared the threatening shadow of the highway. The same spot she'd seen a car sitting before, on the road that led to the tidy row of houses, but not close enough to be parked in the neighborhood. This time when she drove past, the car pulled out and followed her.

"What the hell?" she whispered, staring into the rearview mirror as she drove. It wasn't dark, but the sun was setting, and she knew the business park would be deserted at this time on a Saturday.

She could keep driving, though. She could pull a U-turn and head back to town, drop into the library like she'd wanted to. She could even pull into the storage center and close the gate behind her, although it didn't move that quickly.

She jerked her eyes back to the road before they found their way to the mirror again. The fading sunlight glowed from behind her, so whoever was driving was just a silhouette, a shadow of a threat.

It could be anyone, but she had a terrible feeling it was Mendelson. Still, what if it was a stranger? Jesus, it could even be Jones.

She was supposed to trust her instincts, they all were, but her instincts had failed her disastrously in life, hadn't they? Or had she just shoved them down because she hadn't wanted the truth?

Shaking her head, she decided her instincts didn't deserve her trust. It could be the cop or it could be a madman. She had absolutely nothing to lose by turning around and fleeing, and far too much to lose if she didn't.

Lily hit the gas for the last fifty yards of road, then pulled quickly into her driveway, pulling the steering wheel as hard as she could. The wheels squealed at the tight circle, and then lights flashed, and she slammed on the brakes in panic, trapped between the road and the gate.

The car that had been following her was now stopped at an angle, blocking her path, and the front had lit up in flashing blue and red lights. Her eyes locked with the driver's.

Detective Mendelson.

The surge of relief that washed over her was kind of funny in the face of the police lights, but he couldn't be there to arrest her. She hadn't done anything illegal, not for a long time, anyway.

He opened his car door and approached. Lily stared at him until he'd reached her window, and then she patted her door, looking for the control.

When she finally got the window open, she first heard the sound of his engine, then the scrape of his shoe as he stepped back and bent down.

"Mrs. Arthur," he said solemnly. "I didn't mean to scare you."

This again. This *Mrs. Arthur* bullshit, the ghost she'd left behind, stirred back to life by whatever stick was up this guy's backside.

"What do you want?" she ground out.

"I told you I'd be by to talk, ma'am. Maybe you could pull on in?"

She desperately wanted to bite out, *Talk to my lawyer,* but there were two problems with that. One, she didn't have a lawyer, and two, she did not want to piss off this man any more than she had to. So she snapped, "Park here," then eased her car backward and curved around to the gate to enter the code.

The gate closed behind her after she pulled in. For a moment, she thought about simply heading inside and locking her door, but she knew Barbara would be dropping off Everett soon. It wouldn't be fair to him to present his friend and her mom with a spectacle like that, so she took a deep breath and unlocked the pedestrian gate to let herself through.

"I have no idea where Jones is, if that's what you're after. I'd direct you anywhere but here. Try Costa Rica. Try Guatemala. Try Greenland. Wherever he is, I haven't seen him in six years. If you do find him, tell him to send money for the son he abandoned. Cool?"

"Well, ma'am . . . I wasn't looking for him the first time I came out, but as I said, your behavior caught my attention. If you're not hiding Jones Arthur out here, you're hiding something else."

Her heart pumped a flush to her face almost immediately, so Lily shoved her hands in her pockets and paced away. "What *were* you looking for, Detective? You've never said."

A heartbeat ticked by in silence before he spoke. "A woman was reported missing by her husband. Amber's last reported location was nearby, though I can't reveal more than that."

The hot blood in her face was quickly overtaken by a flood of icy fear. Amber? This was about *Amber*?

Her abusive husband had reported her missing, which shouldn't have surprised Lily. Of course he would go to the police if his wife didn't come home, even if he was a violent bastard.

But Amber wasn't missing. She'd *left*. Lily couldn't be guilty of covering up a crime if there had been no crime.

"Her husband says there may have been drug use involved and that her friends were an . . . unsavory sort. I spoke to every business owner in the park and knocked on every front door. As I said, you're the only one who reacted like you had something to hide."

Yes, she had. Lily took a shallow breath, then another, trying to disguise that she was composing herself before she turned back to him. "So what does this have to do with my ex?"

"I have no idea. I'm just asking questions."

Unfortunately, Detective Mendelson's instincts were spot on. Lily had been hiding something. Now she had to throw him off the scent if she could. But how?

"I'm sorry," she said. "But now that you know about Jones, you know why talking to you upset me. There were a lot of *interviews* after he ran. Years of them. I'm just . . ." She shook her head and paced back toward him to hide that she wanted to run the other way. "I get scared by police now. If I was nervous the first time you came by, it was because talking to a detective brings back a lot of terrible memories of the worst time of my life. That's all." A little truth to sweeten the lie.

He watched silently as she crossed her arms over her chest to hide her shaking hands. "It's just me and my little boy out here, and this is a fairly quiet business. If anything weird happened or anyone was hurt on my property, I'd certainly notice it. I'm always on guard, that's part of my job." When he didn't respond right away, she added, "We're not even open after dark. The gate can't be accessed. That's it. I can't tell you anything more than that."

"And you checked the surveillance?"

"I did. There's nothing there." Another truth, but only because she'd erased a few minutes. "She was seen nearby?" Lily knew she shouldn't have asked, but she felt alarmed at that. What did that mean? Someone had seen her dropped off at Lily's front door? "I don't even know where anyone would go out here."

Detective Mendelson ignored her, his head now cocked to peer at her expression. "When was the last time you saw Jones Arthur?"

"I just told you. Almost seven years ago."

"Surely he's been in touch. A pretty wife. A big, strong son."

"Ex-wife," she growled, hoping he would assume the shake in her voice was just anger. "And no."

"Very strange," he murmured, "considering."

Lily told herself not to ask. She ground her teeth together. Squeezed her fists. Still, a tight, hoarse "Why?" escaped her control.

"Because five days ago, someone saw a prowler in their backyard in the middle of the night. Can you guess where?"

She held up her hands in an impatient shrug.

"Your old house, Ms. Brown."

She had no idea what he was implying, but he kept talking, and each word was a pinprick of ice against her skin.

"The neighbor's dog wouldn't stop barking, and when the owner of *your* old house turned on the porch light, he saw someone crouched down near the backyard shed. Digging."

Digging? She frowned hard, her pulse pattering faster, though she wasn't sure why. "Okay, that is strange."

"Isn't it? The officer who responded found a big ol' hole dug in the ground, twelve inches wide, six inches deep. Why would a prowler dig a hole in a stranger's backyard?"

She started to shake her head, but it hit her then. What it must mean. The cops had found a bundle of ten thousand in cash hidden in their home. Jones must have buried more in the yard. And he'd come back for it. He'd come back *here*.

"Yeah," Mendelson drawled. "I think you can probably take a guess. After I met you, and I looked you up, I started putting the pieces together, and . . . Well, you can see why I was a little *curious* what might be making you so nervous out here."

She nodded again. And again. The memory of her ex-husband's voice scraped through her brain, telling her he wanted his son. Calling and hoping to reach him. Why now? He'd called before too, even a month ago, but not like this. Was it truly possible he was in Herriman?

No. If he had been, he was long gone with his money now.

"I have nothing to do with Jones," she explained, her words distant in her own ears. "I divorced him. He left us with nothing but heartache. I abandoned his name. He's had no contact with his son."

"Hmm."

"Detective Mendelson, I'm still trying to claw my way back up from the hole he left us in. If he is here, and I have no idea if he is, he's not welcome near my property or near my child."

As if her words had summoned Everett, headlights appeared on the road, tiny, then small, then growing larger, until she could make out Barbara Woodbridge's car.

Shit. A pain lanced through Lily's chest. She didn't want this for Everett, to pull up with his new friend and discover his mom being questioned by a cop. Mendelson had turned off his red and blue lights, thank God, but he could make it look bad if he wanted to. And Everett had just had those awful dreams.

Mendelson smiled in a deliberate way, and a new fear blossomed in Lily's heart and quickly took over all the others. What if he mentioned Jones to Everett?

Her feet were moving before she could think, and suddenly she was at the curb, flagging down Barbara so she could open the back door and usher Everett out. "Thank you so much for taking the kids! Sorry to be rushed, there's a security thing with one of the customers." She waved her hand toward Mendelson, who stared hard at her.

"Oh my gosh, no worries. We had a great time. Thank you for having Josephine over so often!"

Lily got her arm around Everett's shoulders and leaned close as she shut the door. "Just go straight in. No stopping, all right?"

"Mom, what's wrong?"

"Everything's fine. Straight inside, okay?"

She subtly pushed him toward the gate, offered Barbara a wave and a wildly fake grin, then hurried back toward Mendelson, putting her body between the detective and her child.

Barbara pulled away, and Lily could hear Everett's footsteps behind her, moving far more slowly than she wanted. She didn't dare look at him, as if Mendelson would somehow notice him only if Lily drew his attention.

Her caution didn't pay off. "How are you doing, Everett?" Mendelson called.

Her son's footsteps didn't stop, thank God. The pedestrian gate rattled loudly before banging shut. The security lights gradually glowed to life above her, casting them into a strange and seamy vignette.

"He has nightmares," she said quietly. "I don't want him hearing anything about his dad. Please. I'm begging you. He's just a little boy."

Mendelson held up his hands. "Listen, I'm out here trying to find a missing woman. What I want from you is some honesty."

"I am being honest, and I'd help if I could." An outright lie, but Amber had a right to disappear if she wanted to.

"You didn't see her?"

"I don't know anything about her. And Jones has *nothing* to do with us, with our family, and I have no idea where he is. I swear."

He stared at her. She held his gaze until he finally shrugged. "You have my card. Call me if you see anything. I'll be sure to check on you and your boy soon."

She watched him walk back to his car. She waited, making sure he started the engine, eyeing him as he pulled away. She didn't want to go inside, didn't want to lie to her son. And she certainly didn't want to tell him the truth. Full darkness had fallen suddenly, and spring frogs sang somewhere beyond the buildings, living whole lives in rain puddles that would disappear by summer.

She heard a door open, and then Everett's small voice. "Mom?"

After taking a deep breath, she set her face into cheerful calm and turned toward him. "How was dinner?"

"Um . . . good. What's wrong?"

"Nothing's wrong."

"That was a cop?"

Clearing her throat, she pushed through the gate and locked it behind her. "Yes, just some stuff that was stolen from a unit. No big deal."

His eyes went wide as she moved past him to the door. "You're acting weird," he said to her back. "What's wrong?"

"Just worried about the theft, that's all."

"What was stolen?" His voice had turned slightly squeaky, so Lily held up her hands.

"Sweetie, it was only a divorce dispute. Furniture, that kind of thing. There aren't dangerous thieves around."

He visibly deflated, his shoulders lowering from around his ears to their normal place. Determined to change the subject, Lily unlocked the apartment and said, "Barbara texted that she took you two to the library. Did you get anything good?"

His backpack rubbed against his shirt, signaling a shrug.

Desperate to take his mind off the cop, Lily almost mentioned her own night out and had to snap her mouth closed on the idea as she locked the apartment door behind them. She couldn't believe that had been just tonight, just an hour ago. She'd had so much fun. A handsome man had flirted with her. She'd felt freer than she had in a long time.

And now her past was back, stomping her down again. What if Jones was back too?

No. She wasn't scared of him, not physically, but she felt terrified all the same. Because what the hell did he want?

"Where were you?" Everett asked, glancing at her purse as she set it on the table.

Jesus, what a time for him to actually start paying attention. "I, uh, went out to dinner."

He frowned. "By yourself?"

"No."

His frown deepened. "With who, then?"

"Just . . . just a new customer I ran into. He's in town for a couple of weeks taking care of some things for his uncle. He was by himself and asked me to . . ."

His frown went crooked. "So you were on a date?"

Lily blanched. "No! We had dinner at Mia's. That's all. Then I came home. Obviously, because I'm right here."

"You're allowed to date," he grumbled. "I was just worried about the police." He glanced at her, eyes narrowed a bit. "Was it about Dad?"

"*Dad?* Everett, why are you asking that?"

"Because he's wanted by the police?" he snapped back.

She squeezed her eyes shut. Yes, it had been a stupid question, but Everett seemed more and more on edge these days. "I'm sorry," she said in the most even voice she could muster. "I already told you the police were here about some missing items. It wasn't about your dad," she added, lying through her teeth. "Ev, are you doing okay?"

"Yes," he said, but that was all.

"Do you . . . do you want to talk about your dad?" God, she hoped he said no.

He did, thank God.

Lily let out a long sigh. He could have been more polite, but the truth was he had a right to be snippy. And he wasn't even wrong. Detective Mendelson *had* been here about his dad. Oh, he was using Amber as an excuse, but he'd obviously caught Jones's scent. Because Jones was *here.*

No. No, she didn't know that. He couldn't be here. If he'd buried a bunch of money in the backyard, that would certainly be a reason to stop by but definitely not a reason to stay. He wouldn't risk that.

Maybe seeing their old house had made him think more of Everett. Maybe even someone like Jones had regrets, and that's why he'd phoned only a month after the last call.

She needed to think this through. "I'm going to take a bath. Unless you wanted to watch a movie?"

Everett shook his head, looking sorry now, his head ducked low. She knew this wasn't easy for him. He probably felt lost, unable to control his life or any of the adults in it. She could understand that because she felt the same.

If she had a number for Jones, she'd call him. Demand to know what he was doing and where he was. But for now, all she could do was sift through the rubble of his destruction and try to interpret the pieces. He'd never given her any answers before, and he definitely wasn't going to start now.

CHAPTER 16

He'd tried to have fun with Josephine tonight, but anytime he relaxed just a little, his brain would jolt back to anticipation. *You need to get home. You need to check your messages. Your dad is waiting.*

He kept telling his brain to shut up. Dad hadn't been on Discord this morning or this afternoon, and Everett didn't want to get his hopes up, because maybe he'd walked away again.

When he did manage to tamp down his own thoughts, he would eventually relax, and then his brain would escape his control and snap right back to Dad again.

He and Josephine had gone to the library to look up school yearbooks, and they'd found all the girls, even Tiffany Miller. But Everett had barely been able to pay attention. He'd just wanted to be back at his computer.

A soft metal click told him his mom had locked the bathroom door; then the rushing roar of the pipes filled the hallway when she turned on the tap. Everett raced to the desk and dropped into the chair to log on.

He hated himself for doing it. Hated that hope buzzed through his muscles. And he really, really hated that he still believed his dad would show up.

But then . . . he did.

Hey, LM, it's me.

LM. Little man. It was a code, kind of, that didn't give him away. Everett flushed hot all the way to his scalp. He checked the timestamp.

The message had come in only one hour before, and Everett felt furiously glad that he hadn't stayed home all afternoon waiting for it. What was his dad busy with, anyway? Stealing cars and robbing old people?

Feeling immediately bad for that, he shook his head as he checked his dad's username. It was just a bunch of letters and numbers. Everett added him as a friend.

You still there? he messaged back, unwilling to act excited to finally hear from him. When the rush of the pipes abruptly cut off, Everett jerked back in fear, then craned his neck toward the bathroom. He waited, holding his breath, until he heard the faint shushing sound of his mom shifting in the water.

He'd just relaxed back in his chair when a new message arrived. Yes! Still here! Sorry it took so long. Things are complicated, and I had to find a safe place to stay.

Where are you? Everett wanted to ask, but he knew his dad couldn't give that away. So he typed, Is everything ok? instead.

Everything is great. I'm talking to you!!!

Everett couldn't stop the smile that popped onto his face. He didn't even want to. His dad hadn't disappeared again. He'd kept his promise. It was a small thing, maybe, but it was something good.

Another message arrived. Can you talk on the phone? Or here on Discord?

I can't, he wrote back with a glance toward the bathroom. Not alone.

Got it. No worries. I've been feeling guilty about the call anyway.

Why?

You're too young for me to ask you to keep a secret this big.

That's not true, he wrote back immediately.

His dad sent a winky face. Oh, you've got practice already, huh?

Everett pressed his lips hard together at that. He could tell his dad about the lockers. Tell him what he found. The missing girls and his suspicions. But when the words formed in his head, they sounded like a dumb campfire story.

But he did know how to keep a secret. I didn't tell her you called, he said. I wouldn't.

Thank you, LM. I've missed you a lot.

Everett felt so full of happiness he had to wait until the shaking of his fingers eased so he could type back. I've missed you too, Dad. He backed up the cursor and erased "Dad" so there'd be no evidence. I've missed you too. A lot. Where have you been?

All over really.

Other countries?

Sure. Brazil. Costa Rica. Dollars go a long way in some of those small villages! It's not so bad, but it's lonely.

He was sweating a little, his armpits prickling strangely under his shirt. It should be nice talking to his father, but instead it felt like time was slipping away, and he wanted to hold tight to it like a rope.

Are you ever coming back? He typed that, then stared at it for a long moment, afraid to send it, afraid for the answer. He tapped the

RETURN key, then squinted his eyes mostly shut as if that would shield him from the reply.

If I did . . . , his dad responded quickly, would you see me?

A strange laugh popped from Everett's throat at that. Yes! Of course!

His dad sent another winking emoji. I'll hold you to it!

Deal, Everett responded. Then he carefully typed, That would be so cool. If you could do that.

Maybe I could.

Really??? Like soon???

His dad didn't respond for a long time. When he finally texted again, it was just a thumbs-up emoji, and then he changed the subject. Everett felt a strange mix of guilt and resentment at that. Had he pushed his dad too quickly? But why *shouldn't* he?

Everett was just answering a question about his favorite video games when a watery burble rose from the pipes in the wall. His heart exploded into flutters. His mom had opened the drain. I need to sign off in a sec. Sorry!!! He didn't want to let go of the connection, and his neck went tight and achy at the thought.

Are you usually online?

He grimaced in frustration. It depends. When Mom's working I can get on, and I can play online games on the weekends.

Ok listen, I'm laying low but I'll send messages when I can. I'll be on the move tomorrow but maybe tomorrow night we can meet up.

Yes!

Stay awesome, LM.

You too!

Tomorrow night. They had a time now, not just a promise and a hope. Everett laughed, then covered his mouth. He didn't want to log off, but he had to. Still, he took the time to reread the whole conversation so he could think about it later. He didn't even click on the message waiting from Josephine before he closed the whole window and put the computer to sleep. He was too busy imagining the kind of road trip he might take with his dad someday.

CHAPTER 17

She'd stolen his son. She'd stolen his *future*.

He knew that the same way he knew everything: he was smarter than other people. He saw through their stupid little lives to the shitty truths that lay beneath. And now Lily walked around like she'd done nothing wrong, playing at being a poor, innocent victim.

Lies. All lies.

He'd lain low for years, hadn't he? Kept quiet and careful, doing what he was supposed to do like all the helpless sheep that milled around him, and this was what he got in return. Disrespect. Falsehoods. And absolute betrayal.

Walking the perimeter of the storage center in the darkness, he stayed far enough from the fence line to avoid tripping any security lights or cameras, but everything inside the fence glowed under those daylight-bright lamps. It looked like a movie playing just for him.

She felt safe in there behind chain link and razor wire, and yet he could get in anytime. He could sit on her patio all night if he wanted. He'd spent a whole hour there already, just waiting, just watching, the boy's open window a delicious welcome that had rushed along his nerves over and over.

He liked that. The power of moving in their space in the dark as they slept, totally unaware, totally vulnerable. Tonight Lily emerged from the false safety of the apartment to bring out a bag of trash and check the lock on one of the gates. A light had burned out nearby, and she stopped to look up at it, hands on her hips. He couldn't see her expression from so far away, but he imagined she looked concerned, worried about that gap in the security when there were a dozen others she would never notice.

The cat arrived to glare at him again, her throat vibrating with a nearly silent growl. The joke was on the cat, though. He'd decided black cats must be good luck instead of bad, because like him they were another shadow sneered at by society. He waved at the cat, then looked back up to find that Lily had retreated inside.

Rage surged through him like a vast, rolling ocean. He picked up a chunk of cement from the ground and threw it hard over the fence, where it hit a building with a sharp clang of metal. The cat shot away into an alley. He threw another rock and another, hoping to lure Lily back out so he could see her face when he aimed one so close it would scare her half to death. He needed her terrified so she'd eventually run to him and give him just what he wanted. His body responded to the idea of her fear and to the sure knowledge that he could punish her for her transgressions. He could rid the world of the burden she brought, pulling everyone else down.

He waited, seething, but she never emerged from her hiding place. She was numbing her brain in front of the TV, maybe, or drinking herself to sleep or swiping through slutty dating apps online, because that was what dumb garbage did with their lives.

He faded back into the night.

Now that he'd calmed down, he could see his outburst had been foolish. Impulsive. His control had slipped already several times this week. But the right moment would come eventually. And he'd be ready.

CHAPTER 18

Lily woke to an email with more bad news, and she was finally starting to feel like she couldn't escape it.

> Hi, Lily! Gretchen again. Please let me know if there's a good time to meet on Monday. I can be in your area as early as 9.

Gretchen was coming back. Gretchen, who'd just been there for a surprise inspection. There could be only one reason, really. She'd found something.

But what? Lily had been so careful. She'd taken care of this place as if it were her own business. It had to be that goddamn detective stirring up trouble.

On top of that, she had her Federal Taxation final in four days, and she felt like she'd dropped the ball on studying since a tornado of anxiety had invaded her brain.

At least Everett was in a great mood, cuddled into the couch with his blanket, laughing at cartoons. He'd looked so cozy she hadn't even asked about his chores. He could do them later.

Speaking of chores . . . Lily stripped the sheets from their beds and stuffed them into the washer, then moved on to the office to clean the front door. People really had trouble using the handle without pressing handprints all over the glass, which boggled her mind. She always cleaned it on Sunday morning so she could go a whole day with clear glass since the office was closed.

She was just finishing up the exterior of the door when the gate rolled open and a car began to ease through. She stood and swung around with a vague customer-service smile that widened into something more real when she saw Alex waving.

"Hey, Lily," he called through his open window. "Come over and say hi if you have time. Help me procrastinate!"

She laughed and waved him on, but honestly she wanted to procrastinate too. She wasn't quite finished with her normal Sunday tasks, but then again she had all day.

When she went back into the apartment, Everett had moved to the computer, though he still had his comforter wrapped around him as he played a game with his headphones on. He jumped when she tapped him on the shoulder. "Want to drive over to Frostee's this afternoon? We haven't gone out for ice cream in a while."

He glanced at the computer. "Maybe. I'm gonna be online with Mikey later."

"I could call his mom and ask if he can come over to play."

"I'm not five, Mom. Don't be weird."

She nodded and hoped to God she could comply.

Lily was turning away when he added, "You don't have to be here all the time. You can go do something on your own." He shot her a meaningful look, as if he were thinking of her not-quite-a-date explanation for that dinner.

She felt for all the world like a junior high kid trying not to look pitiful in front of the high schoolers, which didn't make any sense.

"Maybe I will," she said defensively, but he only nodded and raised his eyebrows in encouragement.

Sheesh.

Goaded into not being a loser, Lily went to the kitchen and filled two of her favorite mugs with coffee before heading outside.

"I brought you a cup of procrastination!" she called as she came around the corner of Alex's building. He hauled a box out of his SUV and set it on the cement before popping up with a smile. He hadn't even opened the unit yet, so she hoped she hadn't too obviously rushed over.

"Coffee? My God, you're a genius."

"Just black, hope that's okay."

"Anything that hasn't been sitting in the kitchen of a break room for fourteen hours is absolutely perfect."

She tipped her head toward the box. "Moving more stuff *in?*"

"Oh yeah. You know. Sorting through it to see what we should keep. Want to sit down?" He gestured to the now-empty cargo area of his vehicle.

"I should probably get back . . ."

"Wow, you truly suck at procrastinating."

She laughed and gave in, handing him her cup so she could scoot herself up. He settled a few inches away.

"Thanks again for dinner," he said.

"It was really nice." She meant it. She'd been thinking about him, she'd even searched for him online that morning.

His byline photo had looked so serious she'd immediately laughed. He hadn't looked that solemn even when she'd told him she couldn't help him with the gate. When she scrolled through a few pages, she noticed he mostly covered local politics, though he'd written several pieces on health and community. He'd also covered a lot of the protests and counterprotests of the past few years, and she cringed as she read about him needing stitches on his scalp after a bottle was thrown.

Alex was older than she'd thought, which she often found with men. No childbearing years to spring back from, and once they got wrinkles, they could grow a beard. She'd pegged him in his midthirties, but he was forty-one. That boyish grin did a lot for him.

Now she worried he'd searched for her too. After all, he was a reporter.

She'd returned to her maiden name, but how hard would it be to see past that? Though Brown was a common surname. She'd stumbled into good camouflage, though she'd really meant it as a public declaration of her rejection of Jones.

"How's school going?" he asked.

Lily groaned. "My final is this week. I can't wait to be done. Two more classes and I'll have my degree."

He tilted his head to watch her, a half smile lifting up one corner of his mouth.

"What?" she asked.

"Nothing. You just look very happy when you say that. Proud."

Her face heated with self-consciousness. "Yeah, I guess I am proud."

"You should be. I certainly didn't work full time and raise a kid while I was in school, so I'm impressed. It's a big deal."

Jesus, he was sweet. "Thanks." She felt a blush heat her cheeks, but the rest of her body prickled with a more complicated tension. Pleasure at his attention, and a kind of animal impulse to run and hide.

"Are you wrapping up here?" she asked, gesturing toward one of the boxes.

"No, still slowly going through things, taking my time. I don't want to get rid of anything important, so I work here for a while, then review a few things with my uncle. We always wind up talking, so it's slower than it should be. What are you up to today?"

"Just chores. I'm hoping to talk Everett into going out later for ice cream. That would have been a given a few years ago, but I guess I'm not cool anymore."

"That means you're a good mom, though, right?"

She laughed at that.

"I'm serious!" he protested. "All the parents I thought were cool at that age . . . Now that I look back? Yikes! They were all badly aging adolescents."

She nodded. "So you're saying I should cancel that freestyle rap class I signed up for?"

"No, you should definitely do that and send me a link to a livestream."

Lily nearly spit out the last of her coffee at that. She was disappointed to realize she'd finished her cup, but it felt like a signal that it was time to retreat. He had work to do, and she . . . well, she couldn't keep nurturing this crush.

"I'd better get back," she said.

"Oh. Got it. I'm going to be back and forth all day. I could bring some lunch later?"

Lily cleared her throat. She glanced down at the fingers he'd wrapped around his coffee mug, and they just looked . . . nice. How in the world could fingers holding a cup somehow be attractive? "Sure," her mouth said before her brain could stop it. "Yeah."

Her phone buzzed in her pocket, and Lily reached for it in desperation, so she wouldn't say more or, worse, *feel* more. It was a text from Zoey.

Call me?

"Oh, I need to get this. Sorry. I'll grab your mug later?"

"Sure! I'll text you about lunch."

She hurried away without even saying goodbye, afraid he'd see all her anxiety bubbling up when she couldn't explain it to him. It was just lunch, and only a severely damaged person would be so nervous about it. She was definitely severely damaged, but she preferred to keep that to herself.

Lily hit the CALL button and walked quickly away. "Hey, what's up?"

"Hi, everything going good there?"

"Things are *good*, yes." She put extra emphasis on *good*, hoping Zoey would persuade her to spill the beans about lunch. But her smile faded at her friend's next words.

"You said I should call you if I need you, but . . ."

Shit. She hadn't really meant that. She'd only been trying to be brave and bold and strong. But she didn't feel like any of those things in the face of this unspoken question.

Feet slowing, she murmured a wordless "Mm," because she couldn't say yes this time. She couldn't do it again with everything swirling so madly around her. Gretchen would be back tomorrow, and—

"I won't ask you to shelter anyone again, but . . . it's Connie."

That brought her to a complete standstill. "Connie?" she whispered.

"You let her have that unit in your name three months ago?"

"Yes, I remember." Of course she remembered. Lily was granted the right to one small storage unit as part of her compensation, but she'd never used it. Zoey had come to her and asked if there was anything she could do for Connie. Connie needed a place to keep furniture she'd acquired from a woman whose house she cleaned. She'd need something to start a new life for her and her son when she finally escaped.

Connie, who'd barely said a word when she arrived, had looked nearly sixty, gray and sunken in on herself. She'd later discovered the woman was only forty-five. Lily had offered the unit for free.

"Is she okay?" she asked.

"Yes. Her father-in-law had a heart attack, so her husband just left for the hospital in Kansas City. He'll be gone until at least tomorrow morning, hopefully much longer. This is her chance to leave."

She could do this. This was easy. "Of course. I'm here now; I can let her in anytime."

"Is tonight okay? Her friend is driving in from Wichita to get her. She has a big van to help, but she won't be here until eight thirty tonight, maybe nine. I know it will be after hours, but can you do that? I'll drop Connie off, her friend will pick her up. The end."

Lily said nothing for a moment, turning over all her fears about Gretchen and Mendelson and everything else.

"Lily?"

"Yes," she blurted. "I can do that."

"Thank you! Thank you, Lil. I'll drop her and her son off at eight thirty on the dot."

"Her son?" Lily glanced around, suddenly worried she wasn't alone. Her senses sharpened, and the drone of a nearby frog sounded like an alarm.

"She has a five-year-old."

Five. Almost the same age Everett had been when their lives imploded. Lily suddenly felt sick. Sick at the risk, but also at the deep blow of her compulsion to help this little boy. Lily hadn't been running for her life with Everett, but she'd still felt so terrified, so overwhelmed, so hopeless. What must Connie be feeling?

"Okay," Lily murmured. "Eight thirty."

"I'll see you then. Thank you!"

She hung up and forced herself to move back toward the office. This wasn't bad. It wasn't illegal. But if Mendelson was pushing her this hard over a grown woman who'd walked away, what might he do about a five-year-old child taken by his mother?

She hoped to God she wouldn't find out.

CHAPTER 19

Everett couldn't stop smiling. His mom had left the apartment again at noon, saying she'd be back in half an hour, which meant he could log on to Discord without worrying she might be over his shoulder. He'd been checking on and off all morning, and now he crossed his fingers for luck as the messages loaded.

It worked. A new message from his dad.

Still, it was only a minor stroke of luck.

Hey, LM! Hoping to have free time later. Maybe at 1 or 2. Let me know if you'll be around.

"Shit," Everett grumbled, glancing at the time. It was only noon, and his mom would be back by 1:00, and then she wanted to go for ice cream, which would have been a great idea on another day.

He looked at the door, then back at the screen. She'd been gone only five minutes, and he'd have plenty of warning if she came back.

Before he could lose his nerve, Everett got up, went into his mom's room, and opened the drawer of her nightstand as his neck prickled with the false warning that she was watching. He tried to ignore it but still looked back at the doorway a couple of times as he lifted a home-and-garden magazine to find her clunky old tablet.

Hoping she didn't use it often, he slipped it free and quietly slid the drawer closed. Every once in a while when Everett was sick, she let him take it to his room to watch cartoons, but otherwise she had a strict "internet in the family room only" policy. The public service propaganda had convinced her he'd get lured into being kidnapped or exploited somehow if he managed to log on outside her supervision.

After opening Discord in the browser window, he logged on, and even though the whole thing moved at a snail's pace and took forever to load, it worked. Everett stowed the tablet under his bed.

Back on the computer, he answered his dad, letting him know he'd do his best to be online between 1:00 and 2:00; then he closed the window and jumped up to reheat the leftovers his mom had left for lunch.

At 12:30, he headed out to do his chores, to ensure his mom wouldn't knock on his door at 1:30 and tell him to get busy. He quickly passed two of the buildings without even bothering to check for open locks. He had more interesting things to occupy him now, and his mom wouldn't know he hadn't checked. But the garbage was another thing entirely. It seemed self-generating and had to be emptied every day.

He quickly hit the four garbage cans placed throughout the complex and found they were stuffed full of the usual forbidden trash listed on the can. Cardboard boxes, packing paper, Styrofoam peanuts. He sighed and switched out the bags, then jogged to the big dumpster with all the overstuffed trash before digging the key out of his pocket.

If they didn't keep it locked up, people would throw away anything. Old furniture, computers, broken televisions, a dozen boxes full of VHS tapes, used tires. Once his mom had seen someone leaving a sleeper sofa next to the dumpster, and she'd had to march out and yell at them. That was the first time he'd ever heard her say curse words in front of him. She'd apologized later and let him get out his popsicle-making kit despite that she always grumbled it was cheaper to buy the store brand instead of using fruit juice. The store-bought kind tasted better too, but he didn't admit that to her.

Everett slammed the trash lid, locked it up, and sprinted back through the complex on his normal route.

He'd already fully passed one of the alleys before he registered the vehicle there at the same moment he heard his mom's laugh. He skidded to a stop. Took three backward steps. Stared in absolute shock.

His mom was perched on the back of an SUV, a sandwich in her hand, her smiling face turned toward a man. He was not an old man. He was dark haired and skinny, maybe his mom's age. But he was parked in front of Alex Bennick's half-open locker.

As Everett gaped at them, his mom glanced up and visibly jumped at the sight of him. "Everett! Oh hi!" She set down the sandwich and slid to her feet. "This is my son, Everett! Ev, this is Alex."

Alex. His name was Alex. And when he got to his feet and smiled, there was no mistaking that face. This was one of the teenagers from those pictures in Alex Bennick's house.

"Hey there, Everett!" Thankfully he didn't come closer or reach out a hand; he just gave a little wave.

Everett gawked at him.

"We're having sandwiches," his mom said, her voice a little strained. When she took a step toward him, the bubble of shock around his brain popped, and a thought floated to the surface. *He's in town taking care of things for his uncle . . .*

Holy shit. Oh *holy shit.*

"Ev?"

"Yeah," he managed to say, because he couldn't let this guy know. He couldn't give anything away. "Sorry," he muttered, moving again, walking past the alley, leaving them alone, because what if he said something, what if he gave something away and this man sensed danger, and—

"I'll be back in a few minutes!" his mom called after him, and that was good, because he would watch carefully until then. Make sure that guy left, and then he could tell his mom, warn her.

He was sprinting again, not back to his dad this time, but to his bedroom and the snapshot he'd hidden in his backpack. He slammed through the front door and raced to kneel next to his bed and dig through his bag. When his fingers touched the stiff corner, he pulled the Polaroid out to check. That guy was definitely the teenage boy in this picture. He had to be. There was no mistaking that stupid wide grin.

But what the hell did it mean? Was he dangerous? Or was he just helping his dangerous uncle?

Shit. Josephine probably wasn't back from church yet. He couldn't text her for advice. But then it didn't matter because he heard the front door open, and he only had time to stuff the picture into his backpack and flop down on the bed.

"Hey, are you all right?" his mom asked as she appeared in the doorway. She was okay. She was home.

"Who was that guy?" Everett blurted out, unable to think of some subtle way to ask.

"The one I had lunch with? That's Alex. He's in town going through his uncle's things."

"His uncle?" When she nodded, a good thought seized Everett, and he sat up. "He died?"

"What? No, his uncle is in a nursing home in town. He can't take care of himself anymore, so Alex is here to help go through his things and make some decisions for him."

"Oh. So is that who you had dinner with too?"

"I . . . Um. Yes. And today he was working here so he picked up lunch for me. That's all. It's not . . ." Whatever she'd been about to say, she decided not to say it and closed her mouth.

"But who *is* he? Do you know anything about him?"

She shrugged. "I mean . . . He lives in Memphis. He worked for a newspaper."

Memphis. "But he grew up here?"

"No, he didn't. I think he said Ohio."

Everett relaxed a little. That was good news. Very good news. Tennessee and Ohio, those places were far away from the murders. And if he wasn't involved . . . Was it possible Everett could ask him why his uncle had collected the information? But he couldn't ask without revealing his trespassing.

His mom moved closer, then sat on his bed, her hand reaching for his knee. "Ev, are you upset that I went on a date?"

"No," he protested immediately.

"Because it wasn't even really—"

"I'm not upset about that."

"Well . . . you did tell me to do something on my own."

He frowned at the awkward smile his mom pulled. "What?"

Sighing, she slumped a little. "Nothing. Look, I'm home now, so it doesn't matter."

"Is he gone?"

"I'm not sure. Probably. He was just grabbing a few more things. And he's leaving town soon." She patted his leg. "Want to go get ice cream?"

Everett's eyes slid away toward the open door and the computer beyond it.

His mom sighed again, and he felt guilty, though he wasn't sure why. "It's fine. I need to study, anyway. Maybe later." She sounded tired. But she was safe, and that was all that mattered.

When she went to her room, Everett tensed, waiting for the slide of a drawer, a shout of outrage, but instead she emerged quickly with a textbook and a stack of papers. He heard her quietly arranging stuff on the kitchen table with none of her usual humming.

Everett couldn't log on to Discord on the computer with her out there, but he had a solution now. "I'm going to read and listen to music," he shouted before closing his door. Although he tucked his earbuds in, he didn't turn anything on as he slid down to sit on the floor between the window and his bed. He carefully arranged a paperback open on the floor beside him, then slipped the tablet out from under his bed and fired it up.

No message from his dad yet. Everett reached out to Josephine, but as he suspected, she wasn't online. He started typing out a message anyway, but it seemed less alarming the more he typed. This wasn't the man who'd rented that locker. Everett had seen the driver's license. Probably this Alex was just doing what he said he was. Everett deleted half of his exclamation points before sending.

When he got up to open his window, Shadow was there, waiting patiently for her food. The sight of her relaxed some of the tightness in his shoulders. His mom was here, Shadow was here, and he'd be talking to his dad soon. Everything was okay.

As soon as he set the food on the windowsill, a bubble popped open on the tablet.

You there, LM?

Everett gasped and dropped back to the floor. Yes! I'm here!

How's it going?

After glancing over his shoulder in nervous guilt, he decided to tell his dad what was going on. He probably knew all about criminals, right? Maybe he could offer advice. Today was kind of crazy, actually. I've been looking into these murders from like 20 years ago. Or I guess they're technically missing women since they've never been found.

Wow! Sounds cool! Unfortunately today was crazy for me too. I
had to move again. Things aren't good.

The tentative smile that had spread over Everett's mouth faded.
What did that mean? Were the cops closing in?

Lips parting in shock, he typed, Are you okay???

For now but I need your help, his dad responded immediately, and
Everett's heart leapt into a wild rhythm.

He had to type and retype his response several times as he cursed
his clumsy hands. Absolutely! Yes! What do you need?

Maybe I shouldn't ask.

He was shaking his head as he wrote back. No. Go ahead. Tell me.
He'd do anything if it meant his dad could keep talking to him.

Ok. I didn't want to ask this but . . . Your mom has something of
mine. It's nothing dangerous, I swear. But if I don't get it soon, I'll
have to turn myself in.

Everett's eyes went so wide he felt an ache at the strain of it. What
is it?

Just a notebook.

"Oh." The word came out on a grunt, like Everett had been punched
in the gut. A notebook. Something he'd left behind. Something he
needed.

Are you . . . ? Everett shook the chaos from his head and tried to
form a clear thought. Are you nearby?

I'm not far. You think I wouldn't check on you, LM? I have to make sure you're doing ok every once in a while.

His eyes flew past Shadow to the space beyond the window as if his dad might be standing right there on the patio. He was here? Somewhere *close*?

Have you seen me??? Everett asked, but his dad's message arrived at the same time.

It's brown leather.

What?

The notebook. It's small. About 6 inches tall. Nice brown leather with some decoration. Do you think you've seen it around?

Everett tucked his hands into his lap. He stared at the messages, the balloons shaking and wavering past his tears. His dad was close by. He had to be if he wanted to pick something up. He was close enough to come see him.

And that was why he'd reached out. Not for Everett. Not at all. It was because he wanted something. And he needed Everett to get it for him.

LM?

No, Everett typed very slowly, I haven't seen it.

Could you look for it for me? It's probably in a box or in a closet or something?

Everett realized he was crying, crying quietly but hard, snot running from his nose and tears dripping down his cheeks. He wiped a sleeve across his face and tried to take a few deep breaths. He clenched his hands into fists to stop himself from lifting the tablet and smashing it against the floor, smashing it until he could break his dad's words apart.

He wanted the notebook, and then he'd go away again. And maybe that would be better. Maybe he *should* disappear forever and never come back.

But how could Everett ever let him go?

CHAPTER 20

Lily glanced toward her son as he stared out the car window at the rain coming down in sheets. His temple rested on the glass, and his bent neck looked so pale in the gray light. He'd been subdued at dinner too, despite the rare treat of a twenty-minute drive for his favorite chili dogs and soft serve.

"Everett, are you sure everything is okay?" she finally asked.

"Yeah."

"You've been quiet all day." She reached over to squeeze his elbow. "Are you fighting with Josephine or something?"

"No."

"All right." She grimaced and tried again. "Did you get your homework done for tomorrow?"

"No, I'll need the computer tonight."

"No problem."

"Thanks." He turned to flash a wan smile, and Lily felt more sure about the sick feeling swelling in her gut. This was about Alex. She couldn't forget the moment she'd looked up from her mild flirting and Everett's face had been a grimace of horror.

But if it was about Alex, there was nothing she could say. She was an adult, and it wasn't healthy for Everett to be part of her decisions about casual dating. Anything more she might say to Everett at this point would be painfully awkward for both of them.

They were almost to the gate when he finally spoke. "Did you love Dad?"

Tension snapped so quickly through her body that she accidentally jerked the car toward the shoulder before she could control her arms. "Sorry," she muttered. "I'm sorry. What?"

"Did you love him?"

"Yes. I mean, of course I did. Before all of . . . Well, I wouldn't have had you with him if I didn't."

"So you thought he was a good guy, but he wasn't?"

Lily cleared her throat as she stopped at the gate. Thank God she had to take a moment to lean out and key in the code, so she had a few seconds to think. It didn't help. She should have expected this at some point. She should have been ready. She wasn't.

Lily eased the car through and into her parking place. When she cut the engine, the rain beat down, muffling the outside world until the space felt nearly claustrophobic. She turned toward Everett, thinking of Mendelson, and Alex, and wanting to say, *I don't want to talk about any of this,* but that would be cruel. He had a right to know.

"Yes, I thought your dad was a good guy. I wouldn't have married him otherwise, and I definitely wouldn't have let him near you. He loved you. I know he did. But I don't love him anymore."

Everett stared down at his tightly clasped fingers, the tip of his nose going red. One tear dripped to his hands. "You think he loved me?"

"Oh, baby. Yes. Whatever else he was doing, he took the time to play with you whenever he got home. You were so excited every single time his car pulled into the driveway. And when you were sick, he'd pick you up and rock you for hours no matter how big you got."

His face scrunched up in a frown. "I think maybe I remember that."

Unbuckling, Lily leaned over to wrap him in her arms. "I'm sorry. I'm so sorry. What do you want to know?"

His head rocked against her when he shook it. "I don't know."

"I get that I'm not the most fun mom in the world. I can be too strict. But I love you more than anything. You can ask me whatever you want about your dad, and I'll tell you." Her eyes filled with tears at that, at what she'd kept from him, and what she'd have to be honest about now if he asked. She'd thought he was moving on without his father, but maybe he was in the exact same place he'd been at six, needing his daddy and heartbroken that he'd left.

"I'm sorry he had to leave, Ev. I'm sorry."

He nodded. "He would have been in prison anyway."

True, but he would have been reachable that whole time. Hell, he might have been bored enough to write to Everett every week.

"I'm sorry that—" She choked back a sob. "I'm sorry I didn't know better. I would have . . ." But what could she say? That she wouldn't have had him with Jones? If that were true, then Everett wouldn't exist. "I love you so much."

"I love you too, Mom."

"Is this about Alex? Or about that detective?"

He pulled back with a shrug, though he seemed more composed now. "I don't know."

Maybe he didn't. Or maybe he'd listened in on yet another conversation with Mendelson.

"Thanks for dinner," he said, obviously attempting to end the conversation.

She let him. She had no idea if it was the right thing or not, but she let him reach for the handle and get out. Because what could she say? There was no good way out of this. They just had to keep moving forward.

He hopped right on the computer as soon as they walked in, slipping his headphones on in a clear signal that he was done talking. Lily sat down to study, though she wasn't sure she took anything in. She was too busy staring out the window, alternating between worrying about Everett and worrying about Zoey dropping off Connie and her son.

She'd be an ideal mom after this. No more sneaking around at night, no more lies, and no more suspicious activity that would bring that bastard detective back to disturb her son.

Her skin buzzed as if she'd been enveloped by static electricity, and her shoulders ached under the heavy grip of stress. When Zoey finally texted her with a simple Be there in 15, Lily took her first deep breath in an hour.

All she had to do was meet Zoey at the gate, unlock the unit, and open the gate when Connie's friend arrived. It wasn't illegal, and it wasn't precisely against Neighborhood Storage rules. On the books, after-hours visits weren't allowed, but she had some discretion. Or to be more precise, no one had ever told her she didn't.

Lily paced to the window, watching the last drops of rain streak through the halos of security lights. Then she paced back to her bed before returning to the window again.

When her phone buzzed to life, she puffed out a breath of surprise to see Alex's name appear like magic. Can I treat you to breakfast tomorrow? he asked. A couple of grocery store donuts, maybe? Her tense frown relaxed a little. It was nice to be asked even though she was way too overwhelmed to agree.

Sorry, I can't tomorrow.

Ok, got it. But I'll be coming out there, so please don't think I'm stalking you. I'm only after the storage space.

She sent him a laughing face in response, then put her phone away with a sad sigh, reluctant to return to reality.

She had only digital clocks in her place, but Lily could swear she heard ticking as she stared out, waiting for the telltale glow of headlights to appear. When she couldn't stay still any longer, she finally excused herself to the office. "I'll be back in a few minutes," she murmured to Everett, who didn't seem to notice as she grabbed her windbreaker and left the apartment. She watched out the front window until she finally spotted lights on the road.

Zoey's boxy SUV, usually packed to the gills with donated supplies or bulk food purchases, pulled up to the gate, and the back door immediately opened. A woman slipped silently out, pulling a big bag after her. A second passed, and then a little boy jumped free, landing on the drive with a glowing splash illuminated by his light-up tennis shoes.

Lily's heart twisted at the sight of him. He was so small. Before she'd had Everett, she'd never thought about how small five-years-olds were, their little bodies far too tiny for those first backpacks they wore to school. They were babies still, and this little boy's shock of tousled black hair and his too-large jacket made her want to weep with the thought of what he'd already been through.

Jones had only been a grifter, and look how traumatized Everett still was. His little life had been blown up. But this poor boy . . . This boy must have seen terrible things. And felt terrible things.

Lily unlocked the pedestrian gate to let Connie and her son through, and Zoey pulled away once Lily waved. They all moved silently, even the boy, through the pale circles of light and wavering puddles toward the storage unit. He glanced at her once, then tucked his face back against his mother's side, pulled along by the hand she'd wrapped tight around his. Her other hand clutched a duffel bag that looked as if it might burst at the seams if she dropped it.

When Lily opened the locker, the metal rollers shattered the quiet of the night, and they all flinched at the sound. She turned on the electric lantern she'd brought to reveal a space that didn't hold much. A beige recliner. A small kitchen table and two chairs. A half-dozen cardboard boxes. One tiny wooden bookshelf. A full-size mattress.

She imagined mother and son both sleeping on that mattress on the blank floor of a carpeted bedroom somewhere. It would be a start for them. It was something.

"If you want to stay here and get things organized, I'll go watch the gate."

"Thank you," Connie said softly. "She'll be in a white van."

Lily slipped back into the office and grabbed a sack she'd filled that afternoon with some juice boxes and fruit snacks along with bananas and bottled water. She'd also gathered up a few Matchbox cars in a plastic baggie. Everett hadn't opened their squeaky old toy box in months.

Clutching her small offering, she waited at the gate for ten minutes, feeling strangely powerful after all the powerlessness of the past days. She was doing something right tonight. Something decent.

She felt hidden and safe in the warm, damp wind, tucked against a dark corner of her building. The steady drip of the passing rain echoed off metal buildings, clogging her ears with soothing noise. For a moment, she was totally alone, and it was such a relief. No one looking at her. No one asking questions.

Still, when the van approached, she was ready for it and rushed over to hit the override button near the gate. She closed it again after the van passed, then directed the woman to the right building before following behind.

Connie was clearly eager to get moving. By the time Lily joined them, they'd already wrestled the recliner up into the van and were pushing it to the back. Lily winked at the little boy and handed him the baggie of toy cars, thrilled to see his eyes light up as he accepted them and held them tight to his chest.

Between the three of them, it took only a few minutes to get everything packed, and then Connie's friend was slamming the doors and getting back behind the wheel. There had been no introductions, and there were no goodbyes.

Connie lifted her son up and buckled him into the middle of the bench seat; then she followed. "Thank you so much," she said solemnly.

"Stay safe," Lily murmured before hurrying back toward the front gate to open it for them.

The van was starting through the opening when the night exploded with white light.

She thought it was lightning at first, but it didn't flash out; it didn't fade. These were headlights.

The van had jerked to a stop next to her, and Lily looked through the window to see Connie's face contorted in a terrified grimace, her son's head pressed to her side, her arms shielding him from whatever might come.

Lily had a terrible, booming thought of an enraged husband with a gun, cutting down everyone near his wife. Thank God Everett was inside. Thank God he was safe.

"Just go!" she said, thinking they'd all have a better chance if the van were moving, but then a car door closed somewhere, and footsteps approached. Lily could hear her own panting breath as she raised shaking hands to ward off an attack. "Go," she croaked again.

"What do we have here?" a man's voice drawled from the dark. She recognized the voice but didn't place it until he stepped into the headlights of the van. Detective Mendelson.

Lily slumped with relief. "Jesus Christ," she whispered, clutching her chest. His face, never friendly to begin with, now seemed carved from disapproving granite. "Detective? What's wrong now?"

"Oh, you know me, Ms. Brown," he drawled. "Always keeping an eye out for strange goings-on. What are you up to this fine evening?"

"Just helping out a customer," she said.

He looked into the van, shining his flashlight into each woman's face for long seconds, then dipping it down toward the mop of hair visible in Connie's arms. Lily heard the little boy whimper.

"You said the gates were shut after six on Sundays, didn't you? Thought you were closed for the night."

Lily felt her jaw spasm with sudden fury. How dare he? How dare he scare this woman and child and question Lily's right to manage this place how she saw fit? "Jones isn't here," she bit out. "I'm not hiding him, I'm not smuggling him out, so please leave us in peace."

"There's a woman missing," he said.

"I still don't know anything about her!"

"I meant another woman."

That froze Lily's anger, cracking through it like ice. "What? What do you mean?"

"An eighteen-year-old has been reported missing, last seen two days ago."

"Near *here*?" she squeaked.

"Near enough. Would you mind if I look in the back?"

She was almost sure they could say no, but she glanced at the driver and was greeted with the barest nod. Lily waved him around. She heard him open the doors. A few heartbeats passed, thundering in her ears. Then the doors closed with a heavy thunk that shook the van.

"Can my customer leave now?" she asked. "It's late, and she's in the middle of a move."

"It is late for a move," he said dryly, "as you say." But he tipped his head at the driver, and she immediately hit the gas, taking them away into the night. And leaving Lily with a cop who seemed to think it was equally likely that she could be hiding a fugitive or kidnapping local women. Maybe both.

"What happened to this girl?" she asked as Mendelson stepped back outside the fence line. He was watching the taillights of the van—or memorizing the license plate—and didn't notice Lily step back. She hit the button to close the gate and lock him out, taking petty joy in his annoyance when he swung around in surprise to peer at her past the chain link.

He blew out an annoyed breath and shook his head. "I'm not at liberty to discuss the details. You'll see it in the paper tomorrow."

"Don't you want me on the lookout for her? Are you going to describe her? Or are you really just here looking for Jones again?" When he didn't answer, she rolled her eyes. "He's not here. He's never been here. I haven't seen him in six years!"

"She's eighteen," he said as if she hadn't just yelled at him. "Skinny. Long blond hair. You seen anyone like that driving off through your gates, Mrs. Arthur?"

Mrs. Arthur again. God, she wanted to slap him. That probably wouldn't help the situation, but it would almost be worth it. "No. No, I haven't seen a teenager around here. What happened?"

He spread his hands. "She's missing. Drug problems and whatnot. Probably ran off, but you never know."

She shook her head in weary exasperation. He wasn't here looking for that missing girl. "Did anyone really see my ex-husband in town? Honestly?"

"All I said was someone called in a prowler. You're the one confirming it was Jones."

"I'm not confirming anything. I don't *know* anything. Have you . . . ?" God, she didn't want to ask him for even one thing, but she needed to know. "Have you heard more about Jones? Do you really think he was here?"

His eyes narrowed. He stared at her for a long moment. "Seems unwise to fill you in, doesn't it?"

Lily wanted to scream. She needed to know if Jones was back in Kansas.

But she couldn't trust this man. He thought she was running a human smuggling ring or something, so he could be making the whole thing up just to put pressure on her, have an excuse to hassle her and spy on her at night.

"I'm going inside," she said tiredly.

"Good night, Mrs. Arthur. I'll see you again soon."

She moved back to her dark corner, then turned to watch Mendelson leave. He walked across the road to the parking area in front of the plumbing shop. His spotlight blazed for another two minutes before he finally switched it off, revealing the dark silhouette of his sedan.

When he pulled away, she let her head fall back against the rough brick, closing her eyes and trying to pull the peaceful night back around her. It didn't work. A girl had gone missing, perhaps really missing this time, and now Lily felt eyes on her in the dark.

Shivering, she pushed off the wall and headed back into the high walls and shuddering metal of the buildings to close everything up. She refused to give in to the paranoia that crawled over her skin and look behind her for shadows in the night. The fence rattled somewhere. Something scurried up ahead. But she was so tired of being a coward, so Lily walked on.

She pulled the door down with a clatter that echoed like thunder through the empty complex. Feeling vulnerable with her back to all the lurking shadows, she quickly snapped on the lock. Despite her nerves, she felt grateful. Grateful that Connie had gotten free, and grateful that her last promise to Zoey was fulfilled.

Zoey was amazing, but she made Lily feel too small in comparison. She'd tell her tomorrow that she couldn't help anymore. The idea made her sad, because Lily knew that without this thing connecting them, it would be too easy for her to withdraw and hide out here, keep invisible at the edge of town.

She bent to grab her darkened lantern, and that was when she heard it. The worst sound she could imagine: the terrifying, wavering scream of her son.

"Mom!" he shrieked, his scraping, straining voice barely reaching her past the metal and cement of the buildings.

She dropped the lantern and leaned into a sprint. "Everett!" she cried out.

"Mom!" he yelled again. "Mom!"

"I'm coming!" she cried, the syllables bursting from her like blows as her feet hit the ground. "Everett! I'm coming!"

If he screamed again, she couldn't hear it over her pounding feet and galloping heart, but she made it past the corner faster than she could've imagined and bent a wide arc toward his voice. She thought of the missing girl. Of Jones. Of Connie's cruel husband. Even of Detective Mendelson.

A sob wrenched from her when she saw him standing on the wet cement of their front walk, barefoot and shivering.

He cried out one more time when he saw her, and then she was barreling into him, snatching him up into her arms to squeeze him to her.

"Everett, what's wrong? What happened?" He clung hard as she twisted in a circle, looking for threats, covering his head with one hand as if to ward off blows.

"I thought he took you!" he rasped.

"What? Who?"

"I thought you were in the office, and I couldn't find you. I thought he took you, and I'd never see you again."

"Oh, honey," she gasped. "Oh, baby, I'm fine. I was just checking on something. Everything's okay. I'm right here."

He quieted then, only his gasping, tortured breath breaking the silence of the night. She pressed her chin to the top of his head as she hugged him closer, breathing in the scent of the new shampoo he'd recently started buying, infused with manly smells like sandalwood and cedar instead of the softer scent of strawberry.

"It was only that police officer again," she whispered. "That's all."

He grew heavy in her arms as her terror wore off, but she shifted her weight, trying to balance her strength so she wouldn't have to let him go, until he took one more shuddering breath and straightened his body to slide free of her.

"Why was he here?" he whispered. "Is he here for Dad?"

Fucking Mendelson. "Don't worry about it. Let's go in before you catch cold."

She ushered him inside to the couch and tucked the throw tight around his pale skin. "You want some milk?" When he nodded, she went to pour milk into a mug, then warmed it in the microwave before adding a little sugar and vanilla. His hands were still shaking when she delivered the treat, but his cheeks grew pinker when he caught the scent. "Thanks, Mom."

All of this bullshit with Mendelson and Jones seemed to have tapped into the same overwhelming fears he'd felt as a little boy. She scooted in next to him on the couch and snuggled close. "Your dad isn't coming to take me away, Everett. No one is."

"Not Dad," he said, nose half-buried in the mug.

"What?" She stared down at him in surprise. "Then who?"

He shot her a wary, sideways glance, and Lily realized what was wrong. "Honey, that was just a nightmare you had. No one was outside your window, so you don't have to worry—"

"It's Alex," he blurted out, sounding defiant.

Lily froze. "Alex?"

"It's him I'm worried about."

"Everett," she said carefully. "Alex is just someone I had dinner with. That's all. I didn't even mean to tell you about that, because he has nothing to do with our lives."

"Something is weird about him."

She tried to keep her brows from tugging down into a deep frown at that. "Baby, you don't even know him. I'm sure it's strange for you, but—"

"There's a bunch of creepy stuff in that storage unit, Mom. Stuff about missing women. And I looked it up and those women have never been found. They're probably all dead."

Lily pulled sharply back, her frown finally overcoming her efforts to keep it contained. "What in the world are you talking about?

How would you know what's in his storage unit? That's his private property."

She watched him chew the inside of his cheek before he spoke. "I just . . . I looked in there once when he was working. That's all. There's a big board with pictures of missing women, and his uncle wasn't a cop or anything like that. So why would he collect pictures and files about missing girls?"

"What?" she yelped. "How do you know who his uncle is? Did you go into his space? *Everett!*"

"I didn't take anything!" he cried in a panicked response that confirmed her fears. "I only looked! And I checked out his uncle online, and that guy used to work for the school system. He worked at schools and he's obsessed with missing girls? What the hell, Mom?"

She let the cussing slide, tamped down her rising panic, and thought of the eighteen-year-old Mendelson had mentioned. "What missing girls?"

"They disappeared from here a long time ago, like in the '90s."

Lily felt one brief moment of relief, but that only cleared the way for her deeper, darker fears. Fear for Everett. Fear over who he was or could be. "How do you know any of this?" she asked quietly. "How did you know his name to look him up?"

"Uh," he grunted in response, and then his eyes darted back and forth, searching for a solution. "I don't know," he said, lying.

And what did it mean that her son was lying and sneaking around and trespassing? What did it mean about how she'd raised him or who he was?

He's not his father, she reminded herself in a desperate wish. *This isn't about his father.*

"Did you go into that storage unit? And how did you get his name? Tell me the truth. Now."

His big brown eyes filled with tears. "I don't take anything. I just look."

"Look at what?"

"Sometimes . . . sometimes people leave their locks open. That's all."

Lily thought her eyes might bulge right out of her head and bounce across the floor. Her whole body went hot with a toxic mix of anger and that not-so-deeply buried fear exploding to the surface.

"You don't have any *right*, Everett! I asked you to check locks to keep people's belongings safe, not so you can break in and—"

"*You said I could talk to you,*" he shouted. "How am I supposed to talk to you about important stuff if you just get mad?"

She took a deep breath, and then another, trying to control her horror. He was like his father. She'd tried so hard to make sure he wasn't. "You can talk to me. I'm not yelling, am I?"

He huffed out a sigh that sounded clogged with tears. "You're mad."

"Of course I'm mad, Everett. How could you have broken my trust that way? It's illegal. It's trespassing. It's a *violation*, and I'll be *fired* if anyone finds out."

"All you care about is your stupid job." He jerked away, sliding the half-filled mug onto the table with a reckless shove. "And it's not even a good job."

That burn of terrified anger rose higher, warming her face. "It's the job I have, and I'm thankful for it, and you should be too. Nothing is guaranteed in this life. *Nothing*. We have a place to sleep and food to eat, no thanks to your fa—"

She cut herself off, her breath coming too fast and hard, anger pushing her to say something awful about his dad. She wouldn't do that to him. She never had, and she couldn't start now when he was finally wrestling with all those questions. After a few deep breaths, the anger had faded enough for her to push past it. "Have you stolen anything?"

"I told you already I didn't!"

"And are you telling the truth?"

He glared at the wall, his little chest rising and falling with gulps of air.

"Everett? Are you lying to me?"

"Who cares if I am? You lie to me all the time, don't you?"

Lily jerked back as if she'd been struck, but this blow hurt all over; there was no specific injury she could clutch and protect. He knew. Oh God, he knew that she'd spoken to his dad. This week, last month, a year ago. How many times had Jones called in the past few years? Four? Five?

She felt none of the relief of having a terrible secret exposed; she felt only fear. "Everett . . ."

"I heard you tell that cop you never went outside at night, but you left the night before. You left for a long time, and I was worried, and you pretended it never happened. And then tonight? Why was that cop here again? What are you lying about?"

He was crying now, and Lily pulled him into her arms before he could resist. She wanted to cry too. Cry because she'd scared him, but also because he didn't know. He still didn't know the truth.

"Oh God, baby, I'm sorry. I didn't mean to frighten you."

"What's *wrong*? Something's wrong and you won't tell me! It's about Dad, isn't it?"

She could give him a little truth, anyway. She could stop lying about one thing. "I was helping Zoey," she whispered.

"Zoey?" He went still. "With what?"

"I . . ." She cleared her throat. "You're right. I did something wrong too. I let a woman stay here . . . more than once, actually. I let women stay here overnight when they needed to hide. I'm not supposed to, and that's why I was hiding it from you and from that detective."

"That's illegal?"

"Not . . . not really. Except that I used a customer's vehicle, and that was wrong, and I could get in a lot of trouble. It's a violation, just like going through their things. So I'm sorry I acted like you were risking my job when I was already doing that. That wasn't fair."

He sniffed, pulling away from her a bit, but he seemed calmer now. Spent from his outburst. His anger about her other lies wouldn't be so easy to assuage if he found out. *When* he found out. Like a child, she wanted to put off the consequences as long as she could, hoping they might just disappear into ash.

"You did something wrong to help someone," he said.

"Yes."

His gaze dropped to his lap, to the fingers he'd twisted together into a knot of worry.

Now that her initial alarm had faded, she could think about what he'd told her. "Everett, what did you mean about seeing pictures in Alex's storage unit? What kind of pictures?"

He shrugged.

"Scary pictures?"

"No. Photos from the paper. Printouts. Stuff like that."

Oh, thank God. "Sweetie, Alex lives in Tennessee. He recently lost his job at a newspaper. So first off, he's a reporter who probably researches a lot of things. Second, I told you he came here to help because his uncle can't take care of himself. Even if you think he was someone bad, his uncle is a harmless old man now, Ev."

"You're sure?"

"Yes. He had to move out of his home and into a place with nurses and helpers. So there's nothing at all to worry about. No one is coming to get me."

His body quieted a little, relaxing under her hand. "Okay."

"Does that make you feel better?"

"A little."

She sighed, suddenly unbearably exhausted. "I'm sorry I got upset, but you can't go through people's things. Not ever again. I know this is our home, but people trust us to take care of their belongings and respect their privacy."

"Yeah," he agreed before shifting away. "I know that."

"Is that what you've been so worried about? Is that what brought on your nightmare?"

"No. I'm fine."

She wanted to say, *You're obviously not fine,* but she squeezed his arm instead, then gave him a sideways hug and a kiss on his temple. "I'm sorry I scared you tonight. And I'm sorry I lied to you."

"I'm sorry too," he whispered.

She took his mug, then followed him to his bedroom to tuck him in. "It's late," she said, turning off the light. "Time for bed." But she left his door slightly ajar before heading into her own room to close the door. She leaned her back against it and let a tear slide down her face.

Jones had started out with small crimes around Everett's age. His transgressions had spread from there, like rot and mold creeping out to decay everything around it. After stints in and out of juvenile detention for breaking and entering, he'd stayed out of trouble long enough to get a degree in accounting, but only because he'd decided to graduate to the big leagues and steal from the inside instead. He'd probably cheated his way through school too.

Everything Jones had ever told her about his childhood was a lie. He hadn't been raised by a single dad in Idaho. He'd been taken from an abusive home in Kansas City and stuck into foster care at age nine.

His truth might have elicited pity if he'd pled his case, but he hadn't bothered. She'd learned his history from the detective banging on a table in the interview room. The same place she'd learned about the extent of his theft in their own town. From their friends. His coworkers. People whose children she knew.

And the whole time—the whole damn time—she'd thought he was a caring, sensitive guy. Just like Everett.

"No," she whispered, shaking her head, pressing it hard against the wood so she could feel the rolling contours of her own skull, the faint crunch of her hair against cheap paint. No, not like Everett.

He was her boy, she'd raised him. He hadn't been abused and neglected and taught that there was no love or safety in the world. He'd always been a good son, and she just had to keep loving him and protecting him.

After all, she hadn't exactly transitioned smoothly through adolescence herself. By fourteen she'd been babysitting for neighborhood moms and using her money to buy clove cigarettes or wine coolers from older teenagers on the weekends. And she'd turned out just fine, hadn't she?

She had to cover her mouth to smother a horrified laugh at that.

Everett was okay. He was good. She knew that was true because it had to be. And if Jones was somehow still nearby . . . The only danger to her was that he might tell Everett the truth, which meant she needed to gather up the guts to tell him herself.

Such a simple, impossible thing. *Tomorrow,* she thought. *Or the next day. Just not tonight.*

CHAPTER 21

Everett waited. He waited probably an hour until he heard his mom get ready for bed.

He listened to the sound of water as his mom washed her face in the bathroom. Her footsteps then went to the kitchen, and he heard the clink of dishes as she moved around. It seemed like forever until the lights clicked off in the rest of the apartment and her bedroom door closed.

He kept waiting after that, hoping the house would stay dark and quiet until he could be sure she was asleep. When he finally ran out of patience, he got up, tiptoed to his door, and closed it as softly as he could.

He got a flashlight from his bedside table, turned it on, then slid his hand beneath his mattress to feel around. He touched paper, then the point of something plastic, and finally he felt it: soft leather.

He tugged the notebook from its hiding place and climbed into bed.

The first pages were blank. It wasn't until near the middle of the thin journal that any writing appeared, and that was all nonsense words. When he was little, he'd thought it was a special code for him, a message left from his father that he needed to figure out.

He didn't remember much from that night. He'd been six or maybe five, and he'd watched his dad walk past his open door in the moonlight. When he hadn't come right back, Everett had climbed out of his treasured race car bed, tucked his Winnie the Pooh under his arm, and made his way downstairs. There'd been one small light on in the kitchen, but his dad wasn't there.

Then he'd seen a flash of brightness through a window. He must have crawled past the curtains, because he knew he'd stood there watching, the fabric wrapped around him like a butterfly's cocoon. His dad had been digging in the backyard, illuminated by the super-cool forehead light he used when he was fixing things in the house.

The only other thing Everett remembered was his dad pulling something from his jacket pocket and dropping it in the hole. Then he'd looked up. Everett must have moved in some way, because his dad looked right at the window, and Everett had quickly dropped down to crawl beneath the curtains and run back to his bed.

Why? He wasn't sure. It must have been the angry frown on his dad's face. He'd waited to get in trouble, but it hadn't happened. It had faded like a dream.

Now he realized his dad must have suspected it was Mom who'd been watching. And Mom who'd dug up the prize he'd buried.

But after his dad had disappeared, Everett had assumed it must be a secret treasure just for him, because he was the one who'd watched his dad bury it in the dark.

He knew from the way his mom talked about those days that he'd been inconsolable when they were forced to move. The bank had given them forty-eight hours to move out. But Everett didn't remember that part. All he remembered was sneaking into the yard while his mom was crying on the phone. He went to the side of the shed where he'd seen his father, and Everett had dug up the secret his dad had left for him.

But it hadn't been treasure. Or at least it hadn't been meant for Everett.

At the Quiet Edge

Now as he looked over the long strings of handwritten numbers and letters, he recognized them as access codes or passwords. Something his dad needed to help himself. Something to do with money.

How long could Everett pretend to his father that he was looking for this book that was already in his hands? Days certainly, and probably weeks.

But should he even want to keep his dad close? Everett had been thinking about him so much that he'd forgotten all about Alex Bennick, and now look what had happened. His mom was hanging out with the man's relative.

He shoved the notebook back under his mattress and fired up the tablet to open Discord.

There was no secret message waiting. After all, Dad didn't want to have a conversation; he just wanted the book. He hadn't even listened when Everett had started his story about the murders.

But Josephine had. She'd responded with all the exclamation points that Everett had deleted and included a whole line of OMGOMGOMGOMGOMG! He felt a little vindicated at the sight of it. It was creepy as hell that his mom had gone on a date with someone *else* named Alex Bennick. But Josephine had pointed out that if that Alex was forty or so, he would have been barely an adult in 1999, but if he hadn't lived here, it didn't matter.

She'd sent a message with another link too. This is so sad. People never even talk about these women anymore. The link took him to a Facebook post.

> Crazy story: my aunt went missing twenty years
> ago, and I didn't even know about it until LAST
> YEAR!!! Over Christmas break I heard my dad
> talking about his sister to another relative, and I
> thought he meant my aunt Lucy. He said no, he

had an older sister named Mary who disappeared in 2001. Like, how had he never told me this???

He said she always wanted to get out of their town and she was kind of a wild child. She dropped out of high school her senior year so she could work and save money to buy a van so she could like cruise around the country, camping out and shit. She wanted to get to California and live up in the mountains somewhere.

He wasn't even sure when she disappeared because she used to take off sometimes, and their dad (my grandpa is NOT NICE) didn't really notice she was gone at first. Dad was the one who started wondering, and he was only 17 at the time. So he only knows she disappeared sometime in the spring of 2001, and they finally told the police, but they didn't even have any information to give them. She hadn't bought her van yet, so it didn't make sense that she'd leave, but the police said she'd turn up, and even her family figured she'd tumble back into town in a few months, and then it just . . . didn't happen. Nothing.

When my dad turned eighteen, he went back to the police to file an official report. I'm not sure they even questioned anyone! Just filed it and moved on.

She's literally never been heard from again. Her name is Mary Elizabeth Sooner. I haven't been to

church in a long time, but I'm going to go light a
candle for her after I post this.

Anyway, stay safe out there, chicas.

Everett shivered. He couldn't believe how little people paid attention. If you got stuck with a parent who didn't love you, no one else
cared what happened either.

What would have become of him if he didn't have Mom? Would
his dad have taken off and left him at daycare or school, and never
returned?

Probably.

Strangely, that made him feel a little steadier. Dad was going to do
what he was going to do. Everett's focus had to be on his mom.

And Alex Bennick.

He opened a new message for Josephine. I'll tell my mom I have
robotics again tomorrow. Can you meet me after school? I've got an idea.
We need to go to that nursing home.

Without leaving a message for his dad, he closed the window and
tucked the tablet under his bed. Dad could wait. He'd sure made Everett
wait long enough.

CHAPTER 22

It was a hobby of hers, ruining families and betraying husbands. Inserting her nose into other families' business, probably because she'd been abandoned over and over and couldn't stand to see other women thrive with what she lacked. What a waste.

She was one of those women who'd been thrown away. Her own father had tossed her aside, her mother was a whore, and now she was riddled with weakness like so many others.

These women simply didn't matter, not even to those who made a show of pretending they cared. Some people were discarded by life so quickly they never left even a hint of a mark on it.

Back then, only four women had ever been officially reported as missing, but he knew there were five. The fifth girl so used up and discarded by age seventeen that no one had bothered looking for her. If no one notices a girl disappear, was she ever really there?

No. No, she wasn't. She was nothing but a phantom stain on the world.

Lily Brown had found a toehold of sorts in life. One little edge of solid ground to stop her descent. A job and a place to live, even if that place was on the boundary of society, the quiet, empty border of town.

But she didn't deserve that little toehold at the margins. She was a lying, conniving bitch, and she didn't respect fatherhood or family or loyalty. She'd proven that. She'd *lived* that belief.

She lied about everything. Lied like the deceitful, whoring piece of crap she was. She couldn't open her mouth without bullshit falling from it like blood from a wound. And she'd been doing it so long she thought she could fool everyone.

But he wasn't everyone. He knew her. He knew women like her. And she needed to learn a very important lesson about honesty.

He was just the man to teach her. Like he'd taught so many others.

They'd say, *She lived out here all alone, what did she expect?* They'd say, *With a husband like that, who's even surprised she disappeared?* Then they wouldn't say anything at all because someone else would fill her place and the world would move on and on, churning out more girls just like her. More girls to fall through the cracks into his arms, where he saved them from the misery that floated around them and fouled others.

And Lily Brown deserved that more than any other woman he'd ever met. Because she'd stolen his heart.

CHAPTER 23

Lily grimaced as she watched Alex's vehicle pull in on her monitor. She should confess to him. Tell him her son had been looking through his things. She should, but she wouldn't. She couldn't risk that, couldn't risk her job.

She felt even more guilty when he waved at the camera as he drove by, flashing his cute grin just in case she was watching.

"Ugh," she complained to herself. How the hell had a simple flirtation become so fraught?

Whatever it was, the guilt that was mixed up in her attraction to him was compelling her to go see him.

To make sure he didn't suspect anything? Or just to see him again? Everett's story *had* made her curious. What the hell was in that storage unit? Alex had been acting self-conscious about the locker the whole time.

She'd found herself turning over Everett's claims this morning, calculating Alex's age in the '90s. That had been reassuring, at least. He'd still been a kid, a teenager or a college student. But what if he was covering up something his uncle had done?

She'd tried googling a few things, but she'd found only two missing women from Herriman and a couple of teenagers who'd run away.

She imagined a lot of kids wanted to run away from small Midwestern towns. Hell, it was basically the same story in the paper this morning.

Mendelson had been trying to scare her, obviously. The eighteen-year-old girl who'd gone missing was only reported as an "at-risk" adult in the town's police blotter. It said she'd gotten out of drug treatment a week before. Her name was withheld for privacy. It wasn't exactly being pursued as a kidnapping.

Poor Everett. He'd been so freaked out about all of this. He read too many scary books, but she really didn't want to smother his love for reading. She was already so strict about everything else.

Sighing, she checked the cameras and saw Alex's SUV parked. He was probably already busy. Or maybe he was waiting for her to come by after promising not to stalk her. She stared at the monitor for a while before finally giving in and pushing out the office door.

She heard music as she approached, growing louder as she drew near. Slowing, she finally came to an awkward stop at the back of his SUV because she'd forgotten to come up with an excuse. Alex was inside the unit, already bent over a box. The open windows of his vehicle blasted music she didn't recognize. He probably had all-new music every month after covering the scene in Memphis.

Her foot scraped the cement, and Alex popped up with a pleased smile. "Hey! How's it going?"

"Well," she lied. "How about you? Getting everything organized?" She casually took one step into the doorway, looking around with what she hoped was a normal amount of curiosity. She didn't see any pictures. She didn't see much of anything. Some boxes that had all been shoved toward one wall, and a little furniture. It looked mostly bare. "I guess you cleaned up."

"I'd say I'm about halfway through. I got a lot packed up last time I popped in." That could explain the missing pictures.

"Find anything good yet?"

"Lots of papers. Lots of stuff that needs to be trashed. Want a water?" He pointed toward a little cooler at his feet.

"I'm fine, thanks." She took a step inside. "I like the music. A Memphis band?"

"Yeah. There are so many great indies there. Thousands of talented souls looking for a break. This is just a demo."

Lily touched a brass floor lamp that looked like an antique. "Tell me about your uncle," she suggested. "What's he like?"

Alex smiled easily, not at all like a man who was hiding something. "He's a great guy. One of the best." Even Lily's cynical heart didn't believe a man could lie that sincerely. He loved his uncle a lot.

"My dad, his brother, wasn't exactly a loving parent. My mom was great, but my dad had a bad temper that got worse on the weekends when he drank. We just . . . Well, let's say we didn't get along. I lived at home through high school, but Uncle Alex was the father figure I chose in my life. I spent my college summers living with him and working to save up for the next year's tuition. He's just . . . Yeah. A great guy."

"He sounds amazing."

"He is. What about your dad?"

"Oh boy. That's a long story."

"I get that," he said, letting her off the hook if she wanted that. She did. "Hey, I'm glad you dropped by. I was hoping you would."

"Yeah, I saw your cheesy little wave when you pulled through."

"Cheesy! That was charm!"

"Oh, my bad." She laughed, then opened her eyes to find him watching her mouth, and she turned utterly awkward again. She couldn't be attracted to this man, not after Everett's outburst the night before, but Jesus, her blood pressed beneath her skin, surging against the walls of her veins, wanting closer. How long had it been since she'd felt that?

But no. She couldn't afford these kinds of sparks. Not with him or anyone else. She needed to stay focused on the real world.

Christ, she hated the real world.

She hated Jones, and Mendelson, and her life. Her apartment, her bills, her schoolwork, and she even hated Zoey a little for goading Lily to do things she wasn't brave enough to do. And Everett . . .

She didn't hate Everett, but she hated this new worry she had, that her son was more troubled than she'd imagined. *More like his dad.*

Alex was still watching her, and there was a tension to him today, just beneath the surface, as if he were holding back some intensity she could feel but not see.

Frightened by the sharp response it brought to life deep in her belly, she forced herself to step toward the opening and away from him.

"I'd better get back," she said, though she managed a smile.

"Oh." He blinked like she'd surprised him. "Sure. Of course."

When her phone vibrated, she reached quickly into her pocket. A new email from Gretchen. She'd be there at 3:00.

"Bad news?" Alex asked.

"Just a work thing," she explained without spilling that there'd been an audit and now a supervisor was returning abruptly for an ominous kind of meeting that no one at corporate had ever requested before. "I need to respond to it. See you later?"

"Yeah, absolutely."

Lily hurried through the complex, managing a wave for a customer who drove by, though she couldn't quite return the woman's smile as she raced back to the office.

Everything in her paperwork was correct, legitimate, and clean. It was only guilt making her panic. She rushed into her office and immediately reviewed the tapes from the night before, though she didn't have the guts to erase them.

What if Mendelson had decided to add a little more pressure by calling her boss about Connie's late visit? What if Gretchen wanted to review that footage? Or *all* her footage?

Or what if . . . what if a client had seen Everett breaking into a locker and complained?

The recordings were stored for two full weeks, and with nine camera angles, she couldn't possibly work all the way through them. But she knew where to look, at least.

Pulse fluttering, she called up the records for the camera closest to Alex's unit, the one that currently showed his SUV parked there but didn't quite reach to his doorway. She raced backward at the fastest speed, keeping an eye on the clock for the hours when Everett was home and awake.

Her tension began to ebb as she reversed through hours and then days and found no sign of her son even approaching the Bennick unit. Sunday, Saturday, Friday, and the only person she saw was Alex. And herself. She resisted the urge to slow down and watch those interactions.

But on Thursday, something moved, and she slammed the button to stop the feed. Then she backed up, slowed down, and watched. Everett was good, but he didn't stay quite off camera. She caught the corner of his movements and saw him disappear from the feed right where Alex's unit sat. Josephine followed him. They both reappeared minutes later, hurrying away.

Stomach twisting with the sickness of heartache, Lily backed up again and traced the hours into the past. There he was again, her son, by himself this time, glancing over his shoulder to see that he wasn't being watched.

This time she knew what to expect. Everett disappeared, and even though it had happened days before and he was safely away from the property, Lily felt an urgent need to race outside and save him from his own actions. She eyed the timestamp until he reappeared, looking back over his shoulder. Five minutes. Five minutes of him disappearing right where Alex's locker slipped off the screen. And this time he held something in his hand.

She shoved away from the desk, her chair flying into the metal cabinets behind her with a rattling explosion that ratcheted up her pulse again. She unlocked the apartment and ran to Everett's room, a terrible anxiety burning up from her throat as if she might be able to breathe fire.

She dug through his dresser first, though that was pointless. She was the one who did his laundry, who folded it and put it away. She slammed the drawers closed, fabric now sticking wildly out of all of them, then pulled open his ancient nightstand, scarred by the stickers he'd applied at age six. There she found pens, notepads, dead batteries, and one pocketknife. A very nice pocketknife she hadn't bought for him.

Still, maybe Mikey had given it to him. Lily would never have allowed it, and they would have known that. She cradled the heavy weight in her hand for a moment, then put it back.

His closet was fairly spare and took her only a few minutes to search. She was starting to wind down, draining of adrenaline. And she felt foolish, sticking her hand into his winter boots to check for contraband. At least she hadn't found any drug paraphernalia.

Hands on hips, she stood there for a moment, staring at his bed. She got on her knees and peered under it, pulling out the two shallow bins she'd stashed under there, stuffed with every drawing and craft and award he brought home from school. She also found her old tablet. That would have angered her a week ago. Even a day ago. But now she didn't care at all.

There was one last place to check. Lily took a deep breath and slid both hands beneath her son's mattress. Her fingertips found a smooth edge of plastic.

Praying it was something innocent like porn, she tugged it free. Then she frowned. She stared at it for a long time, her heart sinking as she realized what it must mean.

In her shaking hands lay a Batman comic from the '70s, encased in a protective sleeve. This wasn't something a friend would give him. Kids exchanged comic books that were beat up and creased and reread a hundred times. This comic looked pristine and valuable. Exactly the kind of item people kept in storage.

She slipped her hands under the mattress again, and this time when she touched something, she growled and wrenched the mattress up, tossing it onto the floor so she could see the second comic hidden on the bed slats. And next to it, a clear plastic case that contained four coins. Two silver, two gold. There was also a video game disk inside its packaging, and she knew she hadn't bought it for him.

The last item was a thin notebook of brown leather that gleamed with the quality of something expensive. A journal more than a notepad. The kind of expensive gift business people or writers bought.

Her knees giving way, she slumped down over the bare slats of his childhood bed and wept. Because her son was a thief. He'd lied right to her face, promising he never took anything, but he had. He was only twelve, and he'd already started stealing other people's belongings, just like his father.

Oh God. Oh no.

No, no, no.

She'd get Everett into counseling right now. That would help. It had to. Maybe he was just trying it out to see what it was like, see if he felt closer to dear old Dad.

Feeling like a weeping toddler, she rubbed her eyes hard, as if she could grind the sight of the evidence from her vision. Because maybe this was all her fault. She'd tried so hard to keep him from Jones that she'd forced Everett toward his father instead of away.

Her tears finally subsided. She breathed, sniffed, waited for the anxious buzz in her ears to stop.

She could fix this. He was still a good boy, and she could fix this.

Lily got up, gathered the stolen prizes her son had stashed away like a raven, then fixed his bed. She shut his closet and his door, carrying the five small items to the office. It wasn't so much, really. Her reaction was totally overblown. She could see that, but only from a distance, as if she were a cool ghost floating over her own heated body.

Lily deleted the minutes from the two times she'd caught him at Alex's locker, and then she sat down to review as many other cameras as she could. If Gretchen asked any questions about these missing times, she'd complain about the system glitching. She'd rather be fired for a suspicion than provide proof to them that her son was a delinquent.

One more hour and she'd find out.

CHAPTER 24

"What are you going to tell your mom when she asks about the big robotics competition in May?" Josephine teased as they left the fire station and strolled down Main Street.

He shrugged. "Next week I'll tell her I caught the other kids vaping so I quit."

Her laugh rang out so loudly it bounced off the awning of a shop and rained back down on them. "Couldn't you just say you were going to the library again?"

"She could have said no to that and told me to go another day. But she can't say no to a future in STEM."

"You are devious, Ev."

He looked down at the little blue circle of their location on her phone. After tracing the route, he handed it back to her. "We'll be there in five minutes."

"Okay, my dad is off at four, and he'll pick us up at the library. We should get there early and pick out books so we look legit."

"Got it."

"So do you really think this Alex guy is lying?"

"I don't know. He told Mom his uncle is in the nursing home in town, but he could have made all that up to protect his family. Somebody else was in that house, and it belongs to his uncle."

"Yeah, but maybe he has a dog."

"Dogs don't open doors."

"Fair." She looped her arm through his and pulled him close. "Are you okay? I know you're worried about your mom, but you've been funny lately."

"I'm good."

"Hm. Well, let's make sure your mom's not dating some freak, and then we can relax and hang out."

He rolled his eyes and said, "They're not dating," but Josephine's worry for him made his heart feel so warm and soft that he had a momentary, blinding thought that maybe he wasn't gay. Maybe he liked boys *and* girls. Maybe he even wanted Josie to be his girlfriend?

But no. That wasn't quite right. He didn't feel nervous or shimmery around her like he did with boys he had a crush on. He didn't stare at her mouth, wondering about his first kiss and what it might be like. With Josephine's arm looped through his and her side pressed against his elbow, he just felt . . . *safe*. Like he had more family now.

He loved her, he thought. He loved Josephine like she was his sister or his best friend, and when he was with her, he didn't miss Mikey and his stupid video games at all. Maybe he could even tell her about his dad someday. It would be such a relief. But not now. Not until everything was safe.

A few minutes later, he was definitely feeling nervous and shimmery, but that had nothing to do with attraction and everything to do with walking toward the nursing home. He'd come up with a cover story to find out if Alex Bennick was here, but he was still prepared for a stern nurse to glare at him and accuse him of lying.

Josephine let go of his arm, and he walked on shaky legs past the sign that promised SENIOR LIVING in green cursive letters. When the front door swung open automatically, he was looking straight at a receptionist seated behind a short, curved wall about ten feet away. She sat still as if she'd been waiting for them, her red hair heavy and straight and just brushing her shoulders. He thought he saw the tiny edge of a tattoo peeking up beneath the collar of her shirt.

Everett met her eyes and kept moving, wishing he were still holding Josephine's arm.

"Hello there!" the woman chirped. "How can I help you?" At least she wasn't a mean nurse in a white uniform.

"Hi," Everett said, then stammered it out again. "H-hi. I'd like to drop off a card for one of your patients?"

"Oh, how nice! That's so sweet of you. Who are you looking for?" Here was the moment of truth.

"Alex Bennick?" he ventured, waiting for her to frown and shake her head and prove that his hunch was correct.

But she didn't frown. She smiled wide and gestured toward a row of windows. "You're in luck! Mr. Bennick is out in the courtyard right now! I just talked to him, in fact. And that's such a nice place to have a visit. You don't have to just drop it off; you can go right on in and see him." She slid a clipboard toward him. "Just sign the log."

Alex Bennick was here. He was really in this home, and that other guy wasn't lying to his mom. Relief made his guts shiver like he was getting sick.

He picked up the pen. Josephine poked him in the back. Hard. He couldn't look at her. He was too busy trying to control the tremble in his hand as he put down the fake name he'd already come up with. John Olson.

"Just through those double doors on the other side of the lounge!" the red-haired woman said as if she were biting back an *Aw!* at their adorableness. It was a welcome response, and he'd take it. He and Josephine probably were pretty adorable.

After a few steps in that direction, Josephine threw her arm over his shoulders to slow him down. "What are you doing?" she whispered fiercely.

"I'm going to see him."

"Everett, this isn't okay. You promised no more dangerous ideas."

"This isn't dangerous. I'm just going to talk to him in a public place. He's an old man."

She growled and let go of him. He heard her muttering behind him as he pushed through the double doors and then turned right out the glass door to the interior courtyard. Josephine didn't follow.

He had only planned on proving whether Alex Bennick was here. But now that he knew he was so close, Everett couldn't stop himself. He wanted answers. He wanted answers to *something* in his life.

He stepped out into birdsong and shade and let his eyes adjust for a moment before he recognized Alex Bennick's round cheeks and balding head. Mr. Bennick sat alone at a table toward the left side of the garden. A few women sat chatting together toward the back, but otherwise it was quiet. Maybe no one wanted to sit with him because he was creepy and awful.

His knees trembled, but he walked toward the old man. "Mr. Bennick?" His voice cracked against the words.

The man's caterpillar brows yanked down over pale eyes as he lifted his head. Everett's gut tightened further and then twisted in on itself until he was only seconds away from changing his mind and racing for the door.

But then the man smiled. His whole scary face opened up with warmth, though Everett couldn't tell if it was real or fake.

"Well, hello there," Alex Bennick croaked.

"Hello," Everett responded automatically.

"How is your school year going, young man? Do you like your teachers?"

"Um." He glanced around before remembering he was alone. "Sure. They're pretty good."

"Let me guess . . ." The brows fell again, giving him a thundery look as he studied Everett. "Sixth grade?"

"Ha. Yeah, that's right."

"Haven't lost my touch! I'm spot on ninety-nine percent of the time. So what can I do for you today, son?" When Everett just stared at him for a moment, Mr. Bennick said, "Sit down! Pull up a chair!"

Eyes wide, Everett thought about it for a long moment before deciding it was probably safe since there were still other people in the courtyard. He scraped a heavy chair over the stone tiles to sit at the small round table.

Mr. Bennick only smiled at him for a long while until Everett cleared his throat and steeled his spine. He could do this. He'd come this far, hadn't he?

"Mr. Bennick . . . I wanted to ask you about this girl." He unzipped his backpack and pulled out a picture of the last woman who'd gone missing. Marti Herrera had been only twenty-one, and her family had mounted a tireless campaign for information. He placed the grainy ink-jet picture on the table, and the man's face deflated from open friendliness to a darkness Everett couldn't read. "Marti," he said simply.

"Yes! That's right. Marti Herrera. Did you know her?"

"Just a little. I worked for the school district, you know."

"I know," Everett answered. Still, goose bumps rose on his arms at the confirmation. "I thought . . . Well, I wondered if you might know anything about her disappearance."

The man seemed lost in the picture that he now cradled in his hands, his eyes sad and watery. "She was a rude young lady," he said, and the knot that had almost begun to loosen in Everett's stomach snapped tight again. He felt himself edging back in his seat at the idea that this man would say something so harsh about a missing woman.

But then Mr. Bennick smiled and shook his head. "But she was smart as a whip and so, so funny. That was what teachers didn't like about her, you know." He chortled at some memory. "Lots of kids are rude, but Marti could get everyone laughing. No one wants rebellion in their classroom! Still, we worked out a deal to keep her in school, and she did finish. She graduated. Marti was a success story."

"Until she disappeared?" Everett prompted, and Mr. Bennick's smile melted again, sagging into that hangdog sadness.

"Yes. Just like the others."

Everett leaned forward. "The others? Mr. Bennick . . ." He held his breath for a moment before daring to ask. "Do you know what happened to them?"

The old man drew himself up with sudden speed, sitting straight and pointing a finger at Everett. "Stay out of that mess, young man. It is not safe. You understand that? Why are you asking questions about this? It's been too long."

"She's my cousin." Everett spit out the prepared lie without hesitation. Heck, in this small town it could even be true. He wasn't exactly sure who his dad's family might be related to.

Mr. Bennick glared for a moment before sinking down into sadness again with a sigh. "I'm sorry, son. I really am. But this is dangerous stuff. Not a subject for a book report or . . . or . . ." He started to wave his hand, then paused and cocked his head. "How did you come by my name? Do I know you?"

"No. But someone told me you were interested in these missing girls."

"Someone . . ." The man trailed off, his eyes focusing somewhere past Everett's head. "Well, I'm not really sure . . ."

When he continued staring past him, Everett twisted in his seat to look, hoping Josephine had come in, but there was no one there, just a tree reaching up for the cloudy sky. "Sir?" he asked, but the man shook his head and eased back into his chair, his face a little paler, the picture trembling in his hand.

Everett felt his throat thicken. He'd forgotten his fear of Mr. Bennick, and now he just felt bad for trying to trick him. But when he stood, the old man's hand shot out to grasp Everett's wrist. He nearly squealed in surprise at the strong grip.

"Don't ask any more questions, boy. Don't. My son . . ." His eyebrows covered his eyes so deeply now Everett wondered if he could see. The hair rose on Everett's arms. "Your son?"

"My son," Mr. Bennick repeated, his pink-rimmed eyes filling with tears. "The police wouldn't leave him alone. My poor son . . ."

His grip fell away, and he slumped back, gaze more unfocused than ever. Everett grabbed the printout, then backed up so quickly he almost stumbled over a potted plant.

When he banged through the door into the big open space of the lounge, Josephine wasn't there.

Everett gave the receptionist a sloppy wave when she called out a goodbye, and then he raced out the front doors, onto the grass, and away from danger.

Josephine grabbed him when he reached the WELCOME sign. "I can't believe you did that!" She tried to look mad, but it didn't last long. "What did he say?"

"He said he has a son! I think that guy is his son, not his nephew. I mean, he's named Alex, right? People name their own kids after themselves."

"But what does that mean?"

"I don't know. He said the police wouldn't leave his son alone."

Josephine gasped so loudly that Everett felt more scared than ever. "You think your mom is dating the *killer*?"

"I don't know, but I'm going to find out."

"What does *that* mean?"

He started walking, Josephine trailing behind him. "Don't worry about—" His words choked to nothing when he saw a man stepping up onto the curb, heading for the doors Everett had just left.

It was Alex Bennick. The younger Alex Bennick. And when he spotted Everett, he frowned.

Everett spun on his heel and headed the other direction, nearly plowing right into Josephine. "It's him," he whispered. "Walk!"

Her eyes went wide, and she started to turn, but he said, "Don't look!" They rushed down the sidewalk and across an alley before rounding a corner.

"That was him!" he panted as they slowed. "Alex!"

"Did he see you?"

"Yeah, but I only met him once. I don't think he recognized me."

"What if he did?" Josephine nearly shouted.

"It's fine."

"What do you mean, 'it's fine'? You think that guy is a murderer, *and* he knows who you are."

"But he doesn't know that we know about the women."

"Everett, you need to tell your mom."

He walked on, his mind churning. "I'm already in trouble, Josephine. She knows I looked through his stuff. And I told her about the missing girls. She thought it was stupid. The only new information I have is that I lied my way into an old-folks' home. I need proof."

Josephine grabbed his arm, yanking him to a stop. "This isn't okay. It was supposed to all be in the past, and now you're running into suspects on the street and breaking into houses, and I'm scared."

"I didn't break in!" he protested. "It was unlocked!"

"Who *cares*, Everett? You need to tell your mom. We're just *kids*."

He took a deep breath as they finally turned back onto Main Street and headed for the library. "Okay. I'll tell her. But I need proof first."

"No, you don't."

"Just give me one day, okay?"

She shot him a dark look, but Everett set his jaw and kept walking. He needed to send a message to his dad, and the library was the perfect place to do it.

CHAPTER 25

"What are you saying?" Lily whispered. She couldn't stop staring at a strand of blond hair that had fallen from Gretchen's bangs and now lay draped across her nose.

Lily's mind felt distracted and spinning and so confused. She'd convinced herself this was related to her son, and she couldn't manage to shift her brain out of panic mode.

Gretchen grinned at her.

"I thought this was about the audit," Lily murmured.

"Well, it is! In a way. The audit was the last step, after all. Just a quick double checking of our records. So tell me: What do you think?"

Lily blinked several times. She'd expected this meeting would cause the floor to fall from beneath her feet, but now it was rising fast, launching her through the air, everything moving in the wrong direction. "We live here," she said weakly, her hand barely rising to indicate the door to the apartment behind her. "My son and I."

"I understand that could be an issue," Gretchen agreed. "In fact, we actually discussed it. You'll need time to find a new place. And there's always the chance that your replacement might not be open to on-site housing. If that happened, you could stay if you liked."

Stay? Lily shook her head. Why would she want to stay?

"This is just an offer, of course. The regional manager position would mean local travel, and maybe that's not appealing to you since you have a son. But I've personally found it's easy to adjust the schedule so you're never away overnight."

Regional manager. She'd supervise eleven different locations in Kansas and Oklahoma. She could base her work from home, Gretchen had said. Which meant she'd have to *find* a home. Something with a yard, a deck, a tree to shade them on hot days.

Her head swam, dizzy with the whiplash between what she'd feared and what had been offered. "This is . . ." She shook her head again, but nothing cleared. "Wow. I really wasn't expecting this. I'm in shock, I think."

Gretchen looked like a proud mama, though Lily barely knew her. "I love surprising people," she gushed. "I could tell you had no idea, but you've been our top performer for a couple of years now. So meticulous! And now that this position has opened up . . . Well, we're really excited about this opportunity."

It finally began to sink in. There were no suspicions. There was no investigation. Instead she'd been offered a *raise*. A rather big raise, though she'd have to pay rent or a mortgage.

But she and Everett could move, just as she'd dreamed. Live in a real neighborhood with real neighbors. Move to whatever nearby place would make her son happy.

"This is amazing," she finally said, and the smile that had begun to slip a little from Gretchen's face blazed back to life. "I do need to think it over, though. Talk to my son. It would be a big change."

"Of course!" She slid a piece of paper closer to Lily. "Here are the details. You talk to your son and give me a call in a couple of days, if that works for you. And call with any questions at all, of course. We'll be working together a lot if you say yes!"

Lily nodded, biting back the urge to immediately shout that she'd take the promotion. It was a good offer, more than she'd make with an entry-level accounting position, and the job would still involve a lot of the accounting work she loved. But she'd also have to deal with human resources issues, managing personnel, and then there was the travel.

After she shook Gretchen's hand, Lily walked her outside into a day filled with sunbeams filtering through angry gray clouds. Once Gretchen was in her car and safely away, Lily balled up her hands, closed her eyes, and let out a scream. She bounced as high as she could, then jumped again. "Yes, yes, yes!"

She'd done it. She'd put her head down, worked her ass off, and she'd pulled her future out of the deep muck that could have sucked her under for the rest of her life. This was good. It was really good. And Everett wasn't in danger. Maybe if she got him away from here, away from the isolation and boredom and the temptation of unattended goods . . .

"What's going on?" a voice called, making Lily yelp. She opened her eyes to find Sharon already across the street and walking up to the gate, a big smile on her face.

"Hi, Sharon. I got some good news, that's all. Sorry about the screaming."

"Oh yeah? What kind of good news?"

"A raise," she fudged, since the decision wasn't made yet.

"That is good news! I know how hard you work. You deserve it."

"Thank you."

"I have a little wine in the fridge! Why don't you come over? We should celebrate. It's been way too long."

"Oh, I . . . I can't today. I'm sorry. Everett will be home soon."

Sharon's face fell for a moment but quickly brightened again. "Nour saw Everett with that cute friend of his again."

"Josephine?"

"Yeah, they were tearing out across the meadow on their bikes. Doing some exploring. Nice to see kids their age playing outside instead of permanently hooked up to video games."

It was nice, but Lily couldn't help but think of Everett's lies, and that footage of them disappearing into Alex's unit. But biking was good. Biking was positive.

Everything was positive today. The dizziness returned, and she had to blink back a threat of exhausted tears.

Sharon moved a little closer. "Anything more from that detective?"

"No. Nothing. Why?"

"Well, I've been keeping my eyes peeled, and there have definitely been a lot of lurkers around."

Sharon could spot a threat anywhere, so Lily wanted to be clear. "Just the cops? Or other people?"

"I told Mendelson he could use our lot anytime, of course. But I've definitely noticed more cars in general. Haven't you? You keep an eye on that boy of yours."

Keep an eye on her boy. She hadn't been doing a very good job of that, clearly. "I'm trying. He's more independent now, and I'm trying not to hover. Have you . . . ?" She couldn't ask, but she had to, didn't she? For all her nosiness, Sharon cared about Everett. She'd once whispered to Lily that Everett could come talk to them *any*time, about *any*thing, and he needed people like that in his life. Other gay people navigating a small town in the Midwest. Sharon and Nour could be there for Everett in ways that his own mother couldn't.

"He's twelve," she finally said weakly. "He's not a baby, but . . . adolescent boys can find trouble. You'll tell me if you see anything I should know about, won't you?"

Of course it was too late for that question if they were moving out. She should have asked it a year ago. But now she could tell herself she'd asked.

She hadn't anticipated the guilty side-eye Sharon threw in her direction.

"What?" she snapped. "What is it?" Had he stolen from Sharon and Nour too? He moved freely in and out of their work area when Nour was around. "Sharon, please tell me."

She sighed, but once she opened her mouth, her eyes were as bright and eager as always. "I said I wouldn't tell you, but . . ."

Oh God. Lily braced herself.

"I did see him and his friend up on the roof of the big building over there. I told him not to do it again or I'd tell you."

"The big building?" Lily spun to look at the two-story structure and the top loop of the metal ladder just visible from here. "That's all?" She laughed a little, then caught herself when she turned back to find Sharon frowning. "I'm sorry. Thank you so much for telling me." She scowled with mock seriousness, knowing she should be freaked out over that kind of danger, but she just wanted to hoot with relief.

"I guess kids will stretch their wings," Sharon said a little doubtfully.

"They will. They really will."

"Well, try not to worry. Detective Mendelson asked us to report anything at all unusual, so we turned one of our cameras out toward the street." She winked. "I'll let you know if I catch Everett up to no good."

"Great," Lily said weakly. "Thanks." She was just starting to turn away when Sharon dipped her head closer to speak in a loud whisper. "Nour found two energy drink cans behind the shop this morning. Like someone has been lurking there after hours."

Lily's heart stopped. She spun back to look at Sharon, then toward her shop. "Energy drinks?"

"I hope it's not Everett. That stuff is so bad for kids his age, but I know they love it."

Energy drinks. Jones used to down energy drinks constantly. So many that Lily had worried about his health.

"I put them in a bag for Mendelson," Sharon continued. "Nour said it wasn't illegal to drink caffeine. But he said a woman went missing around here, and I think we can't be too safe."

"Sharon," Lily interrupted. "I think it was Everett. I found an energy drink in his backpack a couple of weeks ago, and I told him it wasn't allowed, so he probably snuck some over there. He and Josephine, maybe. After their bike ride?"

Sharon frowned. "Oh. I hate to think he'd just leave them on the ground. That doesn't seem like him."

"They probably forgot!" Her words were far too loud. She needed to dial it back. "I'll . . . I'll talk to him, Sharon. I'm really sorry."

She sighed. "All right, I'll just toss them, then. Wouldn't want Everett's prints on file at age twelve." She laughed at that, as if that were impossible. "There was nothing on the camera, so you're probably right. He must have walked around back from your place."

Around back from your place. Lily turned in a slow circle, her gaze catching on the cameras, her fence, the partial brick wall that shielded part of the office and apartment from outside view. That far corner toward the field was out of camera view, wasn't it?

She looked around at the meadow that surrounded them, the open space beyond the business park. Jones could have parked anywhere and moved behind the buildings, watching them and waiting.

Waiting for what?

"Oh my God!" Sharon gasped, and Lily actually stumbled a little in shock. "I almost forgot to tell you! I have gossip! Kimmy Ross was in, and do you know what she told me this time? Just guess."

Lily shook her head.

"She's pregnant! Can you imagine starting over at fifty-one? Not me. I'm fifty-five, and you couldn't pay me to raise a baby at this age. But Dr. Ross is in pretty good shape. He's a jogger."

"He is."

Sharon threw up her hands in joyful exasperation. "I guess that's what happens when you marry a young new wife! But God bless him, his youngest daughter checked herself out of rehab and came home, and she must have been really upset about the new baby, because she took off. They reported it to the police. Kimmy is worried sick."

"*Rebecca Ross* is the runaway?"

"I'm not even sure you can call her a runaway at eighteen, can you? Poor girl. I hope she doesn't become one of those lost souls wandering into darker and darker places."

Lily felt almost guilty about her smaller worries now. "That's awful. That poor family. I'll keep them in my thoughts." She took a step back toward safety. "Listen, I'd better get to work."

"Come over for wine!" Sharon suggested again, and Lily ignored her, despite a sudden rush of gratitude. She *was* grateful. Grateful for Everett to have an extended family of sorts, two more adults looking out for him. Two people who might keep him safe from the big, bad world out there.

A world that apparently included his father. The energy drinks were probably a coincidence. But if they weren't . . . why had she jumped in to protect Jones?

Still . . . she sighed because she knew exactly why. If the police caught him here, right in her backyard, they'd be determined to bring Lily down too, sure she'd been aiding him. And everyone in this town would know the same thing. They'd feel it in their bones. She'd be a villain again, and this time Everett would be included, a little family gang of thieves, permanently tattooed with their crimes.

She couldn't believe he'd managed to do it again. Pull her into his grimy web just enough to get her stuck, wrapped with the phantom threads for the rest of her life. Lying to everyone again. Lying for *him*.

Damn him.

She wanted to call Jones now. She'd thought she had the upper hand before, thought he'd been far away and she'd been above it all. But now she was flailing, off balance, desperate to protect her son and this bright new future shining right at her fingertips.

Maybe they could move immediately. She had enough money saved for a security deposit. They could move fifty miles away. One hundred. They could leave this place behind. Leave Jones and Mendelson and even Alex and his uncle. Just walk away, get a new phone number, and start fresh.

Lily sat down at her computer and pulled up a map of all the Neighborhood Storage locations she'd be managing. Then she searched for towns that would provide easy access.

They could go to Oklahoma. A different state entirely, no charges against Jones Arthur there, and not one person who knew them.

She was doing a virtual tour of a house in Stillwater, Oklahoma, when a car pulled through the gate, a man she thought might have been Dr. Ross, though he didn't turn toward her as he inched past.

Why was she so nervous? Mendelson didn't even know about the drink cans.

When the police had first taken her in for questioning, she hadn't quite believed what they'd told her about her husband. After they'd insisted she must have been involved too, she *really* hadn't believed them. They had everything wrong. She hadn't done anything illegal, so Jones probably hadn't either.

When she'd finally gotten home and retrieved Everett from a kind neighbor, walking through her front door had been the breaking point. They'd destroyed Jones's home office, torn each drawer out of her kitchen, left every single room of her house in chaos. Even Everett's clothes had been removed from his dresser and tossed on the floor to be trampled by their shoes.

Monsters. That's what they'd been. Monsters who'd come to devour her life.

Jones couldn't have stolen all that money. They didn't *have* money, aside from a modest savings account and Jones's small retirement fund.

She'd set her jaw and started cleaning, beginning with Everett's room so he could go to bed that night without one thought of what had happened.

By 6:00 she'd been watching for Jones to pull into the driveway. By 7:00 she'd assumed he was spending the night in jail. By 8:00 she'd locked all the doors and shut herself and Everett in the bathroom so he could play in the tub and she could hide.

She'd been primed for his phone call when it finally came at 1:00 a.m. and had snatched up the receiver, gasping out his name.

"You know the place Everett likes to skip rocks?" he'd said. "Meet me there. Bring your keys. Please. I need help, baby."

And so she'd gone. As soon as Jones hung up, she'd left Everett deeply asleep, and she'd stolen out her back door to jog the three blocks to the duck pond at the local park. The cold had seeped into her as she stood there, vulnerable, waiting for a police spotlight to explode on her at any moment, to illuminate her like a flamethrower and consume her.

Instead she'd heard the whisper of her name from a line of fir trees and moved closer as if there were a rope pulling her toward a pit. "Jones?"

And then his arms had been around her, his face buried in her neck. "I don't know what's happening," he'd sobbed over and over.

She'd held him tight until he'd calmed enough to speak. "I'm being set up. I think I found incriminating evidence in the books at the dealership. I told the manager about it. That's the only thing I can think of. It must be him. It must be Rolly."

"Oh my God," she'd breathed over and over. "Oh my God."

"I've hired an attorney," he promised. "He knows what's up, and he's willing to help. But I am not going to turn myself in to those bastards. Rolly's cousin is the chief of police. If they get their hands on me, I'll never be seen again."

"They can't do that!" she'd responded.

"I'll get railroaded into prison, Lily. I just need to lay low for a couple of days until the real evidence works its way through the system. I've contacted the newspaper already. It'll go public. I won't let them get away with this."

"Where are you going to hide? I'm sure they're watching the house!"

"I have a spot. But . . . I need your car. They're on the lookout for mine."

Lily had thrust over her keys immediately. "Take it. We're fine. I can walk to the store for a couple of days, and we'll figure it out from there."

He immediately gave them back. "When you get home, move the car one block over. Under that willow. You got that?"

"Yes. Absolutely. Are you okay?"

He shook his head. She didn't realize until much later that he hadn't asked about her. Or about Everett.

That was the last time she'd seen him. The last time she'd seen her car. There'd been no attorney. No conspiracy. No article in the paper. Just more lies.

And she'd added to them. Her lies to the police after that night had given Jones a five-day head start before they'd realized her car was gone. Even then, even when doubts about Jones had begun to creep along her limbs at night, she'd still told the police she believed the car had been impounded along with everything else they'd taken. She'd lied about a lot of things that first week, scared that Jones was being framed.

It was no wonder they thought she'd helped him. She had.

Was it her guilt and hatred that made her keep Everett from his father? She told herself she was protecting him, but maybe she was making his pain worse.

When her text alert dinged, it finally occurred to Lily that she should be in a good mood. She should be texting Zoey to tell her the news or baking cupcakes to surprise Everett. Instead she was chewing her thumbnail and freaking out.

But when she flipped her phone over and saw the text, Lily's heart froze.

Ms. Brown, I'm worried about Everett.

CHAPTER 26

"Come on, come on," Everett muttered to the computer monitor. He'd sent the message five minutes ago, and so far there'd been no response. Josephine's dad would be at the library in fifteen minutes.

He watched Josephine emerge from the bathroom, and he hunched in defensiveness. But she didn't join him. Instead, she glanced at him with a deep frown and turned away, making her way to the YA section of the library.

She was upset. He knew she was upset, but he'd explain everything once it was done. She'd understand. Maybe she'd even enjoy the story.

When a bubble popped up, Everett nearly shouted with triumph.

Hey, LM. Find anything?

Everett set his jaw and curved over the keyboard. Maybe. You need the notebook for money, right?

He held his breath, waiting for a return message, but his dad took so long to respond that Everett had no choice but to draw another deep breath, and then another.

The message finally arrived. I guess you're old enough for honesty. Yeah. I'm struggling & that's my last back-up plan. I need those codes.

Everett's fingers hovered over the keyboard for a long time. He didn't want to ask. He didn't want to know. But if his dad was going to disappear again, why shouldn't he? He typed it out and hit SEND.

Is that the only reason you came back?

He couldn't cry here. He couldn't, but his face burned as he waited for the response. Finally, it came.

Don't think I don't love you, LM. I always have. And I wanted to get in touch. I tried. Did you get my cards?

Everett blinked. Cards? I got your birthday card when I turned 7.

Yeah. Yeah, ok. I fucked up. I dropped off the face of the earth for a long time and then . . . Well, that was my fault. But now we can talk whenever you want.

You promise?

I promise. I can't stay nearby. It's too dangerous. But I can be online when it's safe. I can find you again here, right? Whenever we want?

Everett nodded, breathing carefully through his nose so he wouldn't cry. As much as he wanted his dad close, he needed him gone now. But they could always find each other again. Couldn't they?

I have the notebook, he wrote. He hit the button to send it, and then he closed his eyes. His dad would have what he wanted, and he'd leave. Then it would be safe for Everett to call the police. He'd tell them about Alex Bennick, about the storage unit, about the missing girls. They'd come and investigate, and his mom would be safe. His dad would be nowhere to be found, and more important, he'd be nowhere to be *caught*.

A tiny pop alerted him to a new window. Everett forced his eyes open.

LM? Can you meet me somewhere tonight?

He shook his head, ignoring the little bolt of lightning that shot through his body. He wouldn't be home until almost five, and his mom wasn't going to let him go anywhere after dinner. I don't think so. But I can tomorrow. Neck prickling with alarm, he made his offer. The bus drops me off at school at 8:10.

Everett glanced over his shoulder, then back to the screen.

Do you remember where we used to feed the ducks? his dad asked.

A tear finally leaked from Everett's eye. Because he did remember, and his dad did too.

CHAPTER 27

Lily grabbed a piece of packing paper that had blown up next to the fence and walked it over to the trash can, her eyes still scanning the road.

Any minute now. Any minute. Josephine had texted when they left the library.

Finally she heard wheels on the road and retreated to her hidden corner. Josephine's dad was driving them home, and Lily hadn't met him yet. She was far too upset to summon up pleasantries and friendly talk right now. She'd look like a madwoman. Better to stay in the shadows. She heard a door open; then she heard her son calling goodbye. The small gate opened, and the car pulled away. Lily stepped onto the walk.

"We need to talk," she said, and Everett skidded to a stop, hands flying up in surprise.

"Mom! What? Why?"

"A lot of reasons, actually. Starting with the things I found under your bed."

She saw the color drain from his face. His eyes went wide and wild as he took a step back. "Mom!" He shouted it, but it was more like a yelp of fear than outrage.

"You promised me you didn't steal anything."

"Mom, I—"

"I know you've been struggling with some things lately, and I know I've let you down. I avoided talking about Jones with you because . . . because I didn't know what to say. I'm sorry, Ev. But what you did, that's not all right."

When she heard the sound of another car approaching, she winced, assuming it was Josephine's dad returning for some reason. "Let's just . . ."

But it wasn't him. Instead Alex's SUV turned in. Cursing his timing, she managed a small wave of greeting.

Everett made a strangled sound, and this time the pure alarm on his face didn't surprise her at all.

"Mom, I do need to talk to you," he said, the words rushed and tripping over each other. "Now. Can we go inside? Please?"

Alex parked outside the gate instead of pulling in.

"Mom!" Everett said as Alex opened his door and began to get out.

"Everett, stop it. I know why you're upset, and we need to talk about that too."

When he grabbed her hand and tried to pull her toward the door, she yanked her hand back. "Stop that."

Alex's mouth was a tight line of serious concern as he stepped toward the pedestrian gate. She hadn't locked it, but he stayed outside, his gaze shifting from Lily to Everett, one eyebrow cocked in question.

"Whatever he says, don't listen to him," Everett cried, and her chest ached at the sound of fear in his voice.

"Alex?" she asked. "What's going on?"

Everett bleated out a sound of protest or alarm. His entire body coiled tight with tension as if he were about to flee, and she was already reaching toward him to try to hold him still. But then he froze, his face setting into a firmer expression. She watched the struggle on his face, bravery trying to defeat his panic, and her heart broke for him. Finally he planted his feet and squared his shoulders to face Alex through the links of the fence.

After a long moment of silence, Alex sighed. "Well, Everett went to visit my uncle today."

She'd been ready for that. Josephine's message had been concise. He went to go see Mr. Bennick today & he thinks the Alex Bennick you know is dangerous. I'm not sure what's true but I'm worried about it and think you should know.

But Lily had thought she'd be the one explaining this to Alex. Had Everett upset the old man?

"I saw Everett walking out," Alex said, answering her as if she'd asked. "Apparently he was there to ask my uncle a few questions."

Lily squeezed her eyes shut in shame. "I'm so sorry."

"Mom, he's not who he says he is!" Everett protested. "He's Alex Bennick's son! He lives in his house, and there's someone else there too, I don't know who."

"What house? What are you talking about?" Dumbfounded, she gaped at Alex, waiting for an answer, but his head was bowed now, fists braced on his hips as he stared at his feet. "Alex, what is he talking about?"

"Well, I'm definitely not his son," he finally answered with a sad smile.

"I know he has a son!" Everett shouted. "He told me!"

"He does have a son. I'm his nephew."

"Why are you named after him, then, huh?"

"We're both named after my grandfather. That's all."

Lily's mind spun, buffeted by deception from every side. "Wait. Everett, how would you know anything about where Alex is living?"

Alex cleared his throat for a longer period than seemed necessary. Then he grimaced. "I think Everett might have broken in."

"What?" The word left her throat like the fall of an axe, cracking through the air hard enough to make Everett wince.

"No, I . . . I just looked inside," he whined.

Lily's world seemed to tilt. She'd thought she knew what this new trauma would be, and now it was a monster with a whole new shape. "Looked inside *what*? What is happening? Alex, you have a house? I thought you were living in a hotel!"

"I, um . . . No, I never said that."

She shook her head. "You let me think that, though. Didn't you?"

"I'm sorry," Alex said, holding up his hands. "It's really complicated. It's not my house, and . . . It's my uncle's home, and my cousin lives there. Brian. His *son*. He moved back home this winter after his wife left. He's . . . yeah. Brian has had some problems. But he's doing better now, and I'm just staying with him for a little while."

"I don't believe him," Everett snapped.

Lily rounded on him. "Did you break into this man's home? Tell me the truth."

Her son shook his head, the tips of his ears bright red against his pale skin.

"Alex? Did he?"

"On Friday, while I was gone, my cousin thought he heard someone downstairs. He found a broken picture frame on the floor. I think maybe . . ." He trailed off, waiting for Everett's reaction.

Everett sniffed hard and scrubbed a hand over his eyes. "I knew something was wrong. That's all. Something isn't right, Mom! I wanted to protect you. I didn't break in. It was unlocked."

Lily blinked back her own tears. She wanted to scream at him. Wanted to squeeze him and never let him go. She tried to calm her breathing. "Alex, I'm very sorry. You have every right to be furious. I didn't realize how far this had gone. I—"

"It's okay," he said quickly. "I understand curiosity. I may even have stepped over the line a time or two during an investigation. It's fine."

"It's *not* fine. Everett, this is outrageous. You're grounded for starters. You're not going anywhere except school. No friends over. No internet. But first you're going to apologize to Alex."

"You haven't even asked him about the girls!" Everett yelled. "Ask him about the women and the pictures!" His voice pitched up into panic. "Ask him who did it!"

She was still inhaling a sharp, shocked breath when another car pulled up. Lily recognized Detective Mendelson's vehicle immediately and wanted to scream in frustration. But then a thought occurred to her. A terrible, soul-breaking thought that seized her like snapping teeth.

She swung back around to look at Alex. "Did you . . . ? Oh my God, did you call the police about Everett?"

"Of course not," he scoffed, but then he followed the path of her eyes to the man parking behind him, and fear stretched over Alex's face. He finally opened the gate and stepped in.

Everett backed away, pulling her along.

"Lily, no. Absolutely not. I would never do that to you or Everett. Listen to me, please. Don't say anything to the cop about this. About any of it. I'll explain later, I swear."

"Why?" Goose bumps rose on her arms at the panic twisting his features as he stepped closer.

"I'm begging both of you not to say anything. I won't say anything about what Everett did either. Nobody needs to know that."

Her gaze darted from him to the detective rising from his car to glare at them past his mirrored sunglasses. "Why?" she whispered. "What's wrong?"

But it was too late. Detective Mendelson was already walking toward the gate. "Ms. Brown," he drawled. "Everything okay here?"

They must've all looked terrified. She could feel the horror on her own face. But an expression was proof of absolutely nothing. "Everything's fine," she said, trying her best to sound light. "Everett, go on inside. Get started on your homework."

Everett didn't move. She *felt* his stillness beside her. Felt the tight wire of tension stretched between them, pulling her nerves so taut they hurt. She swung casually toward him, hiding her face from Mendelson so she could screw her expression into a caricature of urgency.

Go! she mouthed to Everett. But he wasn't looking at her. His eyes rolled wildly from Alex to the police detective, back and forth. "Everett," she growled. "Homework now."

He finally looked up at her, and her heart wrenched at the violent uncertainty that seemed to tremble through him like an awful quake. "It's okay," she whispered. "I've got this." She slid her eyes toward the door and tipped her head, and he finally relented, his body easing toward the office.

She knew he was lurking at the door, though. She could still feel him, her son, flesh of her flesh. And she'd do whatever it took to keep him safe, even if he wasn't quite an innocent baby anymore.

"Detective Mendelson," she said, swinging back around to stare at him with as little emotion as possible. "Checking in again?"

He shrugged one shoulder and sucked in air through his teeth. "I'm following up on everything."

"I've still seen nothing around here. Just me, my son, and our friends and family."

His mirrored sunglasses shifted toward Alex. "That you? Friends and family?"

Alex crossed his arms and lifted his chin a little. "I'm a renter, actually. Is something wrong?" He glanced around like he might be worried about the security of the place. "Do I need to be concerned about my stuff?"

Mendelson stared at him silently for far too long. "You look familiar. Do I know you?"

"I don't see how. I just moved here a couple of weeks ago."

The detective stared longer, then longer still. Something felt wrong here. Some*one* felt wrong. Was she putting her son in danger by ignoring his instincts about Alex? After all, he was nothing more than a stranger who'd shown up at her door with a charming smile.

And hadn't she fallen for that exact con before? Zoey told her all the time how important it was for women to trust their instincts in dangerous situations, but Lily couldn't trust herself at all. Her track record was as bad as they got.

Her lips were parting to ask Mendelson exactly what he was hinting at when a dark blur began racing up the road toward them. She frowned in confusion, then registered the whir of bike tires and realized it was Mac. She'd never seen him approaching before, and she'd assumed it would be a leisurely ramble.

Wrong again. He was flying down the road.

"Hey there!" he called out as he came to a stop with a scream of rubber against asphalt. He typed in his code, and the gate squeaked open. "Detective, what brings you out? Arresting our little Lily here?"

"Mac," Mendelson drawled, holding out a hand to shake. "Still on the bike, I see."

"I've got a checkup next month, so light a candle for me, folks." He winked at Lily, flashed Alex a friendly grin, and then he was through the gate and heading off to visit his stranded boat.

Mendelson finally cracked a flat smile in Alex's direction. "A couple of weeks, huh? Well then, welcome to Herriman."

"Thanks," Alex said curtly.

"Ms. Brown, I'll come back later," Mendelson offered in farewell before he retreated to his car.

Alex gestured toward the office as if they'd been headed there, but Lily wasn't going to take him inside. She glanced in that direction and saw Everett's dark waves of hair at the edge of the glass, one eye shining out at them with vigilant caution.

"What the hell is going on?" she snapped, rounding on Alex.

He blinked owlishly at her.

"No more bullshit, Alex. I want the full truth from you. What are you doing here? Who are you?"

"Can I . . . ? Can I come in?"

"No," she said with no remorse. "Absolutely not. We'll stay right here by the camera and discuss this."

He glanced up at the gate camera and sighed before tipping his head toward the bench near the parking area. "Can we sit down, anyway?"

She walked over and sat without answering. Once he'd taken a seat on the opposite side, Everett came out. She held up a hand to make sure he stayed close to the door.

Alex stared into the distance for a few heartbeats before shaking his head. "I know when I told you I didn't have the space to look through my uncle's things you assumed I was staying in a hotel. And I let you keep thinking that. I'm sorry."

"That isn't really the biggest issue here," she said past clenched teeth.

"Of course. But it's the reason . . ." He hesitated and smiled, though it looked more like another grimace. "You definitely have a very smart son."

Everett glared at his attempt to be friendly, and Lily felt proud of him in that moment. She believed that he genuinely thought this man was dangerous. Maybe he was. But he still stood there like a guard dog, if only in puppy form.

"My uncle did know those girls who disappeared back then," Alex started. "He's a good guy. Exactly the kind of caring administrator you'd want working in a school district. He hated to see any kids drop out. He fought for them." Eyes on the ground now, he nodded to himself.

"What about you?" Everett demanded. "Maybe you did it!"

"I wasn't here when most of those girls disappeared. You can look that up if you want to. I was in school in Ohio, writing for my college paper." He waved a hand. "It's all on record."

Everett demanded the name of the paper. Alex gave it, but then said, "That's not the problem. I wasn't here, but . . . but my cousin was. Brian. And he was the last one seen with Mary Elizabeth Sooner."

"She disappeared in 2001," Everett blurted.

"Yes. Someone saw them talking outside a party; then she was reported missing a few weeks later. No one is even sure what day she vanished, but Brian got pulled in and questioned several times."

Alex scrubbed a hand through his hair, and Lily thought she caught a sheen of tears in his eyes. "He'd already had some major depressive episodes, and he spiraled after that. He felt responsible, you know? Like, if he'd done one thing differently, maybe she'd still be here. If he'd invited her to hang out, or grab dinner, or just walked her home. It really messed him up. He started drinking heavily. He tried to kill himself."

"Oh no."

"He was too young to be a kidnapper. Like, fifteen-year-olds don't start kidnapping adult women out of the blue, and that was how old he was when the first girl disappeared. He was eighteen the day he was seen with Mary. But it wasn't him. I know it wasn't. He didn't even have a car. But when he attempted suicide, the police kept bothering him. It went on for months until Uncle Alex finally sent him away to get in-patient treatment. He never came back. He hated this place."

"But are you *sure* it wasn't him?" Lily asked.

"I thought I was. But of course doubts have crept in over the years. That was why I wanted to keep my uncle's papers here. I didn't want Brian to know I was looking into this."

"Because now you think your cousin could have kidnapped those women?"

He bent his head as if the weight of the world were bowing his spine, but he finally pushed himself straight and sucked in a breath. "No. Because either he was involved—and I don't think he was—or I'd be triggering the worst memories of his life. Those are both really bad options. But no, he wasn't involved. I'm ninety-nine percent sure."

"Why?"

"First, like I said, I don't think he was capable as a teenager without a car. But mostly because of the boy he was. He wasn't angry. He wasn't dangerous, not to anyone but himself. He still isn't. He's a gentle, thoughtful man struggling with demons that can only harm him."

Everett finally spoke up. "You look like him."

"People mistake us for brothers, yes."

"So maybe it was you who was seen with Mary. Maybe he was never involved at all."

Alex smiled a little sadly. "That's a smart theory, but I really was in college in Ohio at the time." He held up a hand when Everett opened his mouth. "And I know just what a savvy investigator would say, so I'll tell you right now to go check the dates of all those articles. I wasn't here, Everett. I swear."

Lily cleared her throat. "Okay, but what about your uncle? You already said he knew those girls."

Alex's head was shaking before she'd even finished talking. "I know him, Lily. He's a wonderful man."

Everett snorted. "Everyone always says that until the truth comes out."

Lily tipped her head in question, because everyone did always say that. *He was quiet, he was involved with the community, he never gave any indication . . .*

"Uncle Alex asked for my help a few years ago. He wouldn't have done that if he were involved. Yes, he got a little obsessed with the cases, but that seems normal, doesn't it? His son was accused. He knew these women. Heck, in a town this size, most people knew these women."

"True," Lily said. "So why wasn't everyone else obsessed?"

"My uncle says the town considered them throwaways. People expected the worst for them, and hardly anyone blinked an eye when the worst happened. And no bodies have ever been found, so it's not even murder. Hell, most people barely remember the girls at this point, and those who do will say they're just runaways. Lord knows teenagers around here are still desperate to get away from Herriman."

Everett protested. "The Herrera family doesn't say that."

"No, you're right. The Herrera family never believed their daughter ran away, and they were absolutely the most vocal. They raised a fuss, they organized search parties, and they wouldn't let it drop. And the funny thing is that girls stopped disappearing after that."

"I'll be right back," Everett abruptly said, aiming a hard look at Alex that would have made Lily smile under any other circumstance. She could see a bit of the man he'd be in that narrow look, the muscles beneath his skin tightening enough to square off the round edges of his face.

Lily and Alex both stared at the door after he disappeared, until Alex finally spoke. "He's going to check my alibi, isn't he?"

"I think so."

"Good boy." Alex leaned back and tipped his head toward the blue sky. "I'm sorry I didn't tell you the whole truth."

She turned to look at him, studying his face, his closed eyes, listening for the rest of the truth, because that wasn't all. Alex was practically still holding his breath, waiting for the other shoe to drop.

"Are you going to?" she finally asked.

"Yeah." He turned his head and opened his eyes, and she felt struck by the way his face had already become familiar. "I didn't just come here to organize my uncle's things."

"He seems to have a son who could do that."

"He does. I came here because I'm working on the story."

That surprised her, though she had no idea why. She'd thought maybe he'd come to find proof for his dying uncle or fulfill a promise to help with the research. "For your newspaper?"

"No. I did leave the paper. That wasn't a lie. I'm thinking about a book or maybe even a podcast." He flashed a nervous smile, but she ignored it. "Trying to keep up with the times, you know. Print journalism isn't exactly thriving."

Everett banged outside again, the door flying wide to reveal him still glaring. "Well, it checks out," he snapped. "He was publishing stories in Ohio during a couple of the disappearances. He even did a video interview at a basketball game."

Lily was surprised by the deep relief that sank through her at Everett's declaration. She felt thankful for her own sake, of course, but more than that, she felt a sense of near deliverance that she hadn't brought a dangerous man into her son's life. If Alex had been revealed as a monster, she could never begin to trust herself again. Not with her own safety, and certainly not with her child's.

"You'd make a great reporter," Alex said. "Good work."

Everett's eyes still hadn't softened from their narrowed glare, but at least he didn't accuse Alex of murder again. Sadly, Lily took that as a positive sign.

But it wasn't the end of this. Not by far.

CHAPTER 28

"I want to see what Everett saw," his mother said. "He said there were photos? Articles?"

Alex nodded. "Sure, come to the locker."

Everett glared at that and lifted his chin toward the camera when his mom looked at him.

She nodded. "No. Bring them here."

"Oh." Alex glanced up at the camera too. "Got it. Sure."

After he walked away, his mom turned to him and opened her arms. Everett took three quick steps and sank into the safety of her hug. "I'm sorry, Mom. I'm sorry."

"It's okay. You were trying to do the right thing. I know that. We're all just trying to do the right thing, and we all screw up."

He felt a few tears slip from her cheek into his hair. He tightened his hold on her and pressed his face harder into her shirt, sure that she still loved him, sure that she must. When he heard Alex's footsteps returning, Everett didn't scoot away; instead he stayed close to her side.

"Is there anything he shouldn't see?" his mom asked.

Alex shook his head. "It's nothing like that. I only hid it behind some boxes so there wouldn't be any questions."

Everett looked at the board with his mom. The women's eyes met his, most of them happy and bright, the lids rimmed with dark makeup, staring right into the camera lens.

"They're so young," his mom whispered, and he knew they were, though they seemed mostly grown up to Everett.

All of them had long hair, some natural blondes, some with darker roots peeking out. With less makeup and different hairstyles, they'd look like the senior girls that gathered near the steps of Everett's school.

"I've been trying to keep my head down," Alex said. "Stay under the radar while I research the stories."

"Why?" his mom asked. When he hesitated, she pressed harder. "Why did you look scared when the detective showed up?"

"It's nothing concrete," he said. He glanced toward Everett. She glanced toward him too.

The irritated meow of a cat drifted toward them from not too far away. "Everett, go feed your cat."

He shook his head.

She looked like she'd protest, but then she slumped a little, weariness dragging her face down.

Alex reached out to touch the border of one of the photographs. It was an inkjet copy of a family shot, a laughing blond girl holding a tiny brown dog.

"This is Marti Herrera," he said. "She's the last woman who disappeared. The kidnappings or killings stopped after that, so either the guy died or moved away or went to prison for something else."

"Right. People like that don't just stop and take up car restoration. But if he's gone . . . If he's dead or in prison, that means there's no danger in looking into it, right?"

"It's not danger I'm worried about, exactly. It's just . . . Nobody has ever done anything about these missing women. The police never connected the cases. All they did was blow off the disappearances, saying the girls ran away or moved on to a new life somewhere. At the very least, they displayed callousness, but it was likely absolute incompetence. They wouldn't want anyone exposing that, would they? Not even now."

"I'd imagine not. And I know how persistent they can be when something pisses them off."

Alex cleared his throat and glanced at Everett. "In the interest of full honesty, Lily, I should tell you I looked you up online. After our dinner."

"Oh." It was all she said, but Everett felt his face prickle with self-consciousness for her and for himself.

"I'm sorry you two went through that," Alex said.

"Everett," his mom said, her voice harder this time. "Please go feed your cat. Alex and I will stay right here, and I'll be inside in a few minutes."

Shadow yowled as if she'd heard her. Everett hesitated, shifting back and forth on his feet a bit. He didn't know what to think, didn't know what to feel. But he'd confirmed for himself that this Alex Bennick couldn't have been responsible.

"I'll be watching the camera," he finally said, shooting out the words as if he could lay down a line of defense for his mom.

"Understood," Alex said.

Still, Everett watched over his shoulder as he went inside. Instead of going to feed Shadow, he walked immediately to his mom's work computer and watched the tiny square that held miniature versions of his mom and Alex.

His head felt a little floaty now, like a balloon, and the only real thought he could hold on to was that he needed to talk to Josephine, tell her everything was fine and it wasn't Alex. Hopefully she wouldn't be too mad at him about today.

When his mom and Alex barely moved on the screen, Everett felt silly watching them, as if he were overreacting again. And that thought let the shame in. He should have apologized to Alex for going into his house, for lying to his uncle.

He would, he decided. He'd go back out and say he was sorry as soon as he'd fed his cat.

When he hurried to his room and opened the blinds, Shadow's bright gold eyes were staring right at him, and he had to feel guilty about that too, because her food was two hours late now. "Sorry," he muttered as he pushed the window up.

She hopped right in, and he let her, filling her dish and setting it on the floor. He squished down into the corner next to her so he could pet her perfect, sleek fur while she ate. The motion of it soothed him. Her purring made him feel tired. The balloon of his head was deflating now, and he suddenly wished he could curl up on his bed and sleep. Sleep through dinner and all the way until morning.

One corner of his sheet had popped off the mattress and risen up, and that was when he remembered the other horrible thing. The things he'd stolen. His mom finding them. And . . .

"No," Everett breathed, shifting up to his knees and lunging for the mattress. He shoved his hands under it, splaying his fingers and reaching. They touched only fabric and wooden slats. He waved his arms wide and still felt nothing. Shadow bolted for the window when Everett sobbed out a strangled "No!"

He bucked up in a panic, and the mattress tilted high, slipping off the bed. Everett found his hands had been right. There was nothing there. No comics, no coins, and no brown leather notebook.

CHAPTER 29

Lily felt frozen with embarrassment once Everett left. She could see that it was a silly response. After all, Alex was dealing with a cousin suspected of murdering young women, and her ex-husband had only been a thief. Still, there would always be this surreal film clinging to her, that her life had been so completely defined by a terrible thing *she* hadn't done. Would she be forced to apologize for Jones until she died?

"I am sorry," Alex repeated. "And I assume that's why you're not tripping over yourself to trust the Herriman police either."

Lily crossed her arms. "I definitely have a complicated history with the cops here. When they couldn't get access to my ex-husband, I was the only person they could put pressure on."

"That sounds awful."

"It wasn't pleasant."

"So you understand why I don't want to piss off the local cops. No fuss was made about these women disappearing because they were already living on the edges. Already discarded by polite society. They came from poor families, some were dropouts, some were drug users."

He tapped a picture. It was the girl with the dog. The corner of a picnic table edged into the scene, loaded with barbecue fixings. A hand reached toward the girl, the gesture a sign of her bond with family or friends, people who missed her and probably always would.

"Marti had been arrested for shoplifting the month before. Now it could be that their lifestyles simply put them in the way of a predator. Criminologists refer to them as high-risk victims, which has always sounded a little like victim blaming to me, but it's meant to convey that some people are more likely to be in the wrong place at the wrong time."

Lily couldn't help but glance over at the rows of buildings and wonder if she was a high-risk victim. She lived alone in a business park instead of sheltering herself within a safer community. What would they say about her if something happened out here?

"That said, there's also a history of predators purposefully targeting victims no one will miss. Their victimization isn't a byproduct of habit; it's strategy."

"And you think that's what happened here?"

He touched the paper again. "When Marti disappeared, her family raised hell. Her aunt lived down in Dallas and was an executive at a microchip company. She had money to spend on organizing, and she did. There were flyers and searches and news reports. Pressure was applied to the Herriman Police Department."

"And after that attention this supposed serial killer stopped killing?"

"Yes. I think he moved on after things got too hot. But that means they could have stopped this killer sooner." He gestured toward another photo.

This dark-eyed girl smiled for the camera, but only with her mouth. There were no crinkles of happiness around her eyes. No bunching of the muscles of her cheeks. This looked like a forced school portrait, and she'd barely played along, hopelessness glowing from her eyes.

"Tiffany Miller was so far off the radar that I can't really say if she disappeared or not. She was in foster care, no family here in Herriman. I have a tape of two officers discussing the case with some crony reporter of theirs. They're laughing about Tiffany, calling her trash. One of those officers is the chief now."

"Jesus. That's so sad." She thought of Detective Mendelson so diligently searching for the young woman Lily had helped disappear. It broke her heart that the old Herriman Police Department had just let these girls vanish without any alarm raised. "I assume the department never acknowledged they might be connected?"

"No. Never. Marti Herrera's aunt was the one insisting her disappearance must be related to some of the other girls, but the police kept repeating there wasn't a bit of evidence of any foul play, much less connection between them."

She shook her head and sighed, looking over the sad board and its sad contents. They all looked like girls she'd known herself. Girls who were trying too hard, just as she had, swinging too far into fads and trends, even if you could only afford an approximation of the look. The growing pains of trying to find your place in the universe during adolescence.

She sighed. "I'd better get inside with Everett before he . . . I don't know. Becomes a cat burglar spy in my absence? Thank you for explaining everything."

"It's all right."

"No. You have every right to be furious about what Everett did, so I can't thank you enough for understanding."

"He was worried about you. How could I be mad at that?"

"Well . . . he did violate your privacy and your uncle's privacy."

Alex shrugged. "It's a small town. There isn't much to begin with. And Uncle Alex said he was a nice boy. He really does love kids. He'd love it if Everett came to see him again."

"That's a kind offer," she said, her heart twisting at the idea of Everett having a grandfather figure in his life. He'd missed out on so many normal things. What if she'd already irrevocably warped him with this isolation?

"I might stay in Herriman for a while to work . . . ," he said.

Lily cleared her throat and decided to ignore the careful question in those words. "Are you already writing?"

"I'm still researching and contemplating who to contact for—"

"Hey there!"

Lily looked up to see Mac riding back toward the entrance. "Next checkup's in a month, and I should be cleared for driving. Your boy wants to go fishing, you know! Thought it'd be nice to take you out for a day on the water."

That *would* be nice. It would be really nice. But Lily had no idea if she'd be here in a month.

She let Mac through the gate, and then waited there, giving Alex a clear signal he should go. He took it, offering her a tired wave of farewell. "I'll check in in a couple of days, if that's all right."

"Thank you."

Lily didn't know what to feel as she headed back into the office, carefully locking the door behind her. Horrified? Grateful? Plain old exhausted? All of them fit the bill. What she didn't feel was fear, but it sprang fully formed into existence when she opened the apartment door and heard Everett's hoarse cry.

"Nooo!"

"Everett!" Skin crawling with terror, she raced to his room to find him crouched on the floor with his hands over his eyes. "What's wrong?"

"The notebook, Mom! It's gone!"

"I told you I found everything you—"

"I didn't steal that! It's mine, and I need it. I *need* it!" He scrambled to his feet, arms spread wide as if he might start flailing them like someone calling for help. He wasn't crying, though. His eyes were dry and desperate, hot with panic. Lily wanted to cry out too. Wanted to wail and thrash and demand that it all stop.

Instead she pitched her voice to a soothing tone. "Okay, Everett, calm down. I'll get the notebook and we'll talk about it. All right? Just breathe."

What the hell was this about? She spun to rush back to her office, pulling her keys from her pocket. She unlocked the bottom drawer, smashed all the files tightly toward the front, and fumbled behind them for the contraband she'd locked there. Once she had the notebook, she carried it back toward his room, but stopped halfway across the living room to open it.

She didn't want to invade his privacy, but his panic had terrified her, the irrationality of it crawling beneath her skin like writhing bugs. Something was wrong with her son. Something more than she knew, and the endless possibilities of how she could fail him loomed over her like a giant wall of dark water.

But when she opened the book, the pages were blank. She flipped through, half expecting contraband to fall out, but nothing did. Then she caught a glimpse of light scratches in the middle, and flipped back. She didn't believe it at first. She couldn't.

"Mom?" Everett stuck his head out, and when he saw her with the book he jumped forward to grab it, but Lily had already seen enough. She stepped back and held the notebook up, hand trembling with fear.

"Everett, what is this?"

"It's mine!"

"This is your father's writing. *Where did you get this?*" She was yelling, she realized dimly, as if the sound had come from someone else. She spun in a slow circle, looking toward the patio doors, toward Everett's room, toward the scuffed door to the office, as if Jones might step out from any one of them, a trickster ghost. "Is he here?"

"No! No, it's mine. From before."

"Before when?"

"Before he left. Before . . . everything. I . . ." He gazed up at the notebook as if he needed it so much he might grab it from her. Lily's heart ached at the misery that twisted his precious face. "I found it in the backyard!"

"The backyard?" It all fell on her then, every little clue dropping like embers that burned through the tender, exposed spots of her soul. The phone calls. The prowler digging a hole. The notebook. Everett's panic.

When he drew closer, she let him take the book from her limp fingers. He clutched it to his chest like a talisman, his despair wilting into relief.

"He called you," Lily said dully.

Her son may have been lying to her about a hundred things, but he wasn't good at it yet, or not quick, at least. His eyes flared with alarm even as he tried to stammer out a denial.

"Everett," she said wearily. "Just tell me what he said. I know he was looking for something he hid; I just didn't know what."

He shook his head, but then he whispered, "How did you know?"

"The person who lives in our old house called the police about a prowler. That's why that detective has been around. And . . ." She caught her breath and questioned herself for a moment, but she couldn't do this anymore, she couldn't wonder and fear every day for years. "Jones called here one night and asked if he could speak to you. I said no. I said you were too young."

She was surprised when he didn't look angry or even hurt. He just stared up at her, the rectangle of leather clutched tight to his heart. After a long moment, his chin dipped in a nod.

"He only wanted this," he said softly. "I thought he wanted to talk to me, but he just wanted this. That's why he called."

Oh God, the soft grief in his voice struck her harder than any blow ever could. As angry as she was with Jones, she couldn't let Everett think that. "That's not the only reason, Everett. I know it's not."

"Mom, it's okay."

"No. He's called before. He even . . ." She had to pause to choke back tears. "He started sending cards a few years ago."

"He did?"

"Yes, but after that first one, when you turned seven . . . You were devastated when you didn't get a Christmas card that year. And then no birthday card the next year. After a couple of years passed, I decided it wasn't fair to . . ." A little stitch of hurt creased the space between his eyebrows. "I'm sorry. I'm not sure I had the right to decide that, but I did. When he finally got in touch again, I didn't give you the cards. I destroyed them."

"Oh."

Oh. Just that small, awful sound of pain. She wanted to wail. Beg for forgiveness or rage against the unfairness or anything to get some of this fear out of her soul. But she didn't have the right. Not now. "I'm so sorry. I was afraid he'd . . . It's no excuse, I suppose, but I thought he'd try to manipulate you and cause more pain, and—"

"He did."

"Ev—"

"He wanted me to bring him this." He shook it.

Lily gasped. He wanted Everett to bring the notebook *to him*? Fury clapped through her like lightning. "When? When is that supposed to happen?"

"Tomorrow. When I get to school. And I wanted to see him. I wanted to see him, so . . ." His face fell into sadness. Her poor son.

"Tomorrow," Lily whispered, the word catching against her teeth. Tomorrow.

Now she knew exactly what she needed to do.

CHAPTER 30

When his mom grew quiet with her own thoughts, Everett's panic subsided, and he realized his mistake.

He didn't need the notebook anymore. He didn't need his dad to leave. Whatever Alex Bennick was, he wasn't the killer, so there was no urgency to call the police, and no need to chase his dad off.

It had been a crazed moment of frenzy, and it had been *wrong*. Or maybe . . . maybe he'd just wanted the book for himself because it was his dad's and it was his, and he needed it for that reason.

His fingers loosened on the leather, but he kept it close to his body, afraid to move too quickly and draw his mom's attention back to it.

His ploy failed, because she inclined her head toward his hands. "This has to be about money, some account somewhere, and that money isn't his, Everett. It never was. He stole it from hardworking people."

He nodded. Because he knew it was true, yes, but also because it didn't matter now. He could keep the book with him, a memory he could hold and feel.

"I'll take you to school tomorrow," his mom said darkly. "No bus. And I'll pick you up."

"Okay."

Squeezing her eyes shut, she pressed a hand hard to her forehead, turning her fingertips white. "Maybe I should just keep you home," she murmured.

He could hear the fear in her voice, and it had to be bad because she never let him stay home if he wasn't sick. Her face twisted in something that looked like physical pain. Everett dared to set his treasure down on the table and go to her.

She sucked in a breath when he put his arms around her; then she clasped him tightly. "I love you so much," she rasped. "You're the best thing in my world. And none of this is a disaster. It's not. You're just . . . You know it's wrong to take things, right?"

He nodded desperately, afraid she might change her mind about loving him, after all. Afraid she'd think it over and realize he hadn't ever been worth loving. "I know. I'm sorry."

"That has to stop right now," she said, squeezing him even harder. "You're twelve now, and this is something a twelve-year-old might do, a mistake, but what happens when you're sixteen? Eighteen? Thirty?"

"I'm sorry," he croaked. "I don't even know why I did it."

"Do you remember where you got those things? Because we should return them."

"Most of them."

"Okay. Okay." She took a deep breath that felt like it lifted his body up. "And you need to write a letter apologizing to Alex."

"I will."

When she pressed a long kiss to the top of his head, everything inside him went soft. In this moment, right now, he could feel that she still loved him, that she hadn't given up. "I love you, Mom."

"I love you like crazy, Ev."

After one last squeeze, she pulled away to look down at him. "I need to lock that back up."

"It's mine," he said quickly, regretting it immediately. He'd just been worried she might stop loving him. So why had he said that? He couldn't think straight.

"I know it's yours. And once things settle down, you and I will decide what to do with it. But right now your dad is hunting for this and the police are circling, and a locked cabinet is a safer place than under your bed."

He knew she was right, but he still wanted to grab it and hold it like he was some kind of baby who needed his toy. But he wasn't a baby, so he nodded. "Okay."

His mom took it without waiting a beat, and he heard the clinking of her keys as she locked it up in the office. It was there. He knew where it was. He could probably even sneak the keys if he needed to.

This was fine.

His mom closed the apartment door softly when she came back in. "It's only six," she muttered. He watched her glance around as if she'd lost something. "We need to have dinner still. I don't think I can cook. Pizza?"

"Yeah."

"All right." She smiled tiredly, her eyes puffy and pulling down at the edges like they couldn't hold themselves up anymore. "Hey, you know what? There's some good news too. I got a promotion today."

"You did?" Everett asked in shock.

"Yeah. You're looking at the new regional manager of Neighborhood Storage District Three."

"Whoa. That's cool."

"You know what the coolest part is? We can live anywhere. Well, anywhere in the district. So we have some big decisions to make, you and I. We can look online tonight if you want. See what kind of houses are out there for rent."

"Oh. Wow. We're moving out of here?" He glanced at the tiny living room. "Cool. Hey, can I bring Shadow?"

He didn't know why, but her eyes filled with tears at that. "Yes, sweetie, you can bring Shadow. We'll find a house that allows pets, okay?"

"Thanks, Mom."

"A boy should have a pet," she murmured. "I'll order the pizza, and then I have to do a little work. Go ahead and do your homework. Tomorrow, we'll . . ." She waved a choppy hand. "Figure out everything else, all right?"

Everett nodded. After hesitating to see if they were really done, he went to his room, closing his door softly behind him. He'd noticed her tablet still on the floor beneath his bed. She hadn't seen it or had forgotten it, and thank God for that.

Shadow was lying on the floor, cleaning her paws, and Everett hunkered back down next to her, relieved to be alone. Because he had to fix something. Or maybe it was something more like pulling off a Band-Aid. He didn't want to do it, but he had to.

For once when he logged in, his dad was actually waiting.

LM! You there? Are we set for tomorrow?

He'd sent it fifteen minutes earlier, and he was still logged on.

For a moment Everett imagined what he might say. Imagined he could meet his dad a little later, even if his mom dropped him off. He could skip out during PE or lunch hour. Meet his dad at the park and spend some time with him before admitting he didn't actually have the notebook. He could see him, at least. Remember what his face looked like.

Sorry, he typed instead. I was wrong. It was just some kind of calendar book for Mom's work. I don't know where your notebook is.

There was no response, not for a long time. Everett hung his head, so tired of trying to figure out what to say to who and how they might respond. Why couldn't he just have a dad who'd do the right thing no matter what? Wasn't that what dads were supposed to do?

Finally a bubble popped up. Oh. That's bad news. I really need that, can you keep looking?

Well, at least he wasn't angry. Yeah I guess. I pretty much looked everywhere but maybe you can check back once a week or something just in case.

Sure. Of course. You're positive it's not the right one?

100% And I can't look more this week bcuz I'm grounded & don't need more trouble. Maybe I'll look more later. Sorry Dad.

When he felt a tickle, Everett wiped his cheek and realized he was crying. Last night when he was falling asleep, Everett had imagined seeing his dad. He'd imagined they might go away together. Not tomorrow, but sometime. A summer trip to Mexico or something. They could stay at the beach. Have adventures. Be a family just for a little while. He didn't want to leave his mom, but he wanted Dad too, and for a couple of days, it had felt possible.

But that had been imagination, and this was reality. This was good-bye. For now.

A window popped up. And it didn't say goodbye. Instead it said, Grounded, huh? Is everything okay? You want to tell me about it?

Surprised, Everett stared for a full minute, wondering if it was a trick. But if it was, he could be ready for it, right? And if it wasn't . . .

He shot a worried glance at the door. Then he started typing. Well, I saw something weird in one of the lockers a week ago . . .

CHAPTER 31

Lily had been exhausted and gritty-eyed by 7:00 p.m., but somehow she'd managed to stay awake until midnight, waiting for a response from Mendelson.

She'd tried calling him before dinner, but he hadn't answered, so she'd texted a message. I believe you are right about Jones. If he's still in town, he will be near the school at 8AM tomorrow. That's all I know.

Mendelson's response, strangely, had been to ask about Alex. Was that your husband's contact?

No, he's really just a customer.

From Tennessee?

At first that had scared her, that he would know that. But then she'd realized of course he'd seen Alex's plates. Maybe even run them. So much for him staying under the radar.

He's in town taking care of his uncle & has nothing to do with this. I'm worried for my son. Are you going to watch for Jones or not?

He hadn't responded to that at all. She'd checked incessantly all through dinner, all through a quiet evening on the couch with Everett looking through rental listings, and now as she struggled to stay awake.

But did it matter? She'd told him what she knew. She'd set it in motion.

Tomorrow she'd decide whether she would take Everett to school or keep him home. Shit, maybe she should call in sick and get him the hell out of town for a day or two. She'd never even used a sick day before. They could drive to Wichita, go to the zoo, stay in a place with an indoor pool for Everett. Pretend everything was more than okay, pretend it was good. Paranoid that Everett would see what she'd done, she deleted her texts to Mendelson and waited.

Phone clutched to her chest, she fell asleep with half the lights on.

When the wind kicked up around 5:00 a.m., Lily jerked awake, sure she'd only been asleep a few minutes. It certainly felt that way. A glance at her phone showed no messages. Lily closed her bleary eyes and tried to get back to sleep despite the howling storm.

Jones and his goddamn selfishness. He'd probably sent this wind too, just to torment her and keep her awake. Within a few minutes she was staring into the dark, eyes wide open and not one bit of sleepiness left. She checked her phone frequently to break up the seconds.

She finally wanted to talk to this Mendelson asshole, and now he was ignoring her? Typical.

Turning over, she tried to find a comfortable spot on her ancient mattress. Maybe she could toss this one and have a new one delivered to a new home. A new home. That was something good to think about.

Still, the security deposit would put a big dent into her savings, so a new mattress might be out of the picture. At least she had very good access to a dolly and moving supplies. Laughing humorlessly into the dark as she turned over for the fifth time, she finally gave up and got out of bed.

Outside her window, the wind whipped the metal doors of the nearest units, rattling them. If she tried hard, she could imagine it was the distant rumble of waves or even the whoosh of shaking leaves, but there was always that faint ring of metal beneath the sound. She wouldn't miss that.

A sudden, louder clang of metal startled her. Jones? Could it be Jones? She went to the window to peer out at clouds scudding past a faint edge of dawn.

She didn't think he'd hurt her—she'd never seen that in him—but he was certainly capable of skulking around. The metal sound came again, softer this time. The garbage can must have rolled over into the fence. That was probably what had woken her up. Her neck ached and her back screamed with tension, but that was all left over from last night. At least she'd slept a little.

Lily trudged to the bathroom and hit the light switch, then hit it again. Nothing. The storm had knocked out the power. She stifled a weary groan.

It was the first time this year, but she had plenty of experience. Their area was too isolated to put it high on the list of the power company's priorities. One time she'd had to manually haul the gate open and closed for three days in a row. But Everett had loved camping in her bedroom with lanterns.

Using her phone as a flashlight, Lily found one of the battery-operated lanterns and turned it on. She washed an apple in the sink and put the coffee on, staring blankly at the machine for far too long before remembering it had no electricity.

"Oh God. No coffee." She should really crawl back into bed and try to sleep.

For a few long seconds, she thought the buzz that began to tickle her ears was another rattle kicked up by the storm, a vibration plucked from the endless yards of chain link surrounding her home. It was only when the vibration stopped abruptly that Lily realized it had been her phone.

It started buzzing again as she reached for it. Was Mendelson finally calling back? "Hello?" she croaked.

"You're not going to believe who I found sneaking around outside your fence, Lily."

She cleared her scratchy throat as her pulse banged in her ears. "Jones?"

"Yes. I have him outside in my car. I'd like you to come identify him, please."

That snapped her wide awake. Her eyes rolled toward Everett's closed door. "I'll be right there," she whispered.

She hung up and stuffed her phone into her sweatpants. Thunder rolled in, starting with a purr before it grew to a roar. Then a flash of faraway lightning crept past her blinds like slashing fingers.

She needed to sneak out, confirm it was Jones, and let Mendelson gloat for a moment, since that was clearly what he was looking for. She felt strangely calm at the idea of laying eyes on Jones again. She wasn't sure what she'd feel if he weren't in custody. Scared or just angry? But at this exact moment, she felt nothing, like her mind had switched off her emotions for safety.

Pulling on a hoodie that lay over the corner of the couch, she moved quietly to the door to slide her feet into tennis shoes. Then she slipped out, locking the apartment door up tight behind her. The office was dark without the lantern, but a bit of light filtered through the windows from the business park across the street.

Jones had finally screwed up. He'd finally gotten too desperate and taken too many risks. She no longer cared about the optics of having him caught here, because Everett would be safe, and they were free now. She and Everett could walk away from Herriman and never set foot in this town again if they wanted. Well, aside from her supervisory duties, of course. But Everett could start over far away.

She opened the office door and was nearly tugged out by a gust of wind that spat rain beneath the hood of her sweatshirt. She rushed down the walk, wondering what this would all look like on Sharon's security cameras.

Right, they wouldn't work without power.

And yet . . . She was two steps from the pedestrian gate when she realized there were still a few lights on above the doors in the business park. Weird. She squinted into the dark maw of her driveway, trying to make out Mendelson's car. She was surprised he didn't have the spotlight on to make sure anyone within a two-mile radius could witness her embarrassment.

"Hello?" she called softly. A gust of wind pushed at her. It pushed at the gates. And the pedestrian gate opened an inch before clinking back into place.

What in the world? Why wasn't it locked?

For a split second she felt only confusion as she began a slow turn, searching out the area around the office for Mendelson or Jones or someone. But as her gaze cut through the night, sliding over the driveway gate, over the cement, toward the curb and the sidewalk beyond that, her brain sent a warning. Not even a thought, just a quick rise of the hair on her arms, a sharpening of her vision.

A terrible premonition.

Something was very wrong, and she knew it deep in her animal soul even before Lily saw the rush of a blank, black space in the storm, the reaching out of a shadowed arm, and the dull glint of light on a leather glove.

She had one heartbeat to grab for her phone, but no time to pull it free. She sucked in a breath, but her scream was caught by rough leather and the hard, strong hand beneath it.

She fought. She kicked and bucked and twisted, but she was already fighting against the crushing crook of an arm, and it was too late. She could only manage to whimper and wish she'd done a thousand things differently in her life.

"Shhhh," he shushed into her ear. When she drew in a sharp breath through her nose, she was horrified to realize he smelled bright and fresh, like minty toothpaste and nice shampoo. That couldn't be right. It couldn't.

"All I need is a little information."

Mendelson.

Mendelson? That made no sense.

Why would he do this to get Jones? She'd already given him the information, and now he thought she'd stay quiet about being assaulted by a cop?

Oh God. That meant he was crazy. Or . . . was it possible Mendelson was one of Jones's victims and couldn't see past his own need for revenge?

She found herself whimpering against his gloved hand again.

"Where did you take my wife?" he growled.

That shocked Lily into shutting up. What the hell was he talking about?

"I'm going to move my hand, and you tell me where you took my wife and child."

Wife and child? No. That couldn't be. Only Connie had brought a child with her, and Mendelson had looked straight into Connie's face without a word. But . . . When it hit her, her veins flooded with ice water. A wife. With a child.

"Amber?" she whispered as he slowly eased the pressure on her mouth.

But saying her name had been a mistake. His fingertips dug hard into her chin and jaw. "Yes," he sneered, ruthlessly grabbing her face. Her teeth cut into her cheeks, and she tasted blood.

"Amber. My wife. My little angel girl. I know she came here. Her cellphone turned off just past the highway there. And I saw that bitch

Zoey Cain drive that whore out here the other night. I get your fucking scheme, you bitch. *Where did you take my wife?*"

"She . . ." Lily tried to choke down her terror and think. He loosened his brutal hold a little. "She only came here to stay the night. That's all. Then she left."

"She slept in your apartment?"

"No."

"Where, then? In a locker?"

She shook her head.

He laughed. "You'd better answer me, bitch, or we'll go wake your boy and see if he remembers my wife."

"No! No, he didn't even see her. There's a camper. An RV. She spent the night and then she left in the morning. I don't know where she went. Please. I'm so sorry."

"I want to see it." He wrenched her arm up behind her back, and Lily did her best not to cry out. Everett was still asleep. He would sleep through this, whatever happened to her.

She'd brought this on them, brought danger to her door. She'd brought Amber here first, and then she'd practically invited Mendelson in this morning. She would accept the consequences all for herself. At least if she was taking him to the RV she was taking him away from her son.

She moved as quickly as she could without putting more pressure on her arm, her mind spinning, her stomach rolling. *The most dangerous time for a woman was when she was trying to leave.* The most dangerous time for any woman, apparently, even one who was just trying to help.

She realized suddenly that her free hand was tight against her side and still clutching the phone in her pocket. But there was nothing she could do with his arm curled so hard around her. If she tried pushing buttons, Siri was liable to wake up and ask her loudly what she wanted.

Could she jerk away and run? Just for a few seconds? Just for the time it would take to dial 911? She knew this place, after all, far better than he did.

Lightning tore through the sky ahead, and she took it as a sign. When the thunder clapped a few seconds later, she yanked herself to the side, hoping to twist her arm free and run. She twisted, she took two steps, she got the phone free of her pocket, and then he tackled her.

"You bitch," he growled, rain or spittle landing on the side of her face. "You bitch." When he kneed her in the ribs, she let the phone drop, tossing her arm as she opened her fingers. But that was something. At least he couldn't take it from her. At least someone would find it, and they'd know she fought. Know she'd been grabbed and hadn't just run away from her high-risk life out here on the edge of society. He kneed her again, forcing the air from her in a jolt of pain.

Zoey would take care of Everett, wouldn't she? Zoey would take her boy and love him, because she loved everyone. Grief twisted through her, wanting to scream.

Mendelson climbed off, then yanked Lily to her feet by her hair. She scrambled up, trying to ease the searing fire across her scalp.

"You've got one more chance to show me, you whore. You're not going to like your next punishment, I promise."

Lily nodded and pointed her body in the right direction, hating the tight hold of his hands on both her arms as she walked him through the vehicles. Hating the sharp ache in her ribs and her shoulders. Afraid to imagine how much more pain was coming. She couldn't think about that. She had to stay blank and focused on keeping him far from her son.

"This is it," she finally gasped, slowing in front of the RV's door. "Right there."

He reached for the handle and pulled it open, then shoved her inside, banging her knees hard against the metal edge of the step. She scrambled in and cowered against the kitchenette.

Mendelson walked up the two steps, seeming to grow impossibly tall above Lily in the small space. A giant. A demon who'd lost his angel. "I'm sorry," she said. "I'm sorry. I didn't know."

"You did know. You knew exactly what you were doing."

He pulled the door shut behind him and withdrew a flashlight, then stepped toward the little bed that made up most of the room. When he reached out to reverently touch the bare mattress, Lily's face crumpled because this man wasn't in his right mind. Not at all. No wonder Amber had been so scared. His eyes looked too big, too wild, taking in everything and nothing. In the dimness of the RV, his irises looked black and bottomless.

"Where's my girl?" he asked quietly, calmly, then in the next breath he let loose a terrifying roar. *"Where's my girl?"*

"I don't have any idea!" Lily babbled, raising her hands to cover her face when he lunged toward her.

"Give me your phone. Where is it?"

He began slapping at her, a couple of slaps to the side of her head before he worked his way down her body. He tugged up her sweatshirt, then stuffed his hands into her pockets, nearly pulling off her pants. "Where is it? You have her number. You know where she went."

"I don't know!" she shrieked. "I don't know!"

He grabbed at her, rougher now, yanking her up so he could scream in her face. *"Where's my wife and son?"*

But she couldn't answer, because his hands were around her neck then. She tried to speak, then she tried to breathe, and then she only tried to pry his fingers open as her lungs caught fire and began to eat her alive. She burned for air, and then the world turned red, then gray, then, finally, black.

Lily floated. Nothing hurt; she didn't even feel that sad, really. Her deep, dark sorrow was a phantom she couldn't touch from this high up.

"I'm sorry . . . ," she heard vaguely from somewhere far away. A spirit, maybe, leading her up? Or perhaps she was about to be pulled down beneath the earth and deeper still.

"I'm sorry I did that," the voice purred. "I just need you to tell me the truth. We have to find Amber; it's very important. If we don't find Amber, very bad things will happen."

Yes. Yes, she knew that. Very bad things were already happening.

Lily drew a deep breath that scalded her throat and sent her into a violent, wrenching coughing fit. When that finally cleared, every breath burned, but she could see gray light stealing past the edges of the ugly curtains above the sink. How much time had passed? Was Everett awake?

"I took her somewhere," she croaked. Because she knew what she had to do now. She needed to lead Mendelson off the grounds so he could kill her somewhere very far away from her son.

"What?" he asked, leaning closer.

She coughed again, harder, until he finally got up to search through the cabinets until he found a water bottle. "I took her somewhere," she tried again, and this time she knew he heard it, because he smiled.

And Lily immediately wished she were in the black void again.

CHAPTER 32

Everett was having a dream about being in a boy band, which was odd because he didn't like boy bands. They all looked like cartoon characters to him.

But not his band. He was a member of a singing group of guys from his old soccer team, and they all wore their soccer stuff onstage. He was so frantically stressed about the new song he'd forgotten to memorize he felt nothing but a gasp of gratitude when his alarm woke him up.

Granted it wasn't so much gratitude that he jumped out of bed. He had already fallen back asleep when a crack of lightning hit somewhere close, and he woke again with a start. He glanced at his clock and realized he'd now passed his second alarm. He must have hit SNOOZE during one of the dream's dance numbers.

"Shit," he cursed, then threw a wince at the door in case his mom was standing there.

She wasn't. His door was still closed tight. Weird.

Getting up, he pulled on jeans that weren't too dirty, then grabbed a pair of socks to head straight toward the bathroom to pee and brush his teeth. The whole apartment was dark, and the bathroom light didn't respond when he hit the switch. "Mom?" he called, pausing for a moment in the doorway.

No answer. Storm damage, probably.

He raced through his morning routine in the near dark, then suddenly remembered that maybe he didn't have to go to school today. He wandered out into the living room. Still no mom.

If he were taking the bus, he'd already be late for it, but maybe she'd let him sleep in because she was going to drive him.

Fingers crossed, he reached to tug the apartment door open. It didn't budge. He turned the lock in confusion and looked into the office.

His mom wasn't inside, and she'd locked the apartment door behind her. So she'd gone out onto the property, maybe to check for damage?

The morning hit him with beauty when he stepped outside, no sign of any bad weather now, just clean, crisp air and a few damp spots on the sidewalk. "Mom?" he ventured.

He hadn't quite expected her to respond, but he still felt himself wilt a little when she didn't answer. She was always there in the mornings. Always waking him up with a smile even when he could see the lines of worry around her mouth. She'd never been the type of mom to cook up eggs and pancakes before school like they did on TV, but she'd ruffle his hair and call him sleepyhead before offering milk or orange juice.

His questions over whether she'd take him to school faded into a new worry. Maybe she was still mad. Maybe she didn't want to see him this morning. "Mom?" he called.

After a few moments of waiting, Everett went back inside and moved tentatively around the kitchen. Everything felt too . . . empty. No clinking dishes. No smell of coffee. But there wouldn't be, would there? The power was out. Still, there wasn't even a glass or bowl in the sink. His scalp crawled with prickling anxiety.

Where was his mom?

He went to the office and dialed her cell number. One ring. Two. Three.

On the fourth ring, he began to frown. On the sixth ring, he had to swallow past a thickening clog in his throat. When her voicemail answered, he listened hard to her voice and told himself things were fine.

"Mom? Where are you? Am I going to school?"

He hung up. He thought they'd made up yesterday, but maybe she'd gotten angrier and angrier the more she thought about his lying and stealing. He called her again. Then again. There was no answer.

He wasn't going to freak out this time. He wasn't going to scream and run and cry wolf. His mom worked here, so she was working. It was that simple. And if the power was out, maybe cell service was too.

This time he decided to search the grounds methodically, quickly moving along the alleys of the storage center, looking for any open doors or signs of tools being used. He'd made it through three sets of buildings and was walking at the edge of the vehicle storage area when he spotted it. Not a clue. Nothing so innocuous. What he saw was a shiny white rectangle tilted into the dead grass under the long end of an old RV.

His mom's phone.

A strange little hum began around him, and it took Everett a moment to realize he was making the noise, a shaking in his throat, pressing up. A cry wanting to come out, like he was a scared toddler.

Everett crouched down and reached beneath the vehicle to retrieve the phone. When he turned it over, his call notifications still glowed on the screen, and it made him feel like he'd just missed her. That she'd just been right there a few seconds before.

"Mom?" he asked, his voice cracking and breaking in the space of that single syllable. She didn't respond.

He didn't feel even a whisper of guilt when he unlocked her phone with a security code he wasn't supposed to know. No strange texts had come in. He found no phone messages except his. But she had gotten a phone call early this morning.

He looked up, turning in a slow circle. That was when he heard a door open somewhere ahead. The squeak of a spring compressing and releasing. A footstep.

Everett was just about to call out for her when he heard her voice. She was talking to someone.

"It's not in the apartment!" she said frantically.

Everett frowned.

"I told you I dropped it when you tackled me. It's here somewhere. Just call it. You'll see."

He was confused for a moment. Someone had tackled his mom? Then the phone in his hand buzzed, and a ringtone sang out. Everett looked up, and a man stepped into his sight, dragging Everett's mom alongside him. Everett noticed the man's black gloves first and the way one of them gripped his mom's arm and held it too high.

But then his brain finished clicking through the connections of his memories, and he realized it was just a cop, and everything was fine.

Caught between relief and wariness, Everett stilled and watched for a long moment as the police detective smiled. "Hey, buddy! Checking out a possible theft!" His voice sang with cheer. "Come on over. Your mom is—"

His mom suddenly grew. She expanded, her body uncoiling and launching straight up at the man's face.

She seemed to move in slow motion, her hands curving into claws as she landed on him. The police detective twisted and stepped back, but he couldn't catch himself. He landed hard on his back just as Everett heard his mom shout, *"Run!"* in the loudest roar he'd ever heard, as if those claws had turned her into a beast.

But Everett couldn't run. He was frozen in place, watching his mom wrestle with the cop, who was already struggling up.

Her face craned toward him, looking over her shoulder with huge, round eyes. "Run, Everett! Run!" He met her gaze, trying to convey that

277

he couldn't leave her, but she was roaring again. "*Run!* Call 911! Hide and don't come back!"

"Shut the fuck up," the cop wheezed as he raised up enough to dump his mom off him. His face was bleeding from a long scratch.

Everett saw the gun in a leather holster against the man's side, so he squeezed the phone hard in his hand and he did exactly what his mom had yelled. He ran.

Hide, she'd said. *Run. Hide. Call 911,* and for the first time in his life, Everett was lucky to live in this place, because he could hide anywhere. He could choose from a thousand places, and this monster would never find him.

He vaguely heard the man cursing, heard his mom still yelling, *Run,* but mostly all he heard was his thundering heart and the crunching impact of his feet and his straining, keening breath as he ran as fast as he could through the vehicles. His mind tripped and fumbled, throwing up ideas for hiding places and dropping them before he could grab hold.

He'd just settled on sliding beneath the cover of a boat when his eye caught on the tall building that housed the biggest RVs. *There,* his brain ordered, and he zigzagged away from the last of the motorhomes and bolted for the structure.

Forty steps felt like four hundred, but he was finally, *finally* sliding safely around the far corner of the building. He raced immediately toward the metal ladder, but halfway there, he skidded to a stop and hurried back to the edge of the wall. Forcing his head out to peek around the corner was the hardest thing he'd ever done, but he had to be sure.

The cop hadn't tracked him. If the guy had caught him going up the ladder, Everett would have been trapped, but when he caught a flash of movement, it was still far off inside the warren of wheels and boats and trucks.

Muttering some curse-filled prayer beneath his breath, he switched off the ringer of the phone, determined not to lose this chance to some stupid cellphone song. Then he raced to the ladder and scaled it far too quickly for safety, his sweaty hands slipping on the rungs before he threw himself over the lip of the roof.

Everything stopped then.

For a moment he was just Everett Brown, lying on his back, rough bits of the asphalt digging into his shoulder blades, thick white clouds sliding peacefully across the sky as he tried to catch his breath.

He could hear a bird singing somewhere, smell the damp earth of the meadow, and he suddenly pictured Josephine on the school bus. It was probably just pulling up to the school, and she was about to walk in, wondering where Everett was. But at least she was safe. He should never have involved her in this, and he was so happy she wasn't here now.

The quiet moment passed in a few heartbeats, and then the phone lit up, but it only buzzed quietly in his hand. He'd done something right, then.

He forced himself to his feet so he could move toward the roof wall and peek over it. Another terrifying moment of forcing his body to make itself vulnerable. His guts shook, zinging with a strange electricity as he crouched low and sidled to the edge.

But he never had to force his head to rise and his neck to angle it over the ledge, because someone shouted his name.

"Everett! Come on out!"

He dropped down to his belly, cheek against the pebbled surface, his nose nearly touching the rough white wall. Had he heard the vibrating phone?

"Everett!" the detective shouted again. "Come on out! If you come out now, I won't shoot your mom."

His own whimper slunk into his ears as Everett whined in horror at the thought. He squeezed his eyes shut and felt his hands shaking and wanted it all to just stop. What was going on? Why would a police detective have his mom hostage? Why would he threaten to shoot her? It was Everett's theft or investigation or his contact with Jones. He'd brought this on.

"Oh God," he breathed to himself, squeezing his eyes harder. What had he done?

But then the man called his name again, and it came out so hollow and distant that Everett knew he was facing away. He knew, and this might be the only time he'd know that he wouldn't be spotted. "Oh God," he whispered again before he shoved himself up to his knees and raised his head only a couple of inches past the wall.

He spotted the cop immediately, his back turned to Everett while he looked out over the field of vehicles. When he started turning back toward the tall building, Everett ducked down again.

His mom wasn't with him. Maybe she'd gotten away.

"Everett," the bastard called again, sounding disappointed this time. "I've got your mom handcuffed to a truck, and if you don't come out, I will shoot her right in the head, and I'll get rid of her body, and no one will ever even know. Is that what you want to happen? You want your mom to disappear forever?"

Pressing his hands to his face, Everett dropped his head and began to cry.

"You come out right now, and she'll be safe. I promise. If you call 911, you'll watch her die."

He had to. Oh God, he had to come out because he couldn't let this man shoot his mom.

He had to do it, but he didn't have to be stupid. Everett got out the phone and dialed 911.

Before the first ring, the detective was shouting into the sky again, "You've got ten seconds, and then it's all over for your mommy. Ten! Nine!"

Everett sped toward the ladder, feet sliding in grit as he pinwheeled his arms to give him more momentum. He heard a tiny voice ask, "What's your emergency?" just as he reached the metal handholds, and he hesitated for one moment.

If he took the phone with him, the detective would get on and talk to the dispatcher himself. He'd claim Everett was just a kid crank-calling 911 and he had everything taken care of, no need to send a car out. And then he'd shoot Mom.

So Everett set the phone on the ledge of the roof, and he spoke quietly toward it, even as he placed his foot on the first rung.

"I'm Everett Brown, I'm at Neighborhood Storage on Ranch Road, and there's a crazy cop here threatening to shoot my mom. Please send help." As he descended past the lip of the roof, he raised his face toward the phone. "He's a detective, but I can't remember his name, and he has my mom handcuffed to a truck! He's going to kill her! Send help, please! Please!"

Then Everett scrambled down the ladder and threw himself straight into the sights of a monster.

CHAPTER 33

He'd gotten away. Thank God Everett had gotten away.

After she'd pounced on Mendelson, he'd punished her by punching her temple so hard she'd seen nothing but stars. But Everett had gotten away, so she'd let herself be dragged to a truck and handcuffed to the frame.

The sound of Mendelson screaming for Everett loosed a deep primal roar of joy inside her own body. That meant he didn't have him. That meant her son was free.

She managed to twist her feet to the side. When she tried to brace herself more thoroughly against the truck so she could stand, his shouts were dulled by the scrape of her shoes on gravel. Her head pounded with pain. She got her feet under her, but had no strength left in her legs.

Then she made out some of the words Mendelson was screaming into the sky, and her joy dried into dust. "No," she whispered. Then she screamed, "No!"

He couldn't come back for her. He wouldn't, would he? He'd stay hidden and safe. He'd stay alive. He had to. She didn't care if she was shot; Everett had to stay gone.

Mendelson's footsteps moved away. She prayed. She cried. She yelled, "No, no, no!" as if the words would float up to Everett on a gust of wind. But the wind had died down. The sun emerged.

"Mom?" she heard an impossibly tiny voice say, and her heart exploded into a thousand bits of torn and bleeding grief.

"Evvie?" she sobbed. "Evvie, no!"

Then he was crying too, his voice pitched back into childhood instead of the young man he was so close to being. "Mom, he said he'd shoot you if I didn't come back. I'm sorry."

He stumbled into view, her perfect little baby. When Mendelson shoved him, Everett cried out, throwing out his hands to keep from falling onto her face. "Mom? Are you okay? You're bleeding."

When he curled his body around hers, all she could do was cry and say, "I'm sorry," over and over. Because she was so, so sorry she had done this to him.

It was her fault. All of it was.

"It's okay," she whispered into his keening throat. "It's okay, baby. Shhh."

"No, it's definitely not okay," Mendelson sneered. "Where's the phone?"

He shook his head against her, then yelped when Mendelson grabbed him by the back of the neck and pulled him off.

"Leave him alone!" Lily yelled.

"Where is the phone?" he ground out through clenched teeth.

"I-I don't know. I dropped it when I was running. Then I didn't know what to do; that's why I came back."

"Liar. You called it in, didn't you?" He shuffled his hands roughly over Everett's body, patting him down for the phone.

"I didn't!" Everett cried.

"Let's find out." Mendelson flashed an evil smile, then pulled a police radio from his belt. The radio flared to life with a crackle and a grating explosion of digital voices.

He scowled at it for quite a long time while Lily kissed Everett's head and breathed in his smell, wishing she could just put her arms around him.

Mendelson finally looked up with a little chuckle that raised the hair on Lily's neck. "Looks like you were telling the truth, kid. Nothing on the radio. Aren't we lucky? Regardless, it's time to go."

"Go where?" Lily pressed.

"Wherever I say."

She cringed back when he crouched next to her to unlock the handcuffs. She could see from the genuine warmth of his smile that he liked her flinching and afraid. After locking her wrists behind her, he slapped her thigh and winked when she nearly jumped from her skin.

"Please don't," she begged. "I swear I've told you everything."

"I don't believe you," he countered calmly. He sneered at Everett as he gestured toward Lily. "Christ, what a crybaby. Get her up."

Everett scrambled to his feet and grabbed Lily beneath her arm right where Mendelson had hurt her.

"I'm sorry," he said at her gasp of pain as she did her best to stand. "I'm sorry, Mom."

"Let's go," Mendelson ordered, as if it were her fault she could barely move. Lily imagined he'd barked at his wife this way after he'd beaten her, annoyed with the very suffering he'd caused, irritated that she was bothered by his violence. But his anger served its purpose, and Lily's muscles surged with adrenaline. Finally, she was on her feet.

Everett tucked himself beneath her chin, and she kissed his head over and over. "It's okay," she repeated.

Mendelson waved them forward. When Everett took a step, that bastard grabbed his shoulder to swing him around before he pulled a zip tie out to restrain her son's hands behind him.

Not her baby. No. This couldn't be happening. He'd already had so many nightmares. She didn't want him scared anymore. She didn't want him hurt.

Everett met her eyes, and he looked surprisingly calm, when she wanted to scream at the sky and tear at her hair. He stared at her intently, trying to communicate in some way, but she couldn't tell if he was attempting to ask something or say something. She shook her head slightly, confused.

His lips parted as if he meant to speak or mouth a word, but then he was shoved ahead. "Let's go. Back gate. If you try anything, I'll beat your mom to a pulp."

Everett hunched his shoulders and started walking.

She'd heard the wisdom that you should never allow yourself to be taken to a second location. That you should challenge an attacker to the death if he wanted to move you. But what did they say about behaving when your precious child was being taken too? She had to stay alive long enough to save him, so she kept her eyes focused on her son's moving, breathing body.

How could she get him out of this? How could she keep him alive? "Please just leave him here," she begged.

He answered with a huff of hard laughter. "Where's my fucking wife?"

"I've told you a thousand times, I don't know! Yes, I admit to helping her. You were right. I *was* working with Zoey, and I took Amber in, and I hid her here, but we're not supposed to exchange information. That's one of the rules."

"Where did you take her?"

"I just . . . I just drove her to the Quik Trip. Over in Highbank. I drove her there."

"Why?"

Lily didn't care about Amber anymore. She'd sacrifice anyone to save her son. "She caught the bus. She stayed for a night, and then I drove her to Highbank to catch the eleven forty-three bus."

"Ah, that's more like it," Mendelson drawled. "Now we're getting facts."

Everett slowed when he neared the back gate, where an old black Suburban was parked on the other side.

She looked hopefully up at the camera, but it was dark, of course. No power. Detective Mendelson had obviously parked here in the middle of the night and spent plenty of time preparing for this attack.

He'd planned so well. If anyone saw anything suspicious, he would've heard it on the radio and vanished. How was she supposed to stay ahead of that kind of thinking when he'd likely been masterminding this for days?

"It's unlocked," he said to Everett. "Open it."

Everett shoved until the gate slid open on its metal wheels, and when he slipped through, she had the brief hope that he might bolt, but that hope struck her at the same time with the blinding fear that he would. This bastard might shoot her son if he tried to run again. Her skin crawled with the waves of anger pouring off him.

But Everett didn't run. He'd come back for her, and he meant to stay to protect her. He looked pale and scared, head bowed to frown at the ground beneath him. He was such a good boy. She'd been so stupid to be worried when he was an amazing, loving son. Why had she wasted time obsessing over stupid things?

She was so full of regret now. She was nothing but regret. She just wanted this over and Everett safe, and it didn't matter what happened to her. She tried to make her brain cough up an idea, any idea for how to save him. But suddenly they were through the gate, and he was leading them toward the SUV.

"She got on the bus to head south," Lily choked out. "Maybe . . ." She swallowed hard against her dry fear. "Maybe she has family in Texas? Oklahoma? You can track them down."

"She does not. Get in." He pushed her toward the front seat. "Son, you get in back."

She nearly gagged at the sound of him calling her child *son*. He yanked open the back door and pointed Everett toward it.

"But I told you everything!" she yelled.

"Funny, for the past hour you've been claiming you'd already told me everything, and now here's a very important fucking detail you left out. Now the only thing I can trust is that you're a lying, conniving bitch who needs quite a bit of persuasion to find the spirit of God in your heart." He wrapped his fingers in her hair and jerked her head around to face him. "Isn't that right?"

She couldn't help her whimper. He was snarling and red-faced, and her scalp felt as if he were ripping it off her skull. Lily drew in a breath, opened her mouth, and lunged for his nose.

Her teeth caught on him. She clamped her jaw down hard. He'd turned away at the last minute, but she had his cheek, and if she could just stay on him, Everett could run. Run to the business park. Run to Nour or Sharon or the plumbers she called neighbors, and he'd be free.

She felt Mendelson's hand cup the side of her head. She felt glass crack against her skull. And then the world blazed into shooting stars that trailed white tails until they faded into a deep, dark black. And she was gone again.

CHAPTER 34

He knew he shouldn't be crying. He knew he didn't have time to cry, but Everett had discovered that the scariest thing in the world wasn't a crazy man with a gun; it was watching his own mother be hurt. His strong mom, his one parent in the world. Watching her cry out in pain, watching her wince at a rough hand, and now watching her slump limp against the door after that sharp crack of glass against her head . . . it was way more than he could handle.

The cop grabbed a fistful of tissues and pressed them tight against his bleeding cheek before gunning the vehicle into reverse. When he swung onto the road, Everett's whole body slid over to the door, and he tried his best to brace himself against it, raising his feet up to push against the back of the driver's seat.

He pressed his forehead to the window and swept his eyes over the back of Nour's workshop, hoping she might be there, but everything was shut up tight. The detective cursed and grabbed for more tissues.

Just as Everett felt his control slipping, just as he thought he might start screaming in helpless terror, he saw someone at the front of the shop. Right outside the door, Sharon was there, her back to the road, her hand at the lock, and Everett willed her to turn around, turn around, turn—

She did. She turned, frowning at the sound of a vehicle where it shouldn't be, because she always knew where things shouldn't be, and Everett sat up straight, opened his eyes wide, and mouthed, *Help,* as clearly as he could. Then he mouthed it several more times, bouncing up and down just a bit, trying to meet her gaze as they sped too quickly past.

He looked back as long as he could, pressing his temple to the window to keep the shop in sight for a moment longer. Then he faced forward and scooted more toward the middle to stare down the road toward the highway.

Were the police on their way? If there wasn't radio chatter, was it because they weren't coming or because they'd taken seriously his warning that their attacker was a cop? They wouldn't broadcast that all over a cop radio, would they?

But they might have just considered the call a prank from a stupid kid. He thought the whole police force would have been racing down the road by now. Then again that could be something that happened only in TV shows, and maybe everything moved more slowly if they didn't use the radio.

If it was possible to stare hard enough to make the entire police department appear, Everett gave it his best. Unfortunately they made it all the way to the highway undisturbed, only one other car passed, and then, instead of turning right toward town, they turned left.

As they turned, Everett glanced back down the road, and he saw a gray car pull out of Josephine's neighborhood, right where he caught the bus. A man was behind the wheel, face shadowed by a ball cap. Then the cop sped onto the freeway, and Everett couldn't see well behind them no matter how much he twisted.

This evil cop could be taking them anywhere. To another town, to a city, or just to a field where this monster could shoot them and bury them in plowed dirt so that wheat would grow from their bodies.

He hiccuped a little at the thought, but then his mom groaned, and he was so thankful she wasn't dead that he began to cry in earnest, tears falling freely down his cheeks because he couldn't reach them. She rolled her head back and forth for a second, but that was her only movement even after he watched her for long minutes.

Everett decided his only strength at this point was observation, so he blinked the grief from his eyes and read each sign that came up, each mile marker. They hadn't driven far when they got off the highway and turned left again.

"Where are we going?" he forced himself to ask, but he got no answer except a raspy sigh from his mom, who seemed to be struggling to sit up again.

They weren't far out of town, but out here there was nothing but farm roads, paved and unpaved, no real landmarks. He felt thankful that they stuck to the paved streets, because the isolation of a dirt road would be too terrifying in this situation.

When they turned left one more time, a strange stir of interest bloomed inside Everett's brain. He squinted, studying every structure he could see. A farmhouse on one side. A bigger farm with a cattle pen on another. A group of huge cottonwoods near a drainage ditch. And far up the road, getting larger every second, stood a group of three houses.

A chill bloomed over the back of his neck and raced down his spine.

Despite all his careful research and investigation, despite his many suspicions, Everett had been wrong about everything and everyone. Because this monster wasn't taking them to some random spot in the country.

He was delivering them straight to Alex Bennick, and that suddenly seemed like the scariest possibility of all.

CHAPTER 35

The side of her head burned, and a deeper pain throbbed there with every beat of her heart. A concussion surely, because she could barely force her eyes open, and the world spun around her.

Or perhaps the world was flying by, greens and browns and blues sliding past. Yes. She was in a vehicle. She was with . . .

Lily cut her eyes hard to the side, and she saw him. *Him.* The man who'd put terror in Everett's eyes. It all rushed back, and she clamped her teeth hard to hold back the nausea that rolled over her. She tasted metal and pain and sour blood. Her heart fluttered at the sight of the oozing wound on Mendelson's cheek. She'd marked him. She'd hurt him.

But where were they?

She didn't think her head was injured badly, more of a goose egg than a skull fracture, but combined with the pain in her temple, she felt caught in a vise. Still, she forced herself to twist around and look for Everett. The sight of him stabbed her with relief and horror. He looked sickly white and shocked, but he met her eyes and even tried to smile for her. His attempt choked her with a wave of painful love.

She tried to raise a hand to her head, but of course her hands were cuffed behind her, so she only made her ribs twinge with sharp pain.

There had to be a way out of this.

Wherever they were going, Mendelson would get out of the car before her. He'd take the key with him, so even if her hands were free, she couldn't drive away, but he'd have to open her door for her at least. Maybe she could kick it into him. Or she could throw herself at him, give Everett enough time to flee.

But where would he run out here in the middle of cow pastures and turned fields of dirt? There was nowhere to hide.

Except that when the vehicle began to slow, they weren't in the middle of nowhere. Instead he turned onto a short drive that sprouted off in three directions to three houses. Everett would only need to make it to one of those.

She tensed, drawing her body up from its woozy sprawl. She could do this. She didn't need her arms. She would launch herself at him and bite him again, tear his nose off this time, fill his throat with blood, and Everett could run, run, *run*.

Elation spread its wings inside her for a moment. She could see it happening. Feel herself fly through the air. Taste the flood of his blood as his flesh gave way beneath her teeth. She could even hear the slapping of her son's shoes against the drive, then the whoosh of his steps sinking into the dried lawn of the house next door.

Then the home they were driving toward opened like a mouth, the garage door rising to swallow them, and her hope dissolved and sank to the ground to soak uselessly into dirt.

"This is Alex's house," Everett whispered from the back seat.

"What?" she rasped.

"This is Alex Bennick's house, Mom!"

She was swinging toward him in horrified confusion when she caught sight of Mendelson's face. His smirking, gloating face. At least there was blood still leaking from that curving wound.

"What?" she managed before her tongue went too heavy and dry to function and they pulled into a garage crowded with boxes and tools and detritus.

When the door closed behind them, all her hopes for Everett were shut out with the sunlight.

The relative darkness helped her headache, at least, and her brain began churning with possibilities, none of them good. "What's happening?" she demanded, but Mendelson just turned his smirk at her and winked.

Were he and Alex actually working together? To what end? What the hell could this possibly have to do with poor Amber running for her life?

Unless it didn't have anything to do with her at all.

Maybe Alex really was a serial killer. Maybe the two men were some kind of ghoulish tag team. Her mind spiraled as Mendelson got out and shut the door, and she was spinning so hard she almost missed what Everett said. "Mom, I called 911. They know we're in trouble. And they know he's a cop. I couldn't remember his name. I—"

And then Mendelson was opening her door and pulling her out, and she could only stare wide-eyed back at her son.

He'd called for help?

She huffed out a bark of pain or laughter, she wasn't sure which. It didn't matter. If help was coming, they could get through this. The whole force couldn't be dirty. She just had to drag it out for as long as she could.

When Mendelson pulled Everett out, she rushed toward her son even though she couldn't put her arms around him. "I love you," she said into his sweaty hair. "I'm so proud of you, baby."

"I love you, Mom," he whispered back before Mendelson shoved them both toward the scarred wooden door past the front of the vehicle. She knew it wouldn't change a thing, but she desperately wanted her hands free so she could touch her son, hold him and offer comfort. Instead, she only pressed her left arm as tightly as she could to his shoulder as they moved together.

"Let me go first," she murmured, approaching the three steps that led up. *Just get through this. Just draw it out. Just keep him talking.*

Mendelson reached past her, turned the knob . . . and the horror awaiting her was just a laundry room. No one loomed with an axe or a gun. No one appeared at all. Mendelson shoved her through the doorway, and Everett followed right after.

"Turn right. Go sit on the couch. Both of you."

She glanced back in question. "What are you going to do to us?"

"Go sit on the goddamn couch!"

She hurried forward, trying to rush without losing her balance, and stepped out into a very short hallway. A stairway in front of her led up to a second story. A dimly lit living room loomed to the right. To the left she caught sight of white linoleum. The kitchen.

But something that hadn't registered in her vision dragged against her brain, and after one step toward the living room, she stopped and peered deeper into the shadows of the kitchen. At the very edge, the floor turned from white to blood red. She took a step back in that direction, pulled along by fear. She saw a limp arm on the floor. A body. Another victim.

Her stomach lurched, acid burned high in her throat. Then Mendelson shoved her hard.

"Want to join him?"

Pressing her body against Everett's, she herded him in the other direction, toward the couch and away from the blood.

What the hell was happening? Either Alex was involved or he wasn't. It didn't make any sense to drag him in as another victim of Mendelson's search for his wife.

She wanted to call out for Alex, but she wouldn't let herself. She couldn't bear it if he walked into the room wearing the same sick smile

Mendelson had flashed. Something inside her would give way to animal panic, and she needed to be able to think.

The ancient hulk of a couch in that strange living room became an unexpected refuge, because as soon as she reached it, Everett sat right next to her and pressed himself to her side, halfway crawling onto her lap. They were together again.

Mendelson didn't turn on any lights, but enough of the curtains were open that she could see easily as he set his radio on a shelf and turned to face them. "Your son is extraneous," he said flatly. "You're the one with the information."

Panic crawled up her spine like a scurrying animal, and Lily shook her head hard, sending sparks through her damaged brain. "That's not true! You know I'll cooperate if he's here. I'll help you find her. I'll do anything."

He tipped his head, studying her with that little smirk. "That's also true. So let's keep him for now."

Stomach turning, she strained her ears for any distant promise of sirens approaching, but the silence around their dim nest felt like a wall. The police had no idea they were here. Why would they?

"We have all the time in the world," he said, stretching his back a little. "No one is looking for you or me. So let's get way down deep to the real truth. Where is my wife?"

Lily would throw anyone to this wolf if it would save her son. "Zoey set it up. Just like you said. Maybe she knows! She said someone needed help—Amber—and she couldn't come to the shelter."

"And if some whining bitch calls to lie about a woman's husband, you just accept everything she says? No investigation, no trial, no defense?"

"She . . . she's an adult. She doesn't need my permission to leave."

"She needs *my* permission," he roared, suddenly lunging toward Lily to loom over her. "She needs *my* permission to take my child, doesn't she?"

"I don't know," she whimpered, sliding her shoulder in front of Everett's to shield him.

"No, you don't know *anything*, but you sure as hell thought you should insert yourself into my life, didn't you? What happened next?"

"She dropped Amber off outside the gate. It was late. After nine. I met her there, and I took her to the RV. The one I showed you."

"Then what?"

"She stayed for a night, and then the next night I drove her to the bus stop."

He clucked his tongue and paced away. "That's very interesting, Lily, because I've been wondering something. Why did she spend the night?"

"Wh-what?" she ventured.

"You hid my wife while I was desperately trying to find her."

"I'm sorry. I didn't know. I hadn't even met you."

"True, but you knew she belonged to someone."

Belonged. Belonged, like she was a child or an object.

"So . . . why in the world did Amber need to stay with you? Why didn't that woman take her right to the QT to catch the bus? Would've been quicker, wouldn't it?"

Everything inside her clenched with fear, her organs drawing in to protect themselves from attack. "There's something else. If you just let Everett go . . ."

His laugh was so loud and brief it rang out like a gunshot. "You're not a strong, independent woman in the power position here, you dumbass bitch. If you want to make a deal, here's the deal. Here's *my* deal. You tell me everything—and I mean every single thing—or in four or five days, maybe a week, the cops will find this house reeking of the five rotting bodies inside."

She blinked rapidly, trying to count. Five bodies. *Five?*

He winked, recognizing her confusion. "You and your son, of course. And your new boyfriend there." He tipped his head jauntily toward the kitchen, confirming who that arm belonged to. Who the blood belonged to. Alex. She heard the tiny sound that leaked from Everett's throat.

"And upstairs they'll find the body of his cousin, the murderer, a man long ago suspected of being a disturbed psychopath preying on the women in this town. And his last victim, of course."

Air leaked from her lungs, escaping in a strange whine.

"He came back, you know. Just recently. I checked it all out. Brian Bennick. So sad. This fucking loser psychopath gets dumped by his wife, he moves back in to his dad's house, and suddenly, there's another missing girl in Herriman, Kansas! Isn't that funny?"

Lily frowned, she couldn't think, and it felt very important to think. "Amber?"

"Jesus, you're dumb as a rock. No, not Amber. It's that druggie slut."

Her eyes darted over the room, trying to think. What missing girl? "Rebecca Ross?"

"That one's on you, Lily," he said, almost cheerfully. "That one is totally on you. You took my sweet Amber. You took my girl, and she kept me *clean*. Do you get that? She kept me pure and righteous." He'd paced away from her, then back again. "You took my beautiful angel and my *son*, and someone had to pay for that. How the fuck was I supposed to know some junkie whore was a doctor's daughter? Huh? How was I supposed to know that?" He threw his hands high.

"Now the town will need *answers*, so here they are." He gestured so widely that Lily flinched back from the motion, afraid to be hit again. She had to stay conscious. Had to figure out some way to save her son.

Mendelson reached into his jacket for an envelope. He opened it and drew out a necklace. "After a long search, they'll find some of the souvenirs Brian Bennick collected from the girls he killed. And that will be the end of this tragedy. Everything tied up with a neat little bow for those backwater idiots down at the station. His journalist cousin was getting too close to the truth, and you two were just collateral damage. So sad. I'll be front and center at the memorial, don't worry. And I'll be front and center for the work of the investigation, making sure all the pieces fit. And then I *will* find my wife, Lily."

The universe seemed to slow around her. The dim parts went dimmer and the light parts brighter, and her head was a hollow bell ringing with her heartbeat and whooshing breath and the faint vibration of Everett's trembling bones.

Everett. Everett. She had to save him.

The delicate necklace dangled from Mendelson's gloved hand, and her gaze caught on its faint sway like a deer caught in headlights.

He could promise whatever bargain he liked, but she and Everett weren't leaving this house alive. Not if Mendelson had any say in it. The town would need answers, and he had them, and he could not let any witnesses live.

Mendelson shoved the coffee table away with his foot, then crouched in front of her, tipping his head again in that eerie way of his. She'd thought him handsome before, but now he looked like a ghoul. Like tan skin stretched over a skull. "So, Lily? Are you ready to make a deal?"

"Yes," she said, because it was the only choice. A deal for a few more seconds of life and a tiny chance for her son. She tried to swallow, and her dry throat ticked. "The reason Amber stayed the night," she said, "is because she was waiting for a new ID, and a cash card, and a disposable phone."

"What was the name on the ID?"

"I don't know. It was sealed. I just gave her the envelope." His eyes flashed with fury, so she lied. "But I saw her open it. I think . . . I think it said Jennifer."

"Jennifer. And the new phone number?"

"I don't know."

"Wow. We don't have a lot to work with here, Lily."

"Someone left the envelope in my mailbox," she blurted. "I don't know who. But we could find out. They would know. They'd know her new name, at least. Someone made it for her."

"But your friend Zoey arranged that, right? Not you?"

He was going to hurt Zoey. But first he'd hurt Everett. She opened her mouth to speak, but a deep groan of pain emerged. "Please, I . . . I . . ."

Everett had called 911. He asked for help. And he'd left the phone behind. The police didn't know about this place, but they knew about the storage facility. Her brain fired, spinning and sparking. What did that mean? What could she do?

"My phone!" she yelled.

Mendelson pulled his chin in, frowning. "What about it?"

"Her new number is in my phone!" She settled into the lie, warming to it, letting it drown her with hope. "She called me from the trailer once. Amber. Her back hurt. She was afraid it would get worse on the bus. She needed Tylenol. So her number is there, even though I never called her!"

"You told me ten times you didn't have it."

Lily shook her head. "I . . . Like I said, I never called her. I wasn't thinking. I was just so scared."

He walked to the window and looked out before pacing back to her. "It's on your phone. The one that's back where we started."

"Yes. Just leave Everett here. Tie him up. Lock him in a bathroom so you know he won't get out. We'll go find it."

He snorted. "You don't even know where it is." His gaze slid to Everett like a snail leaving a trail of slime over them. "The boy and I will go. A little adventure, right, son?"

"I can go, Mom," Everett offered quietly, his voice shaking.

"No. No. You lost it! You said that. But I know that place like the back of my hand. I'll find it, I swear. I've lived and worked there for six years."

That head tip again, like a lizard studying a beetle. His eyes narrowed, glinting in the dim room. "No. I'll take the boy. And if the number isn't on your phone when we find it, I'll shoot him."

"No!" she screeched, throwing herself in front of Everett's body.

"It's okay, Mom," he said on a sob. But it wasn't okay. She couldn't let Everett get caught in some sort of cross fire between Mendelson and the Herriman police. It had to be her. She angled her whole body in front of him, pressing him back into the couch.

"Take me. I'm begging you. You can be damn sure I'll find the phone, because I need to keep my child safe. I don't have an option here. I don't. You'll have complete control of me, and I'll just want to get back to him. You know that's true."

He laughed again. "Nah. You want to get me away from him. You want to control *me*. See the difference?"

She did see the difference, because he was one hundred percent right. She also, through her haze of frantic panic, saw movement in the window, and she had to fight the urge to jerk her head toward it.

What the hell had that been? Had the police somehow found them?

Movement flickered again while she tried to keep her cool. She sat up straight. "You need my thumbprint! To get her number! It's a fingerprint passcode. You need me with you." She had to keep talking.

A head outside? A face? But as the figure beyond the window coalesced into recognizable features, she nearly gasped. How was that possible? It wasn't. She was seeing things.

But as she watched, Jones, his eyebrows raised, held a hand high and pointed up. Up? Then he disappeared. Jones. He was actually here, still here, and . . . he'd arrived to *help* them? Or maybe she was hallucinating. Maybe her brain was bleeding and she'd had some weird stroke.

Mendelson paced away, his head bowed. "Shit," he cursed. "All right." For one brief moment, she felt triumph and sweet, sweet hope. He'd lock Everett in a bathroom where he was safe, and then between her and Jones, surely they could take out Mendelson.

He picked up his gun and stepped close, trying to shove Lily out of the way. She resisted but he pointed the gun over her shoulder. "You're right. We don't need him at all."

"No!" she screamed, trying to push up to her feet. He was reaching for her hair when something cracked upstairs. Nothing loud, just a pop of sound. Mendelson froze, his gaze jumping to the ceiling.

If Jones had been trying to get inside upstairs, Mendelson was now ready for him. He shoved Lily back down and stepped toward the stairway. If he went up, she could get to the front door, unlock it, get Everett out . . .

But he didn't go upstairs; he only stared up toward the second floor. Movement drew her gaze again, and she was shocked to see Jones right there, back at the window. Something poked past the frame, sliding inside along the wood—a file, a knife—and it easily slipped the window lock free of its hasp. He started to raise the glass, but a tiny squeak stopped his progress.

Lily cleared her throat. "What is it?" she called to Mendelson.

"Shut up," he ordered, pointing the gun toward her without even looking.

"Is someone alive? Are they still alive?" She had to keep talking. The window scraped gently higher. "Please, I just want my son to live, that's all. Please let us go."

"I said *shut up!*" he bellowed; then he swung toward her, neck bulging, eyes glinting with fury. "Are you deaf, you whore? I said shut your mouth, or I'll gut your precious son in front of you."

"Get down," she whispered to Everett, but she didn't feel him move.

The window was only half-open, but Mendelson was coming back toward them. Jones had disappeared, but the curtains drew slightly toward the open space, sucked out by the wind.

"I'm sorry!" she cried out, keeping his attention on her.

He grinned at her, pleased with her wild cries.

"I'm begging you not to hurt us." She stood up as he rounded an ottoman. "Just take me back and I'll find the phone and call your wife. I'll find her for you." She stepped toward Mendelson instead of away, focusing on the little bleeding wounds her teeth had left in his awful face. "I'll do anything for you." Another step.

He laughed. "Jesus, you're pitiful. You all beg the same in the end."

The curtain shifted. Lily heard Everett gasp. Just a few more seconds . . .

And then there were no more seconds because Jones was only halfway through and the wood creaked, and Mendelson was swinging toward him, gun raised. Jones was stuck in the window, trapped, and all Lily could do was leap.

She hit Mendelson just as the gun went off, knocking him off balance, so he stumbled to the side, arms flailing.

Eyes on the gun, Lily roared and barreled forward, forcing him down just as Jones slid inside and fell to the floor, grabbing for Mendelson's ankle.

The evil bastard went down hard. Lily heard the dull clunk of his head hitting the wood floor, then the sharper clatter of his gun falling, and she could not let him have it, she could not let him hurt Everett, so she dove for the gun, covering it with her body. "Get down!" she yelled to Everett.

Mendelson roared with fury. She felt an iron grip around her ankle, and she kicked hard with her other foot. A fleshy crack. A deep scream. His grip left her, and she scrambled up, kicking the gun away before she spun to see Mendelson with a hand to his face, blood streaming between his fingers. She hauled back her foot and kicked him again.

And again. His hand fell away. His nose was a pulpy mess of blood and flesh. His eyes drifted to half-lidded slits, but they still watched her, glittering with hate.

Lily held his gaze, bracing her body, drawing in a deep breath. "You won't ever touch my son again," she said. Then she drew her foot back and kicked him as hard as she could in the temple. His eyes rolled up to show the whites, and he wasn't looking at anything anymore. Hopefully he never would again.

CHAPTER 36

"I guess I can let him go now," a man's voice said dryly.

Everett kept his face pressed into the sofa, eyes squeezed shut, ears ringing and muffled from the gunshot. He didn't feel anything, didn't think he'd been hit by a bullet, but what if he had? Or what if his mom had? He didn't want to know. He couldn't look.

"Everett," his mom sobbed, and then she was next to him, her body curved over his, her voice in his ear. "It's all right, baby. I'm here. You're fine. We're fine."

"Mom?" he cried, as he turned into her, the curtain of her hair shielding him from everything else in the world. He could smell her skin and feel her forehead against his cheek. "Are you okay?"

"I'm okay. I'm not hurt."

"Hold on," the man's voice said. Footsteps moved away, then came back. "Everett, can you sit up?"

He felt his mom's weight lift from him, and then Everett scrambled to right himself in the soft cushions of the couch. A stranger stood before him, a small knife in his hand. Everett stared wide-eyed at the blade for a long moment before his eyes rose to the man's face. And he wasn't actually a stranger. He was someone Everett remembered.

"Dad?" he asked.

The man smiled, and then there was no question, because that smile had filled Everett's days, once upon a time. "Dad!"

"Come on, little man, let's get those ties off you."

Everett jumped up and twisted around. There was a quick snap, and one hand was free, then the other.

"All right, Son," his dad was saying, but Everett had already spun back to wrap his arms around his waist. He felt solid and real, strong and warm. But not quite as big as Everett remembered. Not a giant. Just a man. He sighed, "All right," into Everett's hair and hugged him tight.

"Jones," his mom snapped, her voice cracking like a whip. "What the . . . ?"

Everett opened his eyes to see his mom still on the couch, blood dried in a fan of trickles down her face. She *was* hurt. He let his dad go and dropped down to hug her. "Mom, are you okay?"

"I'm fine," she reassured him. "Don't you worry about me. Are you hurt anywhere?" He shook his head.

His dad clicked his tongue. "Sorry, Lily. I can't do anything about the cuffs unless—"

His mom gasped sharply, cutting off his words. "Jones, you're bleeding! He shot you!"

When Everett saw the bright-red stain blooming over his dad's sleeve, he was on his feet again.

"Merely a flesh wound," he said with a wink for Everett, but he winced a little when he tried to lift his arm. There was a hole in the fabric of his shirt. From a bullet.

Everett gulped hard as his stomach rolled, but he shook it off. "Dad, what are you even doing here?"

"I wanted to see my son, of course." When Everett just stared at him, brain spinning, everything jumbling up like a clog in his mind, his dad sighed and sagged a bit. "I was leaving the state, but my motel was only thirty miles away, and I just thought . . . well, even if I only get to see you drive by on your way to school, that'd be something. Right?"

Everett didn't want to cry in front of his dad. He didn't. But after all the horrible and scary and awful things that had just happened, this drop of brightness overwhelmed him. It was too much, and everything inside drew tight and painful as Everett's throat closed.

Because his dad really had wanted him. Not just the notebook. He'd wanted Everett too.

"Jones," his mom said. "You need to call for . . ." But her words faded and then died out. "Wait, are those sirens?"

"Yes."

Everett glanced back and forth between them, torn between being worried about his mom and wanting to really look at his dad. His hair was longish, curling a bit like Everett's in waves that covered his ears and reached his collar.

"Jones," he heard his mom whisper as she stood up. "You actually called the police?"

"Sure. Anything for my boy."

"But that means . . ."

"Yeah, I should probably find a back way out of here while I can."

"You're leaving?" Everett croaked past the lump that was choking him half to death.

"Sorry, little man." His smile creased his eyes into bright crescents of warmth. He had scruffy stubble, but he somehow looked healthy instead of disheveled. The deep tan probably helped. Everett imagined him on a beach in sunglasses, smiling at the waves.

His gaze dropped to the wet blood on his dad's light-blue shirt. "There's a back door in the kitchen," he suggested softly. He was sure Mom would protest, say that Dad needed to face the consequences of his actions, but she only blew out a deep breath and tipped her head toward the doorway.

His dad threw his good arm around Everett's shoulders and pulled him in tight. "Lead the way, Son."

When his mom stepped ahead of them, Everett moved forward, and then he saw Mendelson and yanked back. The cop wasn't moving, maybe not even breathing. His ruined face was a smash of different wounds, blood coating his skin. But he *was* breathing, because a bubble of blood swelled from a crooked nostril. It popped, and the next one slowly began to form many seconds later. So he wasn't dead, but he looked close. His mom kicked the gun even farther away, sliding it toward the kitchen.

Everett was holding tight to his dad and watching his mom's cuffed hands ahead of him when she jerked to a stop at the kitchen doorway. The sirens were drawing nearer, not close yet, but not far, and they needed to keep moving.

"Mom—"

"Don't look, Everett," she ordered. "Jones, you keep him with you." Then she peeled off to the right, away from the door.

Everett looked, of course, and his mom was bent over a puddle of blood. He spied a man's arm, and legs in a pair of jeans, but then his dad was guiding him to the doorway.

"How will you get away?" Everett asked, worried that his cracking voice sounded like a whine to his dad, who was somehow still joking and cool even though the patch of blood had soaked through more cotton.

"Don't worry about it. I left the car in another driveway, but . . . Well, let's just say it's not in my name anyway. So I'll hike out. No worries." He said no worries, but his eyes darted nervously toward the door. "Speaking of, I'd better be going."

"Yeah." Everett followed him out when he opened the door. The sirens were louder now. "Bye, Dad," he said, trying to be strong and calm, but his dad laughed at that, and swept him into a huge hug.

"I love you, Everett. Take care of your mom. I'll be in touch."

"I love you too," he said, which seemed like an odd thing to say to someone he didn't know, but it felt true. It felt like he loved him.

And then he was gone, slipping straight back from the house and angling the opposite way from how Josephine and Everett had escaped. Everett watched him as the whine of the sirens grew more piercing.

"He's breathing!" his mom yelled. "Alex is still breathing!"

Everett spun around and stumbled over the threshold, rushing back into the house. He still couldn't see much of Alex Bennick past his mom's back, but he did see a bloody knife in a pool of horrible red next to her foot.

"Everett, go sit on the couch, keep your hands up. When the police get here, yell to them that it's safe and we need an ambulance. Don't go near Mendelson."

Everett didn't think. He wasn't scared. For the first time in forever, he wasn't scared at all. He raced into the living room as he heard car doors slamming out front. He dropped to the couch, and he raised his hands.

Then he heard his mom begin to cry in quiet, choking sobs, and he finally felt safe to cry too. His mom and dad had saved him. And they would all be okay.

CHAPTER 37

"Are you seriously working at a party?" Lily asked as she strolled beneath the trailing edge of the weeping willow and into the shade beneath.

Alex lay in a cheap lounger he'd brought over, a tattered spiral notebook in his hands. "You already put me to work at a party, remember?"

"It seemed like you'd be a natural DJ."

She bent down to give him a kiss on the cheek, then dropped into the chair next to him. They were taking it slow to keep things steady for Everett, but after three months of dating, they weren't actually hiding things from anyone.

"Any trouble with that scar lately?" she asked when his hand settled on his stomach.

"No, that last surgery made a huge difference. I'm right as rain." He wasn't right as rain; he'd never grow back the missing lobe of his right lung, and he'd never get his cousin back either, but he was starting to seem more like his old self.

His uncle, thankfully, often forgot that his only child had died. Lily hoped that made it easier for him. The rest of the town was reeling from losing two people who'd grown up there, and they wrestled with the truth of who'd done it. And still, there was no sign of the long-missing girls lost to so many families.

Lily tipped her head back to stare up through the swaying leaves of her new backyard tree. "How's the book research coming?"

"There's a lot to dig into. I leave for Omaha in eight days, and I don't feel close to ready."

"Maybe that's because you're barely recovered, and you shouldn't be traveling this soon."

"I think it's because I just started a book that will take me at least a year to finish, and I'm feeling a lot of pressure."

"Good thing they paid you six figures." She reached over to take his hand, letting her head fall to the side so she could study him and the new frown lines that seemed permanently etched between his brows. "You'll be ready for Omaha."

"Maybe," he said softly. "They think they've identified nine now."

Nine. Not bodies. Just missing women.

None of the bodies had been found in either state. Their killer was a cop, so he'd known exactly how to hide a victim so well they might never be found. And Mendelson wasn't talking.

Maybe that was Lily's fault. His attorneys claimed he had brain damage and couldn't recall his crimes, and perhaps that was true. But she felt only an intellectual level of regret over that. She would've killed him a hundred times over to save her son, the investigation be damned. She frankly regretted that she could claim only to have massacred half the bones in his face. She wished she'd gotten all of them.

Alex's working theory was that Mendelson had left Herriman to join the Omaha Police Department because Marti Herrera's family had forced an actual investigation. His game of hunting local women had suddenly become dangerous. He'd needed more anonymity, a larger territory to stalk, and Omaha had provided that.

He'd risen to detective there. He'd even been assigned to investigate several of the disappearances he was suspected of causing. Then he'd met his "angel," Amber, and he'd brought her back to Herriman to start over, to raise a family.

Lily still shivered every time she considered that strange parallel in their lives. It had to be a coincidence, but it felt dirty, like something stuck to her, somehow. Like she'd caused it.

"Amber wrote to say she's back with her mom in Nebraska," Lily said softly. "She hasn't responded to you?"

"No. Not yet. I told her I'd be in touch and ready to talk whenever she wants. But I think she's still afraid of him. She probably always will be."

"Me too," she whispered.

"He'll never get out."

"I know." Yes, she knew it, but she didn't feel it. Everything was still too raw, the fear too huge to work around. Amber had to be experiencing that a thousand times over. And Mendelson had left her with another, much more horrifying legacy.

It was her fault he'd lost control, Amber had written to Lily. He'd always told her that she kept his monsters at bay. That he'd done terrible things before he'd met her five years earlier. Her virginity, her innocence, had cleansed him on their wedding night, and now she feared she'd let the monster loose when she'd left him. It was exactly what he'd told her would happen.

And now she had his son.

Lily felt like she would need a PhD in psychology to respond adequately to this poor woman's request for forgiveness, but she planned to take her time and do her best. And she would honor the one request Amber had made of her.

When her phone buzzed, she glanced at it with a sigh. "Everett is now texting me from his bedroom. Which is twenty feet away. I never should have gotten him a phone."

Alex chuckled at the running joke. Of course, one of their first stops after Lily had been released from the hospital had been to buy Everett a cellphone. It hadn't left his hand since, and she was damn grateful for that constant connection. She wasn't sure she'd have ever let him out of her sight without it.

Her phone buzzed again. "Update: he confirms that Shadow likes her new cat condo, in case you were wondering."

"That makes me happy. I was thinking I should get a cat." He sighed. "Brian really missed his cat, you know? I think he'd be honored if I named a cat after him. I could talk to him like I used to talk to Brian. The house wouldn't feel so damn big either."

She wasn't sure how he lived out there after the terrifying tragedy he'd dealt with, but he said that was where he'd spent all his time with Brian in both childhood and adulthood, so he felt close to him there.

"And he'd be okay with the cat having his name?" she asked with a smile.

"I mean, he *really* missed his cat. Maybe even more than his wife, I swear to God. I guess the relationship with the cat was a little simpler. I think he'd like it."

Brian had been found shot through the head in a way that would have suggested suicide if Mendelson had been able to complete his plans. They'd found more than Yolanda's necklace in Mendelson's possession. He'd also had an anklet identified as Mary's, and an earring that must have belonged to one of the other girls. He'd meant to leave them all hidden in Brian's room, as proof of Brian's evil soul and of the past that had motivated him to kill Alex, Lily, and Everett.

But instead Mendelson had left three fewer victims behind, thank God. Four if she counted Amber.

Alex squeezed her hand and gave her a quick kiss that pulled her out of the past and brought her back to the party.

A panel of the backyard privacy fence had been removed and a metal archway placed there with new honeysuckle vines now reaching up it, and Lily watched Sharon walk through with two cases of soda in her arms. "More party supplies!" she called out to Nour, who was manning the smoker they'd rolled over to Lily's yard that morning.

"I still can't believe I agreed to this," Lily murmured.

"You love it," Alex countered, and she rolled her eyes.

"I'd better get back to it."

He raised his iPhone. "Don't worry about the music. I won't let you down."

"Coward," she said, but she was smiling when she walked back out into the sun.

Everett had decided he wanted to stay in Herriman. She would have denied him nothing at that point, but even she had started feeling glad about the decision. The choice of rental house she wasn't quite so sure of, but she couldn't deny that Everett finding a vacant three-bedroom directly next door to Nour and Sharon's house must have been a sign. Right?

And she couldn't deny that it really did feel like having family, even if she still squirmed occasionally under those tight binds. But Sharon . . . Sharon had helped save Everett. She'd seen him in the back seat, face a mask of fear, and she'd seen Mendelson too, and recognized him. She hadn't hesitated for a moment to call 911 and report that something was very wrong.

Granted, they'd already known that because of Everett's call, but Sharon's follow-up had confirmed that it was no joke, that everyone needed to mobilize, that one of their own had gone rogue. If Sharon hadn't called . . . well, there was a good chance they might have sent out only a couple of officers to check on a hoax.

She followed Sharon to the deck and gave her another big hug. She hugged Nour too. "Thank you again for the ribs. They're amazing. Thank you for everything."

"Where's Everett?" Sharon asked. "I promised him a water-gun fight."

Lily laughed and rolled her eyes. "He's in his room. I'll go roust him."

Lily waved at Mac, who was talking to Josephine's parents near the beer cooler. It was more of a family party than a kid's party, but that was what Everett had wanted. He'd gone to the water park with Josephine, Mikey, and three other friends last weekend, which had been Lily's gift to him. But today he'd wanted just family, so that's what he'd gotten.

The house was quiet with everyone outside. Peaceful. It was a bit more than they could afford, but it had felt so right when they'd walked in. Everett had lit up, and he'd very solemnly explained how convenient it would be to have Nour and Sharon next door if Lily got stuck late on the road when she traveled.

The move seemed to have helped him. The daily night terrors had come roaring back after Mendelson's attack, which was hardly shocking after what he'd been through. But they'd faded since they'd left the apartment. And his therapist had helped. Lily's was helping too.

She walked down the short hallway toward Everett's bedroom. He'd chosen the one next to hers, and she still felt a little teary-eyed about it. That even at thirteen, he'd chosen to stay close to her. When she reached his doorway, she stood quiet for a moment, hoping he was as happy as he seemed.

He and Josephine lounged on a giant beanbag that took up a whole corner of his room. Josephine had gotten him a set of wireless earbuds, which made it easier for them to each have one in their ear to listen to the same music. He already had a Bluetooth speaker, but apparently that wasn't as much fun.

Shadow seemed to be ignoring her new cat condo to stretch out between the two kids on the warmth of the chair. The beanbag had been another birthday gift. Not from Lily. It had come from Cheyenne, Everett's stepgrandmother.

Lily wasn't quite sure how to take that. The strangest part was that Cheyenne still hadn't met Everett. She'd had the chair delivered along with a note that read, *Happy Birthday from Cheyenne and the boys!*

"What a fucking weirdo," Lily had muttered to Zoey. "Who does that?" But Everett had seemed quietly pleased, so that was something. Lily would reach out at some point, but she wasn't quite ready for that minefield. Soon, maybe.

"Hey, kids!" she finally called. They looked up from Everett's phone with matching smiles. "Cake in ten minutes. And Sharon says you promised her a water-gun fight."

"Aw yeah!" Everett cried, and Josephine pumped her fist.

"Ten minutes!" Lily warned. He was addicted to his new phone, just as she'd feared, but Lily no longer gave one good goddamn about that. Such was the freedom of escaping imminent murder, she supposed.

Speaking of escaping . . . she slipped into her new bedroom without turning on the light. She could see well enough with the sun filtering in.

Not that much was new about the bedroom. She hadn't replaced any of her own furniture or updated her awful mattress yet, but she had plans. The new furniture had gone to the family room and Everett's room, and Lily's new home office. But that felt right. This room could wait. She was doing her best not to hide from the world anymore, so she only used her bedroom for sleeping.

She crossed to her dresser and pulled out the center drawer, then the little jewelry drawer inside it to retrieve the two letters there. She stared at the top one.

It shouldn't feel significant. Just another birthday card from Jones like the others. But it did. This one was thicker, and she suspected there was a real letter inside on real paper, not just a hastily scrawled message scribbled into a card.

She hadn't been surprised by its arrival. He'd only vanished three months earlier, and Everett was fresh in his mind. But what would happen next year? Or the year after that?

Lily couldn't know. And she couldn't control it.

"Hey, there you are!"

She spun to see Zoey step into the room, then her friend hesitated until Lily tipped her head to gesture her closer.

"Cake's ready," Zoey said. "Thirteen relighting candles, and I handed out the sparklers to everyone."

"Thanks, Zoey. The cake looks amazing."

"I hope he likes it," her friend said as she joined Lily at the dresser. She looked down at the card in her hands. "Ah. Is that what I think it is?"

"Yeah." She'd told Zoey everything once she'd finally recovered from the immediate effects of the ordeal. Well, not quite everything. No one knew Jones had been there. The police had assumed the stolen car had something to do with Mendelson's scheme and the opened window had been Lily's attempt to escape.

In the end, she'd taught her son to lie to the police, she supposed. But she didn't feel bad about it. This time Jones had earned his head start. One day, when this was long behind them, she'd turn over the access codes from the notebook to the police, but not yet. She still didn't trust them.

"Are you going to give that one to him?" Zoey asked.

She shrugged. "I'm sure he talks to him online anyway. I don't ask."

"Go with your gut."

"I will."

Zoey wrapped her arm around Lily's waist and laid her head on her shoulder. "Have I told you how sorry I am?"

"Oh my God, stop it," Lily said. "You don't have to keep apologizing. None of this was your fault."

Zoey turned to her, tears in her eyes. "I involved you in something dangerous. And you had no support out there, not like we have at the shelter. It was reckless and stupid."

"If you're responsible for putting me in danger, then I'm responsible for putting Everett in danger. Is that what you think? I mean, it's what *I* think, but is that what you're saying to me?" She gave her friend a shake and laughed at the way she groaned.

"You know that's not what I mean!"

"Then stop blaming yourself."

"Only if you stop blaming yourself," Zoey countered.

"Jesus, we're a mess." When Zoey pulled her in for another hug, Lily held on tight for a long time before letting go.

She kissed Zoey's cheek. "Tell the kids to head outside. I'll be right there."

"You got it."

When Zoey left, Lily moved the other letter to the front. She'd barely looked at it since she'd first seen it, and goose bumps prickled her arms now.

She turned it to its side, opened the flap, and let the contents slide out to her palm.

> I told the police I thought he'd stored things somewhere cuz when we first moved to Herriman, he took a bunch of bins from the garage and never brought them back. They didn't believe me. Said nothing showed up in the banking. Said it was probably trash, like I'm stupid enough to think he'd move trash with us from Omaha to Kansas.
>
> Lily, I don't even think those cops are trying. They want this all to go away cuz it looks bad for them. And they're his buddies. I don't trust them at all. So when I was packing up the last of my things from that god-damn house and saw this at the bottom of a drawer . . . I decided to give it to you. You do whatever you want with it.
>
> I'm sorry again.

"You don't have to be sorry," she whispered to Amber as she closed her fingers around the jagged, unforgiving points of the key. The small silver key was stamped with a brand name she recognized. It was the exact kind that fit into the most common padlocks used to lock up units at storage centers.

It wasn't from Lily's place. She knew that. No one had paid so far in advance that she'd never met them, and the only clients of hers who paid with untraceable money orders were a Korean couple who traveled the US in their RV for three months every summer.

But of the six storage places in nearby towns, five of them were owned by Neighborhood Storage. And Lily was now in charge of inspecting every record and all the properties.

She squeezed the key until it hurt, imagining the hundreds of records and names she'd need to dig through, the dozens of units she'd need to visit, the countless locks she'd need to try.

But she would try. And eventually, she'd find Mendelson's secrets, and she would expose every one of them to the world, and he'd never, ever be free of them again.

She tucked the key into Amber's letter and closed it back up in the drawer. But Jones's letter she carried with her, out into the hall and into Everett's room, where she slid it under his pillow.

"I'm sorry," she whispered to the little boy he'd been. And then she took a deep breath and headed back into the sun to celebrate the incredible young man he was now.

ABOUT THE AUTHOR

Victoria Helen Stone is the Amazon Charts bestselling author of *Jane Doe* and *Problem Child* in the Jane Doe series; *The Last One Home*; *Half Past*; *False Step*; and *Evelyn, After*. Winner of the American Library Association's prestigious Reading List award for outstanding genre fiction, she also published twenty-nine books as *USA Today* bestselling author Victoria Dahl. Victoria writes in her home office high in the Wasatch Mountains of Utah, where she enjoys summer trail hikes almost as much as she enjoys staying inside during the winter. She is also passionate about dessert, true crime, and her terror of mosquitoes. For more information, visit www.victoriahelenstone.com.